BROKEN
SILENCE

BROKEN SILENCE

MICHELE C. WHITE

To order additional copies of this book, contact:
Xlibris Corporation
1-888-795-4274
www.Xlibris.com
Orders@Xlibris.com
39821

Rainbows live within your heart, so do not fear the darkness of night, because you'll never be alone. A rainbow will always be safely tucked deep inside you.

—Ethan Ashton White

To my husband, who taught me how to love. To my young son, who not only gave me his endless love but showed me how to laugh again as only an unburdened child can. Then, to my friend Marlena, who has always been there for me. Thanks, I love you all!

1

Ten-year-old Edward Lee tossed the last bag of yard trash into the garbage bin and snapped the lid tightly shut. With a swipe of the back of his hand, he brushed the curly brown hair from his forehead. A glance over his shoulder toward the main house told him the coast was clear. He wanted to leave before Ms. Hanley thought of something else that absolutely needed to be done. He knew his mother was fond of the old woman, but as far as he was concerned, she was a royal pain in the butt. Besides, if he didn't leave now, he'd be late for his real after-school job at the peach farm.

Pressed for time, the fourth grader chose the shortest route to his destination. It was a path he seldom took. In fact, he hadn't used it in months. Not since the last time his mother made him do yard work for Ms. Hanley. It meant he'd have to trudge through an abandoned orange grove, knee-deep in weeds, brambles, and who knew what else that lurked hidden beneath. However, to Edward Lee, who had a great imagination and love for adventure, this only added to the intrigue. He fought his way through the underbrush, creating an adventure movie in his mind as he went.

On approach to the edge of the tree line, he paused. Many of the trees retained the evidence of past frost damage. They stood as ghoulish gray monsters—gnarly arms outstretched in a severe threat to grab anyone foolish, or brave enough, to venture near. Edward Lee considered himself to be such a brave soul and proceeded forth. The boy was totally engrossed in his make-believe adventure when something in the deep grass caused him to stumble. A glimpse of white caught his eye while he used one of the nearby trees to break his fall. Quickly he reached down to untangle the weeds from his ankle and doubled back to investigate.

At first thought, he assumed it was a pile of trash dumped by someone on the highway; then, he reconsidered. The road was too far away and rarely traveled by anyone other than locals. With a cursory look around to make sure no one was watching, he crept closer. With an outstretched arm, he parted the tangle of weeds for a closer look. Still, all he could discern was an outline of white. It forced him to lean in on one knee to move the last remains of undergrowth out of the way. The action revealed a stack of bones.

Although excited by the find, it wasn't exactly unusual. Several creatures inhabited the fields and woods in this area. He'd spent so much time out of doors, he'd come across the skeletal remains of turtles, opossums, raccoons, and deer, even an alligator or two. In general, he was intrigued by all of them. Yet this specimen was different. For one thing, it was in a neat pile, not spread out, except for where his foot had caught on the top bones. He picked up a stick adjacent to his knee and poked at the find. As he did, what appeared to be a piece of spinal column cascaded down. There were no antlers as he had expected due to the large size of the remains. Edward Lee dug the stick in deeper and twisted it to shift the stack. This time the surface bones tumbled off to reveal a skull. This was no animal. It was a human!

"Holy crap!"

The boy scurried back like a crab on a hot beach. He didn't want to believe what he'd seen. His breathing came in quick, raspy, shallow spurts. This was Florida Peach property. How could there be a skull here? A human skull? He sat for a moment in the dense weeds while he tried to catch his breath and make sense out of the situation. He had no idea what to do. He was supposed to be at work, but his boss owned this property. Even though his boss was tough and at times intense, all in all, he seemed like a regular guy. How could he tell him he'd found a body on his land? Then another thought raced through his head. What if his boss actually had something to do with it?

These past few months, the man had acted kind of strange—all stressed out. But then again, most grown-ups did as far as Edward Lee was concerned. (His mother certainly was no exception.) Up to this point, he hadn't given it much thought. After all, the guy's father died not that long ago, and then his girlfriend left him. Maybe it had been enough to make him freak out. Possibly enough to kill somebody.

Edward Lee considered the girlfriend, who was no longer around. He hadn't seen her in months. For two years, she was around constantly. She'd even picked out curtains for the kitchen. Then all of a sudden she vanished. His boss hadn't talked about her since. Could this be her body? He didn't know what she would look like without any skin or fluffy hair, but these looked like they could be girl bones because they were really clean. He remembered that she always wore earrings, but if they were present, he didn't see them. He couldn't make himself move any closer to look for them either.

He realized he had to do something besides sit here and gawk at his discovery. He wanted to be an archeologist one day. A real archeologist would do something like document the location of the find. That's when he remembered the cell phone his mother had given him. It had a GPS device somewhere inside. She'd insisted he carry it at all times. Being a single parent, his mother often had to work late when Edward Lee was out of school and unsupervised. It made her worry constantly. So as a safety net, she bought the phone. He'd been instructed to check in with her periodically. Other than that, he never used it. That was until now. The GPS would locate exactly where the remains lay on the map. Frantically he searched his pockets for his phone. When he found it, instead of dialing his mother's work number, he dialed 911. He figured if there was ever an emergency, the discovery of a human body would have to count. No matter who it turned out to be, or how they got here, this call would document their location and his find.

2

Cooper Davis stepped out of the house into the glittering sunlight. It was another beautiful day, and he hated the fact he'd spent the entire first half of it stressed out at the county tax office without having resolved a thing. He stretched his arms overhead and breathed in deeply to ease the tension in his shoulders. The warm, gentle breeze carried the hint of blossoms. The scent soothed his tight neck muscles, which he massaged with his hand. With his head tilted back, the sky momentarily held his attention. It was an intense, brilliant blue, untainted by the thick veil of humidity that would soon come with the summer heat. He took a few steps, knelt down, and grabbed a fistful of dirt. With a gentle rub, he allowed the soil to slowly sift through his rough fingers. It left a slight cloud of dust in its wake. It was dry, too dry. The farm needed rain.

He walked to the edge of the peach grove and pulled down a limb for inspection. The fruit had the promise of being one of his best crops ever. Although they were only the size of golf balls, with the right amount of rain, they would become the profitable juicy fruit everyone drove for miles around to pick. Irrigation helped, but it couldn't replace a few good afternoon thundershowers. With little over a month to harvest, the danger of a late freeze was all but gone. Spring was definitely here, and his peach crop would once again beat Georgia's by a good six weeks.

He looked over at his wilted watermelons and let out a sigh. They were a different story altogether. He'd decided to give them a try because he'd heard of others who'd made thousands of dollars in a single season, and money was something that was in short supply at the moment.

His problems began a few months back when he'd heard the county was reevaluating everyone who held agricultural-exempt property. Since he was a farmer, he felt he deserved the lower tax rate and had paid no attention to the issue. Then he got an official letter in the mail. They didn't deny he was a farmer. Their claim was that not a hundred percent of his property was currently being used for agriculture. Therefore, the few nonfarmed acres would be taxed at a the usual rate, which was more than three times what he'd paid in the past. To make matters worse, they made their decision retroactive by three years. He now faced a huge tax bill he couldn't pay, along with mounting fines and penalties.

He felt they'd gone overboard and had fought it ever since with no resolution on his behalf. In an act of desperation, he'd planted more acreage in watermelons. It increased the amount of land in farm use, plus, he'd hoped it would turn a decent profit to pay off his looming tax debt. However, things hadn't worked out as planned. It appeared that an opportunistic virus had selected his watermelon crop to take up residence. It had caused the leaves to turn yellow and curl up on the vines. Even with a good rain, his melons were lost. The only upside was the virus didn't attack peaches.

He took another deep breath and tried to focus on matters he had greater control over. Despite all the pitfalls of farming, he couldn't imagine any other lifestyle. He didn't know what he'd do if he lost this place to the tax man. This farm was where he was born. It was where he grew up and, someday soon, where he hoped to raise a family. He was connected to this land. It held his heart and was his legacy. It was spring, time for a fresh start and change. His goal was to bring this farm back to the level it had been before his father had lost hope and was taken ill. He vowed to make it profitable, every square inch of it—even the old orange grove.

A truck rounded the bend and crunched along the dry gravel as it approached. The sound broke Cooper out of his thoughts. He recognized it as Megan, his best friend's little sister and a newly appointed detective. He held his hand up to shield his eyes from the sun and realized she wasn't alone. He hadn't expected company. To have a local detective drive up this time of day piqued his curiosity. Surely the county hadn't sent them to see if he was actually doing any farmwork. Nelly, Cooper's pet pig, ambled over to check out the guests' arrival while Cooper sat down on the top step to wait. Nelly grunted a few times then sat down heavily beside him.

"Wow, what the heck is that thing?" Lacy asked. They pulled up in front of a light blue clapboard house in need of a coat of paint, but it was what sat on the top step that caught her attention.

"He's a single thirty-year-old male Caucasian," Megan replied. "Interested?"

"Not him, that thing next to him."

Lacy was new to the Ocala Police Department, brought in as lead detective a mere month earlier. It was something Megan had taken as a slight and hadn't gotten over yet. Even though she had little experience as detective, she'd been with the force for six years. Her struggle to make detective hadn't been easy. She'd worked days and had taken criminal justice classes at night to finally earn her degree. She felt prepared for her promotion. Then they pulled the rug out from under her by hiring Lacy on as her superior, straight from New York. It seemed her experience as a local qualified her for escort service, proprietor of local customs, trainee, and not much more. The situation had left her with what most folks called a serious attitude and a chip on her shoulder.

"It's what we call a pig round here. What? You never seen one up in New Yourk?" Megan asked with a smirk and exaggerated accent.

Lacy let the insubordination go for the moment and said, "Not sitting up on someone's stoop like that. Does it bite?"

Despite the fact that they were there in an official capacity, Megan couldn't help but grin. Nelly sat there in all her rotund glory, snout in the air, sniffing.

"It's actually a she. Her name is Nelly. She doesn't bite or chase cars, but she can catch a Frisbee like nobody's business. And for the record, we call 'em porches round here, not stoops."

Megan hopped out of her rusted old pickup while the door squeaked in protest. She knew she'd pushed it with Lacy, so she didn't stick around for a retort. The woman *did* have a backbone; that was for sure.

"Hey, Coop," Megan said with a wave. She closed the distance between them with efficient, ample strides. In high school, she was always picked first for basketball and last for dates due to her tall, slim build. Now she was a serious runner. She used it as a way to de-stress and manage her weight. In the past, her lack of curves bothered her; but when she hit twenty-five and her friends complained about their struggles over weight, she'd reconsidered her situation. Sometimes long legs came in handy.

Nelly rocked herself back and forth until she was upright, then trotted over to Megan. The pig snorted and pushed her snout towards Megan's pockets.

"Sorry, girl, I didn't bring any treats today. This is kind of a spur-of-the-moment visit."

"So I take it this isn't a social call," Cooper said.

Nelly snorted loudly and pushed Megan so hard she stumbled back with a laugh. The pig's actions were taken as an act of aggression by the already skeptical Lacy. It was enough to send her flying back to the safety of the truck. She jumped in and slammed the door shut behind her. Once inside, she rolled down the window a crack and called out, "I thought you said she didn't bite."

Megan rolled her eyes and concentrated back on Cooper. "I think she's afraid of pigs."

Megan had a mischievous twinkle in her eye when she spoke, but Cooper didn't seem to notice. He looked past Megan and nodded toward Lacy.

"So who is she, anyway? She doesn't sound like she's from around here."

Megan glanced over her shoulder, and Lacy gave a timid wave. The hostage detective looked down dubiously at Nelly, who had now positioned her ample body outside the passenger door and grunted. Lacy had no experience with pigs whatsoever and dared not leave the security of the cab. As far as she knew, a grunt was an aggressive sign to stay clear or risk loss of limb.

"I'm afraid she's my boss, but don't worry about her," Megan said. "She's new here, from New York. More used to street crime than farm animals."

"So you still haven't told me why you're here. You say it's spur of the moment, and you bring your boss?" Cooper asked.

"Dispatch phoned. Said there was a found body called in," she said.

"Not sure what that has to do with me," Cooper said, obviously still confused.

"The call came in that it's located in the abandoned orange grove on the back of your property. They wanted to send out a patrol unit first to verify, but they're busy setting up the Easter egg hunt for the mayor's campaign speech and press conference Saturday."

"Press conference?"

"Yeah, you know—because Ocala made the top ten best places to live in America. Anyway, dispatch knew we were at the station, so they gave the call to us," Megan explained.

"What?" Cooper said with a laugh. "That can't be. No one goes out there. Is this about not using that piece of land and claiming agricultural exemption on it? Because I plan to reclaim and farm it. As a matter of fact, that's where I was just headed."

"What?" Megan asked, shaking her head. When she did, the breeze blew her long, wavy red hair in her face. Irritated, she swiped it away. She wanted to look professional and be taken seriously. This was possibly her first serious investigation. With her supervisor in the truck, it was also a chance to look good. Instead, Cooper seemed to make light of the situation. "This isn't about taxes or exemptions. There was a body found on your property. I'm serious."

He stood there in disbelief and looked her straight in the eye. He waited for the punch line or the familiar glimmer of mischief. Megan was usually the serious type, but it wouldn't be as if he didn't have it coming. He'd helped her brother, Nate, play enough practical jokes on her through the years; maybe this was retribution. "You've got to be kidding," he said; yet her expression already told him she wasn't.

Cooper didn't know what to think. This was too bizarre. He was a peach farmer with a basically uneventful life. He lived by a schedule and was a creature of habit. Recently there had been a few upheavals, such as his father's death, his dysfunctional romantic life, and his tax problem; but people like him didn't have bodies hidden in the recesses of their farm. This couldn't be real. If it wasn't a joke, it had to be a mistake, and he certainly didn't find it humorous. "I need to sit down," he said and staggered back to the steps. "Did Buddy put you up to this?"

"Buddy Howard? No. What does he have to do with anything?"

"Nothing, I guess. I ran into him this morning and had a few words. I thought maybe he wanted to play a joke on me. Get me back for what I said."

"No. This was a call from dispatch," Megan said and eyed him.

Since Cooper was somewhat of a friend, she was glad she'd been the one to handle this initial call. The guy wasn't taking it so well. Buddy Howard was a county commissioner now. In high school, he'd been two years ahead of her and from the same class as Cooper and Nate. The three had played baseball together, and Buddy was the star of the team. Every girl in the county was in love with him, including half the teachers. Buddy had the charm and good looks that hadn't faded over the past eight years. "Look, Coop, we don't even know what the situation is yet. I say we have a look at this so-called body, then we can decide what to do from there."

Cooper couldn't believe his ears. Moments ago, he stepped out of the house to begin a new positive life. This was certainly not what he had in mind. He ran his hands through his thick brown hair. He usually kept it short, but he was in need of a good trim—he had curls at his collar.

"Are you sure it's not an animal? Some animal skeletons look very humanlike, you know. For example, a bear," Cooper suggested.

"Well, it was called in as human by a little boy, but the kid might be wrong. That's why we're here to investigate. We need to view the body, and I need you to sign this so we can take a look," Megan said. She reached into her back pocket and pulled out a consent-to-search form.

"What's this?"

"It states that you don't mind if we take a look. We didn't have time to get a search warrant," Megan said.

Cooper shrugged his shoulders and signed the paper before he handed it back. "If a kid called it in, it's probably an animal. We can take my tractor. The road is so sandy from lack of rain, your truck would probably get stuck," Cooper said.

Although Megan was pleased at Cooper's cooperation, she felt compelled to tell him the whole story.

"You might want to know it was Edward Lee who called it in."

Cooper instinctively looked at his watch. That was why the boy wasn't here yet. Edward Lee worked for him every day after school, vacations, and during the summers. It was an arrangement brought about to help his mother with after-school care. It gave the boy supervision and pocket money. All without any added expense the mother couldn't spare.

It also meant that Cooper had grown to know Edward Lee very well. The kid was a regular Daniel Boone. When he wasn't at work on the farm or in school, he was outside. The boy could track animals and recognize their footprints. He wanted to be an archeologist when he grew up. That meant he also knew bones. If Edward Lee thought the remains were human, more than likely, they were.

Megan watched as understanding came across Cooper's face. She could tell the man was caught off guard by the situation. She wanted to put him more at ease.

"Your place isn't that far from the railroad tracks through the woods. It could turn out to be a vagrant. The victim very well may have died from natural causes. We won't know until we take a look," Megan said.

"But a body? Way out here?"

"The population of this area has increased rapidly. As more people move here, more things happen. We have an increasing population of homeless and transients," Megan said. "Even out here in the country."

"I don't understand. Why didn't Edward Lee come to me instead of the police?" Cooper asked.

That was a big question for Megan as well. It wouldn't have taken the boy more than five minutes to reach Cooper's house. He was on his way to work, so he knew Cooper would be here. Why didn't he run to someone he knew so well? A place where he felt safe. The place he'd been headed to anyway. That was unless for some reason he didn't feel safe here any longer.

"Well, I say we go take a look before we start to make assumptions or play 'what ifs.' Do you want to come?" Megan asked. "It's the fastest way for you to find out what's going on. Who knows, it may end up to be a bear like you suggested."

"Fine, but we do need to take the tractor. I'll drive," Cooper said.

"Great," Megan said.

Cooper turned toward the tractor, then stopped. Until that moment, he'd forgotten all about the woman in Megan's truck. "What about her?" he asked and nodded in Lacy's direction.

"Oh yeah. Give me a sec," Megan said.

She walked back to bring Lacy up to speed. That was the easy part. It took a good throw of the Frisbee to get Nelly far enough out of the way to gain a clear path that Lacy would trust. However, the hardest part was actually getting her up onto the tractor.

"You want me to what?" Lacy asked, hands on her hips. Her head cocked to the side in disbelief. This wasn't the type of thing a New York City detective was used to.

As the two stood face-to-face, they looked like the odd couple. Where Megan was tall, Lacy was short. Megan's build was closer to a flagpole, and Lacy had definite feminine curves. Megan was fair skinned, Irish. Lacy was dark complected, Hispanic. What they did share in common was they both had an attitude, along with a wide stubborn streak.

"I know it's a bit unusual, but it's the best way to get to the site quickly. It would take twenty minutes to walk," Megan said.

"Are you sure this is safe? Because I have to tell you, it doesn't look safe," Lacy complained.

"It's safe enough. It's safer than your average day at work on the streets of New York City," Megan shot back. "I don't think a crack addict will attack us way out here."

Lacy glared at her new partner. It was obvious Megan enjoyed every moment of her apprehension and discomfort. But she was right. Lacy was used to creeps with guns and women with poor dispositions. She could handle this country girl. She hadn't expected to be welcomed with open arms. If Megan wasn't going to make it easy, that was fine by her. She'd deal with it.

"Whatever," Lacy said and attempted to climb onto the vehicle.

"Just don't hit your leg on the cup holder on your way up and sit over there," Megan instructed.

"Cup holder on a tractor? You can't be serious. This is ridiculous."

"What's wrong with a cup holder? I get thirsty when I work out in the hot sun. I can't exactly balance a drink in my lap when I'm working," Cooper said. He was in no mood for criticism.

"I'm not believing this," Lacy said. Then she noticed that the keys were already in the ignition. "You leave your keys in the tractor all the time?"

"Yeah, that way I don't lose them," Cooper said.

"You're not afraid someone will steal it during the night?"

Cooper laughed. "Like who? I live out in the country. In the middle of nowhere."

"All you have to worry about is to hold on tight so you won't fall off. Coop will take it slow; right, Coop?" Megan said.

"Yeah, sure. I'll even disengage the bush hog. That way if you *do* fall off, you won't get chopped up or anything."

"Is that seriously supposed to reassure me?" Lacy snapped.

Both Megan and Cooper glared at her.

"Look, all I'm trying to say is, you guys do things a lot different down here. But, hey, I'm game. Lead the way," Lacy said, hands in the air. But when the tractor lurched forward, she grabbed hold and held on for dear life.

Cooper then glared at Megan. He'd been told a body had been found on his farm. Told to sign a consent to search form; and if that wasn't bad enough, he realized the boy that worked for him discovered it and ran to the cops instead of him. The last thing he needed was a pig-hating woman Yankee that complained constantly.

Megan leaned over and whispered in his ear, "Be nice please. She's my boss, and this is my big chance to prove myself. I've worked hard for this day."

Cooper looked straight ahead and drove. When he veered away from the main peach orchard, the terrain became rough. Both women held on tightly for fear of being thrown off.

"Where in the world are we headed?" Lacy asked.

"The old orange grove," Megan replied, deadpan. Her stomach was in a knot, unsure if this would turn out to be her first homicide, a vagrant, or an animal.

It was now clear to Lacy why they'd abandoned the truck.

Megan was lost in her own thoughts. She'd known Cooper her whole life. They went to the same high school, with him two years her senior. He was one of her brother's best friends. However, at the moment, he wasn't acting all that friendly. She saw him at the post office or occasionally at the local grocery. She felt comfortable around him. Yet when she actually thought about it, she knew very little about him personally. Most of her opinions were ceded from conversations with her brother, not by firsthand experience. And all were historic.

When they stopped at the edge of the grove, Megan hopped off the large green tractor. Lacy, being only five feet two, was hesitant to make the same leap into the deep grass. Her legs dangled as she contemplated her next move. Cooper reached up and grabbed her by the waist. With a single motion, he lifted her up and plopped her unceremoniously on the ground next to him. It wasn't an act of chivalry. He was anxious to find out what all this ridiculous mess was about. He had no patience to wait around for an apprehensive woman to climb down.

Lacy hadn't expected the assistance and felt self-conscious and a bit flustered. "Thanks," she managed to say and tried to regain her authority. "That's the first time I've ever been on a tractor."

Cooper nodded and began to walk after Megan.

"Wait," Lacy said. "Maybe you should wait here. We'll let you know if we find anything. If it is a body, you don't want your hair or something to be found at or near the scene."

"Right, that's fine," Cooper agreed and went back to lean against the tractor. He crossed his arms over his chest and watched the two women intently as he waited.

It didn't take long to find the remains. Edward Lee had tagged a nearby tree with a bandana. From there they saw the beaten-down grass which lead straight to the bones.

"They're human all right," Megan called out loud enough for Cooper's benefit. "Oh shit."

Despite the low probability, he had held out hope that Edward Lee had been mistaken. He raked his hands through his thick curly hair, a habit he had when upset or nervous. Right now, he was both. Then he started to pace, which wore a good path in the weeds as he strode back and forth.

Lacy watched him trample both the weeds and brightly colored flowers indiscriminately.

"Is he always this uptight?" Lacy asked, low enough so only Megan could hear.

"Not that I remember."

"Remember? I thought the two of you were friends. Kind of tight," Lacy said. Her dark eyes sharply focused on Cooper, not Megan.

"We used to be. Well, actually my brother more than me. I've kind of lost touch the last couple of years. Still, I've only seen him like this once before," Megan said. She left out that it was vaccination day at school, and he freaked out in front of everybody in the cafeteria when he saw the needle. She was in second grade, he the fourth at the time.

"He seems overly anxious to me. He's killing those flowers. That's not right. People just don't go around stomping down flowers for no reason," Lacy said. "Besides, he's supposed to be a farmer. I thought they planted and grew stuff, not killed innocent daisies."

Megan rolled her eyes as she flipped open her cell phone to call the crime scene unit. "The flowers are called phlox. They grow wild everywhere around here. And he's upset because a body was found on his farm. End of story."

"No," Lacy said with a shake of her finger. "It's bigger than that. Something's not right here. I've seen too many guilty people. I can tell when they're holding back. That man has a secret."

"We all have secrets. It doesn't mean anything."

"Maybe you're right," Lacy said and threw her arms in the air in exasperation. "All this nature shit creeps me out. This is a fresh scene; we have no idea what happened to this person. No need to jump to conclusions. But I have to say, I distinctly get the feeling that cops make that man nervous. It may have nothing to do with this body, but there's something going on with him."

"I've known Coop all my life. He's a peaceful guy."

"Thought you said you've been out of touch lately," Lacy challenged.

"True, but he's not a criminal. He's not capable of violence, if that's what you're insinuating."

Lacy cautiously eyed Megan before she continued. "I know you're resentful that I'm here, and I don't blame you. But you have to remember you're new to detective work. Degree or not, I was brought here based on my experience. I can teach you a few things. Another reason I'm here is for objectivity. You know practically everyone in this community. It's possible you're too close to this situation to remain objective," Lacy said. "You can't be defensive or protective of people you think you know. Look, you jumped to that man's defense before I accused him of anything more than being nervous around cops."

Who in the hell does she think she is? Megan thought with a serious pout on her lips. But what really irked her to no end was that Lacy was right. Her resentment over being displaced made her want to argue with everything Lacy said, instead of listening and learning from her.

"I never said he hurt anyone. It was a basic observation. Hell, maybe he has a few pot plants around here he doesn't want us to see. He *is* a farmer; he knows how to grow things," Lacy said.

Megan mulled that over. It was possible. Coop and her brother had smoked marijuana a few times in high school. It was also true that end-stage-cancer patients used it as a treatment for nausea and appetite loss. With Cooper's father's recent death from lung cancer, it made sense. However, before she could speak, her cell rang. It was the crime scene unit, so she took the call. A few moments later, she flipped her cell closed and turned back to Lacy.

"They're at the main road." Then she made eye contact with Lacy and said, "You can trust me to be objective. My knowledge of the people in this area will serve to better allow us to understand what's gone on here and solve our cases."

"Fine, I look forward to it," Lacy said. She matched Megan's posture of arms folded across her ample chest and steady gaze. She didn't enjoy being at odds with her new partner but held her ground like a bulldog. Their relationship was still young, and she needed to secure her position as the superior if they were to ever have a workable future.

"I advised them to gain access via the paved road. It's closer, and I wanted it measured," Megan said.

Lacy nodded. "That was smart. I doubt the CSU van could navigate the road we took to get here."

"Probably not, and if this body was dumped here, they would have done it from the main road, not Cooper's driveway," Megan shot back.

"It's good to have the measurement from both. Anyway, we've got a signed consent-to-search form, and we're here. I say we get to work. You call dispatch to check the missing-persons files for us. We may have stumbled onto someone they've been looking for," Lacy said and strode off, hands behind her back.

Megan watched her make a large circle around the remains. Lacy's eyes searched for evidence while her tentative steps were deliberate and careful. Lacy had a strong personality, even overbearing at times. Yet she was being fair. Megan knew if she could put her wounded ego on the shelf, she could learn a lot from her new partner. She could tell Lacy knew what she was doing.

Megan looked back over at Cooper and tried to see him as Lacy had. He wasn't an overly large man but had a strong build from years of hard physical labor. A shadow had formed along his jawbone from the day's growth of a heavy beard. With his head bent, he worked a path into the deep grass, obviously upset. A body found on your property could do that to a person. Some handled situations like this better than others. She decided to go talk to him while Lacy was busy with preliminary sketches of the area.

"You doing OK?" she asked as she strode up to him.

He looked over at her and gave a shrug. "As good as anyone who's been notified a body was found on their property. It's got me kinda shaken up."

"I can see that. The last time I saw you this upset was when you had to have a tetanus shot."

"I hate needles," Cooper said. He gave an involuntary shiver at the memory.

"I remember."

"Do you think you'll be able to figure out who it was? I mean, who the person was before they turned into a pile of bones?"

"We'll give it our best shot. The bones are so clean, they've obviously been here awhile. Is there anything else you can tell me?"

Cooper looked at her and then toward Lacy. "I know she thinks I had something to do with this, but I didn't. The last thing I expected today was to find out a body was dumped on my property."

"It may turn out to be a transient down here for the winter. He may have died of malnutrition or something. As far as Lacy goes, she's just doing her job. She has a suspicious nature. It's nothing personal—she's a detective."

It felt personal to Cooper since it was all happening here on his farm and to him. He felt invaded and still couldn't believe a once-live person was now dead a mere twenty feet away.

"How about hunters? Have you had any trouble with people out here?" Megan asked.

"No, not really. There's always an occasional poacher, but I doubt it would be them. Their truck would be left around close by."

"It's possible someone shot their hunting partner, panicked, then took the vehicle and fled. It's also possible they shot the person and didn't know it. Some rifles have a range up to a mile. I've heard of cases where people are at target practice and injure a neighbor through the woods."

Cooper ran his hand through his hair again and looked at Megan in thought. "I haven't shot my gun in over a year, and Ms. Hanley doesn't own a gun that I know of. Other than that, the Phillipses live through the woods. They have a son Edward Lee's age, but I'm pretty sure his mother doesn't allow guns in their house."

Megan nodded and jotted that down in her pad.

"You know what really gets me?" Cooper continued, "It's Edward Lee's reaction. I still don't understand why he didn't come to me or at least stop by afterward to tell me about it."

"I'm sure he was pretty shaken up. He'll turn up here sooner or later. He's probably down at the diner with his mom right now."

Copper nodded silently. They both looked up when the crime-scene van arrived. As the team began to unload their equipment, Cooper excused himself to head back to his place.

"I'll take the tractor. It will get it out of your way," Cooper said.

Megan watched for a moment as he left. His shoulders were slumped, and he looked older and more tired than she'd ever remembered. It wasn't the Cooper she was used to, with broad shoulders and a swift stride. She wondered if it were all due to today's events, his father's death, or life in general. All seemed to have taken a greater toll on him than she'd expected. With a shake of her head, she turned and walked back to the activity.

One man began to tape off the area. The other members of the team were in the organization process. She knew the team leader, Mahoney, from her years on the force. He had a reputation of being conscientious in the collection of evidence. He took great care not to contaminate anything during the arduous process.

"So what do you think?" Megan asked.

"I think I like this case," Mahoney said. "There're no soft tissues left to stink."

"You're bound to get lucky every now and then," Megan joked.

"The position of the remains is a bit unusual though," Mahoney said.

"I noticed that too. The person that found it tripped over them. That's why there are a few scattered. Other than that, they appear to be stacked," Megan said.

"So the mystery begins," he said and cautiously moved around the find. "Humm. Looks like there's possibly a few bones missing."

"Really? Like what?" Megan asked. She leaned in for a better view. It looked like a fairly intact skeleton to her.

"Offhand I don't see either humerus. But heck, they might be underneath or buried somewhere in the weeds. It's possible an animal made off with them. Stuff like that happens. We won't know until the photos are taken, and I can dig in."

"Do you think you have enough to go on without any soft tissues to determine much of anything?" Lacy asked as she walked up to join the two. The majority of homicide cases she'd worked in the past had contained a great deal, if not all, of the soft tissue. In the city, bodies were found within hours. A few days at most.

The three stepped to the side to give the photographer room to work. Since the bones were stacked, the process didn't take long.

"Ah, ye of little faith. You must be the new kid on the block," Mahoney said as he reached out to shake her hand. "You don't know our infallible lab guy, Jerry. Or what he will go through to gather information."

"I might have met him once at orientation, I'm not sure. I haven't had the pleasure of working with him on a case yet. He sounds promising. I take it this guy is good," Lacy said.

"One of the best," Mahoney said and acknowledged the photographer when he moved on.

"Let's see; we have the skull—that will give the race. Then there's a pelvic bone, clavicle, and—I'll be darned—both femurs. That's a little odd if the arms are gone. I would have assumed at least one of the leg bones would have been appropriated by some critter by now. They're favorites of dogs. If any bones are gone, it's usually them, not the hands."

"Could that mean they haven't been here long?" Lacy asked.

"Anything's possible, but from the look of them, they appear weathered and sun bleached," Mahoney said.

"Cooper doesn't have a dog," Megan said.

"Really?" Lacy said. "I would have pegged him as a dog person for sure."

"He used to have a bulldog. His name was Butch. He took that dog everywhere. Even bought him double cheeseburgers and chicken nuggets. He died of old age about six months ago. I guess he hasn't gotten over it enough to bring himself to get another pet yet."

"Humm," Lacy said. She hated to be wrong about anything. Even something as trivial as what kind of pet a person owned. "I knew he was a dog person. But still, there has to be someone else close by that has a dog."

"I'm not sure. Ms. Hanley lives closest to here. That way through those woods," Megan said, pointing. "But she doesn't have any pets that I'm aware of. Other than her, no one else lives closer than a mile from here. I guess the Phillipses through those woods. They have a dog."

"Then I say we talk to good old Ms. Hanley and the Phillipses. Pets or not, she might be able to tell us something," Lacy said, making a notation in her pad.

"I also think we should talk to some people down the road that own hunt dogs. The dogs get out every now and then and run this part after deer. I'd be interested to know if they've hunted in this area over the winter," Megan said.

"You think they'd confess that to two detectives?" Lacy asked.

"Probably not, but like you said, you can tell when someone tries to hide something."

Lacy looked at Megan, not sure if the comment was a compliment or a challenge. Then she focused back on Mahoney. "What else do you think Jerry will be able to tell us?"

Mahoney smiled and continued. "We should also be able to determine the sex from the pelvic bone. The odds would dictate it will turn out to be female. From the femurs, we'll be able to give you a good estimate of height. Then with the sutures of the skull and evaluation of the epiphysis of the various long bones, Jerry can give you a close approximation of age. Basically, he'll be able to give you everything but the victim's name and address. That guy's a genius. We're lucky to have him in our lab."

Lacy jotted down more notes as Mahoney spoke, then looked up abruptly. "What about the fact that these bones have been weathered? As you stated, they appear sun bleached. Will this effect the ability to gather any of this information?" She hated to ask, but her past case experience didn't encompass clean bones, and she didn't want to pass on a learning opportunity.

"Not really. They're in pretty good shape aside from the few possible missing ones. Who knows, we might find them before we're through. Anyway, it can affect the quality of DNA. Still, there're so many ways to come up with the information we're after. Between radiological results that can offer the ossification centers of the bones as well as the degree of closure of the cranial sutures, you also have the development of the dentition. If the victim was young—which, again, probability dictates, it's easier."

"Wow, I thought all that took soft tissue," Lacy said.

"There are problems with no soft tissue. Even the most violent crimes can be contained to this area and cause mortal death without damage to the bones. It would be rare to state an absolute cause of death without soft tissue. However, there is still hope. Much information is still there. The body has 206 bones and thirty-two teeth. Then we have the sutures that become closed at a specific rate as growth is complete. Same as tooth eruption. You can still look for wear on the back teeth, but that's more subjective since some people grind their teeth, which makes them wear faster."

"Yeah, I had a brother that did that. It sounded terrible, like he was breaking all his teeth off in the middle of the night. It kept the whole household up," Lacy said.

It was the first reference Lacy had made to her family and caused Megan to realize she had no idea what had prompted Lacy's move from New York to Florida. She'd been so involved with her own displacement on the force, she never asked. As she spoke of her brother, Megan didn't sense any animosity. She felt ashamed of herself for being so self-centered. All she had focused on was that Lacy took her position as superior on the Ocala force. She'd never once given thought to what caused Lacy to make such a career move. Or that Lacy might also feel displaced and need a friend.

Mahoney continued, "Well, in this case, the condition of a few of these molars looks really good. They look young. Youthful teeth can tell you a lot."

"Again, I like the sound of that," Lacy said. "But let me ask you a question. You mentioned probability. Does that mean the majority of the victims in this area are young women? Couldn't this be an elderly person? I mean, Florida's a retirement state. I thought you had old people coming out of the woodwork. Maybe one wandered away, got disorientated, and lost?"

"From where? There are no retirement homes nearby. The majority of those are located either in town, close to the hospitals, or in the southern part of the county, in the villages," Megan said.

Lacy looked at Mahoney for confirmation.

Mahoney nodded. "It's true. Besides, we would have been notified right away if we had a missing senior on the loose. However the real clincher here is the lack of clothing. I don't see any form of clothing on or near the remains. Old people aren't usually naked. It happens, but usually they are pajama clad or in a hospital gown."

"It's possible they had on cotton pajamas, and women don't tend to wear bras to bed. The clothes could have rotten away by now," Lacy suggested. Again, this was new territory for her.

"True. We'll know more when the lab reports come back," Mahoney said and walked away to give his crew room to work. The two detectives followed.

"The no-clothes thing does put a damper on the rifle-accident theory. Most people don't hunt naked although it could still turn out to be a vagrant hit by a stray bullet," Lacy said.

"The biggest problems you face now is how to determine the length of time these bones have been at this site, along with the cause of death. That's where soft tissue comes in really handy. If we had that, there would be bugs. With bugs, a forensic entomologist can give a better estimate of how long the body's been in a particular location. Actually, there's an excellent facility that deals with that in Gainesville," Mahoney said.

"It's good to know bugs are good for something other than personal annoyance," Lacy said.

"Yeah, but then sometimes people are stuffed in a freezer for a while before they're dumped. That messes everything up," Mahoney added. "But still, even without insects, many forms of homicide leave their mark on the skeleton. Except perhaps hypothermia, which I think we can rule out here in Florida. That and carbon monoxide poisoning. However, I think we can all agree this isn't an accidental death."

"Whoa, back up a minute," Lacy said. "We have no proof this isn't death by natural causes."

"It looks suspicious to me too," Megan said. "The bones are in a neat pile, or they were before Edward Lee tripped over them."

"And there are no traces of clothing anywhere," Mahoney added. "Not even a button."

"Fine, both of your opinions are duly noted, but until I get the lab results, my mind will remain open. Once we get these remains back to the lab and take a closer look, it's possible we'll find a nick from a bullet or a knife blade. Until then, the jury's still out on that one," Lacy declared.

"You can bet, if it's there, Jerry will find it," Mahoney said.

"Hey, look at this," one of the men called out.

They all turned to look, but Megan asked first, "What do you have?"

"It's a Wal-Mart Supercenter bag. It was so tangled in with a few of the bones on the bottom of the pile I don't see how it could be unrelated trash."

Recognition of evidence was always a difficult task for both the crime scene unit and the detectives alike. It was equally important to be able to discern unimportant background items from potentially crucial evidence. A stray bag had the possibility to be either, but as Megan walked over to take a closer look, she had to agree with the technician. This bag was significant. "Good call, Tim."

"It's one of the newer white ones. They used to have blue ones; then they changed to really thin white ones. I guess enough people complained about them because they eventually switched to thicker newer white ones."

"Wow, we have us an official Wal-Mart freak here," Lacy stated.

"Hey, give me a break. I'm a technician. We don't rake in the big bucks like you detectives. I happen to be on a tight budget, and my mother taught me how to value shop."

"Value shopping is good, Tim. We might be able to use this bag to determine how long the body's been here," Megan said, then glared at Lacy.

"That's exactly what I thought," Tim said, vindicated.

"Hey look, there's something here stuck on the bottom. I can't tell what it is, but Jerry might want to analyze it. You never know, it might help." It was possible the substance and the bag could be tested for evidence of blood, prints, or saliva. "It's been exposed to weather conditions, but we haven't had much rain lately, so it's worth a try."

"It could work. The bag's plastic and porous enough. It may have absorbed oil from someone's fingertips. the weather being warm and relatively humid without rain will help," Mahoney said. He watched Tim skillfully handle the specimen with tweezers and place it in a stiff paper bag.

Mahoney understood that Tim chose the rigid paper container for two reasons. First of all, paper allowed moisture from the evidence sample to dissipate, whereas plastic caused moisture to remain trapped inside. This caused the evidence to either mold or rot; neither was favorable. It left many collected items unusable—something he'd preached to his crew. Secondly, with the paper bag being so stiff, it wouldn't arbitrarily damage any prints in transfer. This was also the reason why Tim took so much care in retrieval—so as not smear any residual prints.

"You don't by any chance have an idea when Wal-Mart switched bags, do you?" Megan asked.

Tim's eyes shot toward Lacy. He didn't care to become the brunt of any more jokes, but he felt it was more important to ID the killer. He looked back at Detective Callingham and said, "Actually I do. It's been awhile, but I remember at Christmas they still used the cheap white bags because I had one rip open on me with a jar of spaghetti sauce in it. The jar fell to the floor and shattered. It made a major mess in my kitchen. I had sauce everywhere. The floor, cabinets, dishwasher—I'm telling you everywhere! It really ticked me off because that's why I'd gone to the store in the first place. I had to drive all the way back to town to get more sauce. I had a date due for dinner, and I couldn't exactly serve her peanut butter and jelly in an apartment covered in sauce."

Megan's first reaction was to be impressed. She would have served Pop-Tarts or ordered takeout. Then again, she was domestically challenged.

"That means this body had to have been here after Christmas. That makes it no more than three and a half months old," Megan said.

"We need to run that date against the missing persons and runaway data file," Lacy said.

"At this point, it looks like that's all we've got until we hear back from Jerry. With some of the other information like sex, height, and race, we might be able to get a positive identification fairly quickly," Megan said.

Lacy nodded and made a notation in her pad. She'd been standing in the same place for several minutes, intent on the discussion, when suddenly she let out a shriek and began to jump around. She stomped her feet as if she were putting out a fire. "Ohmygod!" she yelled.

In seconds, Megan realized the problem.

"Oh man, Lacy, you're on a fire ant mound." Megan rushed over to pull her partner away from the infested area and swatted frantically at Lacy's pant legs.

"It burns like hell," Lacy shrieked. "The damn things are stuck like glue. They're all over me. I can't get them off."

"This isn't going to work. They've already burrowed into the fabric. You need to take off your shoes and socks, or you'll keep getting bit."

Lacy didn't question the advice. She stripped off not only her footwear but her pants as well. The men from the crime scene unit looked on in total amusement.

Once her skin was exposed, the two women were finally able to brush the tiny invaders off.

"What the hell are these things anyway? I've never heard of ants that attack people like that."

"They're fire ants, and they're really relentless. They crawl on you, hundreds of them at a time, and you don't even realize it. Then they send out a signal which prompts them to all bite simultaneously. That's their mound over there, right where you stood," Megan said and pointed. "You really have to watch where you step."

"Well, that little piece of information would have been helpful earlier," Lacy snapped. She was in the process of putting her pants back on when she noticed her rapt audience.

"Nice flowered panties," Tim said. "They're a nice touch to the high-dollar detective outfit."

Lacy figured she had that coming after her Wal-Mart commentary. The phrase "What goes around, comes around" popped into her head. However, even though the comment may have been deserved, the ant bites certainly were not. They really did burn like hell.

Megan tried to use herself as a visual shield to afford her boss a modicum of privacy, but with her tall lanky build, it wasn't very effective. The men merely leaned to either side to maintain their view of the spectacle.

"Nice butt," one of the men remarked. "No cellulite."

In an attempt to hold on to what tiny shred of dignity that remained, Lacy lifted her head high, jutted out her chin, and said, "I swear, if any of you say a darn thing about this to another living soul, I will get you back." She pointed to each and every one as she spoke. It left no doubt she meant every word. She had balls.

"She's cute and feisty," another whispered.

"You realize they're still going to rush back to the station to tell everyone about this, don't you?" Megan whispered.

"Yes. Unfortunately I will make a huge impression on my first real case. One I'll probably never live down. Too bad it's not the one I was shooting for."

"Gosh, I hope none of them had a camera phone," Megan said. She had to admit, she wanted to prove herself competent in front of her boss. Perhaps even superior. Yet public humiliation was something she hadn't wanted. It certainly wouldn't make their work relationship any easier.

Lacy looked up, horrified. "I never thought of that. Sometimes I hate modern technology."

"I know right now this may seem really bad," Megan said, "but in a week or so, it will all blow over."

"Super. A week of total humiliation to look forward to from the people I have to depend on for answers to solve my first case."

Not sure what more she could do, Megan said, "You finish getting dressed; then we can leave. I need to speak to Mahoney and the crew for a minute."

"Make it quick because I need to get the heck out of here, or I might just die of embarrassment. I strongly feel the need to scratch in places my mother told me to never do in public."

"I understand," Megan said.

Megan watched Lacy stomp off, then walked back over to the men who at least had enough decency to pretend they'd gone back to work. "I need y'all to take some good overall photos of this area as well as a few close-up shots."

"Already done for the overall shots," one of the men said. He had a Polaroid camera draped around his neck. "I did the close-ups before you started to poke around."

Being a student of human nature, Megan held out her hand. "How about you give me the shot of Detective Andina in her panties."

His face flushed at being caught, not out of embarrassment but anger. He'd only worked with Megan once before and knew her reputation as a driven, purpose-minded cop. It was what got her promoted to detective. It was also why she had few friends. Although he would have loved to have the photo to show around, Megan was someone he chose not to go up against. Lacy seemed just as bad, so reluctantly, he reached into his back pocket and turned over the coveted item.

"It was all in fun."

Megan ripped it up in front of him and almost threw it in one of their equipment trunks before she reconsidered and tucked the shreds in her own pocket for safer disposal later. With that little task handled, she reverted back into serious work mode.

"I would like the body's position measured from these two trees separately. It will allow us to triangulate the location of the bones and help with the accuracy of all the distances. I also need the distance from here to the main road. Also, did you catch that abraded area on that tree over there?"

"Uh, no, sorry. Where?"

This further aggravated him. He hated when he missed a piece of potential evidence. It was worse when it was brought to your attention by someone who'd just denounced you.

Megan walked over to a nearby sapling and pointed out a small area of bark that had a faint but distinct red discoloration approximately two inches in length.

"This right here. It appears to be paint along with some damage to the bark."

Megan examined the trunk at the edge of the scar. It was abraded and rough at either end. "This looks recent, but it's healed somewhat. The exposed part isn't as bright white like you would expect from a fresh scrape. This might help date the remains as well."

The photographer's animosity abated when he viewed the potential evidence he'd missed.

"Wow, you've got good eyes. I'll get a close-up for you."

"Thanks, and don't forget to measure how far off the ground it is. Who knows, it might also give us the potential model of the vehicle."

"You got it, Detective. I'll get Tim to take a sample of the paint to send to the lab."

"I appreciate it," Megan said. "We need everything documented. I don't want to trust anything to memory. If we don't come up with a missing-person match, this case may sit on the shelf for a while."

"Sure thing."

Megan felt she'd adequately worked the scene and could leave the rest to their competent crime scene unit, so she turned to walk away, relatively pleased with herself. This was her first real case as a detective. It didn't matter if she wasn't the lead detective; she was going to make a positive identification and prove herself to everyone. If this body was a missing person, soon she hoped she would have a name, and the family could be notified. Not good news, but at least it would offer them a sense of closure. Something whose importance she knew all too well.

3

Megan climbed into the driver's seat of her truck to find Lacy bent over in the passenger side, scratching her legs. She saw no sign of Cooper or Nelly and considered that a positive thing. At least the pig hadn't antagonized her partner any further, and she didn't feel like dealing with Cooper's questions right now. As far as Lacy was concerned, she figured she'd start with sorry, then see where that led.

She started the vehicle and pulled out before she said anything. "Sorry about the ants."

Lacy glowered at Megan, too consumed by her personal misery to make idle chitchat.

Megan had been in the same situation before and hadn't expected any different. Instead, her thoughts kept going back to the remains. The position of them in a stack, the lack of any evidence of clothing, and the possibility of the arms being absent all seemed to point to murder. Missing limbs were the type of thing usually associated with the mob. Although Ocala had grown rapidly, up until this point, they had had few problems with organized crime. It didn't fit, and she hated things that didn't fit. Maybe a big-city detective on the force would come in handy. Lacy had experience with this sort of crime.

"I need to stop by my sister's house on the way back to the station," Megan said.

"I don't feel like driving all over the county right now," Lacy said.

"Don't worry, it's on the way and close."

"I'm not exactly up for a social visit," Lacy scowled. Her focus never wavered from her bites.

"You need to stop that, or you'll make it worse," Megan said.

"How can it get any worse?" Lacy asked. "They burn like crazy, and there's got to be hundreds of them. How long will this last anyway?"

"I'm afraid for a few days. If there was any hot water handy at the scene, we could have rinsed you off. Hot temperature helps denature the formic acid, which is what the little monsters inject into you that makes the bites burn so bad. Unfortunately, it's too late for that now."

"Lovely. What else can you tell me besides after-the-fact information?" Lacy asked. "Like something that can help me now."

"Not much. Some people use home remedies, but I'm not sure how much they help. At this point, things kind of have to run their course. Tomorrow you'll wake up, and each bite will be a tiny pustule. You'll look like you have the chicken pox from the knees down. But seriously, don't scratch, or they'll get infected. That's when things can really get nasty and cause scars. As far as your plan to stay away from fire ants, you can't. They're everywhere in Florida. You have to keep an eye out for them. Always watch where you stand, especially in deep grass. That's the worst—because the grass obstructs your view of their dirt mound."

"Again, that would have been handy to know earlier," Lacy said.

"I really am sorry about this," Megan said.

"I know. I'm being bitchy. I look and feel like shit. Do we really have to stop by your sister's house? I'm not really in the meet-and-greet mood in case you haven't noticed."

Megan had definitely noticed but let that go. "You look fine. It will only take a minute."

"I have sticks in my hair, and my shirt is stuck to me from sweat."

"Beth won't care. If she complains about anyone's hair, it will be mine. It's a hobby of hers. I'm her little sister, so she feels entitled to criticize me on a regular basis," Megan said.

"She sounds lovely, so why do we have to stop by?" Lacy asked and looked up for the first time.

"I promised to drop off some PR information for my nephew's school project. It will only take a minute. It's good for the department, and I know he'll appreciate the effort."

"I hope so because I really don't feel so good."

"It's probably from all the ant bites. We'll get you something to eat when we get to Beth's. That will help, and my sister is an excellent cook."

"Shouldn't you call first?"

"No, Beth won't mind. With the two kids, extended family, and friends, she's used to unannounced visitors. Actually she'd be offended if she got wind I was out this way and didn't stop by to introduce you. She's been hounding me to meet you. Anyway, here we are."

Megan pulled off the road onto a long, winding driveway lined with azaleas in full bloom. It was beautiful enough to take Lacy's mind off her recent trauma.

"Wow, this is incredible. It looks so countrylike."

Megan laughed and got out of the truck. "It ought to be—it's in the middle of a two-hundred-acre peanut farm."

"Oh, stop. You know what I mean. I'd expected another mobile home, like so many people seem to have around here, or a single-story blockhouse. You don't see many two-story Victorian houses. It's absolutely gorgeous. It looks like a postcard for quaint country living or some fancy bed-and-breakfast. I love it."

Megan paused to reappraise her sister's home from Lacy's perspective. It had been her childhood home, but Beth and Mather had really fixed the place up and made it their own. It gave her a renewed appreciation of their old family farm. The two-story yellow clapboard house was immaculately kept, with a wide wraparound porch. Numerous majestic huge ferns hung from above, and several rocking chairs were scattered about in an inviting manner. On the top step, Cleo, their oversized orange cat, lay curled up, sound asleep. Lacy was right. It had a certain charm and warmth. It looked cheerful, happy, and very inviting. It had been the perfect place to grow up.

"Are you really sure your sister won't mind? I mean she's never met me before, and here I am on her doorstep uninvited at lunchtime. Not to mention I look like heck. I think I have sticks in my hair."

"It's only Spanish moss and one twig," Megan said and plucked the offending debris out of Lacy's hair. "There, you look fine now. Besides, things are pretty casual around here."

"Casual is one thing, but site evidence in your hair is another," Lacy said. She tried to smooth out her clothes and fluff up her hair. She took pride in her appearance and didn't like to look so disheveled. She was a city girl at heart. Casual to her was shopping at the Gap in the mall.

Megan shook her head slowly. "I'm serious. I think you'll find Floridians lean toward the informal and relaxed side. Especially way out here in the country. Maybe it's due to the heat and humidity. That messes up everyone's hair. Besides, if we're going to work together, that practically makes you family, so you need to meet my sister. It will explain a lot of my neuroses."

"If you say so," Lacy said.

Megan knocked at the door and hollered a hello before going on in. Cleo followed close behind, never one to miss out on an opportunity for food. The feline always associated Megan with a treat.

Lacy hesitated briefly before she followed. "She doesn't lock her front door?"

"Of course not. No one around here does." This time it was Lacy who shook her head.

Beth heard the jingle of the bell on the screen door and came down the hallway to investigate. She wiped her hands on a dish towel and said, "Megan, sweetie, what a pleasant surprise." The two hugged, then Beth stepped back in appraisal. "And who do we have here?"

Beth extended out her hand to Lacy, who quickly introduced herself.

"I hope you don't mind me here unannounced," Lacy said.

"Don't be silly. Please, come on back to the kitchen. I'll fix y'all a snack to eat."

"Something smells wonderful," Lacy said. She hadn't realized how hungry she was until she smelled the food. It was a definite distraction from the misery of the ant bites.

"I've been in this kitchen all morning cooking for Sunday dinner. Plus, there's a reception Sunday night after the Easter play the children are putting on, and of course, I was put down for two cakes."

"My sister bakes the best cakes," Megan said by way of an explanation.

"Oh, Megan, that's so sweet, but I'm afraid it's an exaggeration. Mary Pearl makes the best triple-fudge cake ever! And her hummingbird cake and cream cheese frosting is to die for."

"Stop. You two are making me hungry. Unless somebody has cake to feed me, I'd just as soon not talk about it," Lacy said.

"Well, I don't have cake as of yet, but you are in luck. I just finished a big batch of greens and some cheese grits," Beth said. "So please excuse the mess."

It was a perfunctory comment since the kitchen was spotless aside from a couple of clean food containers on the table, which Beth swiftly removed. She then went over to the side counter and began to fix two plates loaded down with food.

"It smells like you made a batch of corn bread too," Megan said as she poured three glasses of iced tea.

"Of course, silly. It wouldn't be right to expect folks to eat greens without corn bread. It would be a waste of good pot liquor."

Megan sat the tea down in front of Lacy and noticed her confused look. "Pot liquor is the broth the greens make when you cook them down slowly until they're tender."

"Remember how we used to fight over who got to drink it when we were kids?" Beth asked.

Megan laughed. "Yes. As I remember, you and Nate always beat me to it." She turned back to Lacy and explained, "I was the youngest, who was unfortunately cheated repeatedly by my siblings, who slurped it down right in front of me. With no remorse, whatsoever, I might add. I'm sure I was permanently scarred by the experience."

"What doesn't put you under serves to make you stronger," Beth said.

"Anyway, it's proper etiquette to dunk your corn bread in the pot liquor as you eat," Megan explained.

Beth placed the plates in front of the two women, then took a seat across from them. "So tell me what you two ladies are up to way out here in the middle of the day. And please, don't leave out any details because I am absolutely starved for conversation."

Megan immediately thought of Lacy's fire ant incident but considered it best to leave that story untold. She wanted to build a strong working relationship with Lacy, not an adversarial one as she'd managed to do so far. "We had to go out to Cooper's place," Megan said. "Since we were so close, I figured I'd drop off the pamphlets I promised Camp. He said he needed them for a class project that's due next week."

Lacy was too involved with her food to say anything. That is other than the tiny noises that indicated it was being greatly enjoyed.

Beth smiled in satisfaction, then turned her attention back to her sister. With one eyebrow raised, she questioned, "Cooper's place? Do I sense a romance?"

Ever since Megan had broken up with her last boyfriend, Beth never missed an opportunity to bring up Megan's lack of romantic involvement and current single status. She treated it like it was some type of disease that required immediate treatment and not a personal choice.

"No, Beth, we're friends and will always be just friends. Besides, Cooper was engaged to someone else only a few months ago."

Beth waved her hand in the air to dismiss Megan's protest. "I know he likes you and always has. You're both too stubborn to realize it, and you've already wasted your prime childbearing years. They won't last forever, you know. I still don't know what you had against Todd. He owned his own home and made a good income."

"Cooper was recently engaged?" Lacy managed to ask in between bites.

"He was, but then something must have happened because it was suddenly called off. She moved right afterward," Megan said.

"So who's Todd?" Lacy asked.

"He's someone Megan left in despair. He had a steady job as an accountant," Beth said. "They could have had a family by now. A sound family man if I ever saw one, and she let him go."

"Beth, I didn't love him. The man drove me crazy with his neatness compulsion. He had his pantry alphabetized for god's sake," Megan said.

"He was an accountant?" Lacy asked.

Megan nodded and refocused on her tea.

"What about Cooper's girlfriend?"

"No one's heard from her since she left town," Beth said.

"That's interesting," Lacy said and pushed her plate back.

"So if you weren't at Cooper's for a social visit, what happened? If there's some kind of crime taking place around here, I need to know about it. How else am I supposed to protect my family? Besides, what in the world could happen at the peach farm, for heaven's sake? Crimes don't happen on peach farms—except for that time those boys broke into Coop's shed and stole his golf clubs. Those things are expensive. Is that what happened? Is little Joe back to his antics? That boy is no good, I tell you. Neither was his daddy. It's a shame."

Megan knew the way it worked with Beth. If you answered one question, two followed. It was best to stop the inquiry at the start. "Nothing happened that you need to be concerned about." It had come out clipped, which hadn't been Megan's intention.

Lacy watched the exchange between the two sisters with interest. She wanted to know more about Cooper's ex-girlfriend. Like when she was last seen and did anyone know her current address.

Beth got up and fidgeted with something on the stove. Then she reached in the cupboard and retrieved a bottle. Megan noted her hand shook slightly.

"This isn't your first glass of tea, is it, Beth?" Megan asked.

"No, but what does that have to do with Cooper's shed being vandalized?"

"No one broke into his shed. And I can't talk about it, Beth. You don't need to worry."

"Oh, come on, Megan. I've been stuck in this house alone all day. My work is thankless, and it never ends. I need a little excitement. I'm starved for conversation from someone other than a toddler. My life isn't as stimulating as yours. Sometimes I wish I had a job out in the real world."

"Trust me, the real world isn't all it's cracked up to be. There's some crazy-ass people out there," Lacy said. "But, boy, this food was great. I think I could get used to this place if all the food's this good."

Beth smiled politely at Lacy. She was shocked at her language but didn't let it show. "Thank you, that's very kind of you to say."

Megan on the other hand was irritated. Her sister had what most people would consider to be the perfect life. Two beautiful children, a great husband, who was a good provider, and she lived in a beautiful home. Then there was the added bonus of sex if and when she wanted it.

"Where are the kids, anyway?" Megan asked in an attempt to reroute the conversation.

"Arlene came and picked up Tyler this morning so I could cook for the church reception and Easter Sunday. They should be back anytime now. Campbell's still at school. I have to go pick him up at three thirty after soccer practice. Thursday's my day for carpool. You see? This is what I'm talking about. My life's a bore. When they get home, I have dinner, bath, homework, and bed. All separate for each. If you won't talk to me about Cooper, at least tell me something."

Megan took a deep breath, relieved she'd won this tiny battle of wills with her sister.

"How about you fill me in about Todd," Lacy said with a supercilious grin.

Beth's face lightened. "Certainly. Let me refill your plate."

Megan glared at her partner and grasped her tea glass tighter. She was angry until the realization hit that Lacy had smoothly changed the conversation away from Cooper without causing suspicion.

Beth put down the full plate of food in front of Lacy. This time the slice of corn bread was extra large. Then Beth proceeded to give a rundown of Megan's brief affair with Todd. The memory made Megan roll her eyes and give an involuntary shiver. The man was a total bore.

"Maybe we should get back to work," Megan suggested. "I know you were tight for time."

"I swear, Beth, this is the best food I have ever eaten. I had my doubts about this place, but now I think I'm going to really like it here. But Megan's right—we need to get back to the station."

Beth smiled at her again and said, "Well, you'll be a cracker before you know it."

"Really? I thought I was doomed to be considered a Yankee for the rest of my life," Lacy said.

"Heavens, no. We have people from all over the world who move here and blend in. A 'Yankee' is a word we reserve for people who move to Florida and never adapt. They're afflicted with the 'everything was so much better back home' syndrome. They can't seem to appreciate the way of life here. Or maybe they just miss home too much. I'm not sure. All I know is they complain all the time, and it's intolerable. But, you, on the other hand, have a good start since you enjoy the local food," Beth said, then added quickly, "although that accent of yours needs to be tamed. We can work on that later. I'll help you."

Megan held her tongue. If Beth tried to fix Lacy, as she always did with her, the woman deserved it after the questions she posed about her personal life—like bringing up Todd, of all things—to divert attention from their ongoing investigation. Todd. The memory that wouldn't die.

"As Megan said, we need to go. We have a missing person to identify," Lacy said.

Megan wasn't sure if Lacy forgot whom she addressed, or if she wanted to shock Beth.

"What do you mean? Did they have amnesia?"

"No, it's a body," Lacy said, matter-of-fact.

Beth gasped and staggered back into her chair. She riffled for her medicine and swallowed two pills in one gulp. "You can't be serious!"

"Don't worry. It's more than likely a vagrant," Lacy said.

"I hope so. Not that I wish anything bad on homeless people, but it would be better than a murder here in our community," Beth said.

Lacy could empathize with Beth. Of all the possible crimes, people feared violent death the most. It had fascinated as well as horrified people for centuries. "I wish I could say for certain, but as it stands, I wouldn't be overly concerned about it," Lacy said.

"It kind of reminds me of when Mama went missing," Beth said. "I think that's the last time anything like that happened so close to here."

Lacy looked directly at Beth, then over at Megan. They hadn't worked together long enough to know each other very well. Megan had never mentioned her parents. Certainly not a missing mother.

"What happened to your mother?" Lacy asked.

"I was sixteen when she disappeared. One day she began to paint the porch, then she was gone. They never found her or her body."

"That must have been tough."

"It was. Especially right when it happened because they suspected my father, which was ridiculous. Anyone who knew him knew how much he adored my mother."

"That would make it hard, but the first rule of thumb in that type of investigation is to question the immediate family," Lacy said but then let the subject drop. It was obviously still painful for Megan.

"Well, we've really got to go," Megan said and looked at her watch. She didn't want Beth to ask any more questions or give out any more personal family information. It was bad enough for one day that she'd brought up both their mother and Todd.

"Are you sure?" Beth asked. "It's been such a nice visit."

"We don't want to take up any more of your time," Lacy said.

When Lacy stood up, Beth noticed the bites on her ankle and a few on her wrist. "Oh, those look like fire ant bites. You might want to try some tea tree oil on them. Here, I have some right here in the cupboard." She swiftly accessed the container and handed it over to Lacy. "Just gently rub a dab on the affected areas. Come to think of it, you might need to pick up another bottle."

"Thanks for the tip and the medicine," Lacy said.

"Well, y'all be careful out there. Don't get too close to any homeless people. They don't have a place to wash up. Who knows what kind of germs they have. You should pick up a bottle of that disinfectant hand wash too. Our local drugstore carries that and the tea tree oil for your bites."

Megan shook her head. If her sister only knew what kind of situations her occupation placed her in. "I thought you said you wished you had a job like mine. Remember—work in the real world?"

"Well, it's more interesting than mine, but you don't have to go get a serious disease to prove a point, Megan. Besides, I was talking about the jobs you can dress nice for. You can be fashion conscious and professional. I watch television, I know."

Megan threw her arms in the air. Sometimes it was impossible to talk to her sister. "Thanks for lunch, sis. It was excellent as usual."

"Y'all are welcome. It wasn't much of a snack though. If I knew you were coming, I could have fixed a nice roast or some rotisserie chicken. Call me next time."

"Thanks again," Megan said. "Love you, give the boys a kiss for me."

"You see—I told you we should have called first," Lacy said, a step behind her.

"I'm not going to call in time for her to defrost and roast a chicken, plus buy matching napkins," Megan grumbled under her breath and strode to her truck.

Lacy followed behind, then paused at the bottom of the stairs. "By the way, not many people say thanks to cops either. It's also one of those thankless, endless jobs."

Beth frowned. She was all alone in her world. No one understood the pressures she faced.

"Now I understand what you mean about neurosis," Lacy added once in the cab. "But her food would keep me coming back. I can take a lot of abuse if good food is involved."

Megan smiled. "I like the way you handled her. She thinks you told her everything, but you basically gave her no more than what will be on the evening news. She would have hounded me with questions."

"We just met. She's still in her polite mode, except I think she insulted the way I dress. I told you I looked like crap. You said she wouldn't notice."

"I said she would pick on me. The comment was directed toward me. She's not used to me having a partner. You need to give her time. In time, I'm sure she'll insult you too."

A few miles down the road, Lacy spoke up again, "I think we should look up Cooper's ex-fiancé. It sounds like her disappearance coincides with the time frame of our body. Especially if no one's heard from her since she left town."

Megan looked over at Lacy. "You think the body's hers?"

"Who knows. Until we get the lab data back on the basics, such as height, sex, and age, we have nothing else to go on. If it's not her, she still may know something. From what I've heard, it sounds like she lived at Cooper's near the time the body arrived on the property."

"It sounds reasonable. It's good to cover all the bases," Megan said. "I want to talk to Ms. Hanley and Edward Lee as well."

They rode in silence for a while before Lacy spoke up again.

"You chose a career in police work because of what happened to your mother, didn't you?"

Megan looked over at Lacy, surprised. "What?" She had hoped the mother thing would have been forgotten. Instead she thought she saw pity in her partner's eyes, but it might have been her imagination. Most people felt uncomfortable with such issues. They often couldn't make eye contact. This was not the case with Lacy. She stared her dead in the eye.

"You heard me. I asked about your mother."

God, she wished Beth would have kept her mouth shut. At the moment, she envied other people who didn't have to spend the day riding around with their boss. However, since this was currently her lot in life, she owed it to Lacy to explain. Besides, it was better if Lacy heard it from her than be exposed to other's contrived versions.

"Yes, but I don't spend my time in pursuit of answers in my mother's case at the expense of a current investigation. That's not why they brought you on the force—to reign me in. I worked hard as a uniform for six years while I took night college classes to qualify to make detective."

"Hey there, slow down, girlfriend. I didn't accuse you of anything," Lacy said. "I may be your superior, but I'm also your partner. And I hope that one day, you'll consider me as a friend."

"I'm sorry. I didn't mean to be so defensive. I want you to understand. It was very hard on our family. Not only the suspicion of my father but basically not knowing what happened to my mom. I wanted to become a detective so I could do everything possible to keep other families from that kind of pain. I want to be able to answer their questions and give some sort of closure."

"And if you solve your mother's case, all the better?"

"Sure. I can't say I will never look for evidence to solve that mystery, but I can assure you, it won't impede my work."

"I don't doubt that. The same as I don't doubt how hard you worked to make detective. What are you, like twenty-five?"

"Twenty-eight. But there were many people who doubted my motives."

"That just blows," Lacy said.

Megan had to smile at that.

"I had family on the force. That's how I got involved. Two brothers and my father. I've known I wanted to be a detective since I was seven. I still had to work my ass off to prove myself. Now I'm thirty-one and have a good number of homicides under my belt."

"You think Cooper's involved in this, don't you?"

"Hell, I don't know. He was engaged, she's gone, a woman body's found on his farm? It could be hers. Maybe he changed his mind and didn't want to get married, so he killed her. It happens. People do crazy things. It could have been an argument that got out of control."

"I don't think he had anything to do with it. The story I heard was she took off when his father was diagnosed as terminal. Cooper moved his father into their house, then had hospice come in to help. Cooper might have been an emotional mess, but he wasn't violent. I think she couldn't deal with it, so she took off."

"What does he have to say about it?"

"I never talked to him about it directly, but it was the general consensus around town."

"Who knows, it might turn out to be a homeless person, like I told Beth. But we do need to check it out. We won't know for a few days, and that's only if we get lucky. One thing you'll have to learn about being a detective is not all cases get solved," Lacy said.

"I learned that a long time ago with my mother," Megan said. Her hands were tight on the wheel, her eyes focused straight ahead.

Lacy did a mental head slap for the insensitive comment. Despite it being a touchy subject, Lacy was drawn to ask, "So you worked your way through school?"

"Yes. Plus I threw myself into the job during the day. Heck, I *became* the job. I was determined to be the best. At night I took classes. In my free time, I went over every unsolved file for the past twenty years. Not to find out about my mother but to familiarize myself with what had gone on in Marion County for the last two decades."

"Wow, sounds like you don't get out much. Have you dated before or since Todd?" Lacy asked.

"Well, maybe not a lot, but I've had a few boyfriends."

"I think you did the right thing dumping Todd. I can't see you with an accountant."

"Really?" Megan asked.

"Yeah, but you do really need a boyfriend. Any current ones?"

"No. That makes me all that much better to solve this investigation."

"Girl, there's more to life than work. I'm not saying you shouldn't try to be the best you can be on the job. But seriously, you need to get a little balance," Lacy said.

"God, now you sound like my sister."

"Hey, don't throw me in with her. That woman's stir-crazy, and I never said nothing about marriage and babies. Just a nice dinner, a little fun between the sheets, you know—have a good time. Live a little."

Megan had to repress a smile. She was getting used to Lacy. "Actually, back to those old files and work, there's something that's been bothering me about today's case."

"Besides the fact that we don't know who the hell it is?'

Megan looked over and realized it was a joke. "Seriously. There are a couple of files I would like you to look over."

"Sure, I'd be glad to," Lacy said. "Any reason in particular?"

"Yeah, but I'll let the files speak for themselves."

Lacy nodded, unsure what to make of the request. She wondered if it was part of the search for Megan's mother but knew better than to ask.

The truck lurched to a stop outside the station. The motor gave a few protests before it finally cut off, which left them in silence. Megan looked over at Lacy with a smile and said, "I can check in with the chief and bring him up to speed, and you get to deal with the fallout from your little fire ant incident and the flowered panties."

"My life just keeps getting better and better," Lacy groaned. "I say we stick together." With that, Lacy darted from the truck to the building.

Megan watched her from the cab with a newfound respect. The woman was tough—she had to give her that. Lacy had guts, that was for sure.

4

Lacy made a beeline for the seldom-used but closer side entrance of the station while Megan followed on her heels. Their office was far removed from the main hustle and bustle of the central department. Yet despite their stealthy attempt to avoid attention, they were quickly spotted. Within minutes, a small group of coworkers began to congregate nearby. Lacy and Megan could hear the muffled laughter but were unable to make out individual words. Nonetheless, there was no doubt about their topic of conversation. The story had already begun to spread.

"Remember those old case files you mentioned?" Lacy said.

"Yeah, they're down in the basement. Why?"

"Right now would be a good time for me to take a look at them," Lacy said. She spoke to Megan but held her gaze on the growing number of men in the hallway.

"Actually that would be great," Megan said. "I really would like your opinion. I think a couple may be of some importance to today's case."

"Whoa, how so?"

"I don't really want to say and bias your opinion. It's just there are some aspects that stood out, and I could use an objective eye. Besides, they won't follow you down there," Megan added. She made a gesture with her head to indicate the expanding crowd.

"Then count me in."

Once Lacy was settled in with enough material to last a week, Megan excused herself to speak to the chief, then planned to follow up with the lab.

"You think Jerry's had a chance to accomplish anything yet?" Lacy asked.

"Probably not, but I'd like to let him to know this case is important to me and not just a pile of bones," Megan said. However, what really bothered her was what Mahoney said about the arms. She wanted to find out if they were ever located. "See you later. Happy reading."

Lacy had a hunch that everyone at the station knew how important each case was to Megan, she needn't reiterate it. And if Jerry was as good as everyone said, he'd do his best no matter what. Patience seemed a virtue Megan Callingham didn't possess. Yet she was thankful for the solitude after the day she'd had and to finally be able to scratch her bites in peace.

*   *   *

After a brief stop off at the chief's office, Megan took the back steps to the third floor, which came out directly across from the lab. The classical music Jerry played spilled out into the hallway. She knocked on the doorjamb on her way in. "Hey, Jerry?"

"Over here," a muffled voice announced.

On the far side of the room, a man in his early thirties sat slumped over a lab bench, his eyes pressed against the eyepiece of a microscope. His chin showed the stubble of a long day.

"I hate to interrupt," Megan said.

Jerry recognized his visitor by voice and didn't bother to look up when he spoke. "Hey, Megan. I'm on it right now, and I know you want the results ASAP."

"Am I that bad?" Megan asked. She pulled up a stool and collapsed beside him.

This time he turned toward her with a brilliant wide smile. He had the whitest teeth she had ever seen, and they were perfectly straight. Her stomach did one of those flutter-type things. It happened every time he looked at her with his undivided attention. His deep-set blue eyes gave him an intensity that made her feel as though he could see into the deepest recesses of her soul. He missed nothing in his work, and she assumed that carried over to his personal relationships as well. It captivated her, but at the same time, she found it a little unnerving. She thought Lacy might have a point about the sex thing. Ideas definitely came to mind when she was near him.

"I never said you were bad, just predictable."

She sucked in a deep breath to regain her composure. "What do you have so far?"

"Pretty sure it's a Caucasian from the skull. It displays a narrow face with long bridged nasal bones. Blacks have a wider nasal bridge, and the Mongoloid race has a much shorter, broad face. Although it's getting tougher to distinguish one race from another with all the interracial coupling that occurs nowadays. Still, this skull demonstrates clear Caucasian traits."

Megan was not only interested in this case because it was her first possible homicide but because it was solely skeletal remains. That placed her on more even ground with Lacy. With absolutely no soft tissue to work with, this case was much different from her criminal study cases. They had dealt with bodies in various stages of decomposition. She was intrigued by what could be revealed by bones alone. It posed a definite challenge, and she loved a challenge.

"That's pretty cool you can tell that from the skull, but it won't narrow down our missing-persons search very much."

"Oh, baby, I'm only getting started. Look at this." He moved a section of bone under a large piece of equipment.

"Where did that thing come from? Is it new?"

"Yes, it's on loan from the university. It's a powerful scope, basically a giant magnifiying glass," he said.

"What are you looking for?"

"I requested the scope for the anthropology class I teach. Since it was here, I decided to use it to view the muscle markings on this victim's bones. Smooth-surfaced bones indicate the victim was inactive. Like maybe someone in a nursing home, wheelchair bound, or bedridden. A more definite groove at the area of the muscle attachment indicates a more athletic individual. Most often, I have soft tissue to rely on as well. Without it, this scope has been a lifesaver."

Megan was intrigued. It was one thing to read about cases in class, but to be able to watch the evaluation firsthand and be a part of an ongoing investigation was a thrill. "What did you find?"

"This person looked to be moderately active. Since this is a femur, I'd say we have a runner. See this area?"

Megan leaned in closer. "Wow, yeah. That's pretty cool." She wondered if her own bones would reflect her hobby as an avid runner.

"It would be more cool if I had the radius, ulna, or humerus. With them I would be able to determine if the upper body was used as much as the legs. It would also distinguish which was the dominant side—right or left. Sometimes, if there is a complete skeleton, we can guess the victim's occupation."

"How many bones are there in the human body anyway?"

"Two hundred six, with thirty-two teeth. But that's if the skeleton is complete, which is not the case here," Jerry answered.

Megan sat up straight. "So the arm bones never turned up?"

"Afraid not. Or the hands. It's kind of a Venus de Milo thing going on."

"A what?" Megan asked. Her mind was off, racing with the confirmation of the missing limbs.

Jerry paused and cocked his head when he looked at her. "You know—Venus de Milo. The famous marble statue in the Louvre in Paris. The woman with no arms. It's Greek, late third, early second century BC."

"Oh yeah, I've seen photos of it. Never been there personally," Megan admitted.

"Well, if you ever get the chance, you have to go to Paris. It's a wonderful city. They accept everyone there. So much to see, and the Louvre has so many wonderful pieces. The *Mona Lisa* is housed there too. Anyway, back to our case. I consider both hands and arms missing to be not only significant but quite weird. All the other bones seem to be here."

"Mahoney mentioned something about the arms at the site. He said maybe animals made off with them, but he was surprised that the femurs were still there."

"Yes. The femur is the longest bone in the body, but the humerus is the longest bone in the arm, so animals favor them as well. Still, I expected to find a metacarpal or a phalange at the very least. Additionally, it doesn't appear that any of the bones were damaged by animals, which makes it even more unusual and hard to explain."

"Mahoney figured they'd probably turn up. He thought they could have been scattered or buried in the deep grass."

"Sorry. They scoured the entire area with no luck. I know the guy's work. He's thorough. If he didn't find them, they weren't there."

Megan didn't want to make too much out of it at this point, but it did have her concerned; and she furrowed her brow, deep in thought.

"Do not fear, my sweet," Jerry said. He got up and walked over to retrieve both pelvic bones and brought them back to her. "These are both in good shape, and take a look at this." He held the bones out to Megan and pointed as he explained.

"In general, a female pelvis is proportionally wider than a male's. It's to accommodate for childbirth."

Megan was intrigued by Jerry's findings. "I had no idea that a bone held such information."

"They call it osteobiology. With care, you can discern a human life's story through their bones."

"Such as?" Megan asked, fascinated and excited to watch the puzzle unfold.

"Healed fractures, certain forms of illness, childbirth, infections, and, as I have shown you, the degree of physical activity. At times, even their occupation," Jerry continued with his informative commentary.

"See here, you can measure the subpubic angle formed by both pelvic bones. You can clearly tell this victim is female."

"Maybe you see it clearly, but it's not so obvious to me," Megan said.

Jerry smiled with a laugh. "OK, maybe I've done this a few more times than you have." Then he went on to explain, "It's very simple to remember. If the angle is acute, or less than ninety degrees, you're dealing with a male. If it's obtuse, or greater than ninety degrees, it's female. You see it now?" he said and held them out for her inspection.

"Yeah, you're right. I do see it, and it *is* pretty clear. You're a good teacher."

"Thanks. Also, while I have her pelvic bone, I should point out that she never had any children."

"OK, you've got me again. Are you making this up, trying to mess with me?" Megan asked.

"Never, scout's honor. It's all in knowing what to look for. If you put me out in the field, I would be totally lost. I would have no idea how to distinguish evidence from all the miscellaneous background clutter."

Somehow Megan doubted that. This guy knew what he was doing, and he was modest about it. There was no competition between the two of them. She had one job to do; he another. Together they hopefully would achieve a positive result in the identification of this victim.

Jerry continued. "If a woman's ever carried to full term, you'll find a pattern of pitting in the pelvic bone. If she's had two or more children, there will be a small indentation or depression right around here," he said. He pointed to the area with the blunt end of a pen.

"I see. This one looks smooth."

"Exactly. No children, which actually doesn't surprise me because she was in her early twenties."

"How do you know that?"

"For now, it's a reasonable guess using the skull. Give me a little more time, and we can get radiographic information to confirm my initial results. I could also resort to osteon counting. It's accurate but very tedious, time consuming, and I hate it."

"What is osteon counting?"

"You use a microscope to examine a cross section of bone, like the femur, and count its osteons. They're the little tunnels in each bone that house the nutrient-providing blood vessels and nerves. In general, the more osteons, the older the person. It's kind of like the rings on a tree."

"That's pretty cool. I don't remember ever talking about that in school," Megan said.

Then again, her classes mainly dealt with evidence and documentation. Issues that were important to detectives. Like how to catch the perp. The laboratory evaluation side of evidence was often skimmed over. It was one reason why Megan enjoyed time spent with Jerry. He was an excellent and patient teacher.

"Anyway, like I said, it takes a lot of time. I knew you'd knock on my door soon enough, so I did as much as I could with a good cursory once-over. The age estimate should be close enough to use against the missing-persons list. Osteon counting is more for shelf cases."

Jerry walked back to the box, gently placed the pelvic bones back, and retrieved the skull. Then he picked up another one that sat on a side shelf. With both skulls in hand, he put one down and pointed to a suture on the other one from the shelf. "See this wiggly line on the base of this skull?"

"Yes?"

"It's the suture of the sphenoid bone, which was partially fused prior to death. I happen to know that this individual was in his late teens. I use it as a teaching tool. That's why it's so clean." Then he retrieved the skull from the remains. "You see this suture line at the dome of the cranium?"

Megan leaned in for a closer look. "Humm. Yeah, I see it." But Megan thought both skulls looked alike. They were both pristine.

"These sutures usually begin to close when people are in their midtwenties. As you can see here, this victim has almost none fully closed except right here.

That's why I placed her in her early twenties instead of midtwenties or late teens. More than likely, she was from twenty to twenty-three years old."

"You're unbelievable, Jerry. I owe you big-time for this."

"Don't mention it," he said. "Just doing my job. I have one more piece of the puzzle though. I used the Trotter's formula on the femurs to calculate an estimation of the victim's height from my osteometric chart. It's usually pretty accurate, and I placed her around five feet, four inches tall. It would be more accurate with the arm bones, but with both legs intact, I feel confident. There's also the Rohrer body-build index that takes you a step further with a weight estimate. That places her around 120-128 pounds."

"Thank you so much. This gives me something to go on for sure," Megan said.

"Glad to help. Oh, I almost forgot. I also put a call into our forensic odontologist."

"The guy that works up in Gainesville at the anthropology lab?"

"Yes, he's always good about helping out. I want him to evaluate the dentition. In particular, the third-molar root development. That will help pin down the age."

Megan snapped her notepad shut and hopped off her stool. "Thanks again. I need to get on the computer and feed this information into the system. Catch you later."

*   *   *

Megan went directly from the lab to the basement to tell Lacy the good news before she ran it against the missing-persons report. She burst into the small room where her partner was hidden behind a stack of files.

Lacy looked up, relieved it was Megan. "I've always enjoyed the legwork of our job a lot more than all the paperwork. My eyes feel like they have sand in them."

"It's probably not the reading but the all the dust down here," Megan said.

Lacy wasn't convinced since reading always put her to sleep. Yet she wasn't ready to admit that, especially after Megan revealed how many hours she'd voluntarily spent down here. "So what did the chief say when you told him about our unknown?" Lacy asked to change the subject.

"Not much. Told him we'd go through the missing-persons report and talk to the neighbors. You know, the usual."

"So why do you seem so excited? Your cheeks are all rosy."

"I ran down here from the lab. I have to tell you, Jerry is so awesome. In a matter of hours, he's performed a miracle. Thanks to him, we now know our victim was a white female in her early twenties, no children, athletic, and five four and weighed around 120-128 pounds. That will certainly focus our search against the list of missing persons for the last four months."

"That does sound promising. Have you plugged it in yet?"

"No, I wanted to check in with you first."

"Does Jerry think he could get anything off the bag?" Lacy asked.

"I don't think he got to that yet. When I walked in, he was evaluating each bone, one by one. He talked me through everything he was doing. It was fascinating."

"It was, or he was?" Lacy asked. She leaned back in her chair and studied her partner.

"What? Both, I guess," Megan said.

Lacy wiggled her finger back and forth with a grin. "You like him."

"Well, yes I like him. Everyone likes Jerry. He's a likable guy."

"No, I mean you *like* him."

"Oh, stop. You sound like my sister."

"Aha, you *do* like him," Lacy said. "Now the vein on the side of your forehead is sticking out, and your neck's splotchy." Lacy clapped her hands and laughed. "Oh, how I love being right."

Megan wasn't used to a partner who worked so closely with her. But what was really unnerving was that in less than a month, Lacy had figured out more about her than a lifelong friend ever had. Megan was a loner who liked to keep her cards close to the vest, and Lacy was forcing her into uncharted territory.

"OK, maybe I like him a little," Megan said.

"I knew it. You know what you need? You need one of those miracle push-up bras. They work every time."

Megan glanced down at her drab shirt and flat chest. Her build was great for running but not a real eye-catcher as far as men went. "Maybe you're right."

"We can get you a hot color. We'll go after work."

"Unfortunately, that might be awhile. After I run this information against missing persons, I wanted to find Edward Lee and talk to him," Megan said.

"Sure, we can do both," Lacy said. "I want to check this Jerry guy out for myself. The way Mahoney and you make it sound, he's got skills. I like a man with skills." She began to stack the files up and organize her work space.

"Whoa, wait a minute. What did you think about the cases?" Megan asked.

Lacy became serious again and riffled through the stack until she retrieved the file she wanted. "I found this one interesting."

Megan had given her partner a half dozen unsolved homicides that ranged from fairly recent to over ten years old. It was an attempt to receive a fresh, untainted view of the two in particular that interested her. Megan stepped closer and took the document from Lacy and thumbed through the pages.

"Yeah, I remember this one. You tell me what you think first."

"Well, for one thing, it was similar in the respect that the bones were stacked in a pile and not spread out. I checked the map, and the location appeared to be close to Cooper's farm. Also, there were no clothes found on site, no soft tissue, not even cartilage on the bones. Again, very strong similarities to today's case.

"However what really caught my attention was that most of the bones were present with the exception of the hands and arms. Today, at the retrieval site, Mahoney stated he didn't see either arm. He thought perhaps some animal made off with them. This case made me question that opinion. I've had cases with no head or hands but never no arms. That's weird."

"I thought the same thing," Megan said. "And get this. When I spoke with Jerry, he confirmed that it looked like most of the bones were present with the exception of both arms, including the hands. It was a fact that also jumped out at him as being strange."

"It does seem pretty freaky. Organized criminals don't normally hack off arms," Lacy said.

"It's really odd that both femurs were present if they're the favorite of dogs. Why would animals take the arms instead? Especially since the pile appeared to be basically undisturbed. It didn't sit right with me this morning and kept gnawing away at the back of my mind. It got me thinking. Then these two old cases popped into my head."

"Two?" Lacy said. "I was so immersed in this one, I never got to review the others."

"Yeah, there's another separate case that reported both arms missing. I mixed it in with a few other files so it wouldn't be so conspicuous. I wanted you to see them as I did. It was only after looking through several old files that the second one came up. Right away I made the connection to the first and, now, to today's remains."

Megan went over to the stack to search for what she wanted. It took a moment, but when she found it, she handed it over to Lacy.

"See what you think about this."

Lacy glanced at the date. "This case is over eight years old. The same as the other one. Do you think one of them might be your mother?"

"This isn't about my mother. It's about today's case. They're two separate files with missing arms. They're both eight years old and unsolved. Until today, they've been tucked away and collecting dust due to lack of evidence or leads."

Lacy quickly skimmed through the second file while Megan watched. "Wow, this one was also in a pile, no clothing, and the location seems . . ." Lacy trailed off to look at the map.

"It's close to today's," Megan offered, "all the locations are within two miles of one another."

"OK, so we have close proximity, similar crime scene, no remaining human tissue or any evidence of clothing, not even a snap or button. Then of course, the big thing with the absent limbs. If the integrity of the site was contaminated by wildlife, you would expect damage to the other bones, but I don't see that noted," Lacy said.

"Exactly. I don't think we can write it off to animals. The lost arms are significant. As Jerry said, there wasn't even one carpal, metacarpal, or phalange. Yet none of the other bones were damaged or missing. Plus, if animals were involved, the remains would have been scattered, not stacked. I think the absence of limbs was deliberate in all three cases. It's part of the perp's MO."

"Hold up a sec," Lacy said. She tossed the file down on the table, and it landed with a smack. "I agree with everything you said, up until you mentioned perp. To have a perp, you have to have a crime. Now I'm not saying something fishy isn't going on here, but we've got no clear evidence of a crime, let alone three murders. Which I know is where you're headed. You've got that look in your eye. I know you've got something to prove and all. But until you can come up with some solid evidence, you can speculate until the cows come home. The chief isn't going to run with it. Besides all that, what the hell is a metacarpal anyway? I don't remember them as any arm bone."

"They're the bones in your hand. The significance is they're tiny. If an animal carried off any part of the arm or hand, the tiny finger bones would fall to the ground. It's like you said—there was no cartilage left to connect the smaller bones of the hand to the larger bones of the arm. So they should have been there. Both femurs were. Even the patellas. Eight years ago, no one thought much of it; but in light of today's case, I'd have to say their absence is not only significant but the signature of the killer."

"OK. But what if the cartilage was there when the animal took the arms?"

"A fair-enough question," Megan said, obviously smug. "If that was the case, then why not touch the remainder of the stack? Why not spread the bones out? Sniff around."

"True," Lacy said and threw her arms in the air. She was deep in thought and paced back and forth when another thought popped into her head. "What about the eight-year gap? It seems unlikely that a person would kill two victims, take both arms, then take an eight-year hiatus."

"Not unbelievable if you consider the possibility that they could have ended up in prison for those years on unrelated charges, gone into the military, or even moved," Megan said.

Lacy walked around the room as she considered this theory. When she stopped, she said, "So you think that these three murders are actually all victims of the same killer?"

"I'm saying it's possible," Megan said. "If not probable." She was pleased that Lacy was not only actually listening to her but considering her theory to be plausible.

"But that would mean we might have a serial killer on our hands."

"It kind of looks that way, sorry. Tough break for your first real case on this job."

Lacy liked a challenge, but she wasn't sure she was up for this one. "Then we have to find him. Now!"

5

Megan went straight home from the police station. After a long hard day, she wanted to get out and clear her head with a good run. That's when some of her best ideas came to her, and right now, she needed some sort of insight that would make sense out of today's developments. Lacy, on the other hand, chose to remain in the basement with Chinese takeout. Her new boss was convinced the old files contained a clue they'd overlooked. She forsook shopping at Victoria's Secret and planned to reread all the files. Tomorrow they would both follow up leads, talk to neighbors, look up Cooper's ex, then buy that hot colored push-up bra.

With her hair pulled back in a scrunchie and her Nikes laced up, she took off at an easy pace. As a warm-up, she rounded the periphery of the apartment complex, which was lined with large sprawling oaks. The Spanish moss that dripped from the branches swayed in the light breeze. From the rear of the complex, she headed toward an untraveled dirt road that led out into the countryside. This was one of the nice things about Ocala—it was primarily rural. A person didn't have to go far to end up on a tranquil back road with rolling hills that led you past one scenic horse farm after another. She hoped, despite the town's rapid growth, it would be able to retain its quaint equestrian country atmosphere.

For her, there would always be days like today when she craved solitude. She wanted to live in a place where it was possible to distance yourself from the pressures of daily life. Luckily, this route was close and very secluded. That's what made it so perfect. It offered complete isolation. Not a single home or farm lay along its entire length. Years ago, it'd been an old access road for the power company, long since abandoned for newly built highways. With so much on her mind, she didn't want the distractions or dangers that passing traffic brought. Within minutes, the noise and bustle of the small city drifted away. Soon her breathing grew deeper and steady. With each rhythmic inhalation, her stress melted away. Her footfalls became a melodic chorus as she crunched on the limestone.

She replayed the scene back at Cooper's farm. Rationally, she understood Lacy's concern over his behavior. Even Megan had to concede he'd acted overly nervous. Perhaps he did have something to hide. Truth was, everyone had secrets. It was all a matter of degree.

Then there was the unfortunate disappearance of his ex-fiancée. She'd basically vanished, with no forwarding address. The time period fit their estimate for the body found on his farm. It didn't bode well for Cooper, and she hoped to locate the woman and clear the matter up quickly. She didn't want to waste time on a false lead. In her opinion, Cooper wasn't capable of murder, especially something as nefarious as taking both arms. That would involve a lot of blood.

What really made today's case so hard was that it happened so close to her own home. It's one thing to study old-case files or read about crimes in faraway places. That was an impersonal intellectual activity. But for the evil to lurk this close and endanger those she loved—well, that made it personal. A little too personal, but as a detective, it was something she'd have to learn to deal with. The thought made the hair on the back of her neck stand on end.

This investigation gave her a bad feeling. Even though Lacy couldn't admit it without clear evidence, Megan could sense her concern. Today's case was a homicide and not death by natural causes. To make matters worse, it fit in with a killer who had been a part of their community for almost a decade. A serial killer who had, until now, gone totally unnoticed in his egregious acts. He could be anybody. He obviously blended in with society. Chances were, she knew him. Perhaps even saw him on a daily basis.

She thought about Lacy coming onto the force only a month ago and now faced with a possible serial killer. It would have been easier if they'd been able to get to know each other better before undertaking such a challenge. She berated herself for wasting the time they'd had by acting like a spoiled brat. The truth was, Lacy did have more experience; and Megan knew if she'd only get over her jealousy, she could learn a lot from her new partner. Lacy could teach her what she didn't learn in the classroom. Hands-on experience from a pro.

She thought back to her classes. There, she'd been forced to see up close the horrors that went on in the world. But never before had she been forced to become intimately involved with them. To place herself inside the mind of a killer and become a part of his ugly world. The thought alone made her feel as dirty and tainted as the creep she sought. But she would put forth all she had to offer. In the end, she would either walk away a better detective or defeated. If she won, it would all be worth it. The exhilaration of the chase and the knowledge you took down a degenerate that haunted your own community was all worth the personal turmoil. Her community depended on her for their safety.

She thought back on the day she made detective after six years on the force and years of hard work. She'd been elated and held a piece of cake in her hand when this old codger abruptly confronted her with a warning: "Each time you venture into the darkness in pursuit of a criminal, a little bit of hell rubs off. You can't give your heart and soul to the job without it eventually taking a piece back.

One day, you might step across that threshold and get sucked so far in, you'll never find your way back."

Despite the exertion of her run, Megan got gooseflesh at the memory. At the time, she told herself the old man was blowing steam. Probably wanted to scare a woman off the force. However, at this very moment, she understood the true wisdom of his words. They were spoken from years of experience, and the old man's pain was reflected in his face. Those emotions had nothing to do with gender, and that scared the bejesus out of her. Just as this case today had. She ran harder. Not that it would do any good. She couldn't run from the fear or the faceless entity that stalked their community. The one thing she could do was take this killer down and stop him. That's where the satisfaction would come in. That's why she became a detective. She had to be ready for this challenge. The gauntlet had been thrown down at her feet. In her own town. She wasn't about to turn her back on it and walk away.

Then her thoughts drifted to Beth, who kept her disapproval of Megan's career choice no secret. At times it made her laugh. Other times it drove her crazy. What Beth didn't understand was that being a detective gave Megan a sense of satisfaction and purpose. She enjoyed being part of a team that made their community a safer, better place for everyone that lived there. She could make a difference. As did Beth, but each in totally different ways. Yet her sister couldn't understand that. Why did family have to be so complicated? She loved her sister, but at times, she was too much to deal with. Sometimes she was just easier to avoid.

Megan caught her foot on a rock as she turned the corner. It brought her back to the present reality. She'd been wasting her time in a daydream over inexplicable questions. The same questions she'd had for years. What she needed to do was focus on work. It was certain she would never understand Beth. This case, on the other hand, she had every intention to solve.

She reached the point in the road where she normally turned around. Today she kept on, immersed in thoughts over today's skeleton. Hidden on an isolated part of Cooper's farm, he had the easiest access to the location. But many locals also knew the grove was no longer in use. Heck, even the tax appraiser seemed aware of the fact. Anyone could have dumped the body there months ago. They would feel safe that it'd go unnoticed. Which it evidently had, until now.

Darkness began to descend. An owl swooped out from a tree and crossed Megan's path before it disappeared into the dense woods. The suddenness of the event startled her. She realized it was late, so she abruptly swung around to head home. She picked up her pace, wanting to get back to civilization before darkness fully took hold. On the return trip, she thought about the rate of decomposition of today's remains. The two older cases had bones in similarly good condition yet with no soft tissue. Even if the past detectives had questions, there were no answers. With no leads or other significant evidence, both cases ended up in the dead files. In light of today's discoveries, Megan found that understandable.

As Lacy had noted, one of the similarities was that the bones were in a pile. If animals had disturbed the integrity of the site, it would be expected that the bones would be scattered and gnawed on. This was not noted in either older case, and she saw for herself that the remains at Cooper's were not damaged. What would cause this to happen? There had to be an explanation they were not seeing. If the remains had been abandoned with soft tissue, within twenty-four hours, animals would have disseminated the carcass into a fairly wide radius. But that didn't happen. That had to mean they were all free of flesh when they were deposited. Then there was the fact that they were as clean as the teaching skull that Jerry kept on the shelf.

But what did that mean? Did the perpetrator keep the body until it fully decomposed? A nasty thought at best. What kind of creep kept his kill around to rot? And what about the smell? Did that indicate he had no close neighbors? And what about the marrow? Animals could smell that even if human could not. Did the killer treat the carcass with a chemical to denature the proteins?

Megan didn't know what it was, but something didn't add up. She had to have missed something, and she didn't like loose ends. The rate of decomposition was a loose end for her. The skull seemed too clean. She planned to ask Jerry about it tomorrow. Either way, if her fears were correct, they dealt with a cunning adversary, someone who had killed and gotten away with it for years. To capture such a criminal would look exceptionally good on her resume. With a newfound energy, she sprinted home.

It was well after dark when Megan returned to her apartment, showered, and went in search for food. That took priority over styling her hair. However, many times she would multitask and blow-dry her hair going fifty-five miles per hour in her truck with the windows down en route to a fast-food place.

Today, however, hunger pains reminded her that she hadn't eaten since Beth's house. But she didn't want to waste time. After a quick bite, she planned to look up a few things on the Internet. She padded barefoot into the kitchen in search of something edible. She knew not to set her hopes too high. This was another area where a chasm existed between her and Beth. Megan was no cook; therefore, there was no need to buy foods that required anything more than a few minutes in a microwave for preparation. If she ever did have a child, it would almost certainly be doomed to die of malnourishment.

She found a half loaf of bread without any mold and went about making the old standby of peanut butter and jelly. On the bottom shelf of the fridge was one last bottle of Gatorade. *What more could a Florida girl ask for?* she thought.

6

___

Megan hadn't been seated at her kitchen counter long when the phone rang. With one hand, she reached over to answer it with her sandwich in the other.

"Hello."

"Hey, this is Lacy."

"How's it going? You still at the station?"

"Yeah, I just came from the lab."

Megan thought she detected a grin on her partner's face but decided it was her imagination.

"I spoke to Jerry," Lacy continued. "You're right. He's really cute. You didn't tell me he had blue eyes and dimples. If you don't want him, I do. I have a weakness for dimples."

"You called to tell me you want dibs on Jerry?"

"No, but he'd be a catch. You don't usually find guys that sensitive and kind. Plus he dresses really nice. But actually, I called because I went to ask him a few questions."

"Go on," Megan said, almost afraid to hear what would come next.

"I know I'm new to the area, but there were a few things that didn't feel right about today's case."

"Like what?" Megan asked and took another bite of her sandwich.

"I was curious about the decomposition rate. It seemed too fast to me to be so complete."

Megan's interest was piqued. She put her sandwich down and wiped her hands on a paper towel with the phone tucked between her chin and shoulder. "I thought the same thing. I was going to ask Jerry about it tomorrow."

"Well, I beat you to it, and you're right about him. That man's got it going on upstairs."

Megan felt another stab of jealousy. She knew Jerry was smart, but she didn't want Lacy to be so enamored with him.

"What did he say?"

"Mainly overall information about this area. It doesn't exactly pertain to this case. It was more like background knowledge. Most of my homicide cases have been less than forty-eight hours old."

___

"So you're more familiar with immediate postmortem decomposition?"

"Right, in a much colder, less-humid climate—except for our short summers. For example, bacteria don't really multiply if the ambient temperature dips below thirty-eight degrees Fahrenheit."

"That sounds about right to me," Megan said. She pushed her plate out of the way and picked up a nearby notepad and pencil, ready to take notes. "But that's not the case here very often."

"That's what Jerry said. He went on the Internet and researched the weather records for this past winter. They indicated that the temperature only dropped below thirty-eight degrees Fahrenheit a few times. Each time lasted six hours or less. Therefore, we can assume the bacteria were prolific and busy doing their thing the entire time. The same goes for the colonization of the body with flesh-eating flies and beetles, not to mention the other scavengers, like buzzards."

"I knew this past winter had been mild, but I hadn't paid that close attention. That's a helpful piece of information," Megan said.

"I know. I'm glad Jerry thought to look it up. That guy really is incredible. He knows so much about everything, from classical music and art to forensic sciences."

Megan rolled her eyes and held in a groan.

"Anyway, he also told me that if there are high temperatures with low humidity, mummification can occur. But he said that's never the case in Ocala. Even though the winter yields lower humidity, he stated the humidity predominately remains around 80 percent or above and seldom dips below sixty. Evidently you need twenty or below for mummification."

"Yeah, I knew that."

"I'm looking forward to that," Lacy said.

"What? Looking forward to becoming a mummy?"

"God, no, to the higher humidity. When it gets cold out, my skin gets really chapped. Then again, our winter humidity and temperatures in New York are far below what you guys have here. I hate having to buy expensive moisturizers or having scratchy skin."

Megan ignored Lacy's skin-care issues and said, "So basically you're telling me that Jerry feels three months is an adequate time for complete decomposition of the soft tissue to occur? Even cartilage?"

"Yes. He said the rate of decomposition varies widely. In hot, relatively humid conditions, such as exist in an Ocala summer, a body can be skeletonized within five to seven days. Two weeks tops. However, if a body is buried a few feet below ground, that diminishes access to insects and slows down this rate considerably. He said water also impedes the length of time it takes but not as much. If the body is aboveground, as was our case, then the process happens the fastest."

"So we can assume these remains were devoid of soft tissue due to natural causes without any intervention from the killer?" Megan asked.

"Not so fast," Lacy said. "It's true about the soft tissue decomposition, but Jerry wouldn't go as far as to say that, but he did come up with another inquiry."

"OK, you've got my attention."

"He told me that in moist environments, a substance called adipocere, also known as grave wax, is formed."

Megan had seen and heard a lot of things in the course of her studies and work on the force, but grave wax was new and struck her as particularly disgusting. "That sounds so gross."

"Gross, yes, but possibly helpful," Lacy said.

"How so? And what is it?"

"Adipocere? Well, Jerry explained it as a waxy substance that consist of fatty acids. It's produced by the chemical changes that occur when a dead body's fat and muscle decomposes. He said there are cases reported where the corpse has basically turned into a huge wax candle. He told me of one story where that happened, and the person actually caught on fire."

"Ohmygod. Now that I know what it is, and it's disgusting, how can it possibly be helpful?"

"Evidently, it can be detected in the soil for months, possibly even years, but only if the body was allowed to decompose at that particular site. Sometimes, if a body is dumped fresh and allowed to rot, it will turn the soil black. It can even impede the growth of local vegetation."

Megan sat up straighter. This was hopeful news. "So this grave wax would be in the dirt at the orange grove if those remains had flesh on them when the body was dumped there but absent if the bones were clean when they showed up."

"That's right. Jerry says it lingers much longer than the suspected time frame we're dealing with."

"That's great. If the killer waited for decomposition to be complete, or possibly assisted it, before the skeletal remains were moved, it could explain why no animals bothered the bones," Megan said. "It's possible he did it to hide a positive identification. The soil wasn't black, and there were plenty of weeds."

"Whoa, back up a step. We still have no concrete evidence of murder," Lacy stated.

"You can't believe a person died of natural causes in an isolated area, and their remains ended up naked in a pile," Megan said.

"I'm not saying I don't have questions, but the facts have to speak for themselves," Lacy said.

"Absence of evidence is not evidence of absence," Megan shot back.

"What the hell is that supposed to mean?" Lacy asked.

"It's a quote from Carl Sagan. All it means is, just because we haven't found the smoking gun, doesn't mean it doesn't exist. We need to keep looking. The world isn't flat."

"I agree with Columbus, but we need evidence. So far we have nothing but speculation. Speculation doesn't hold up in court. Another snag is, Jerry doesn't test soil samples here in his lab. He said all nonbiological trace evidence is sent out to the state lab in Tallahassee. Evidently it requires some kind of really expensive equipment that local jurisdictions can't afford, so the state has taken a multicounty-share approach."

"That's right, I forgot," Megan said. "That means the paint samples went out too."

"Everything like that. Paint, fibers, glass, soil samples, even bullet casings," Lacy said.

"When did he say we'd get the results back?"

Lacy laughed and said, "He told me that would be your first question after finding out. That guy's got you pegged."

Megan imagined Lacy and Jerry sitting head to head in his lab, sharing a laugh at her expense. She took a deep breath and said, "So what was his answer?"

Lacy picked up on the annoyance in Megan's voice. Apparently, she'd overstepped her partner's comfort zone. "He didn't mean anything bad by it," she offered.

"No biggie," Megan said. "He's already told me I'm predictable and demanding."

"That's a good thing. It means he's paid enough attention to you that he understands you."

"Whether it's good or not is debatable," Megan said. "I think it's the general consensus around the station, but I'm sure the other guys phrase it a bit differently."

"I think right now everyone is still too busy talking about my underwear. But to get back to your question, Jerry said he didn't know when the results would be in since it's not up to him. He knows they're backed up, so he called and told them to put a rush on it. They're supposed to fax the results ASAP. He promised to call us as soon as he got them."

"Thanks," Megan said. Then she had another thought but wasn't sure if it was something she wanted to take up with Lacy since it was better answered by Jerry. She made a note to herself and absently underlined it several times.

"Oh, one more thing," Lacy said.

"What's that?"

"I got in touch with Wal-Mart's corporate office to verify the time frame for the changeover of the bags. They told me they officially switched to the thicker white ones on January first of this year, but they'd have to get back to me if we needed a more exact date for the individual stores. It seems that some locations had a large inventory they were supposed to use up before they placed the new bags out."

"Always got to watch that bottom line, I guess. But that's great," Megan said. "I say until we hear back from them, we can go on the New Year's date."

"Sounds good to me. See you tomorrow," Lacy said, then hung up.

Megan hung up the phone, impressed by how efficient and hardworking Lacy was but also wondering about her advice for balance in her personal life. Lacy seemed to be spending all her time on this case. Then again, she was new to the town, so she had few friends. She was someone she could learn a great deal from, and again she admonished herself for not realizing that earlier. She'd basically walked around with a chip on her shoulder and been a bitch to Lacy since she got here. With this new case, they would be working closer than ever, for long hours. There was no point in being emotionally closed off. After all, Lacy was trying. She deserved better than what Megan had given her so far. If Lacy could venture out to make a fresh start in a new state, she could meet her halfway.

Megan finished her sandwich, threw her paper plate in the trash, and went to the computer to access some of the information Lacy had given her. In general, she wasn't a technology person, but the Internet aided her immensely. Although she loved her visits with Ms. Marilyn at the local library, it was times like this that she made use of the Internet, where speed and anonymity were what she sought.

Whether the body had turned up on Cooper's farm as a corpse and been left to rot or was dumped as a clean skeleton would be contingent on the adipocere results. If the results came back negative, it lent credence toward her theory of murder. It would also enable her to better profile the perpetrator. If the killer had assisted in the decomposition, then moved the remains, they dealt with a different breed of criminal. Someone who was not only mentally deranged but perversely evil. A sociopath who more than likely lived among them. She became a detective to protect the society in which she lived, and from what she'd learned, a sociopath could blend in well. The enormity of the situation scared her.

Their community was open and trusting. No one locked their doors or windows at night. People often left their vehicles running while they darted into a nearby store. It was what she'd grown up with and never questioned until Lacy arrived. Lacy had been so astounded by people's lack of concern for security that Megan had begun to view the situation differently. In light of the danger out there now, it seemed foolish. But then again, the citizens of her community didn't know what she suspected. They were all vulnerable. Megan felt her left eye began to twitch. She placed her finger to the muscle and willed it to stop, citing it as a sign of weakness. But despite her attempts, the spasm continued beneath the pad of her fingertip.

For the most part, the murder rate in Marion County was low. Those that occurred usually involved simple motives and provided an easy resolution. Random murders were uncommon, and few cases had remained unsolved over the last twenty years.

Along the same thought line, Megan toyed with the idea that the killer might have a personal grudge against Cooper. It was a distinct possibility. Cooper had lived here his entire life. The killer she suspected used this community to abandon his bodies for at least eight years. But there was the problem that Cooper was liked by most everyone who knew him. She couldn't think of anyone who'd want to set him up in such a horrible way. Even if they did, it would still entail the death of an innocent woman. Then there were the two older cases to consider—that is, if they were actually connected. Cooper was in high school when they were discovered. His senior year.

Her apartment seemed small and closed in. She wondered if Cooper was with Nate right now, confiding about what happened. They'd been best friends since kindergarten, but she hadn't seen them together much since Cooper's father became ill. Still, she imagined they'd be sharing a beer over it at this very moment. She contemplated joining them. They would be at either one of two locations, so they wouldn't be hard to find. But that hinted of what Lacy had accused her of earlier. She was too close to be objective. Besides, she had other work to do, such as jotting down a few questions to ask Jerry in the morning.

The phone rang before she could write anything down.

"Hello."

"Hey there, sunshine," Jerry said.

"Jerry?" She hated to admit how happy she was to hear his voice yet tried to remain casual.

"Sorry to bother you at home," Jerry said, "but I discovered something I thought you needed to be aware of right away."

"Wow, OK, you've got my attention."

"Remember how I was looking at the bones under that large magnifying lens?"

"Yeah, you showed me the marks of the muscle attachment areas and how they related to the person's activity level."

"Glad to know you were listening. You're a great student."

Megan rolled her eyes and tried not to sound exasperated. "Jerry, I always listen to you. As a matter of fact, I'm anxiously listening to you at this very moment."

"OK. After a short dinner break, I looked at one of the clavicles. Actually, I'm not sure what possessed me to examine it so closely, but I'm glad I did."

"You're killing me here, Jerry. What did you find?"

"Are you sitting down?"

"*Yes!* With pen in hand, ready to write down this very significant discovery, so spill it."

"I found some unusual marks on the clavicle, so I took the mate out and evaluated it as well. It had almost identical marks on it," Jerry said.

"OK, now I feel like I didn't get the punch line. Do you mean like some kind of birth defect or rare disease that would help us identify the victim?" Megan said.

"No. These marks were man-made."

"Now I'm really confused."

"They're more like nicks caused by a blade of some kind."

Megan spoke up before Jerry could finish. "Ohmygod. You mean a scarring of bone from where the arms were dissected off the body?"

"Exactly," Jerry said, a bit let down and confused that she'd guessed what he had to say.

"Could you tell what kind of knife it was from?"

"That's gonna be a problem. It looks like they were made by a chain saw. Almost everyone in the Fort McCoy or northern part of Marion County has at least one chain saw or access to one."

"Humm," Megan said. "That's true. Especially of the people that live on acreage."

"But now I'm the one who's confused. I thought you'd be more surprised. What's the deal?"

"Lacy and I had already considered this possibility. We thought it was no accident that both arms were gone while all the other bones were present. Especially when you mentioned that the metacarpals and phalanges were absent too. I had planned to ask you about it tomorrow."

"I guess our minds were running along the same thought line. I supposed that's what prompted me to take a closer look at the clavicles."

"Well, I'm glad you did. But I don't like the outcome," Megan said. She was pleased to have evidence of murder to back up her suspicions, but it was a hollow victory to be right about such a heinous crime.

"To remove someone's arms with a chain saw is pretty disconcerting to say the least," Jerry said. "I remember one case awhile back where a divorced man went through his ex-wife's house cutting everything in half. Somehow he ended up cutting his own arm off and bled to death."

"Wow, but this woman couldn't have cut both her arms off. Do you think it's possible to distinguish the markings enough to link them up with a particular brand of chain saw?"

"No, I'm afraid not. I already checked into that. The different manufacturers don't discriminate in that respect. Their only variation is the length of the chain, but the tooth size on the blade still basically remains the same. Plus, anyone can go to the hardware store and buy a generic chain to fit the blade length. It's kind of like vacuum-cleaner bags."

"Trust me, Jerry, you don't want to go there. But for the record, I've never bought a chain saw blade, so I'll take your word on that. Thanks for all the hard work."

"You're welcome. If you come up with a particular suspect, we can search their premises for the saw and run a luminol test on it."

"You make it sound so easy."

"Always here to help, sunshine," Jerry said with a smile in his voice.

"You did. It gives us a solid piece of evidence for murder and will also help profile the perp."

"I can tell you that—creepy and seriously disturbed; but that aspect is kind of out of my league. And I don't want to sound sexist, but if you want my opinion, I think it'd have to be a male. You have to have some serious upper-body strength to cut a human's arm off. Even at a joint with a chain saw. Besides, it would be extremely messy and very bloody. Not a girl kind of thing at all."

Megan agreed Jerry was right and thanked him before she hung up. She remained on her sofa, deep in thought. What would cause a person to become so warped and full of rage they would hack off a woman's arms? In light of this new discovery, she wanted Jerry to evaluate the two older cases more than ever. She'd speak to Lacy and the chief about it first thing in the morning. If they had similar markings, there was little doubt they dealt with a serial killer on their hands. He took eight years off, but now he was back and would kill again. Unfortunately, his next victim could very well be one of her friends or even a family member. She would have to step through that threshold for the first time. Possibly to save someone she loved. Her eye twitched, but this time she ignored it.

7

Megan rose early the next morning with a bad case of bedhead and in desperate need of caffeine. She'd tossed and turned all night from one fitful dream to another. When she wasn't in the midst of a horrible nightmare, she'd lie there and stare at the shadows on her wall. She couldn't get the conversation with Jerry out of her mind—or, more to the point, what it implied. By 5:00 a.m. and exhausted, she gave up and shuffled into her small kitchen to start the coffeemaker. With that going, she shuffled back to her bathroom and hopped into the shower.

After the first few sips of hot coffee, she started to feel almost human. Out of habit, she retrieved the paper at her door and settled down with her Pop-Tarts. Soon, word of the remains at Cooper's peach farm would be all over town, but as yet, she saw no mention of it in the paper. She supposed the chief would issue a statement to deal with the inquiries if need be. With the murder estimated to be in January, most of the leads would be cold. It was possible he might request an article in the paper to help rekindle people's memory and aid in the investigation. If what Jerry said was true, and the woman's arms were sawed off with a chain saw, it seemed like someone would have to had seen or heard something. Then there were the missing limbs. They were still out there somewhere. Two human arms. Something not to be ignored.

Megan got out a pad to jot down some of the people she wanted to talk to and information she wanted to look up with regards to this investigation. One of the first items for the day would be to meet with the chief. The last conversation they had, he considered the case to be an unidentified remains. With no clear evidence of it being anything other than a vagrant, he wasn't overly concerned. For once Megan was glad she wasn't the lead detective. Lacy was her superior; she could break the bad news to him. If the two older cases turned out to be similar, it would be a charged situation. And if the chief didn't handle it with the right amount of finesse, he risked a widespread panic on his hands.

She poured a second cup of coffee and drank it slowly, savoring the medicinal qualities it bestowed. Caffeine was indeed a good thing, second only to chocolate and, if her memory served her, good sex. Soon enough, it began to alleviate her headache, along with the fog that clouded her mind when she'd gotten up. She took another nibble of her Pop-Tart and looked at it disparagingly. As a runner, she knew a great deal about nutrition—for example, to eat better. It was one of those things in life that everyone knew but few put into practice. She considered a nutritious breakfast as something reserved for those with time to shop or, God forbid, enjoyed cooking. Neither activity appealed to her. A domestic goddess she was not. Breakfast bars were invented for people such as herself.

While she conscientiously reviewed her notes for the day and basically tried to enjoy the calmness of the early morning, the phone rang. Other than when she ran, early morning was her time for thought and organization. Of course, that was after her first cup of coffee and a hot shower. The phone was an unwelcome distraction. It wasn't even seven in the morning. Much too early for telemarketers. That meant it was either police headquarters or Beth.

"Hello," Megan said with a bit of apprehension in her voice.

"Oh, Megan, great, you're home," her sister said. "I was afraid you'd already left for the station. I have a sort of an emergency here."

Megan's heart leapt to her throat. The first thought that came to mind was the killer had struck again, taking one of her nephews during the night. "What is it? Are the children all right?"

"Tyler's got the flu, and Campbell needs me to make a batch of cupcakes for his school's Easter party. I had planned to stop off at the grocery store after I dropped Camp off at school. The party's not until one, but I can't go anywhere with Tyler throwing up like this."

Megan let out a sigh in relief. What her sister considered to be a dire emergency was much different from her own definition. Yet despite her relief over knowing the children were safe, she was irritated.

"Beth, I have to work today. It's not like I have nothing better to do than run errands for you. Can't you get Arlene to help out?"

"I know you have to work. I'm so sorry. I tried Arlene, but she's got the same thing Tyler has. I wouldn't ask if it wasn't an absolute emergency," her sister pleaded. "Matt left early this morning, before I knew Tyler was so sick, or I would have had him do it."

"Beth, I'm in the middle of my first serious investigation as a detective. I want to look good to my new boss and the chief."

"I'm sorry. I didn't know who else to call. Besides, Lacy seems like she would understand. It won't take long, and it's still early. You could run to the store and be back at the station before Lacy gets there."

All Megan could think was she didn't have time to make an early-morning cupcake run. She lived five minutes from the station for a reason. Beth lived twenty. That meant she'd have to drive all the way out there and back to where she started. But then she thought of her nephew and relented.

"OK, tell me what you need," Megan said. She reached over and grabbed a pen and sticky note.

Beth reeled off several items that ranged from cake mix to medicines, then hung up. With Tyler in need of medicine, the confidence that Megan wouldn't let her down came through in Beth's voice, which further irritated her. She hated being so damn predictable.

* * *

Beth anxiously greeted Megan at the door to help carry the two sacks of groceries inside.

"You are an absolute lifesaver," Beth gushed and took the last bag from her. "Please come in and have a cup of coffee."

Megan followed Beth back to the kitchen and helped herself to the coffee while her sister put the items away.

"Humm," she said as she took the first sip. The coffee was sooo much better than her own. "So where's Tyler?"

"He's in the next room, finally asleep."

Beth glanced at her watch, then added, "It's been seventeen whole minutes since he's thrown up. The poor little thing's exhausted."

Megan thought it couldn't have been a piece of cake for her sister either. Even though Matt was a good father, it was true that the majority of child care fell on Beth's shoulders. It made it more understandable why Beth felt trapped and considered police work so glamorous and exciting. Most jobs would beat cleaning up barf in her book, even from your own kid.

"I hope he'll be all right."

"I'm sure it's just one of those twenty-four-hour bugs. He'll be up and about tomorrow like nothing happened." Beth finished with the groceries and started on the cupcakes.

"I hope you know I would have waited on the cake mix if I could have, but Camp's party is today. Then they're off for Easter break."

Megan nodded and sipped her coffee. "This is really good."

"Thanks. I'm glad you like it. It's a special blend. I ground the beans myself. Anyways, he would have been heartbroken to be the only child whose mother didn't bother to bake anything."

Megan gave an eye roll at the dramatics, but Beth was too busy to notice. She was surprised that Beth hadn't grown the coffee beans.

"To top it off, there are twenty-six kids in his class, plus the teacher, so I need twenty-seven cupcakes. It couldn't be twenty-four—that would be too easy. If it were twenty-five, I could have stretched one batch and be done with it. But with twenty-seven, I have to make two batches. No getting around it."

"No problem. Glad I could help," Megan said.

She was actually surprised by how much she meant it. Lately, more often than not, there was tension between the two of them. Today Megan saw her sister in a different light. Beth was notoriously perky in the morning. Without fail, she was up before dawn doing something or other. Although Beth worked efficiently, with smooth movements, her eyes revealed how tired she actually was. Megan considered being a detective demanding and stressful, but she'd never considered her sister's life to be, until today. There was no shift change for a stay-at-home mom.

"Can I help you do anything?" Megan asked.

Beth looked up, a bit surprised. It had been a long time since anyone asked her that. She gave a weary smile and said, "Please stay and talk if you can spare a few minutes. We don't get to talk much anymore. We're both always rushing around."

Megan glanced down at her watch. "Sure, I can stay for a little bit. Can I pour you a cup of coffee?" she asked as she refilled her own cup.

"That would be wonderful, thanks."

"Have you heard from Coop since I saw you yesterday?" Megan asked.

Beth looked up from her work with a wry grin. "I thought we weren't allowed to discuss police business."

Megan cast her eyes downward into her mug. "As a general rule, that still holds true, but I understand Coop's your friend too. But yesterday I needed to look good in front of Lacy."

"Whom, by the way, I really liked. She strikes me as the type of person who tells it like it is, very straightforward. She just needs to do something about that accent," Beth said. She had yet to sit down and join Megan at the table. As soon as she placed the first batch of cupcakes in the oven, the dryer buzzed. She folded the sheets and carried on their conversation over her shoulder.

"Is Lacy married?"

"No, single with no kids," Megan said, then added, "Your coffee's gonna get cold."

Beth chuckled, "I haven't had a hot cup since Camp was born. Besides, these are Tyler's sheets. I need to get them ready in case bout two of the throwing up starts all over again."

Megan cringed at the thought. It wasn't so much about the bodily fluids and functions that got to her—it was the smells. Vomit had to be close to the top of her list of offensive smells, and with little kids, it seemed to be especially potent. She loved her two nephews dearly, but they caused her to doubt her ability to raise children of her own. She didn't know how other women did it all, plus hold down a paying job. Here Beth was, superorganized, and she still had difficulty juggling her responsibilities without a job outside the home. Maybe the women in her family lacked a certain gene, and her mother had run off from the pressure after all. Many people thought it, at the time.

Megan shook away the thought and turned the conversation back toward safer ground. "So what about Coop?"

Beth finally came over and sat down at the table. She leaned forward and savored a sip of coffee before she spoke.

"He called Nate last night, and the two of them went to T. J.'s for a couple of beers."

"Really? I didn't think they hung out together that much anymore," Megan said.

"They don't. You know how Nate's wife is about him being home after dark. But Nate said Coop needed a friend. It's been a tough year for him. First, his father's death, then his dog, and to top it off, his fiancée walked out on him. Can you believe that woman could be so callous?"

"I know. It sounds more like lyrics to a country music ballad than real life. But then again, maybe her leaving was for the best. If she's the type to bail when things get tough, it's better to find out before the marriage ceremony and kids. Besides, he seemed to get over it pretty well."

"That or he's good at hiding his feelings," Beth said.

"What's that supposed to mean?" Megan asked. Beth was the second person to tell her Cooper had something to hide since the body was discovered.

"It means Coop really didn't want to marry her in the first place. I believe he wanted to get married and have a family so badly, he settled for that hussy. Now, you, on the other hand, would be a perfect match for Coop."

"Beth! That's ridiculous. Coop and I are just friends."

"I know you say that, but it's a shame because he's such a great guy. Don't you think?" Beth asked. She had one eyebrow raised and circled the rim of her mug with her index finger.

"Well, I think the split was a mutual agreement," Megan said and ignored Beth's implication. She wanted to divert the subject away from the well-traveled path of her single status. "What did Nate have to say?"

"Not much. You know men. But Ms. Hanley had an interesting comment."

Beth let that linger in the air as she checked on the cupcakes. Since they were almost done, she started on the second batch.

Megan sat expectantly. She had planned to talk with Ms. Hanley today, but it wouldn't hurt to hear what the woman had told Beth. Sometimes, people became nervous and forgot important information in an interview with a detective. "Sooo, what did Ms. Hanley have to say?"

"That a couple of months ago, she heard noises coming from the old grove. She wrote it off as teenagers, probably doing drugs, so she called the police."

"Ms. Hanley says anyone under the age of thirty or anyone that gets a new vehicle is either on drugs or sells them," Megan said. "Did the police respond?"

"Yes. She saw a police car drive past, but they must not have seen anything because nothing came of it. That's when she thought something might have happened to Cooper. She's very fond of him, you know. He helps out a lot with the upkeep of her house. She asked around the next day and found out he went fishing in the gulf. Cooper's not in any trouble, is he? I mean it's not his fault the bones were on his farm."

"Is that what people are saying?" Megan asked.

"Well, yes, some. You know how people can be, always want to believe the worst of others. They love to talk about other's misfortunes, and Cooper has had more than his share recently."

"What about you? Do you think he's capable of something so horrible?"

"Megan, you know I don't think he did anything bad. We grew up with Coop. He doesn't have a mean bone in his body, and he has to have the biggest heart of any man—other than Matt, of course. But there are those who think he had enough bad luck to push him over the edge. When Ms. Hanley heard that noise, it was close to the time that woman walked out on him. She worried it might have been the break-up fight and that he went fishing to clear his head."

It made Megan sad that anyone from this community could even doubt Cooper. "Well, as far as the police are concerned, he's not under suspicion at this time. There are no charges pending against him or any grounds to bring any up."

"Well, that's a relief. I can't imagine he could hurt anyone."

"So back to Ms. Hanley. What time did she hear all this?" Megan asked.

Beth took a sip of her cold coffee and continued to mix the batter while she spoke.

"It was late in the evening, around ten. She'd just gotten home from church. She told me she was there to clean up after the last show of the Christmas play."

"The last show? Does that mean it was right after Christmas?" Megan asked. She took out her notepad and flipped it open to make a notation.

"Yes. They run it for a few days afterward so the people who went out of town can see it too. Anyway, she rode with Mrs. Stevens, who dropped her off. On the way up the driveway to her house, she heard a car engine start up in the direction of Cooper's place. She recalled that it was a cold, clear night, so the sound traveled. Usually, she said, it's very quiet that time of night."

"You said she thought it might have been an argument. Did she hear voices, angry words?"

"No. She didn't say that. She described it as a commotion. Mainly a noisy car that speed off. Then screeching tires on the road. I guess that's why she thought it was that woman because no one has seen her since. It was the next day that she found out Cooper went fishing with Nate."

"I remember that. They caught a bunch of grouper."

"That's right. We had a wonderful fish fry. I think it was the week of New Year's."

"Yeah. It was Nate's birthday party," Megan said.

"That's right. I made him that four-layer cake. I swear, I don't know how many times it almost fell over on the way there. But anyway, what do you think Ms. Hanley's story means?"

Megan had to be careful. She didn't want to compromise an ongoing police investigation or endanger her sister. It was her opinion that the perpetrator was a serial killer who possibly lived close to Beth. She wanted her family to remain as uninvolved as possible. Her nephews needed their mother alive. Hell, she needed them all alive and safe.

Ms. Hanley, on the other hand, thrived on secrets and anything out of the ordinary. She'd be the one to speak to. She underlined the woman's name in her notepad, then looked up at Beth. "I plan to pay Ms. Hanley a visit and find out. Did Nate say anything else?"

"Oh, he did say they ran into Buddy. You know how Nate has hated him ever since he stole his senior prom date," Beth said.

"Buddy Howard? I saw him the other day. He's a good-looking man. He could have gotten any girl in high school," Megan said. Even her, but she left that out.

"From what I heard, he still does."

"Beth!" Megan said and covered her mouth with her hand.

"It's true. Everyone in town knows about it. I feel sorry for his wife, Sissy."

"Well, I don't know if those rumors are true or not, but he seems to be a reasonable politician," Megan said. She looked up to him as an athletic god in school. But she didn't know him as well as her sister or brother, being two years younger than Nate and three behind Beth.

"Nate said he was an ass to him and Cooper."

"Now, Beth, that doesn't sound very Christian of you," Megan said. It was something Beth usually accused her of. That and not going to church every Sunday. It felt good to be able to throw it back for a change.

"I know, but it's true. Those three have been at odds for years. It irks Nate that he became county commissioner of our district at the age of thirty. That's young to hold that position."

"Well, politics runs in his family. I'm sure it was expected of him. His father's been a big-time judge since we were kids and has more money than God. He practically owns this town. I'm sure the Honorable Angus Howard threw plenty of money toward his son's election campaign. So much so, I can't even remember who ran against him."

"That's because I don't think anyone did. Everyone else is busy with work and trying to raise a family. They don't have that kind of money to mount a campaign against Buddy Howard."

"Maybe, but remember, not everyone dislikes Buddy. Nate just happens to have a personal grudge against the man. I don't think it was just his prom date either. They didn't get along very well when they played on the same baseball team either. Buddy was always the one who hit the winning run. He kind of stole all the team's glory."

"Well, it didn't seem like he was back in town six months before he was elected," Beth said.

"No matter how he got there, he seems to take being county commissioner seriously. He does a good job. He grew up here, so he knows the area well," Megan said.

"I guess you're right, and Sissy is nice enough. She's very active in the community. But there are times when she acts like the queen of Ocala with her fancy clothes and thoroughbred farm."

"Do I detect a hint of jealousy?"

"No, it's not that. I don't have the energy half the time to dress nice. It's more like she thinks she's better than the rest of us because she owns that horse farm and racehorses."

"From what I've read, she's won several trophies. She must know what she's doing."

"Evidently not enough, or she'd rein in Buddy and remind him he's married," Beth said.

They both laughed at that. Buddy was handsome, with a nice build, and he certainly knew how to pour on the charm. Yet Megan understood that just because a few rumors floated around, it didn't mean they were true. She found herself attracted to Buddy but had never acted on it.

"Maybe you should stop by and see Cooper to check on him. You know—as a friend."

Megan said, "I already planned on it." She had a few questions she wanted to ask him.

Beth stood there, a glob of cupcake batter in her hair and a concerned look on her face. "I wish I could do something for the sake of our community. I mean, what kind of world is this when a body turns up a mile from where you're trying to raise two small children."

This was one of those rare occasions when Megan and her sister shared the same view.

"Or maybe I really could help," Beth suggested. "Seriously, Megan, just think about it. People would be more free to talk to me than a detective. It would be like I had a real job."

The alacrity in Beth's voice went straight to Megan's heart. "You *do* have a real job, Beth—several as a matter of fact. Besides, Lacy and I can't have you questioning witnesses. You need to stay out of this. I mean it, Beth. No snooping. This is serious police business."

"It'd be more fun than cleaning up vomit."

"No doubt, but you're needed here. You're obviously busy enough as it is."

Beth laughed nervously. "You act like there's a maniacal killer out there stalking us. It's probably like Lacy said yesterday. Some homeless person who rode the freight trains. Those people carry diseases like TB, you know. Or it could have been a mentally ill person who wandered away."

Megan wanted to reassure her sister that everything would be all right, that the children were safe, but it would be a lie that brought about a false sense of security. The truth was, she believed there had been a murder in their community. The remains at Cooper's farm were proof. She also suspected the perp to be part of their community. Someone who blended into everyday life. She wanted Beth to be warned as well as all the citizens of their community. But that was not her call to make. Soon, the chief would issue a statement. Until then, she had to keep quiet.

"That may be what happened," Megan said and gave a weak smile, meant to reassure. "Just the same, for the time being, I'd keep the doors locked and make the children play close by."

Beth's head shot up from her work, and she looked at her sister. "Megan, you're scaring me."

"I'm sorry," Megan said, getting up from the table. "Don't listen to me. I'm trying to make this missing-person ID into something bigger because it's my first case as detective. I want to feel important. You know, make a big splash. Besides, I have to go to work. Thanks for the coffee."

Her sister cocked her head to the side. "You sure you're OK?"

Megan gave her best convincing smile and said, "With two cups of your fresh ground coffee under my belt, I'll be fine. You know I'm not a morning person."

"All right, if you're sure," Beth said and followed her sister down the hallway to the front door. "Thanks for coming to my rescue."

"No problem. Glad I could help."

"Oh, I almost forgot—we're going to the sunrise service this Sunday. That way the children can do their Easter egg hunt early. Please come with us. I could really use your help. I'm greatly outnumbered, and you're so good with kids. It's a shame you don't have any of your own."

Megan gave a genuine laugh. "Now I know that's my cue to leave, but don't worry, I'll be there Sunday to help."

Beth watched as her sister drove away. Then, for the first time that she could remember on a warm, sunny day, she closed and locked her front door. Then she went to check on Tyler.

8

By the time Megan arrived at the station late that morning, Lacy was nowhere to be seen. An empty Styrofoam cup sat on her desk. With a quick evaluation, Megan deduced it was a recent addition. The leftover coffee and lipstick mark were a dead giveaway. That meant Lacy was more than likely somewhere in the building. Megan had wanted to beat her there this morning to make a good impression, but it appeared that Lacy was just as eager to get a jump on her day, without family ties to hold her back. She thought about calling her cell but didn't want to intrude if Lacy was in the chief's office. She could join them, of course, but opted to avoid any possible confrontation. She had no doubt that Lacy could hold her own against that man all by herself.

She then considered a run to the lab. But decided against that as well. She wanted to speak to Lacy about the chain saw marks before she spoke to Jerry again and asked him to evaluate the two older cases. With those options shot, she chose to descend to the safety of the basement instead. There had been a forensic illustration from one of the old cases she wanted to review. It was only a black-and-white sketch based on the skeletal remains of what the artist imagined the victim to look like alive. There was a slim possibility it held a clue, but she didn't like to wait around idle.

More often than not, serial killers selected individuals who shared certain occupational or physical commonalities. If it were a physical trait or characteristic, she hoped to be able to discern what it was. It was a common question of the grieving families and press alike; therefore, she felt it was worthwhile to check it out. If Lacy needed her, she could call her cell.

She needed to stop this predator. To do so, she had to get inside his mind. Find out what it was about a particular person that made him or her stand out in the killer's eye. Or were they simply in the wrong place at the wrong time? The problem was, for the most part, it was impossible to give rational explanations for irrational acts.

However, one avenue to take was through an artist working with the forensic lab. In the past, some police departments hired artists to do a three-dimensional reconstruction with the use of the skull. Unfortunately, this was expensive, time consuming, and only utilized by larger metropolitan areas. She was certain her department wouldn't have felt such an expense to be justified in the two older cases. Ocala was far too small for such extravagant detective techniques. Especially eight years ago.

Nonetheless, the process fascinated her. With the use of numerous measurements, the forensic artist virtually recreated a three-dimensional head of the deceased person. It was a tedious and arduous process that utilized clay, along with the actual human skull. The technician had to combine his artistic skills with those of a forensic anthropologist. The end result produced an eerie likeness of the deceased individual. This inevitably aided in identification. It also left a haunting reminder of a life cut short.

With the department's financial limitations, it was fortunate for Megan that computers had primarily taken the place of the more costly forensic sculptors. Megan planned to utilize the much cheaper version of computerized image modification. There was a department in Gainesville they often used as an outsource for a minimal fee. Since she had no idea who the perpetrator was, she planned to gain the identity of the victim first, then work from there.

Once the deceased was known, she could question their friends, family, and coworkers about their habits and schedule. That would hopefully lead to where and when the victim was last seen. Possibly even with whom. With any luck, it would ultimately give her the identity of the killer.

As she rounded the corner of the basement, Megan was surprised to see Lacy hunched over a thick file. She took a few steps forward without being noticed. From that vantage point, she read the name of the case Lacy was so intently focused on. Immediately, her face flushed with anger.

"What are you doing with that file? It has nothing to do with you."

Lacy was so deep in thought, she hadn't heard Megan enter. The abrupt sound of her raised voice startled her so much, she jumped and almost slid out of the chair and on to the floor.

"Megan! Why in the hell did you scare me like that?" she said, holding her hand to her heart.

Megan was embarrassed by her outburst. She'd come down here to avoid conflict with the chief. Now here she was, making a scene.

"Sorry, I didn't mean for that to come out like that, but you still didn't answer my question."

"Well, I wasn't trying to upset you, that's for sure. You told me you wanted a fresh perspective on the old cases. I don't recall any exception for your mother's case. It's not like I read your personal diary, for heaven's sake. Lighten up," Lacy said.

Megan went over and sat down heavily in the opposite chair and breathed a deep sigh. She wanted to make a change in her life—to be more open and treat Lacy better. This was a good opportunity to act on that resolution.

"Sorry. You're right. You didn't do anything wrong." This time she said it with more sincerity. "I guess seeing her name freaked me out. I hadn't expected it."

Lacy leaned forward, concerned for her friend. "That's all right, but you sure you're OK?"

"Yeah, I'm fine."

"OK, since you're here, and I have the file out, there were some questions I wanted to pose."

"What for? I've been over the file a thousand times. There's nothing there. The case is unsolvable," Megan said and slumped back in her seat.

"Ah, well, that's the point of having a fresh, untainted perspective, isn't it?" Lacy shuffled through the stack of papers in search for what she wanted. "This here," she said and slid the paper across the table to Megan.

"The Coke can? What about it? They ran it for prints and came up with no match."

"They were run against your mother's to make sure they weren't hers and came up negative?"

"Correct. Despite the fact there was no reason to. She wouldn't have touched the stuff."

"Why not? Helen would be the first person to run them against so you could rule hers out."

The sound of her mother's name set Megan back for a second. She took a deep breath to clear away the emotions that boiled just beneath the surface, then spoke slowly and as professionally as possible. "Because my mother would never drink a Coke, plain and simple."

Lacy raised her eyebrows in question. "Never? Why, was she a Pepsi person?"

Megan chuckled. "No, she was against soft drinks, period. My mother was a kind, generous person. She raised us with an abundance of love and had few rules, but the ones she did have were fiercely upheld, consistently. One primary rule was no soda. Ever."

"Wow, I can't even imagine life without soda. It's like being raised Quaker or something."

Megan had to smile at that. "Not really. None of us children were ever allowed to drink soda. It wasn't a punishment or anything. We knew no difference. It's not like we missed it."

"What about special occasions or holidays?" Lacy asked.

"Not even then. My mom wanted to make a stand against the soft drink companies. She said sodas were empty calories loaded with far too much sugar and caffeine. You have to remember, this was way before her stance was popular."

"I hate to break it to you, Megan, but I still don't think that stance is very popular. I live for sugar and caffeine. They're the basis of my food pyramid."

"Well, she put the fear of God into us that soft drinks would rot our teeth and deteriorate our growing bones the very second we drank it. We drank water and milk instead, that's it. So that's why there was no question in my mind that the Coke can found on the porch that day, any Coke can, could not have belonged to her."

"That's interesting," Lacy said. "But they still ran the prints to eliminate hers?"

"Yes, of course. No one else could imagine such a rule being adhered to. It was their theory since her children were at school, she'd sneak a drink, and we'd be none the wiser. But, like I said, it wasn't a match."

"Sorry," Lacy said.

"About not being able to drink Coke as a child? Don't be. My mother did us all a huge favor, and I grew up with no cavities," Megan said and opened wide. "See, no fillings."

"No, not that. About the detectives not listening to you."

"I was a kid. I was used to adults ignoring me. I was more shook-up about my mother's disappearance and the effect that had on my father. No one took her absence all that seriously. With no body, they assumed she'd left on her own free will. There was no evidence of foul play."

"The police did have a point with your dad. That sort of behavior does occur. I'm not saying that's what happened in your mother's case, but they had to consider it as a possibility."

"I know that now. Even her running away. I see how stressed-out Beth is. I know she loves her husband and children. But for some women stuck at home, they reach a point and lose it. Something about being with toddlers all day long without a break. It can drive a normal person half insane from time to time. Still, even if she did something so radical, after she blew off a little steam, she would have called home. But that call never came."

"So no one else thought it was strange that even though your mother never drank the stuff, a half-empty soda can sat on the front porch?"

"Some would call it half full," Megan said with a wry smile.

"Very funny," Lacy shot back but was relieved Megan could joke about it.

Megan held up her hands. "Seriously, no one outside our family really understood the significance. The prints proved they weren't hers, but that went unnoticed. I'd just turned sixteen, and like I said, no one listened to me. They said I was overemotional. I heard one of the policemen tell another that it was probably 'that time of month for me.' To my face. They said it could have been left there by anyone. My mom had been painting the porch. They figured a friend or neighbor could have stopped by, sat a spell while they drank their drink, then left."

"Did they question her friends? Take their prints?"

"I'm sure people were questioned, but it would have been considered rude to fingerprint them. Like I said, there was no evidence of foul play. To fingerprint her friends would imply they might have something to do with her disappearance."

"Rude hell," Lacy said. She was indignant. "And that shit about you being on your period is just offensive. No, more than that. It's incredulous, not to mention ridiculous. Your mother was missing. My god, now I understand why you became a detective. Somebody had to change the way cases were handled. I'm glad I came here. Things will be different now."

"Well, there's no point in getting all riled up about it now," Megan said.

Lacy opened her mouth to speak when Megan held up her hand to stop her.

"It's over with. Basically they told me I had read too much into the leftover drink. It was a soda can, no big deal. To this day, the situation remains unchanged."

"OK, for the sake of argument, let's say it was possible that the Coke can was left by just about anybody. Still, it wasn't your mother's, right?"

"Not according to the prints."

"Whoever was drinking the Coke never finished it."

"So?"

"Don't you think that's strange? If I remember correctly, this happened somewhere in the middle of May."

"That's right, May twelfth," Megan said to save Lacy the trouble of digging through the file again.

"I know I'm new here and not used to the temperatures, so I looked it up. May has temperatures in the mid—to upper eighties every day with an increasing humidity. It's basically summer by anyone's standards."

"True, but I don't see your point. Don't tell me you're gonna complain about the heat already," Megan said. She leaned back in her chair and folded her arms across her chest.

"No, what I want to say is, the person drinking the Coke would have normally finished it off. That is, unless something happened to interrupt them. Remember, this was back when cell phones weren't popular; so if the phone rang, it would have been your mother who took the call inside. The visitor would have taken the drink and left. It doesn't take long to down a twelve-ounce soft drink when you're hot."

"I'll have to take your word on soda thing. I still don't drink them."

"Seriously?" Lacy sat back in her chair and evaluated her partner dubiously. "You are so weird sometimes." But it was said with a grin.

"Cross my heart. I didn't even drink sweet tea until Beth married Mather. That's all he drinks, so it's always in their house."

Lacy shook her head in disbelief. "Well, at least someone in your family understands the benefits of a good caffeine-sugar rush. He just might save all of you."

"OK," Megan laughed. "Your point?"

"I think the Coke belonged to the last person to see your mother," Lacy said.

Megan noted Lacy fell short of saying alive but could tell Lacy was pretty certain of this conclusion. Her posture spoke volumes. She was leaning back in the chair, arms folded across her chest, and obviously pleased with herself. Her eyes focused on Megan expectantly.

"That's reasonable logic, and I have to say I've considered the same possibility. The problem is, the prints were run back then. They came up with no match. That pretty much makes it a dead lead. There's no one to question. That means it's irrelevant what we suspect. We have squat."

"What if we run them again, now, through AFIS? The database has increased dramatically in the last eight years. The computers are much more powerful. It's more of an efficient national data compilation than it used to be," Lacy said.

"I don't know."

"I know the prints are old, but it's still worth a shot. Jerry is a wiz. If it can be done, he could do it. Like you said, they didn't take it seriously back then. But I do, and I know you do as well."

Megan shifted nervously in her seat and contemplated the possibility. She knew Lacy's reference was to the automated fingerprint identification system. It stored fingerprint images, not only of criminals, but more recently it had began to accumulate those of all service people and public servants alike. Thus, it had greatly expanded its database since her mother's disappearance. It encompassed anyone who held a government position, whether it involved the military service or a school system, in any capacity, even part-time in the cafeteria. Printing was required.

All of this information was permanently kept on file with the AFIS. It was able to distinguish any new prints and, in minutes, compare them to the millions of others on file. Once that was done, it would print out a list of potential candidates for a match. Finally, a further comparison of the loops and whorls which make each print unique could be done by a human to verify or deny a match.

"What's wrong?" Lacy said. "You don't think Jerry could do it?

Megan saw the challenge in Lacy's eye. "You know this isn't about Jerry. I don't think the chief would go for it. The case is old and considered closed. Plus, you may have forgotten, but we have a murder we're supposed to be working on. It doesn't help that we haven't gotten anywhere on that yet. I don't see him allotting funds, regardless of how trivial, to something so insignificant and old. Basically closed."

"You're afraid people will accuse you again of using your position to serve your personal goals, aren't you?"

Megan gave a subtle shrug and said, "Well, yes. There is that too. It's happened before, and I have to say, in this situation, it would partially be true."

"Like heck it would be. This is an unsolved case, and you're a detective. Heck, we run old DNA samples all the time, and that's much more costly. To have fingerprints run on an old piece of evidence won't take any time on our part. It certainly won't interrupt this current investigation. Especially since we don't actually have any leads to pursue. Basically all we can do is interview neighbors until the lab results come back. I say we do it."

"When you put it that way, it sounds OK. But we still need the chief to sign off on it."

"Speaking of the devil," Lacy said and looked down at her vibrating cell phone.

After an extremely brief conversation, Lacy turned back to Megan. The look on her face wasn't one of a happy person.

"What now?" Megan asked.

"We've got another one. The chief said it's no more than a half a mile from yesterday's."

"Oh crap," Megan murmured.

"I'm sorry," Lacy said. It was bad enough for her to have two murders to deal with and being new to this job. But she imagined it was even worse for Megan. She'd grown up here and knew almost everyone. With both cases so close to her sister's home, it would be hard not be concerned over her family's safety.

"The chief's not too happy about it. I wish I had something more to tell him about the remains found at Cooper's."

"Well, my god, it hasn't even been twenty-four hours. What does he expect?"

"Answers," Lacy said. "He wants answers to give to the public."

9

In a solemn mood, the two detectives left the station and drove directly to the scene. They were met by a uniformed officer and a somewhat hysterical mother. Uncomfortable with the situation, he briskly walked over to them, obviously relieved by their arrival. "Glad to see you."

When he got closer, Megan recognized him from yesterday at the peach farm. He'd arrived at the scene when she was leaving. "What do you have?" she asked.

"Looks like it could be similar to the last one." He addressed Megan, whom he was familiar with, but made the mistake of talking loud enough for others to hear.

The mother's eyes widened. "The last one—What do you mean, another? What's going on? How many have there been?"

"We'll be with you in just a moment to answer all your questions, ma'am," Megan said. She pulled the officer over to the side so they could discuss the matter in private. She knew that if this turned out to be another body, word would get out sooner or later. But it would have been better if this guy hadn't blurted it out in front of an already anxious civilian. It only served to exacerbate an already pressure-filled situation. General hysteria never boded well for politicians up for reelection. Nor would it make her job any easier.

Lacy looked up at him. "Good going there, Sherlock. Why not scare the shit out of her while you're at it?"

"I'm sorry, but she's been like this ever since I got here. I'm a pile of nerves," he said.

Megan could almost feel sorry for him, but she had enough problems without having to worry about his inability to perform his job adequately.

"OK, tell us what happened."

"Her little boy was out in the yard playing. He tossed the Frisbee, and the dog was supposed to bring it back."

"Yeah, yeah, yeah. We're familiar with the game. It's called fetch," Lacy said. "But it usually doesn't involve a dead body."

The officer glared at Lacy, but she didn't care. She held the reputation from the day before as a smart-mouth. Albeit one with fancy panties.

"Anyway," the officer continued, "the boy said he threw the Frisbee, and the wind caught it. It ended up in the woods. The dog took off in pursuit and came back with that."

The officer pointed down to a large bone on the ground. To Megan, it looked disturbingly like the human femur that Jerry had shown her yesterday. For a moment, she thought, *OK, a femur. It's just one bone, no big deal. One large bone. It could be from a cow or deer. Maybe this will be OK.*

The problem was, it appeared too small to be a cow and too big to be a deer. In fact, it really did look identical to the one in the lab. It looked human. That meant it once belonged to a live person. A person who was now deceased without a leg bone. Which also meant the rest of the remains had to be out there somewhere. Because as far as Megan could figure, you couldn't lose a femur without it coming to your attention unless you were dead. That brought about all the questions and headaches that were associated with an unidentified corpse. Such as, who was this individual? How did they end up here, and when did it happen? "Oh crap," she mumbled.

She noticed her head began to throb, and her left eye started to twitch again. She tried to ignore it and focus back on the officer. "Please, go on."

"You OK?" he asked. His concern for her was evident.

"I've had better days, but please continue."

"The boy thought it was kind of cool. But he wanted the dog to bring back the Frisbee. He said the bone was too heavy to throw. Since his mother told him to stay out of the woods because of all the snakes, he kept throwing the bone back into the woods in the hopes the dog would get the toy instead of the bone."

"Snakes? What do you mean there are snakes in the woods?" Lacy asked.

Both Megan and the officer looked over at her as if she were crazy. Then the officer continued. "After a while, his mother came out to check on him and saw the bone. Her husband's a hunter, so she knew right off it wasn't from a deer. That's when she called the police. Dispatch sent me to check it out. I wish I'd been on break when the call came in. When I saw it, I immediately phoned the station for y'all to come out and take a look because it looked human to me. She overheard my conversation and freaked out. She started to scream and ask one question after another. It hasn't stopped. It's too much. I can't take hysterical women."

Lacy rolled her eyes and said, "Have you looked in the woods yet?"

"No. I didn't want to disturb any evidence."

"Why is it that uniform cops always say that kind of junk when things get dirty?" Lacy asked.

The officer glared at her again, then spoke to Megan, "Since y'all are here, I'll head on back to file my report."

"That's fine," Megan said and watched him go. Then she turned to Lacy. "What is it with you? You don't have to antagonize these guys. If you want them to accept you, I suggest you curb your sarcasm. You already have the fire-ant fiasco to live down."

Lacy held her hands up in surrender. "I know, I know. Sometimes I just can't help it. They leave themselves so wide open. Besides, I'm not shooting to be one of the guys. I'll find my own niche."

"Like wearing flowered panties?"

"Hey, it's my way of making up for having to wear such conservative outerwear. I have to express my hidden creative side somehow," Lacy said. "They make me feel pretty."

With absolutely no fashion sense whatsoever, Megan just stared at her and shook her head.

Lacy stood by while Megan phoned the crime scene unit for the second time in two days. After relating all the pertinent information and directions to the site, she turned back to Lacy for further instruction.

"How about we question the mother and the kid while we wait for CSU. By the sound of it, I doubt the officer was able to get much information out of either one of them," Lacy said.

On the way to the house, Lacy asked Megan to bag and label the femur as evidence. She didn't want it to end up as a chew toy. Jerry could decide whether it was human or not. Megan did as instructed, chucked it in the bed of her truck, then walked over to join Lacy.

"Hello," Lacy called out. She knocked on the open white gate that led up to the house.

The woman was in the yard, fussing with the flower garden.

"I'm Detective Lacy Andina, and this is my partner, Detective Megan Callingham. You can call us Lacy and Megan."

They shook hands, and Megan thought the woman reminded her very much of her sister. They both lived in a beautiful home and appeared to be living the American dream. This house looked to be on ten acres of well-kept land. Well-tended flower beds lined both the home and driveway. It looked like a perfect place to grow up. That is, except for the suspected dead body hidden somewhere in their woods.

"I know you," the woman said to Megan. "Well, sort of anyway. Your sister's name is Beth?"

"That's right. She lives down the road from here on the peanut farm."

"Yes, the big yellow house. Her azaleas are always so pretty this time of year."

Lacy stood there amazed and wondered if there was anyone in Marion County who didn't know either Megan or her family. It made her feel like a lone wolf. A thousand miles away from her friends and family. She knew no one besides Megan and Beth. Then again, she was hiding from her past. Since they knew everyone, she'd make friends soon enough.

"I'm sorry I yelled at that poor man. I'm usually not like that. Is that why he left?" the woman asked.

"It's understandable under the circumstances, but that's not why he left. He got another call," Megan said. She didn't make a habit to lie to people, but this woman was upset enough as it was. Besides, it wasn't her fault that 99 percent of men didn't know what to do when a woman cried.

"My name's Darcey Phillips, and my son's name is Roy. I sent him on into the house. I can get him if you like."

"That would be helpful," Megan said. "I promise I won't ask too many questions or upset him."

The woman nodded, then leaned in the house to call the boy. Roy must have been pushed up against the door listening because it caught him in the head when it opened. After a brief recovery, Roy and his dog, Rosie, bounded down the porch steps.

"I never heard of a girl detective," the boy declared.

"Well, now you've met two of them," Lacy said.

"Wow, you're here about the big bone, aren't you?"

"That's right. We need to ask you a few questions."

"OK," Roy said. He looked at the two detectives in wide-eyed awe. This was probably the most exciting thing that had ever happened to him in the entire ten years of his life.

Megan was the type of person to note discrepancies, no matter how minor. It was a character flaw that, in the past, had inhibited her success with long-term relationships. Yet she'd found it useful as a detective. Lean on your strengths and downplay your weaknesses, her guidance counselor in high school told her, so she had.

Earlier, Beth needed to make cupcakes for Camp's school party this afternoon. Therefore, it was odd that this child was home, active in the yard. He didn't appear sick, and it wasn't time for school to let out. Although it didn't exactly tie in with the bone, it made her curious.

"How come you're not in school today?" Megan asked. "Are you homeschooled?"

Roy's mom stepped up and answered before the child could. "He goes to a private Christian school. They have today off because it's Good Friday."

Megan nodded and jotted the information down. She had no idea if it would make any difference, but it made her feel more detectivelike in front of Mrs. Phillips. The woman watched her intently—as if she expected Megan to solve the mystery of the bone right then and there from that single question. It made her eye twitch faster, and she hoped no one would notice.

"You said you were outside with your dog?" Lacy asked to move things along.

"That's right," Roy answered, full of enthusiasm from the attention. "We were playing fetch. Rosie's real good at it."

Megan wondered how often the dog had access to the woods. She recalled Mahoney's statement yesterday about femurs being a favorite of dogs. Today's incident seemed to validate that little piece of information. The question was, why hadn't the dog retrieved the bone prior to today—unless of course it was dumped there very recently?

Lacy must have had similar thoughts because she asked, "How often do you play fetch with Rosie?"

"Whenever I can. But if I have school, I usually have a ton of homework, so I don't get much time to play outside with her. But she sits by my desk while I work and keeps me company. She's a good dog. Everyone that comes to visit says so. They all leave wanting a dog just like her."

Megan would have liked a more specific answer. This was like a conversation with her nephews. Children always viewed the world through different eyes. What was important to adults was often of no consequence to them. She looked over pleadingly at Darcey, who was wringing her hands from nerves.

"Do you have any idea when was the last time they were out there together?" Megan gestured to the general direction of the woods.

"Not offhand," she said. "Let me think. The last couple of weeks he's had terrible allergies. You know how spring is, with all the oak pollen and flowers in bloom. I've had to dust every day. There isn't one thing in our house that isn't coated in a greenish-yellow tint. You should have seen my car the other day. Gosh, it looked as if it'd never been washed. Can you imagine?"

Megan realized that it wasn't just children who held a different view of what was important. People like Beth and Darcey were in a world all of their own.

Lacy cleared her throat. She wasn't interested in a weather update, pollen count, or this woman's housecleaning schedule. They had an investigation to deal with. She let out a sigh. She hadn't intended to be rude, but she'd lost her patience about five minutes ago.

Darcey looked over at Lacy then back at Megan and went on, "Anyway, because of his allergies, after school and on weekends I've kept him inside. I think today's the first time they've played in the side yard for weeks. Maybe even a month."

Now that was something she could use. Megan jotted down the fact, next to Roy's reason for being out of school.

"Even when he does play out there," Darcey continued, "he's not allowed in the woods. They've been flooded since the hurricanes last summer and are just infested with water moccasins and mosquitoes. I'm so afraid he'll be bitten or come down with the West Nile virus or some strain of that new Asian bird flu."

"Great," Lacy mumbled. "I hate snakes."

"Well, at least so far there hasn't been any reported cases of the Asian bird flu in the U.S.," Megan said.

Lacy knew as soon as they finished with this woman, they'd head straight to snake and mosquito land. It didn't go unnoticed either that Megan didn't argue over the West Nile virus or the snakes. Only the Asian flu. "Super."

"Pardon me?" Darcey asked.

"Nothing. Please go on," Lacy said. She saw Megan look grimly at her, so she forced a smile of encouragement toward Mrs. Phillips. "I'm sorry, it's just that I'm not used to all the wildlife around here yet."

Mrs. Phillips nodded. "I could tell you're not from around here. You have a funny accent."

Lacy wanted to point out that it was everyone else that had an accent to her but stayed quiet.

"I'm not afraid of snakes," Roy blurted out. "My mom just worries a lot. You know how moms are. My allergies aren't that bad either."

Megan smiled down at the boy. She could feel how uncomfortable all this talk had made him. They'd talked about the bone he'd found and acted as if he wasn't here to speak for himself. He wanted credit for the discovery. She could identify with that emotion.

"Yeah, I know," Megan said with a twinge. He was a cute kid. She wouldn't mind a kid like Roy or having a mother to fuss over her every now and then.

"But still, afraid or not, you need to be careful of any snake, especially the poisonous ones. Besides, it's good to listen to your mother; she knows what she's talking about."

"Yes, ma'am," Roy said, totally discouraged. Then a thought struck him to impress the detectives. "Did you know that water moccasins are pit vipers? I heard if you get bit by one in the arm, they've got to cut your arm right off. If they don't do it real quick like, you die," Roy said with a hacking motion with his hand to emphasize the action.

"Wow, you have quite a knowledge of snakes," Megan said.

Lacy began to feel a little woozy. She wondered how her career choice had gone so wrong. She was supposed to be encompassed by warm tropical breezes, white sandy beaches lined with coconut palms, and muscular, buff guys. She had pictured her daily work schedule more like the occasional pickpocket or vacation fraud. It wasn't supposed to involve dead bodies or poisonous snakes. And this concern over African and Asian diseases was intolerable. How did Megan know there wasn't a case of it here? She needed another transfer, but she couldn't go back home.

Roy continued quite animated. "And, when I throw the Frisbee, it goes right where I want it. Well, usually anyway. Today the wind caught it, so it went into the woods. But that hardly ever happens. I've even trained Rosie to catch it in the air. She's getting real good at it."

"Wow, that sounds like you're an expert on dog training and snakes," Megan said.

This made Roy beam with delight. "Yes, ma'am. I read a lot and watch *Animal Planet*."

"Have either of you seen or heard anything unusual in the last month or so in the direction of the woods?" Lacy asked. She wanted to get off the topic of snakes and the sawing off of limbs. If the kid only knew.

"We had a wild monkey in there a few weeks ago," Roy said.

"What?" Lacy shrieked. "You can't be serious."

"Yeah, a real live one," Roy said.

"It screamed all the time," Darcey said. "We called animal control, but they wouldn't come."

"I don't blame them," Lacy mumbled.

"We think it was a rhesus monkey from Silver Springs. The park's not that far from here through the woods. After all the summer storms last year, all kind of animals were displaced. Normally I love animals, but this thing had a bad disposition. I kept Roy and Rosie away from the woods until we didn't hear it anymore. They can become aggressive and bite, you know."

"I'm not believing this," Lacy said.

Megan leaned over toward her partner to whisper in her ear, "It's OK, you've dealt with much worse than a skinny, two-and-a-half-foot-tall monkey."

"Damn right I have. I could whoop that monkey's ass if I have to," Lacy shot back.

It came out a little louder than intended and brought a smile to Megan and Roy's face. But his mother's face went taut.

"Excuse me?" Darcey inquired.

They all turned when the crime scene unit drove up. Lacy excused herself to go met them. Behind it was one of the canine vans. Megan assumed they'd brought along a cadaver dog to speed up the search for the remainder of the body.

When Megan finished up with Roy and his mother, she walked back to Lacy. The others had already gone to work, transporting equipment toward the woods. Lacy lay in wait. She had a few unresolved issues she wanted to discuss before she stepped foot into the dark swamp.

"Look, Megan, I don't mean to seem like a lightweight, but I don't want to go stomp through those woods ankle deep in snakes with some wild, crazy-ass monkey in wait to attack me. Not to mention the Asian bird flu or West Nile virus infected mosquitoes ready to have at me. They don't give us hazard pay for crap like this."

"OK, here's the deal. There is no Asian bird flu in the United States, and if you watch your step, which you would do anyway because it's a potential crime scene, you won't step on any more fire ant mounds or snakes. I carry mosquito repellant in my truck at all times. We can spray each other down before we go in the woods. Usually, if you don't mess with the snakes, they won't mess with you."

"Usually?" She stood there with her hands on her hips and glared at Megan in disbelief. "What about the monkeys?"

"Darcey's right. They can be nasty. The thing to remember with them is not to stare. It's best not to even make eye contact. But above all, never, never smile at one. If you do, and show your teeth, they will take that as an act of aggression and attack for sure."

"Since they'll only see my backside as I run away for my life, that shouldn't be a problem. I mean, what the hell? I didn't sign on to be a nature cop. I don't do nature," Lacy said and waved her finger at Megan. "I work on pavement, asphalt, and carpet. I don't like mud, muck, or dirt."

Megan repressed a smile. This was the first time she felt like she was on top. Lacy might have more knowledge of detective investigation, but she had more experience with Florida wildlife. "I understand. A lot of people feel that way when they get here. It takes awhile to get over the heebie-jeebies. Snakes and large spiders tend to evoke that reaction in everyone."

"Large spiders? I know you want to reassure me, but so far it isn't working so good."

"So a few of the monkeys are aggressive toward humans. If you don't smile or make eye contact, you'll be all right," Megan said.

"What the heck am I supposed to do if something jumps out of a tree and screams at me? Of course I'm gonna turn my head and look at it. You'd have to be in a coma not to do that."

"OK, but don't smile at it. Look away immediately," Megan said.

"What if my mouth gapes wide open in freakin' shock? Will they attack then? Because that's exactly what's gonna happen. I'm a detective, not a zookeeper."

Megan reached out and gripped her partner by the shoulders. "You can do this. That monkey isn't any worse than a gangbanger with a knife. Or what about a crazed-out crackhead? You know how to handle yourself in those situations. This may be a little new and different, but it certainly isn't any harder. I'll teach you about wildlife, and you can teach me everything you know about being a good detective. I need you. We need each other. We can do this together."

Lacy stood there for a moment to process this information. Megan was right. She was tougher than any sorry-ass monkey or spider. Hell, she had a service revolver tucked in her waistband. Her spine stiffened in determination. This was a war of wills, and she had a stubborn streak a mile wide.

"So let's go," Lacy said with a newfound resolve. "I don't want to waste any more time."

"Great," Megan responded. "I'll get the bug spray."

Off the two went to Megan's truck in search of the aerosol can.

"There probably was only that one isolated monkey, right? I mean, Silver Spring keeps them all locked up tight in a cage, don't they? Probably a head count every night."

Megan didn't want to tell her partner the truth—that it wasn't monkey boot camp. But Lacy did need to be aware of the situation, especially after the fire ant incident.

"Well, not exactly. There is actually a free-range colony with a population of several hundred monkeys. They were left behind after they filmed the Tarzan movies years ago. Silver Springs does feed them, so most of them stay close to the park. It's only every now and then they wander off into the woods. Usually if there's a bad storm or something."

"Yeah, probably the sick ones," Lacy said. She had every intention of shooting one if it posed a problem.

Megan left out the fact that indeed a large percentage the community had had enough of the monkey invasions. There were even staged protests to have them eradicated. The animals were a nuisance. Some were considerable in size, with enough strength to cause serious damage to any unsuspecting passerby or house pet. Plus, there remained the valid concern over disease.

At one point, it appeared as if the local citizens had made progress. The county planned to catch and destroy all the diseased monkeys they could. After all, they were not native to the state. As such, they were considered exotics, and their presence caused a great deal of damage to the local vegetation. All local house pets, beware!

But once word got out, there was vocal opposition by offended citizens, many of whom lived safely away from the animals. And although their numbers were low, they were more than the political officials were willing to alienate. It never sounded good in the press that, as a community leader, you had attempted to kill innocent furry animals. Especially when the opponents showed photos of the faces of cute, healthy baby monkeys that looked so humanlike. Therefore, the program was scrubbed while the monkeys continued to breed unchecked and unmedicated; so they constantly increased in number.

"OK, let me put it another way. The monkeys are the least of our problems if we have a second body in these woods," Megan said.

"That's true. I do know the chief is pretty upset that yesterday's case turned out to be a homicide and not a transient of natural causes," Lacy said.

"He's probably under pressure from Angus Howard. That man's up for reelection this year. He's good friends with the chief and a big-time judge around here. He's rich, powerful, and wants to make a show of how tough he is on crime. Our community ranked one of the safest places to live in *Newsweek* a few years in a row, and he wants to keep it that way."

"Well, damn, it's only been one day," Lacy said. "We still haven't gotten any official results back from the lab yet. You let me handle the chief. If he dares to say a thing, I will show him my muddy pants. Hell, if we aren't working, he can come out here and muck through this shit."

Megan smiled. She had no doubt that Lacy could stand up for the both of them, but before she could respond, a yell came from the woods. They both turned at the sound.

"We found it," came a voice from the dense undergrowth. "It's over here."

Megan hadn't realized how badly she'd hoped there would be no body. That somehow it was an isolated femur. Now, that hope was crushed, and the discovery meant another murder to solve.

"That's our cue," Lacy said. She bite down on her lower lip and strode off toward the commotion. She was now forced to have her own, personal, and up-close encounter with Florida's wildlife. It would have been nicer on the nature channel, but she'd be damned if she would look weak in front of Megan or the crime-scene-unit men. Hell, maybe she could start her own crime-scene reality show in the wilds of Florida. Anything was possible if she set her mind to it.

10

Lacy opted to handle the chief, and Megan wound up in the lab with Jerry for the second day in a row. She wished it were a social visit so she could at least enjoy his dimples, but it was not.

"You said they called in the cadaver dog for this one?" Jerry asked.

It was his initial contact with the remains found at the Phillipses' place. Megan perched on the edge of her stool and intently watched his every move. She was too impatient to leave and wait for the results. She needed to know what his preliminary impressions were, firsthand.

"That's right. We actually owe the original find to a dog as well. That's why there's one femur in a separate bag."

"Ah yeah, I see. What's the story on that?"

Megan told Jerry about Roy and Rosie, along with their game of fetch.

"Roy's mom must have been kinda freaked out," Jerry said.

"That's an understatement. Actually this find has a lot of people on edge. We have a ton of questions but no answers. Mahoney noticed a small amount of soft tissue. Do you think it will help date the remains or possibly figure out how long they've been hidden in the woods?"

"It might. One thing I do know is that these bones are definitely nasty," Jerry said. "I really hate swamp muck."

"That makes you and Lacy both," Megan said absently.

Jerry walked over to a side counter where the labeled bones sat covered in leaves and swamp goo. "Mahoney was right. A few of these have the last vestiges of putrefied flesh still on them. It's more than likely what aided the cadaver dog. They're trained to detect decomposing material. Without the nastiness, this body wouldn't have been found so easily. Unfortunately, it makes my job a lot less pleasant. Thank God for latex gloves and mints," Jerry stated.

"The dog didn't go straight to the bones. She sniffed around quite a bit before she found them. I figure that means the trail from the perp who dumped the body was too old for her."

"Not necessarily. The dogs aren't trained to sniff for the killer's trail, only the cadaver, and there's not much left for her to smell," Jerry explained.

"Humm," Megan said as she mulled this over. "Does that mean the body was fairly clean of soft tissue when it was dumped?"

"That, or the individual's death occurred in the swamp. If that was the case, there would be no drag track for the cadaver dog to smell. You see, that's what she sniffs for—decaying flesh."

Megan shuddered involuntarily. "I think at this point you can call it a murder."

"It's not up to me to decide that. Plus, I want to keep my job. You're the detective. So far, all I see is remains. I believe them to be human, but I see no evidence of foul play," Jerry said.

"So the person went for a stroll naked in the swamp and died of a heart attack?"

"I guess you've got your work cut out for you," Jerry said with a grin.

"What about adipocere? Would it be present in this case?"

"You do listen to me. I love that about you, Megan. You have a thirst for knowledge."

Jerry took the skull out and placed it on a clean stainless-steel table for examination. "At least this is relatively clean." He picked off a few particles of tissue and placed them in a solution to the side. "Oh, look at this."

Megan was encouraged by his sudden optimism. She scooted the stool closer and leaned in to get a better view. "What? I don't see anything."

"Oh my, little one, that's because you do not seek with your mind. Look harder," he said.

Even though this was serious, Megan smiled. It was truly enjoyable being around someone who loved his job so much. Jerry was so positive, especially when he was involved in a new case. He radiated pleasure and satisfaction from his work, all the while taking a great deal of gratification in sharing his knowledge with anyone who wanted to listen and learn.

"Do you mean the suture line?" Megan asked.

"No, we'll get to that in a minute. Look at this here," he said. He picked up the forceps he'd used to retrieve the tissue samples. With them, he pointed to something unfamiliar.

"This is an empty pupa casing left behind by a bluebottle fly."

"A pupa?"

"Yes, it's a stage in the fly's life. It's what makes some insects forensically important. They go through a complete or holometabolous development."

"I really don't understand what that means," Megan said. "Homeo what?"

"Holometabolous. Some insects and beetles are born as eggs, then hatch into a larval form. From there, they undergo a series of incremental growths. This pattern is caused by successive molts that the larva must go through before they finally enter the inactive pupal stage."

"And a molt is the shedding of the skin?"

"Almost. Instead of skin, it's the exoskeleton. When it becomes outgrown, it's sloughed off. The pupa is the hardened last larval stage. In that, the adult remains protected to develop. The various stages are easily differentiated and occur on a predictable timetable. That's why we can use forensic entomology to help place the time of death. The insect activity directly correlates with the destruction of the body's soft tissue. For example, here, we have the egg of the typical bluebottle fly. It develops into mature fly in about twenty to twenty-one days. Then that insect flies away to leave behind a characteristic empty pupa case. Such as we have here," Jerry said and raised the skull for Megan to see. "That makes these remains at least twenty-plus days old."

"You never fail to amaze me," Megan said.

"Actually, in this case I would have to say it's more luck. These pupae are often overlooked because they resemble rat droppings. Plus, you also have to consider the majority of these bones were in water or water-soaked soil. That affects the rate of decomposition which will have to be factored into the final determination of time of death."

"It decreases it, right? But not as much as if they were buried in solid ground."

Jerry smiled at her, pleased. "So you do listen to me, my young Jedi. I like you more and more every day. One day I see you as a great forensic warrior."

Megan enjoyed the compliment. She respected Jerry, and it made her feel as if she was growing as a detective.

"Although these were in wet soil—swamp muck, I believe, is the scientific term," he said with a smile. "It's enough to make a difference. This kind of muck also prohibits the use of soil staining to help date the find. The swamp is too rich in minerals and botanical refuse."

Jerry teased the tiny insect casing off of the bone, placed it in a separate specimen bottle, then labeled it. "I'll send this to the forensic entomology lab in Gainesville." He continued on with his work and gave Megan a narrative as he went. "I'd say this is a female, approximately the same age range as yesterday's. You can tell by the size of the skull. And look at the thickness of the mandible. A male's would be much wider and more dense, especially in this area here," Jerry said and pointed to the angle of the lower jawbone.

"Then you have this area here—the superciliary arch and the glabella. They're also much thicker in men."

This time Jerry pointed to the bone above the orbits, where the eyebrows would have been in life. An image of a boy she'd known in high school came to mind. The poor kid looked like a Neanderthal because he had such a thick boney prominence above his eyes. It didn't do much for his social status even though he was actually rather kindhearted and intelligent.

"Yeah, I can see what you mean. And the nose gives away it's a Caucasian, right?"

"Very good. But I'll wait for a final say-so until I've looked at everything. I hope we have at least one of the pelvic bones. With all the leaves and gook, it's hard to tell offhand what's here."

"They're there," Megan said. "I already asked when they were documenting the site."

Megan was so impressed by how much information the other set of pelvic bones provided, she was relieved when Tim told her this victim's was intact. She had also inquired about the presence of the arms. His negative response sent a chill down her spine and caused a knot to form in the pit of her stomach. Four female skeletons without arms was too much to be mere coincidence. It appeared as if there was a serial killer out there. Soon the town would be abuzz with the news.

Jerry walked over to a separate box—of the bones he'd already examined—then placed the skull next to the others. Back at the table, he looked through the remainder. He gently moved the ones on top to see what lay underneath. As he did, a tiny bone filtered through to the bottom and caught his attention as it fell. He retrieved it and brought it over to the lab bench.

"This is curious," he stated.

He pulled the overhead light closer to get a better look. His facial expression was pensive. Megan was intrigued and lured in by his interest. She leaned forward, eyes intent on the object in Jerry's hands. She'd hoped to see what he found so interesting. The thing was so small, it seemed insignificant. But Jerry's expression conveyed otherwise.

"What?" she asked. It came out in a raspy whisper.

"See this here?" Jerry pointed to an area of the tiny bone. But unlike the last time, the question was rhetorical. He didn't wait for an answer. He was too deep in his own thoughts. "This is the hyoid bone. It's small, especially on women. This particular one appears to have a craze line."

"What does that mean?"

"Maybe nothing, but let me give you a little background in anatomy." He retrieved the skull. Then he held the skull in one hand and the small bone in the other in a manner that depicted what their relationship would be in a life.

"You see, the hyoid bone is situated in the anterior part of the neck. In life, it's attached to the styloid process by two slender bands of ligaments."

Jerry placed the bone down on the table and looked up at Megan. With one hand, he drew his finger across her neck, just below her chin, without actually touching her.

"Right about here," he described.

The gesture, although not meant to be anything more than instructional, felt intimate. With the fact that he'd been handling the remains of a dead human found in a swamp, she considered repulsion to be a reasonable reaction. Instead, she felt an electrical current run down her spine. It proved Lacy was right. She seriously needed to get out more. She needed to have sex.

She cleared her throat to speak and said, "OK, I think I follow you so far. The bone is no longer attached to the skull due to the extensive stage of decomposition."

"That's right, but that's not really surprising if you consider how narrow the ligaments are and the extent of tissue damage present. What I do find enlightening is this craze line."

Jerry had to pull a magnifying glass over so Megan could appreciate what he'd just shown her. Under the bright light, with an enhanced image, she could barely discern a faint line. It amazed her how he'd been able to pick up on it to begin with. Under the same circumstances, she doubted whether she would have caught it.

"Impressive, but I'm not clear on its significance," Megan said

"It is possible this tiny bone was damaged in several ways, from animals to the crime-scene guys, but I don't think so," Jerry said. "If that was the case, it would have most likely been broken in two and lost. The fact that it was found and packed along with the others leads me to think otherwise."

"Such as?"

"I think this frail bone is our clue to the cause of death. I believe the killer strangled this victim before he dumped her body in the woods. If she was older, there would be a more definite break or fracture of the bone. But because she's so young, it wasn't that brittle. Then again, you're the detective," Jerry said with a grin. "She may have died of a heart attack."

Now she knew he was messing with her. "Seriously, Jerry. You think she was strangled?"

"Maybe. It's a shame we don't have more soft tissue. If we did, I could be more definitive. The soft tissue is where the defense wounds show up. There would either be marks from fingernails or fingertip imprints where he placed his hands around her neck or a distinct bruise from a garrote on the skin of the neck. Plus there would most likely be defense wounds as well, as she tried to escape. Below the skin, there would be thyroid cartilage damage as it cracked under the pressure. But now we're left with just the skeleton and this tiny fractured bone."

Megan shuddered at the thought. Here Jerry was, with a woman's skull and a tiny bone held carefully in his hands. He'd surmised what her last moments of life were like. His gentle treatment of the remains was in harsh contrast to the gruesome and violent murder he described. Even though it was her job, it was hard to be impervious to the blatant malevolence of reality.

She could picture the struggle in her mind between the woman's will to live and the killer's desire to dominate and destroy life. This was when she had to step into the darkness, to get a feel for the monster she sought. To know he strangled his victims was another piece of the puzzle. It gave insight into his personality and state of mental illness.

Jerry looked at her with concern. "Megan? Are you still with me?"

"Yes, yes," Megan said and focused back on Jerry. "I was just thinking. You said this woman probably fought back. That means this guy would have had wounds from the altercation evident on his face and arms."

"Wouldn't really matter. They'd be healed by now."

Megan knew that was true. This woman, however, would never heal. Her body was at least three weeks postmortem. Any superficial injuries of the perp would have healed completely. But that didn't mean someone hadn't noticed them. Especially if he was a local. She watched Jerry place the skull and hyoid bone back. Then he fished around for the pelvic bones.

"It's too bad about the defense wounds. It would be pretty convenient to find some jerk with scabs on his arms," Megan said, more to herself than as conversation.

"Kind of like grasping at straws. That is unless he did something to speed up the decomposition process," Jerry said. "But then again, pupa remains don't lie."

Megan eyes met his. It was something both Lacy and she had considered, but their conversation was strictly conjecture. Jerry dealt with lab results, numbers, and facts. For him to imply the possibility made her wonder if they weren't that far off base.

"Is there something you know that you haven't told me?" she asked.

"No, you just never know. So you tell me. Who do you think we're dealing with?"

"I wish I knew, but it's not so clear-cut. I do know all the victims were young Caucasian females in their early twenties."

This time it was Jerry who looked up with quizzically. His eyes were poignant as he scrutinized Megan's face. "All? As in more than two?"

Megan nodded yes under his fervent gaze. She hadn't meant to bring up the other two cases just yet.

"Are you sneaking around behind my back, using another lab? Because by my count, this case makes two. What is it that you haven't told me?"

"Well, I haven't said anything yet because I'm still kind of unsure about it myself," Megan said. "Plus I wanted to run it by Lacy and the chief first. Anyway, the gist of it is this," she said and explained everything about the two older cases.

"With the two past cases, along with these new ones, we now have a total of four victims with no arms, yet all other bones are present. I may be wrong, but my gut tells me they were all murders committed by the same killer."

"So you really do have an errant criminal who creates his own Venus de Milos from beautiful young women. Man, you can't get much sicker than that," Jerry said.

"Afraid so." Megan didn't want to bring up the fact that she'd actually never been out of the state of Florida. It made her feel unsophisticated compared to Jerry. However, that was the least of her problems right now.

"Please continue. I didn't mean to interrupt," Jerry said.

He gave Megan his undivided attention, which she considered the perfect opportunity to use him as sounding board. If there were any blatant oversights in her reasoning, he would ferret them out with his competent analytical skills.

"First, all four women were found with no clothing in the area of the crime scene. I realize that could be an attempt to hide evidence, but it also could be an indication of sexual assault. Strangulation of young women is often associated with rape. But as you know, the most obvious similarity is that all four women were missing both arms. A hard fact to ignore. I don't think it's coincidence," Megan said.

"I can't negate the significance of the absent limbs. The first one had me freaked, but what about the interim time between the two sets of cases?" Jerry asked. "You said the two earlier cases were eight years ago. Why no activity, then *bam*, the guy's back in business?"

He had stopped cleaning debris from one of the pelvic bones and sat poised, brush in hand, intent on her response. He seemed to enjoy the intellectual aspect of their banter. It demonstrated the utilization of the information he gave her. A melding of their two professions to solve a case.

"I figured the offender either spent time in prison for an unrelated crime or moved away from the area for some reason or other."

"But now he's back?"

"I'm afraid so. Back and quite active."

"These two previous victims you mentioned, you say all the bones were accounted for except the arms. Could they have been removed in a similar fashion?" Jerry asked.

"That's something I'd hoped you could tell me once Lacy and I cleared it with the chief. All I know is that the arms were recorded as absent in the evidence list for both cases. That's what stuck in my head and came back to me when yesterday's remains were found."

"Have you ever viewed the evidence from either of the past victims firsthand?"

"No, only looked over the files. I actually hadn't given them much thought until yesterday. When Mahoney said he didn't see any arms, it gnawed away in my subconscious. Then it was like I had this epiphany, and I finally remembered."

"Wow, that's pretty awesome that you read all the old cases. It's like they were harbingers of what was to come."

"I reviewed all those cases in the hopes it would make me a better detective. I guess in a way it did, but I still don't have a clue as to who the perp is. All I know is that both of the older remains were found in isolated areas, and it was unknown how long either were at the scene prior to their discovery. I'm not sure why nothing became of it. Seems like a glaring oversight."

"Hindsight can be exquisitely clear. If they had a solid lead to follow, I'm sure they would have. Besides, the amputation of both of a victim's arms is a strange statement for a serial killer to make," Jerry said. "It's not what you would expect. But I imagine they still looked for more concurrent evidence and came up empty-handed."

"You're right," Megan said. "And I certainly have no grounds to criticize. I have four cases with no answers. These crimes certainly don't display human nature at its finest."

"I'd say they hit way below finest. I couldn't rationalize cutting off a person's finger, let alone both arms. I have no idea how someone could be so deranged. I mean, what would push a human to do such a thing?" Jerry asked.

Megan chuckled, "That's one of the things I like about you, Jerry—you're so sane."

"Thanks, that's the nicest thing anyone's said to me today."

"That's because you're stuck in this lab all day, usually alone," Megan said.

"Very true."

For a fleeting moment, Megan considered asking him out for a drink. Then reality reared its ugly head. They were both so busy with these latest murders, neither had time for private triviality. Besides, she had no idea what Jerry's private life involved. He could be involved with someone, for all she knew. So instead, as usual, she stuck with the safer ground of work.

"You've got to understand, this type of killer has something to prove. There are several different classifications or models that sexual murders can fall under. From the review of older cases along with the little bits of current evidence, I've been able to piece together a theory."

"I'd love to hear it," Jerry said while he continued to work.

"I think we're dealing with an anger-excitation type. They usually had a domineering parent or some other adult in their life that constantly made them feel inferior. Like they're never good enough. Someone who put them in their place and made them feel insignificant."

"I think that would include quite a few of us," Jerry said. "You've never met my mom, have you? In her mind, I was supposed to be a medical doctor like Brian, my roommate. A lab technician was a grave disappointment."

"I'm sure she's not that bad. After all, you turned out all right."

"She does love me. She just has this relentless drive to try and change everything about me. She's focused to make me better than I actually turned out to be."

"Wow, that sounds like my sister," Megan said with a chuckle.

"My point exactly. We all have issues, but most of us don't snap and kill people."

"Luckily only a small percentage of the population does. But you can't underestimate those that do. There are a number of sociopaths out there who do not feel guilt or perceive what they do as wrong." Megan paused to watch him work.

"Please go on," Jerry prompted. "I like hearing about the other side of my cases. Manifestations of all my hard work."

"OK, if you don't think it will weird you out."

"Do you see what I'm doing?" he asked, engrossed in his evaluation of human remains.

"True. So the deal is, this type of killer enjoys inflicting pain and terror on his victims for personal gratification. It temporarily satisfies their desire for being the one in charge. They need to feel like they're in control—all-powerful. It's possible that this guy removed the victim's arms while they were still alive, just to see the horror in their eyes along with the intense pain it would cause. But in the end, they are never sated, so they kill again. As I'm sure our guy will."

"Oh my god, you're serious?" Jerry stopped his work and looked up at Megan horrified. "I guess I *am* a little weirded out."

"Sorry," Megan said.

"I know, I'm sorry. I don't even know why I said that. It's just so revolting. My mother's never driven me that crazy. I mean, she does drive me nuts, but not like that."

"These people are a different breed. They enjoy the process of death and the fear they instill in the victim even more than the actual deed. They inflict a bizarre ritualistic assault on the victim prior to the actual murder, which they often prolong. With this guy, that would more than likely involve some kind of sexual assault. Then he might partially strangle them or remove their arms or the other way around before he completes the crime. We won't know for sure until we catch the creep and question him."

"That's who you have to find?"

Jerry's face revealed apprehension and anxiety.

"These cases fit the profile. This type of offender often leaves the body nude and takes a souvenir with him. We have no idea where the arms are. But they are out there somewhere, and I intend to find them."

"Two arms as a souvenir? I don't like this, Megan. You need to be careful."

Megan wasn't sure if she should be flattered that Jerry seemed to care about her safety or offended he thought she couldn't handle her job. "Do you think this case is out of my league?"

Jerry shook his head and smiled. "That's not what I meant, and you know it. I realize you and Lacy are trained to deal with all sorts of people. It's just that this joker is off the scale."

"I'm aware we're not dealing with a rational, healthy individual."

"That's the understatement of the year."

"I think he chooses his victims beyond mere opportunity. I think they fit some criteria he's made up. I need to figure out what that is, maybe use some sort of computer-generated image with the aid of the victims' skulls. I don't really know what else to do while we wait for the lab reports to come in, and we need to stop him before he strikes again."

"It sounds reasonable, and I certainly appreciate the urgency, but there might not be enough to go on. We have no idea of their eye or hair color. I found a few strands of hair in the Wal-Mart bag, but that could be the killer's. As far as this goes"—Jerry said and gestured toward the most recent remains—"I'm not sure what lies hidden in this nasty mud."

"At least we can try. Lacy and I figured we could work the case from the angle of the victims."

"That makes sense," Jerry said.

"This guy is smart. He obviously fits into society as most sociopaths do. Even psychotic people can have an average outward appearance. It's not like they walk around with a sign that announces, 'I kill people for fun.' They can be successful and well organized. So much so they have the ability to totally separate their criminal endeavors from their everyday lives. They're very good at hiding their secret life."

"Man, Megan. You make it sound like it could be anybody, even someone we work with. You're giving me the creeps," Jerry said.

"Sorry, but that's basically true. They're not the type of criminals you hear about for getting caught in ridiculous ways. Most sociopaths create positive first impressions. Many are described as charming. The problem is, they have a lack of morals and guilt. Their actions are careful and calculated. Once they're done, they dump the body in a shallow grave or some isolated location they're familiar with. Since they are usually repeat offenders, these dump sites are often geographically close to one another. But he won't leave anything behind to make it easy on us."

"Even close to where they live? It would seem smarter to abandon the body miles away."

"Yes, if you're not insane. But with this type of criminal, once the murder is complete, they just want the body gone. They no longer have any use for it. So with keepsake in hand to remind them of the event, they dump their prey and go home," Megan said.

"But both arms as a keepsake?" Jerry said.

"I know. I'm sure it has some significance in their mental history. They noted it in the older cases, but nothing became of it. I don't know if it was lack of leads or what."

"Unfortunately, it's not uncommon for an unusual signature to go unrecognized at the crime scene because of the extent of decomposition of the body. It sounds to me like they had little to work with. Fortunately for us, technology had grown by leaps and bounds since then," Jerry said.

"That's what I had hoped," Megan said.

"I heard they found yesterday's remains on Cooper's farm, and this one was close by," Jerry said.

"Yes. Are you trying to say something?"

"Not really. It's just that I thought a lot of these guys were unmarried and keep to themselves. Kind of isolated. That sounds like Coop. He doesn't have many close friends. I realize that most everyone around here knows who he is, but that's not the same as letting people get close. Who knows what he does in private. Besides, you said the perp blended into society and is often considered charming. Everyone likes Coop."

"Well, you're wrong in this case. These criminals are able to separate their criminal life from their daily lives so much, they can be married, and the wife remains completely oblivious to their activities. They tend to lie, are self-serving, and manipulate people. But that doesn't become evident to their friends unless they're long term. Cooper has plenty of lifelong friends that would be willing to stand up for him. He's the first to help others."

"OK, didn't mean to offend. All I wanted to say was that you truly don't know most people even if you think you do," Jerry said.

"This is crazy, Jerry. The only reason Cooper's kept to himself this past year was because of his father's illness. He was practically an indentured servant. He had to take the man to doctor's appointments, chemotherapy, and basically care for him in every way. He wanted his dad's last days to be as pleasant as possible, and that left him with no life of his own. I think his selflessness was admirable," Megan said.

"Perhaps, or maybe it was stressful enough to push him over the edge," Jerry said. "It's emotionally exhausting to care for a terminally ill patient. That's the type of experience that changes a person. Sometimes for the better, but other times it can break them. I'm not judging, merely stating a fact."

Jerry knew Cooper was not only Megan's friend, but her brother's best friend. Still, he considered the theory to have enough credence to deserve further scrutiny. Friend or not, Megan had a responsibility to at least consider the prospect. He hated the thought of her placing trust in the wrong person. She could wind up another victim.

"You said it yourself, they can keep their evil activities and that aspect of their personalities well hidden. He's been under pressure lately. His girlfriend left him, then his father passed away. Heck, even his dog died—all in the same year. That's a lot to take in a short amount of time."

Megan glared over at Jerry. She could see that there was no malice in his statement, and that's what scared her. He was the second person to sincerely suggest Cooper as a viable suspect. Beth had told her of the talk around town. Yet to her, it remained inconceivable. Had she missed something? Was she blinded by their past? The fact that they'd grown up together? But the man couldn't even stand the sight of needles. There was no way he could be the killer.

Then another thought struck her. "Cooper has lived here his whole life. His problems you mentioned have been recent. What about the two older cases?"

"You think the killer lived here back then. So did Cooper," Jerry said.

"But Cooper's never moved away for eight years. Besides, he wouldn't hurt a fly. He doesn't have a mean bone in his body, and you know that."

"You do have a point about the eight years," Jerry said.

"Besides, not more than five minutes ago, you said most of us fit the profile somewhat, not just Cooper," Megan shot back.

"OK, OK, you win. You know the guy better than I do. Coop and I haven't hung out together since high school," Jerry said. He saw the concern and hurt in her eyes, and it made him feel bad that he was responsible for it. "Look, I don't have it out for him. I'm just concerned about you and Lacy. But hell, y'all are the detectives, follow your instincts."

"Sorry, Jerry, I know you only want to help, and I'll try harder to stay objective," Megan said and got up from her stool to leave.

"Oh, about those older cases, I'd be glad to take a look at them after I finish with this one."

"Thanks. Lacy is going to speak to the chief about them today. I don't see any problem with the work order. But I do know the chief's not going to be a happy man. I'm supposed to solve cases, not double them," Megan said.

"Sounds like you're getting heat from the powers that be too," Jerry said.

"I haven't spoken to him yet today. It's just a reasonable assumption it won't improve his mood any," Megan said. Then what he said really hit her. "What did you mean 'too'? I didn't know they'd hassled you."

"Not really hassle, but I did receive a visit from Buddy Howard. Seems like his dad's up for reelection this year. He wanted to make sure I was doing my job," Jerry said.

A loud laugh, more like a bark, came out of Megan, and she clapped her hand over her mouth. The thought of the charismatic Buddy inspecting the meticulous Jerry was too much to take. "Excuse me," she said, "I've heard Angus has been all over the chief too."

"Well, it ticks me off big-time that they think I wouldn't do my best to solve a murder unless some higher-up's worried about votes. It's really insulting."

"Tell me about it. If I remember correctly, Buddy was an English major, not involved with forensics," Megan said. "How could he evaluate your work?"

"Exactly. I was thoroughly insulted to have him come in here and watch my every move. It's not as if he could understand anything I did," Jerry said.

In consideration of how well Jerry did his job and how seriously he took his occupation, Megan understand his reaction.

"Well, at least you didn't hit him. You didn't, did you?" she said and tilted her head to the side with a smile.

"No," Jerry said, but the thought of it made him smile too. "It would have been therapeutic, but I need my hands for work. Besides that, Buddy isn't the real problem. That would be his daddy, Angus. He's the one who pulls all the strings."

"You mean the purse strings."

They both laughed at that.

"I imagine Buddy's being groomed for the state senate or Congress. He has the money to back him, the looks, and charisma," Megan said.

"That does sound about right," Jerry said. Then he looked at her. "You like him, don't you?"

Megan looked down at her watch and jumped up. "Oh my gosh, I got to go. I told Lacy I'd meet her twenty minutes ago."

"OK. I'll call you as soon as I find out anything," Jerry said and flashed her a big grin, but she was already gone. He had unanswered questions of his own that he intended to resolve.

11

Edward Lee bolted from the woods, ran full speed through a clearing, then shot behind the Phillipses' shed. Once hidden, he leaned against the building for support and gulped in mouthfuls of air. His lungs as well as his legs burned from the strain. He remained there until his breathing slowed, and he didn't feel so dizzy. He was thankful it was spring because it wasn't so hot. Even so, his T-shirt held damp patches. He wiped his forehead with the back of his hand, then glanced at his watch. Excellent, his effort had paid off. He wasn't late after all.

Anxiously, he looked around the corner toward the house. Everything was quiet. He noticed where Roy's mom had planted two rows of yellow daffodils along the back porch. They were all in bloom and swayed gently from a slight wind. The same breeze made his shirt flutter. It felt good, and the sensation made him smile. He loved life in the country, and he loved holidays. They meant days off from school, and that was always a good thing, as far as he was concerned.

Roy should be here any minute, he thought. He bent down to tie his shoe and almost lost his balance when a shadow crossed over him. He jerked his head up and shielded his eyes from the glare. In front of him stood his best friend.

"Darn, Roy, you scared me. Where'd you come from?" Edward Lee asked.

"I had to take out the garbage, so I came around from the garage. Man, you won't believe what happened here today," Roy said excitedly. Then he proceeded to fill Edward Lee in on every tiny detail from earlier that day of Rosie and the bone.

"That is so cool," Edward Lee said, obviously impressed. "I can't believe the same thing happened to both of us. What do you think it means?"

"It means we better get going, or my mom might think of something else she needs me to do. She cleans when she's upset. And finding that bone, along with all the cops here today, has her plenty upset. Besides that, my grandma's coming this Sunday for Easter. That always puts her in a mood. She runs around and tries to get everything perfect. I can't even leave out one toy. We have to make it look like we don't even live here. But still Gramma finds something."

"Where is Rosie?"

"Inside, asleep. I thought it'd be better to leave her home because she makes so much noise when she walks through the woods, and we need to be superquiet."

"Yeah, but that was so cool she found a human bone. What did it look like? How big was it?" Edward Lee asked. He wanted to hear it all so he could compare it to his find yesterday.

Roy held his hands about a foot and a half apart. "It was about this long."

"Cool, did it have skin and stuff on it?"

"Nah, it was just a bone. Kind of like the ones you see in the museum," Roy said.

"I betcha it was from the same body," Edward Lee said.

"I don't think so. They found the rest of this body in the woods, but I'm not supposed to know about that. I heard my mom and dad talk about it when they thought I wasn't around. I got to talk to two women detectives. They asked me all kinds of questions. They really needed my help to find the body, but I'm not supposed to know that either."

"You're so lucky. Nobody's talked to me yet. I think my mom's afraid it will freak me out or something," Edward Lee said.

"You should have seen this place earlier. There were cops everywhere. There was even one of those canine units with a dog who can smell dead people. She looked a lot like Rosie, but her name was Natty, and she didn't dash around as much as Rosie does. She was all business."

"Man, I wish I could have been here," Edward Lee said with a look of awe. Yesterday, after he found the bones, he'd taken off at a full run straight to Roy's house because it felt safe. He was nowhere around when the cops showed up. Now he was sorry for being such a chicken.

"Yeah, it was pretty cool. Most of them are gone now. But we better sneak around the back, just in case, if we don't want anyone to see us. I think there might still be some of them left over in the side yard. That's where the body was," Roy said.

"Were you scared?"

"No way, Rosie and I used the bone to play fetch with." He left out the part that he hadn't actually seen the body. Or the fact that his mother made him and Rosie stay in the house under her watchful eye for the rest of the day. Instead, he reveled in the attention of his best friend. After Edward Lee's experience yesterday, he needed to sound good.

Edward Lee listened intently, impressed beyond words. He'd been so shaken up after he found the skeleton, he never touched the bones. One day he hoped to be a famous archeologist, and the first time he'd come across human bones, he'd panicked. Roy on the other hand not only touched a bone but had actually played fetch with it.

Roy looked his friend over and said, "Hey, how come you're so sweaty anyway? It ain't hot."

"I had to work at the peach farm today after school. I tried to leave, but then Cooper asked me to move some more limbs for him. I didn't want to complain because I didn't want anyone to know what we were up to. So I moved the stuff and had to run all the way here to make it on time," Edward Lee explained.

Roy nodded with a serious expression. They went to separate schools but had remained best friends through the years. "Did he act weird or anything?"

"No. Mostly we worked separate, but I think it freaked him out that a body was on his farm."

"Are you scared of him? Do you think he killed his girlfriend?"

"No." Edward Lee said automatically. But the truth was, he had felt a little uneasy today.

"Well, we better take off if we're going to meet Pete on time."

The two boys peered around the corner of the shed to scope out the terrain. With no adults visible, they made a mad dash across the clearing and disappeared into the dense woods. Within minutes, they'd made it to the lime-rock road. From there, they struck a more leisurely pace.

"Do you think he'll have it?" Edward Lee asked.

Roy walked along. He stopped occasionally to pick up a rock to throw at some imaginary target. "I think so. He said his brother keeps them under his mattress. It shouldn't be a problem."

"I wish I had an older brother," Edward Lee said.

Being an only child as well, Roy understood. He also felt bad for his friend because he didn't have a dad, and his mom had to work all the time, so he made an attempt to be helpful. "You've got Cooper. He's kind of like a brother, and he's older."

"Yeah, but that's different. He's way older, and I work for him. We don't talk all that much. Mostly we just work," Edward Lee said.

When they got to the old oak tree, the two boys looked around to make sure no one had followed, then disappeared into the woods. This time, each step was slow and deliberate. The companions were careful not to make any noise. They were on a mission to meet their friend Pete, who promised to get his hands on a real *Playboy* magazine. They thought the best place to meet would be their secret hideout. It was so secret no one else knew about it.

It was an abandoned old deer stand that they'd fixed up. All three swore each other to secrecy, never to tell another soul where it was. As far as they knew, they had all kept that promise. It was something the three of them took very seriously. Intent on their goal, they passed through the dense woods until the undergrowth fell away to an old-growth forest. There, the massive tree that held their fort stood towering over the other trees, near a small clearing.

When they reached its base, Roy gave one last look around before he climbed up the makeshift ladder. Edward Lee followed close behind, all the while determined to maintain the secrecy of their mission. Once they entered through a hole in the floor, it took a moment for their eyes to adjust to the darkness.

Pete sat and watched from the corner. "What took you guys so long?"

The abrupt comment took both by surprise. "What, we're not late," Edward Lee shot back. He didn't mean for it to come out so harsh, but all the talk about bodies had him on edge.

"Did you get it?" Roy asked.

"No, man, my brother's been in his room all day, sick," Pete said.

"Aw, man, that blows," Roy said. It was obvious the concern was not for Pete's brother.

"No problem. I got something better," Pete said as he held up a pack of cigarettes. "I swiped them from my old man. Who wants to go first?"

Edward Lee knew smoking was stupid. All last year while he worked on the peach farm, he saw firsthand what it did to a person. Cooper's dad spent the last year of his life hacking up pieces of lung and blood. When he wasn't coughing, he wheezed and tried desperately to suck in air through a little tube in his nose. It was totally creepy and gross. It was also enough to convince him that smoking was one of the dumbest things you could ever do.

Problem was, both his friends looked at him expectantly. Roy had just touched a human bone, where he'd run away scared. And Pete had swiped the cigarettes. If he didn't smoke one, he'd look like a complete loser. A total wimp. Preteen humiliation tenfold.

Reluctantly, Edward Lee reached out and took the pack. He tried to act as if this was no big deal, but inside, his stomach did a flip; his hands shook. What if his mother smelled the smoke on him. She'd probably break down and cry. He couldn't remember how many times she'd made him promise to never smoke. He didn't want to make his mother cry. Then relief swept over him. He didn't have matches.

"Here, you'll need this, unless you've got one of your own," Pete said, tossing him a lighter.

"Thanks, man," Edward Lee said, dejected.

He fumbled with the pack to shake out a single cigarette. Finally he pulled one out and planted it in his mouth. He'd seen enough advertisements to make it look convincing. With the thing lit, he held it to his lips and sucked in deeply. That's when they all heard a loud noise from outside. Edward Lee froze. His stomach did another flip, and his heart pounded so hard he was afraid his friends would hear it. He tried to hold in his cough but failed and coughed violently.

"Quiet, Edward Lee," they both scolded.

"What was that?" Roy whispered. "It sounded close."

"It sounded like a truck door slamming to me. Maybe it's the cops," Edward Lee said. He took another draw off the cigarette out of nerves and to look cool and cover for his coughing episode.

Pete held up his hand to silence them and crawled over to a peephole to look out.

"What do you see?" Roy asked.

It was just a whisper, but it sounded too loud to Edward Lee. He took another puff, then snubbed the thing out. His stomach didn't feel so good. His skin started to turn pale, and his stomach lurched, but he held the vomit down. He was cool, but his turmoil went unnoticed by his friends.

"It's a car but not the cops," Pete said. "It's not very far away either, so be quiet."

Edward Lee and Roy silently crept over next to Pete in an attempt to see out through the warped boards.

"Do you think they followed us here?

"I doubt it. I think they just showed up on their own."

"Shush, I'm trying to listen," Pete said.

"I hope it's not my parents," Roy said.

Edward Lee scooted closer. "I can't see anything."

"Quiet, or he'll hear you," Pete whispered.

"This is so weird. Nobody comes back here but us."

"Can you see who it is?"

"No, all I can see is he's got long pants on and has a red car," Roy said.

"Maybe it's Cooper. His dad had a red sports car. He could be looking for you, Edward Lee."

"I don't feel so good," Edward Lee announced.

"What's he doing?" Roy asked, referring to the intruder, not his woozy friend.

"I can't tell. It looks like he just pulled something out of his trunk."

"What if he's a deer hunter and wants to use this stand? He'll catch us with the cigarettes, and he'll have a gun," Edward Lee said. His sick, wispy voice was thick with panic.

"Don't be such a dork. It's not even close to deer season, and you don't hunt this time of day," Pete said. "Besides, that guy wouldn't care if we smoke. Hell, if anything, he'd probably try to bum one off us, not shoot us. You're such an imbecile."

Edward Lee didn't know any of that. He didn't have a father to teach him that sort of stuff. He'd never actually been deer hunting. All he could think about was how scared and sick he was. Or what would happen if he got caught with a pack of stolen cigarettes. He needed to throw up, but he was partially frozen with fear. The one unfrozen part was unable to hold it in. He vomited. Luckily out the window.

"What's he doing now?" One of then asked, not noticing their sick friend. Soon Edward Lee joined them.

The three of them watched, only able to see snippets of activity through the thick branches of the tree and thin gaps in the wall of their fort. They could make out a man from the waist down. He moved around the back of a red vehicle. Then the guy pulled a large black bag from the trunk. It landed on the dirt with a slight thud, and he began to drag it in their direction. A few minutes later, they heard the sound of a shovel digging in the dirt.

"I bet that's the guy that buried the body near my house," Roy said.

"What if it's another dead body?" Edward Lee asked. It came out louder and more like a screech than he intended. He wiped his mouth on a tissue his mom made him keep in a pocket.

"It can't be. It's not heavy enough," Pete said. He was focused on the man, not his friend.

"The one at my house was just bones. It could be a skeleton body," Roy said. "They're light."

"Same with the one I found," Edward Lee added.

The shoveling stopped abruptly. "Who's there?" the man called out.

All three froze in panic. The voice was that of an adult man, not a teenager; Roy could tell that much. He sounded angry and ominous. He thought of running, but they were too far from any house. He doubted the three of them could make it to Mary Pearl's before the guy caught up with them. She lived the closest to the fort. If this person was the killer, he'd have to kill all of them and bury them along with whoever he already had in the bag. No one would ever know.

"Who's out there?" the man repeated. They could tell by his feet he spun in a circle.

"What do we do?" Pete asked. He peered out of the slat. "He's looking for us."

"Is he coming this way?" Roy asked.

"I don't think so. By his feet, it looks like he's just looking around in a circle. I don't think he knows where we are, but I can't tell for sure. I can't see his face," Pete said.

Edward Lee's head lurched forward, and he managed again to stick it out the side window before he barfed. Between the cigarettes and his nerves, it was more than his system could take. His face was fully visible to the intruder, but Edward Lee was too preoccupied with his own bodily functions to notice.

"Oh my god, he looked right at us. I think he saw you." He pulled his friend back into the fort. "We need to stay quiet. Nobody make a sound," Roy said. "It could be the killer."

Edward Lee wiped his face and nodded. His main hope was that the guy hadn't seen him. If he did, he very well might have recognized him. That meant the odds lay in the killer's favor.

"He just put the bag back in the car," Pete said.

"Maybe he's going to bury the body somewhere else," Roy said.

"We don't know it's a body, but it does look like he's leaving. We must have spooked him."

They heard what sounded like a shovel hit the side of the trunk before it slammed closed. Then they heard a car door slam.

"He's leaving," Roy said. "Maybe that means he didn't see us."

The ignition started; then the car peeled out of the woods. They saw the rear of the vehicle fishtail as it sped through the forest at such speed, it amazed them that the guy didn't wrap the car around a tree.

Before they knew what happened, it was all over. The woods were once again silent except for the sounds of birds, the gentle rustling of leaves in the wind, and their rapid breathing. They sat there dumfounded for a few moments in complete silence, too stunned to speak.

"That was really weird," Pete finally said.

"How did anyone end up out here? We've never seen anybody out here ever before."

"Yeah, that's what makes this place so cool. No one knows about it but us," Roy said.

"Well, I never told anyone," Pete said.

"Me neither," Edward Lee added quickly.

"I betcha that's exactly why that guy was here," Roy said. "Don't you see?"

"No. What are you talking about?" Pete asked.

"Where else would you go to bury a body?" Roy asked. "Not where people would see it."

He had spent the entire day thinking about the cadaver found in the woods next to his house. They lived at the end of a long dirt road on the edge of a swamp. Not exactly a high-traffic area as he'd overheard one of the detectives point out. This fort was kind of the same situation.

"This place is perfect to bury a body. No one would find it for months if ever. That guy didn't know about our fort. He didn't expect anyone else to be out here. I think we scared him just as much as he scared us," Roy said.

Edward Lee was pretty sure he had been scared far worse than the stranger but didn't want to admit to that. It wasn't exactly helpful information.

"You don't know the guy had a body," Pete said. "We didn't actually see a body, only a bag."

"What do you think he was doing then? Why else would he come all the way out here with a bag and a shovel? Jeeze, Pete, use your brain," Roy said. It wasn't that he wanted to be right about this. It was more a need that his friends realized the seriousness of the situation.

"OK fine. You think it's a body. Then what do we do now?" Pete asked.

"I don't know," Roy admitted. "He must not have seen us, or he would have come after us."

"Wait a minute," Edward Lee said. "If this guy's the same creep who dumped the skeleton at Cooper's, then buried the body at your place, and had another in that bag, that makes him like some kind of really weird psycho killer." The thought made cigarettes seem insignificant, and it was all a little too creepy for him. He was also freaked out about being seen, possibly recognized.

"So great. Like I said before, what are we supposed to about it?" Pete asked.

"We can't do anything," Roy said. "If we tell anyone, they'll find out about this place."

The other two boys nodded. They had sworn an sacred oath. You can't take something like that back.

Then Edward Lee had another thought. One he'd wished he hadn't had. "But if this guy has killed people and we don't try to stop him, he'll probably kill someone else. Then it will be kind of like our fault. We have to do something, don't we?"

They all looked at each other while that thought sunk in. It was true. They all knew that if an adult were there, they would instruct them to go straight to the police. Heck, there were probably a few left at Roy's house. But then again, sometimes adults just didn't understand.

"So what are we gonna do then? We can't go to the cops," Pete said.

"Pete's right. We don't know who he is. If we tell the wrong person, it might get back to the killer. Heck, it might even be the killer we ended up talking to. Then he'd have to kill us all."

Edward Lee nodded. His throat was dry and sore. He wasn't sure he wasn't going to make things worse, but he continued. "Roy's right. Look, I found a body at Cooper's place; then Roy and Rosie found one at his own house. Now the guy shows up here. I say that means he lives close by since all three places are so close together. I mean who would want to ride around very long with a dead person in your car?"

The other boys nodded in agreement. "That's true."

"Since we can't tell the cops, and we've got to do something, I say we look for the guy ourselves," Edward Lee finished.

"How do we do that?" Roy asked. He liked the idea. It sounded risky but more exciting than anything else. Still, he was confused how they would go about such an endeavor. After all, they were only kids. "None of us can drive yet."

"Well, for one thing we know he has a red car. We all got a good look at the shade of red, and it looked like a sedan to me. I know it's not a lot to go on, but since a lot of folks around here drive trucks, it might help."

"And the trunk has to be big enough to fit a body and a shovel," Roy added, already getting into it. "Like a Cadillac or something."

The three looked at each other intently; then Pete said, "I'm in, but what do we do if we find him? Are we gonna jump him or something?"

"No. We write an unnomymous letter to the cops," Edward Lee stated.

"I think that's 'anonymous,'" Roy said

"Whatever. You know what I mean. We don't give any names."

The three put there clenched fists together and swore an oath not to tell anyone what they saw or what they were going to do about it until they caught the guy.

"To finding the killer on our own," they sang out in unison.

What Edward Lee didn't say was that while the other two boys were safely hidden in the fort, he had stuck his head out in full view for the killer to see. It was more than likely the killer recognized and knew who Edward Lee was. He had no idea who the killer was. It basically made him a target to silence. If he didn't find the killer soon, he would wind up dead and possibly place his friends in danger as well. It was well known they were best friends. That gave him extra incentive.

12

Megan woke Saturday morning at 7:00 a.m., with a start. She'd sworn the alarm had been set for 5:30 a.m. It'd been a terrible night. The majority of it was spent staring at the ceiling. When she finally did succumb to sleep, she dreamt of little children at an Easter egg hunt; but instead of the hidden eggs, they discovered human bones. She was drenched in sweat, and it was too late for a morning run. She was already going to be late to meet Lacy as it was. Even though she wasn't exactly a morning person, being late was totally out of character for her.

With two murder victims in a single week, she felt the pressure mounting. It made her doubt her ability to become a good detective, and the chip on her shoulder over Lacy being made her superior dissipated somewhat. Instead, she felt a growing relief—thankful that her partner held the reins and had experience. She dressed quickly in comfortable weekend clothes and swept her hair up into a ponytail. Maybe Lacy could give her advice on how to better handle the stress.

By the time Megan made it to the station, where they were to meet, Lacy was gone. Megan's mood grew sullen. It wasn't as if they had big plans. First breakfast, then a quick tour of the town. After the swamp incident yesterday and the fire ant fiasco the day before, Megan had looked forward to showing Lacy some of the brighter aspects of Ocala. So far she hadn't seen the best the community had to offer—or, for that matter, the best side of humanity, herself included.

She dialed Lacy's cell while she looked over her messages. None from the lab regarding evidence reports. No surprise there. Lacy's voice mail came on, indicating a message should be left. Megan did as instructed and flipped her phone closed. "Well, shit."

With no other business to accomplish at the station, Megan decided to take Beth up on her advice to pay Cooper a visit. After that, she'd stop off at her sister's to find out what to bring Sunday. Of course she realized a phone call would suffice, but with a potential serial killer lurking about and a night of bad dreams, she needed to see for herself that they were all safe.

On her way out of town, Megan passed a cheerful house with a brightly decorated tree in the front yard. The colorful eggs reminded her that she'd yet to pick out anything for her nephews for the upcoming holiday, so she swung into the closest drugstore to take care of the matter. It seemed as if lately her job occupied all her thoughts. Ten minutes later, she came out loaded down with twenty-eight dollars' worth of assorted Easter candy, plus two adorable toys that made obnoxious noises. Beth would hate it. The kids would love it all. She began to feel more optimistic about the holiday.

By the time she got to Cooper's farm, her mood had greatly improved. It was early, and the air was cool with a slight breeze that carried the scent of flowers. Nelly dozed in her usual perch on the porch. This time Megan came prepared with a suitable treat of Cheese Nips. When the pig realized who'd driven up, she rocked back and forth until she was able to lumber up onto all fours and trotted over to Megan. Happy snorts erupted from the animal's plump body as she did.

"There you go, sweetie," Megan said and doled out the tiny squares one by one while she scratched the animal's head. The pig snorted with contentment and gobbled up the snack along with the attention. The ease in which it took to make the animal happy lifted Megan's heart. She wished all of life could be so simple and rewarding. "You are such a good piggy," she cooed.

"Hey, Megan," Cooper called out. "You're gonna make her fat. You're always giving her treats."

Megan rolled her eyes. "You do realize that she is a pig, don't you? She weighs over three hundred pounds. A few Cheese Nips aren't gonna hurt her."

"Shush. I don't think Nelly's aware she's a pig, and I don't want to hurt her feelings."

He was at the edge of the peach grove and made his way over to her. "It's a beautiful day," he said as he took a seat on the porch next to Nelly.

Megan leaned back and propped herself up on both elbows to savor the moment. A flock of sandhill cranes passed overhead. They were so far up she could barely make them out, but their call was unmistakable. She was deep in her placid thoughts. Relaxed for the first time in days.

"You got any more Nips?" Cooper asked.

"Sorry. Gave them all to Nelly," Megan said, almost groggy.

"So are you here to feed my pig all the good snacks or arrest me?"

The comment made her sit up straight. She thought she detected an edge to the remark but wasn't sure if it was her imagination. Lately her mind had been obsessed with finding the killer.

"Excuse me?" Megan asked.

"I know folks in town are talking."

No, it wasn't her imagination. The edge was there, but then again, she figured he had a right. "Don't they always?" she said and settled back. "It doesn't mean anything. I'm here as a friend."

"Then I think you only came by to see my pig," he said and smiled.

"I am sweet on Nelly, but she's safe with you. My apartment doesn't allow pigs. Otherwise, I might try to steal her away."

"I still don't understand why you moved all the way into town in the first place. I know you love it out here. So what if Beth and Matt live in the main house. You could live out here too."

"True enough. But my apartment's right next to the station. It's more convenient for the times when I work late. Unfortunately, that's happened a lot lately," Megan said and left it at that. No point in complaining to someone who's had their own share of misery. "I took on the position of detective. I need to be close to the station. Besides, it's close to the dating scene."

She looked over at her friend and grinned. His shirtsleeves were rolled up, and several deep scratches were raw on his forearms. Then she noticed the ones on the side of his face. They were practically gouges. They appeared fresh. She didn't like where it led her thoughts. "Enough about me. I came out here to see how you're doing. It looks like you were in a fight with a Florida panther. What happened?" She was now propped up on one elbow.

"Oh, these scratches," he said and looked at his arms. "Cut down some sour orange trees. Damn thorns tore me up. They really hurt too. They're worse than bougainvilleas."

Megan nodded with relief. Sour orange trees were notorious for having wicked thorns, and as she'd already noted, the wounds were fresh. "That grove's been abandoned for years. Why tackle it now? Is it because of the body?" It concerned her that he wanted to destroy evidence.

"No. They want to take away my ag exemption. I have to use every acre for agriculture."

Megan laughed then realized it wasn't a joke. "But you run a peach farm! That's produce."

"They don't dispute that. They say the peaches take up half the property. The old grove uses the other half. They want to tax me retro on the grove. I can't pay it. With Dad's medical bills still over my head, I'll lose the farm. The only thing I thought I could do is take out the old grove."

"What will you farm there, peaches?"

"I haven't thought that far ahead. I still owe a crapload of taxes, so it might all be in vain. Buddy's been pressuring me to sell out. They want to put a high-density development here."

'You can't do that," Megan said and sat upright.

"You don't understand, Megan. I may not have a choice. This whole situation has me stressed out. This is my home, but the government is pushing me out in the name of progress. Then there were those bones the other day. I don't know how much more I can take."

Megan was concerned for her friend and wished she could offer comfort. But she knew Mather and Beth had been pressured in a similar manner. Progress was headed their way. Farming was the way of the past.

"I'm still freaked out about those remains. I wish I knew who put them there or who the victim was. Hell, we might have known the person all our lives. I couldn't sleep last night. That's why this morning I decided to start on the old grove. I can't stand to think anything like that could happen on my property."

"It's not your fault. Try not to worry. Lacy and I will figure it out," Megan said.

"I know you have to say that, and I'm sure the two of you are working your sweet little backsides off. But that doesn't change the fact that a body was found on my property. My father let it go fallow so long, folks thought it was abandoned. I'm gonna fix that," Cooper said.

Megan leaned back and for a moment drifted off into her own thoughts. She understood exactly what Cooper was talking about. She too wondered about the victim and why the killer chose Cooper's farm to dispose of the body. In fact, it'd become an obsession. She turned toward her friend and said, "They found another body down the road."

Cooper twisted around. The look on his face told her this was the first he'd heard of it. "It was on the Phillipses' property. They own some woods with a patch of swamp on the side," she said.

"I know where they live. It's less than a mile from here," Cooper said. "It's a nice place. The kid that lives there is good friends with Edward Lee."

"Yeah, his name's Roy. He and his dog played a game of fetch, and the dog came back with a femur."

"Maybe that bone belongs to the body found here. A dog could have carried it that far."

It seemed like a genuinely hopeful statement. Cooper had left before the CSU bagged any of the evidence from his farm. There was no way he could have known the skeleton was intact except for both arms unless he was the one who placed it there. That meant Cooper was either hopeful, with a need to believe this hadn't happened in their community, or was fishing.

Megan thought about what to say and decided the truth was best. Coop would see through any deception, and soon it would be common knowledge. "I'm afraid not, Coop. The body in the grove had both femurs."

He nodded silently and placed his head in his hands in a defeated posture.

"We called in a cadaver search dog. The dog found the rest of the body in the swampy area. That gives us two entirely separate bodies in two days," Megan declared.

She edited out the confidential information. It seemed she didn't know whom to trust, and limb amputation wasn't watercooler talk. There was no need to upset people any further. Once news of the Phillips body got out, she feared a widespread hysteria would hit. The community possibly had a crazed serial killer on the loose. For a moment, she pitied both the chief and Lacy.

"Oh, what a happy Easter this has shaped up to be," Megan mumbled.

Cooper stood up and began to pace. This time it appeared to be in thought and not nerves. "Edward Lee was out here yesterday, but he never mentioned another body to me."

"Maybe he didn't know about it," Megan said.

"Or maybe he was afraid to say anything. Roy is his best friend. They tell each other everything," Cooper said and pivoted on one heel to look at her. There was a cloud of dust around his feet where he'd abruptly stopped. "I know your partner thinks I had something to do with the bones found here. What did she say about the ones at the Phillipses' place? Does she think I'm responsible for them too?"

Again, Megan couldn't clearly determine Cooper's motive for the question. "Look, Coop, Lacy is a good detective. She's just wants to do her job. It's nothing personal."

"How 'bout I tell you that when someone thinks you're capable of murder," Cooper shot back. "It doesn't get a whole lot more personal than that."

Megan held up her hands for Cooper to let her speak. "I understand, believe me. But I think you're overreacting. I know what it feels like to be wrongly accused. Remember all that stuff my family went through with my mother's disappearance? Then the accusations that I only joined the force to clear my father's name and find my mother? Any of that ring a bell?"

Cooper nodded in acknowledgment, a little embarrassed. He remembered. He'd felt sorry for Megan at the time. She had seemed defeated and discouraged. Now he worried that people would view him the same way. He wanted to be strong. This was his new beginning. He hadn't torn up the old orange grove merely to avoid taxes as he had told Megan.

Megan stood up on the bottom step so she was eye to eye with Cooper. She was on a roll. "Lacy was doing her job. That's what we do. We gather information to find answers. If we keep it up, soon enough, she will believe the same as I do—that you're innocent," Megan said.

"Yeah, I hope so," Cooper said and suppressed a smile. Megan had red hair through to her bones.

"The very worst-case scenario would be she'd come out here to look around. You have nothing to hide, so don't worry," Megan said, then sat down heavily on the top step again.

"Sure I have nothing to hide, but what if that nutcase killer puts another pile of bones out here? It wouldn't look good for me."

"The only place that could happen is the old orange grove, and you've cleared that out," she said and pointed to the wounds on his face and arms. "The rest of the property you're on all the time. You would see it right off. This killer we're dealing with isn't that careless. But if you find anything call right away."

Cooper nodded and raked his hand through his hair. He looked tired, and Megan felt for him. This hadn't turned out the way she'd planned. She came here to cheer him up, but he seemed even more upset and concerned now than before. She considered giving him one of her nephew's Easter plush toys from her truck.

"Hey, you want to take a ride over to Beth's with me and help decorate?"

Cooper looked at his watch and said, "Can't. I told Ms. Hanley I'd try to get over to her place today and take a look at her kitchen sink. She says it's leaking again."

"That thing leaks every time she wants to wriggle information out of you or butt into your personal business."

That got a chuckle out of him. "Yeah, I know. It *does* leak a lot. Especially over these past holidays when I no longer found myself engaged. But if I go over there and answer all her questions, then just maybe she'll spread it around that I'm not a serial killer."

"Well, luckily our judicial system doesn't depend on gossip," Megan said.

Cooper's expression turned serious. "Maybe not in the courts, but the elections are affected by it. With this being an election year, we've got some antsy politicians who want answers."

Megan didn't even want to go there. She was all too aware of the political concern over how these murders would adversely affect the community's reputation. She stood, brushed the dust off her pants, and said, "I better get going. I told Beth I'd give her a hand with the yard. But I do expect to see you there tomorrow."

"You don't have to worry about me or tiptoe around. I'm fine," Cooper said.

The sharpness of the comment stung Megan. "No need to get defensive. You would have been welcome regardless of the recent murders. I just thought since this is the first Easter without your father, you might not want to be alone." With that, she strode off to her truck at a quick pace.

Cooper felt like a heel and ran to catch up to Megan. He managed to grab her by the arm and swing her around to face him. "I'm so sorry. You're a good friend, and I acted like an idiot."

"So does that mean you'll come?" She stood there, hands on her hips, defiant but smiling.

"Sure, if you're sure I won't be an intrusion," Cooper said.

He walked the remainder of the way to her truck and leaned against the door while she fished out the keys. "Who's going to be there?" he asked.

"Let's see," Megan said. "There will be Nate and his family. Matt of course will be there. Then there's Matt's sister Bailey, her husband, Tater, along with their four kids. His mother, Arlene, myself, and I thought I'd invite Lacy since she's new in town and has nowhere else to go."

"Wow, back up. I'm not sure I want to go if Lacy's going to be there."

"Oh, don't be such a baby. I think it would be good if Lacy got to know you better. Besides, we could use all the adults we can get. With that many children, we're definitely outnumbered. Especially if you factor in they'll be hopped up on sugar. It will be a challenge to keep pace with them for the Easter egg hunt."

"OK, OK, I'll come," Cooper said as if it were a big sacrifice. He backed away from the truck and waved as Megan drove off. He wasn't so sure that a day with Lacy would be that much of a holiday, but the truth was, it would be better than sitting at home alone. He did miss his dad.

13

Megan rounded the bend en route to Beth's house and spotted Lacy's car where she normally parked. "That's one question answered," she said as she got out. She walked over to Lacy's vehicle and noted an abandoned cell phone on the seat. "And that solves another."

The sound of voices and laughter drifted through the air. The front door was propped open as usual, but the noise wasn't coming from inside the house. Instead it seemed to emanate from the backyard. So that's where she headed. There she saw her partner and brother-in-law.

Lacy held one end of a bright yellow streamer while Matt stood precariously on a ladder, ready to nail the other end to the shed. Both were laughing. A quick survey of the yard told her they'd been at it awhile. It made her feel a little left out, almost as if she were the guest.

Lacy looked over as Megan walk up. "So there you are. Our very own MIA."

"Um, well yeah. I thought we were supposed to meet at the station," Megan said.

"True. And I was there on time, but when you didn't show up, I got antsy. It's such a beautiful day, and since it's Saturday I wanted to get out and enjoy it. I probably should have waited a little longer, sorry," Lacy said.

"Hey, Megan," Matt said. He climbed down the ladder and gave her a peck on the cheek. "My favorite sister-in-law." It was a joke between the two of them since she was his only sister-in-law.

"Wow, the yard looks great," Megan managed to recover enough to say.

"Thanks, I used a new fertilizer this year," Matt said, pleased that someone noticed his efforts.

Megan watched him survey the lawn with a look of pride and contentment. He was such a relaxed guy. Kind and good-natured to the core. It was a sharp contrast to his large size and rugged good looks. He was handsome in an outdoors kind of way. It made her a trifle wistful. It would be nice to have a man that would be there for her. Someone to lean on for emotional support. This was the picture of domestic peace and tranquility. It made her angry that some whack-job serial killer was close, ready to destroy another family and destroy the open trust that people who lived here held. It wasn't right that one killer could take away so much from so many innocent people.

She realized that both Lacy and Matt looked at her expectantly. When their gaze registered, she regained focus back on the present and pushed aside the negative thoughts.

"So where are the kids?" Megan asked, not wanting them to see their holiday treats just yet.

"Campbell's with my mom. There was a final dress rehearsal at the church for the Easter play tomorrow night. Tyler's inside with Beth."

"How is he? Last time I was here he had some kind of stomach virus," Megan said. She tried not to grimace when she said it, but even the thought of vomit made her queasy.

"Oh, you know kids. They bounce right back. Yesterday he was sick as a dog. Today he's on the move," Matt said and gave another hearty laugh. "Got to love how resilient kids are."

He walked over and took the other end of the streamer from Lacy. "I'll finish up with this if the two of you could decorate that plum tree. Beth set out some stuff for it." He pointed to a small tree with purple leaves and tiny white blossoms. Next to it sat a basket filled with ornaments.

As Megan walked over to the tree with Lacy, she again found herself full of mixed emotions. On the one hand, she was pleased by how fast Lacy seemed to blend into her family. Yet another part of her felt displaced and a bit jealous. She wrote it off to the stress of her first homicide case.

Megan reached down and extracted a hand-painted egg from the basket. It had a ribbon loop atop, ready for hanging. "This is beautiful," she said, amazed at its intricacy.

Lacy joined her and peered in the basket. "Matt and I must not have been the only ones so busy. All of these are gorgeous." She picked one out and held it gently in her hands, allowing the sunlight to glint off the sparkles. "They're all so complicated. They had to have taken hours to create. Beth must have the patience of a saint."

"When it comes to family, she goes all out. It makes her feel good to make the holidays special for Tyler and Campbell. She's a good mom that way. She'd do anything for her children."

Lacy noted the deep love in her partner's voice when she spoke of her sister and doubted Megan was even aware of how strong it actually was. "You're so lucky to have a sister like her."

Megan frowned. "Are you serious? Most the time she makes me feel inadequate."

Lacy laughed. "Families are like that. They feel free to cross social boundaries and say exactly what they think, but you two do love each other. Lines crossed or not. The love's there."

Megan opened her mouth to protest, then thought better of it. After all, Lacy was merely making an observation. Actually, she'd begun to respect Lacy's opinion and view of the world.

"I'm glad I caught up with you today. I was worried that this past week, yesterday morning in particular, did you in," Megan remarked.

"You mean leaving me stranded in the swamp while you took off to the nonsnake-infested lab to see your would-be lover Jerry? I thought I was the one who was supposed to call the shots."

Megan froze, blinking at her boss. She knew Lacy was afraid. The wildlife in Florida was unfamiliar and could be scary and dangerous. But it wasn't like she'd left her out of spite or totally alone. The CSU crew was still there with her and she was to leave shortly afterwards to deal with the chief.

"I'm sorry," Megan said. "It's just that I'm more familiar with Jerry and the lab protocol—"

"Forget about it. It was a joke," Lacy said with a grin. "I'd leave a girlfriend in the swamp to see that man any day. He's hot. You're lucky you got to him first."

"But it wasn't like that. It was all about work," Megan stammered.

"I know that, or I would have called your ass on it. You realize I can pull the power card if need be. And I have to admit, at first, I was scared to death of getting attacked by some damn wild monkey or step on a poisonous snake. I stayed really close to the CSU team. But at the excavation site, I was OK. Then I realized the woods were so quiet. It was hard to believe that something as ugly as a murder could have happened in such beautiful place. Before I realized it, I was not only into my work, but I enjoyed being outside. I don't think I've ever seen that many shades of green before. The swamp seemed endless, so mysterious. It was totally amazing. I owe you one."

Megan smiled with relief. "You know, my sister was right about you. You *will* be a Florida cracker before long. You can see the beauty. You belong here."

"I think you're both right. I love it here. I gained this new respect for nature when I was out there, deep in the swampy woods, surrounded by giant cypress trees. It was as if I was this tiny, but integral, piece of some incredible world that I never knew existed. It was so strange. Don't get me wrong, I'm still aware of the serious dangers—like poisonous snakes, spiders, and alligators. Which I have to admit, will probably always freak me out to some extent. But more than anything, I was enchanted. I thank you for that. You set the snare and dared me to enter."

Megan looked at her. She had been harsh with Lacy, basically forced her to enter a world she knew nothing about. Lacy was being gracious enough to thank her when, in reality, Megan knew she'd been a bitch.

"Thanks," Megan said. She looked down, not able to meet Lacy's gaze. "It takes most people a long time to see the true beauty of Florida. Unfortunately, more and more newcomers have yet to experience it. Most never venture away from the sidewalks, beaches, or roads—into the pristine woods. I think I automatically and unfairly placed you in that category. I'm truly sorry."

"No problem. Yesterday was a real eye-opener for me. I can understand why you love living here. I especially like it way out here in the country. It's so peaceful here whereas in New York, you're surrounded by people and constant noise everywhere you turn. There's no escape. Without even realizing it, you're strung as tight as a guitar string."

"Stress does sneak up on you that way."

Lacy took in a deep breath and let it out slowly. "Ah, and there's no pollution here. That was something else awesome about yesterday. You could actually smell the earth and leaves beneath your feet. There were no exhaust fumes or crowds to cover up the scent of nature. I've never felt so connected, so alive. I am a part of this earth, God's world. The circle of life. It was wonderful."

Megan always enjoyed the fresh scents of nature when she ran. She could smell when rain approached. Or the aroma of leaves as they returned to the soil. The life cycles existed everywhere. One only had to look for them. They created the subtle changes between the spring and summer. If you spent enough time outside, the changes in seasons were clearly evident. She agreed with Lacy. The natural landscape made an individual feel alive, part of something bigger and more important. It put life in perspective and separated her from the darker aspects of work.

"It is beautiful out there, but it can be dangerous," Megan warned.

"I realize that. It doesn't make it any less awesome. Just like the family you have here."

"So you'll be here for dinner tomorrow?" Megan asked. "You have to view the end result of all your hard work and see the smiles on the children's faces."

"Oh, I wouldn't miss it for the world. The only thing better than a child's smile is to know you helped put it there. But I have to ask, why do they call that one guy Tater?"

Megan chuckled. "Tater is called that because he's a third-generation potato farmer."

Lacy laughed. "OK, I guess that makes sense. But seriously, you've made me feel so welcome. Thanks."

"It's the least we can do seeing you're so far from home, and we've made you work like a dog."

Lacy looked around to make sure no one was within earshot. Matt had moved off and was now busy with a croquet set. "Since you brought up work, I wonder if Jerry will be able to come up with a more accurate time of death for this second victim than he could with the first."

"He's definitely working on it," Megan said and did a similar once-over of the yard. "I told him about the two older cases. He said he'd evaluate them under a scope to determine whether the arms were amputated in the same manner."

Lacy stopped and thought about that for a moment. "If they do have similar marks, it would have to be the same killer. That means we have a serial killer for certain with four deaths."

"True. With no leads, the older cases were shelved quickly. The press never picked it up, so they won't connect the past with these two present cases. It should stay quiet for a while," Megan said.

"Well, it rules out a copycat killer. There has been nothing in the papers, and it'd be too far-fetched to think someone else would contrive such an unusual and insidious torture."

"I agree. But the thought of a longtime serial killer on our hands is hard to take," Megan said.

"Got to love our job. On the one hand, if we reopen the old cases, it adds to our evidence base. Yet, on the other hand, it's gonna dump a heck of a lot more pressure on us while it's kept quiet."

"I'm pretty certain there'll be a lot more from the pressure category than of the helpful evidence category. If you consider yesterday's case fits the same profile, the heat's already been turned up, regardless of the old cases. Jerry's felt it too."

"Jerry? What did he tell you? I thought he was hidden away, safe in the lab," Lacy said.

"He's allowed visitors, welcome or not."

"Like who?"

"Buddy Howard, the son of Angus Howard, the judge. Jerry said he stood over his shoulder to make sure everything was done correctly while he asked all kinds of questions."

That got a hoot out of Lacy. A person didn't have to know Jerry long to realize he was a perfectionist. "Jerry must have loved that. But what in the world would a county commissioner be doing getting involved in a homicide investigation even if his father is a judge?"

"His father happens to be up for reelection. You know as well as I do that unsolved homicides are the number one public relations headache."

"So he sent his politically minded son to push Jerry along? Man, I know that irked Jerry."

"There's more to Buddy than being a slick politician. He cares about his district," Megan said.

"Beth seems to think very little of him," Lacy commented as she hung an ornament.

"That's because Nate and Cooper don't like him. Buddy's actually attractive, intelligent, and can be very charming. You throw in a ton of money to back up his name, and Buddy's always had his fair share of girlfriends. That's why Nate and Coop hate him," Megan said.

"Well, since I don't know the man, I don't hold an opinion, but I find it hard to believe Cooper would dislike him over high school jealousy. So what did Jerry say about yesterday's case?"

"It looks to be the same. We have a female, Caucasian, early twenties, no children. He found some kind of bug casing on the skull which dates the body somewhat. I'm sure he'll come up with more information, given time. He also said the victim might have been strangled."

"Humm, that's interesting. Were the arms removed with a chain saw?"

"He hadn't gotten that far when I was there, and he won't speculate. With so much attention from so many fronts, he's being very cautious."

"Smart man. Cautious is good," Lacy said with a mischievous grin.

Megan wasn't sure what thoughts played across Lacy's mind when it came to Jerry. So far the woman had usurped her position on the force, befriended her family, had taken her parking space, and now seemed to be setting her sights on the same man. Yet it wasn't like she could say Jerry was hers. They worked together, she liked him, and that was it.

"If anyone can unlock the secrets that the deep dark swamp holds, it's Jerry," Megan said.

"I'm a believer. Oh, did you ask him if he would run the old Coke can run for prints yet?"

"I never asked. We were too busy with the Phillipses' case. I didn't want to burden him with something else right now. He's overrun as it is. I left late yesterday, and he was still hard at work."

Megan paused then added, "I really am sorry about this morning. I'm usually on time."

"No problem, you actually did me a favor. I ended up here and had a little fun. It cleared my mind. Work can weigh you down if you don't have something else in your life for balance."

Cleo heard a familiar voice and sauntered through the backyard. She rubbed against Megan's legs affectionately. The purring was so loud, Lacy could hear it from the other side of the tree.

"Animals must have a thing for you, girl. Look at that. I've been here for a couple hours, and that cat hasn't given me the time of day. And then that pig the other day. It ran up to you so fast, it freaked me out. You're like this animal magnet. You should have an animal show," Lacy said.

"It's not much of a secret. It's strictly based on food. I feed them whenever I come over. That ensures their undying love and affection."

"Does that work with men?" Lacy asked. "'Cause I can shop at any deli, but I don't cook."

"I'll have to get back to you on that. The men I meet bolt before I get close enough to find out. Then there's the problem that I can't cook either. I suspect cat treats wouldn't be the same."

Megan reached down and picked up the large orange ball of fluff. Instantly the volume increased. "I'm going to go inside and say hi to Beth. It looks like we're about done out here, and she might need some help."

* * *

As soon as Megan set foot in the house, it was apparent all was not well in paradise. It was a sharp contrast to the tranquility of the backyard. In fact, the house was in a state of total pandemonium.

Tyler sobbed uncontrollably as Beth balanced him on one hip while she attempted to answer the phone with her free hand. "Damn, they hung up," Beth said. "I hate when people don't give me enough time to get to the phone. Here, could you hold him for a minute?"

Beth turned Tyler over to Megan before she could protest. "Here's a tissue. He needs his nose wiped too."

Megan took the tissue and wiped the tears from Tyler's face, then dabbed at his red nose. "Why's he so upset?" Megan asked and made an attempt to soothe the child. She rocked him side to side in her arms, making little cooing noises. "Is he still sick?"

"He's fine, don't worry. He's not going to barf on you."

"He doesn't seem fine."

"He's upset because he wants his Lovey bear. It's in the wash, a casualty of yesterday's sickness. Thank God—that buzz was the dryer. I'll go get them."

Megan nodded in understanding. Lovey bear was a once-white and fuzzy stuffed animal. Now he was limp, gray, and basically threadbare as was the blanket. Tyler loved both dearly.

Beth disappeared around the corner, and when she came back, Tyler spotted Lovey bear and his blanket in his mother's hands. The tears immediately ceased, and a wide grin spread across his pink face. "Luvy, Luvy," he chanted as he clapped his tiny hands in utter joy.

The child's gleeful enthusiasm made Megan a little choked up. This was how life should be, safe and surrounded by love. It was one reason why she'd become a detective. To protect her community and maintain a way of life that she'd enjoyed as a child and one day hoped to give to her children.

Beth took Tyler and placed him on the carpet, away from the stove, with his beloved treasures. With a swipe of her hand, she wiped a bit of sweat from her brow. "Boy, I'm sure glad that ordeal's over. I need a glass of tea, want some?"

"Yeah, thanks," Megan said. She watched her sister reach in the cabinet and shake two small pills out of a prescription bottle. Without water, she tossed them into her mouth and swallowed.

"I have such a headache," Beth complained. She poured two glasses of iced tea, carried them over to the table, then collapsed into a chair. "This has been the worst day."

Megan didn't doubt it for a second. The tension level in the house was off the scale. She'd had a bad-enough week herself but said nothing. Beth needed a good listener right now.

"This place has been a madhouse. I'm telling you, Megan, I'm *this* close to going over the edge." Beth held up her thumb and index finger only a fraction of an inch apart. "I'm exhausted. Matt's family will be here tomorrow, and everyone expects a wonderful Easter buffet. You know how critical they are. They act like I sit around on my rear end all day long. They find fault in everything I do no matter how hard I try."

Megan looked up and nodded. Beth didn't seem to expect a response. Her sister was usually the epitome of control and organization. This, however, was a bona fide meltdown. Uncharted territory. It caused her to feel a bit uneasy. "Maybe you should drink decaf," Megan suggested.

Beth grasped her glass so tightly Megan feared it would shatter in her hands. She was wound tight as a bowstring as it was, without the aid of caffeine.

"If it wasn't for caffeine, I'd be unconscious, which I do not have time for in the near future. Arlene's going to be here any moment, and I just know she's going to comment on my hair."

Beth lifted a wilted lock out to the side and let it drop back limply. "I mean just look at me. I'm a mess. The house is a mess, and I haven't finished half the things I need to do. And don't think his mother and sister won't notice and say something to me, of course away from Matt's ears."

Beth looked close to tears, and Megan wanted to help. "The yard looks great," she offered.

Her sister looked at her, exasperated. "Is that supposed to be funny? Because I have to tell you, Megan, this is serious. I'm not laughing. I am so stressed-out right now."

"Um, yeah, I can see that. It wasn't supposed to be funny. It was to make you feel better. I mean the ornaments you made for the plum tree are gorgeous. I've never seen anything like them."

Beth slowly pulled her eyes up from her tea glass to meet Megan's. "You really think so? Seriously?"

"Yeah, so did Lacy. The kids and even Matt's family are going to love them. They're beautiful. I can't believe you made each one by hand. You're very talented."

"Wow, thanks so much. That actually does make me feel better," Beth said. Then a tear spilled out from the corner of her eye.

"You wait here. I'll be right back," Megan said. She bolted out the back door, almost running Lacy down in the process.

"Whoa, girl, where's the fire?" Lacy asked, regaining her equilibrium.

"Great, Lacy, I was on my way to get you."

"You got me, but shit, girl, you didn't have to run me down. You should be more careful. I could have been hurt. There could have been children around," Lacy scolded.

"I know. I know, and I'm sorry," Megan said, then filled her in on Beth's situation.

"Oh, this sounds serious. Count me in. It's Saturday night. I don't know anyone else in town. I'd much rather be here than alone in my apartment. Have I told you they still haven't connected my cable? It's pissing me off. I've called twelve times. They expect me to wait around for them. Like I don't have nothing else to do. I'm a busy woman."

"Great," Megan groaned and grabbed Lacy by the arm. "We'll deal with that later."

Beth was still at the table, with her face buried in her hands. For a moment, Megan was afraid she'd totally broken down crying but then realized Beth had actually fallen asleep.

"Man, you weren't kidding," Lacy whispered. "This girl needs our help bad."

"Wake up, Beth," Megan said, shaking her shoulder gently. Then she went over to the top drawer to get a notepad and pencil.

"Megan? Lacy? What are you two doing?" Beth said, a bit groggy. She rubbed her eyes.

"We're gonna help you, girlfriend," Lacy said. "But first, I need me some of that tea."

"Help yourself," Beth said. "The glasses are in the cabinet next to the sink."

"This stuff is great," Lacy said and poured a large glass. "I can't believe I've lived this long without it. People in New York are missing out. I could survive on this stuff. This and Panera's bakery. That's the life. It sure beats the hell out of watching Ms. Dolly."

Beth laughed so abruptly she spit tea out her nose. "Ohmygod. I'm so sorry."

Ms. Dolly was a three-hundred-pound local televangelist with flaming red hair, blue eye shadow, and distinct rouge circles on her cheeks. All applied as deftly as a circus clown. She preached of sin, the end of the world, and the immediate need for the viewers to send money. Lots of money. As much as possible. She was on local TV. Cable wasn't required.

"Please, let's not get started on that woman, or I'll pee my pants from laughing," Beth said. "Besides, she's not representative of the average parishioners around here."

"I suspected as much," Lacy said.

After a brief rundown of all the chores that needed to be done, Megan split off to wash sheets and clean while Lacy and Beth worked steadily for more than two hours on the cooking. It was the smell of fresh baked cookies that got the best of all three of them.

Lacy got down three glasses for the milk. "This is kind of fun," she said. "All us girls sitting around like we've known each other all our lives, and it's Saturday night."

"Yes, it *is* fun. I need to have a little more of that in my life," Beth said. It made her feel young.

"What you need is to learn how to say no. That and buy those premade cookies," Lacy said.

"Do you think those people at the church appreciate all the time and trouble you went through to make these? The emotional factor? Heck no, they put them on their cocktail napkins and walk around talking. They probably toss half in the trash as they walk out the door to go home."

"Actually, you'd have to be a fool to throw one of these away," Megan said with her mouth full. "They are the best cookies I've ever eaten."

"That's true. You have a gift," Lacy said. "It shouldn't be wasted on unworthy individuals."

Megan smiled. She'd told Beth that for years. If she'd said it yet again, her sister would have disregarded it as a rebuke. However, since Lacy spoke it, Beth actually sat there and listened.

"You know, you're absolutely right. From now on, I'll save all the homemade cookies for my friends and family," Beth declared.

"Friends and family? I'm talking business here. You are sittin' on a gold mine. You're right. You have two children. Who's gonna pay for their college? You need money, and you have the ability to make a crapload. Baking is your forte, girl. You've got it wrapped up," Lacy said.

"That's sweet to say, but I don't know. I have my hands full with the children now," Beth said.

"It's not that you need more work. It's that you need something to feed your soul. For you, that's baking. You have a talent that should not be denied to this world," Lacy preached.

Beth was taken aback by the emotion and conviction of Lacy's words. "OK, thanks, I'll consider it." Then a look came across her face. "Oh, Megan, I'd forgot. I had something to tell you. Mary Pearl called me this morning."

"Who's Mary Pearl?" Lacy asked. "Is she in the baking industry? Because I can be your spokesman. I can negotiate a deal for you."

"No. She's an older woman who lives down the road. She loves to stick her nose into everyone's business," Megan said. "What did she have to say?"

"Well, you know that retarded boy that works for her every now and then?" Beth asked.

Megan knew exactly who she referred to. He was in her class in school. The man had been completely normal until an unfortunate tractor accident four years ago. Now he made his way on disability and doing odd jobs and chores for the local single women and elderly.

"He's a grown man, not a boy. Besides, I think you're supposed to refer to them as mentally challenged now, Beth."

Beth waved her hand in dismissal. "Whatever. The point is, Farley was working for Mary Pearl yesterday. She wanted him to rake the side yard, but he wasn't doing it the way she wanted, so she went out to talk to him. They were near the edge of the road when a car came tearing out of that old dirt road near the big peanut field. You know, the one directly across from her place that they don't use anymore. The one that got shut down."

Lacy listened intently, intrigued by Megan's interest. This seemed to be important, yet she couldn't fathom how. "What the heck do peanuts have to do with our homicide?" Lacy asked.

Megan spoke up before Beth could. "No one uses that road anymore. They haven't for ages. The property was condemned years ago because it was contaminated with raw human sewage. Sludge, they called it. The peanut farmer wanted to cut corners on his fertilizer and got caught."

"It was Mary Pearl that turned him in. Every time he spread the stuff, the smell drifted into her house. She couldn't stand it. The smell seeped into her clothes and people started to talk. Can you imagine?" Beth asked. "How embarrassing would that be? You can't hide that kinda smell."

"Oh, gross," Lacy said. She rethought the cookie she held in her hand. "And to think how much I used to love peanut butter."

"Well, it's not only gross. At the time, it was illegal," Megan stated emphatically.

"What do you mean 'at the time'? Farmers can use it now?" Lacy asked. The look of distaste told which side of the issue she stood.

"I'm afraid so."

"I've seen it. They call it Milorganite," Beth helpfully added. "But Mather never uses it."

"I may never eat again," Lacy said. "What about mad cow disease?"

"That's BSE or bovine spongiform encephalitis. That has to do with animals eating other animals' brains, not their fecal matter."

Lacy felt queasy at the image. "Lovely. But it can't be good for you. Think of all the prescription medicines people consume that aren't absorbed. Or flushed away. They don't filter the sewage for that, so it would end up in the waste material, then spread into your garden. I don't want to eat someone's heart medicine or antibiotics in my spinach or lettuce," Lacy said.

"I didn't say I agreed with its use," Megan said. "Besides, that's not the point. We're homicide. Those issues are for other agencies with fancy abbreviations."

"Sorry, I know. Go on."

"Anyway, when Mary Pearl turned the farmer in, it was illegal. So, by law, his land was condemned. It was no longer considered useable for crops, pasture, or hay production. Not even houses could be built on it. Basically it became worthless. It's been vacant ever since," Megan explained.

"I'm sure he loved Mary Pearl for that," Lacy said. "I'm surprised he didn't whack her."

Beth brought her hand her mouth to stifle a horrified gasp. "Oh my!"

"We don't do that sort of thing around her," Megan said. "That's city talk."

"Really?" Lacy asked, eyes raised. "Bodies with no arms? Does that ring a bell?"

"Anyway, to see someone come from there now seems suspicious," Megan said.

"I say we check it out. The person was more than likely up to no good, but that can run a wide gamut from illegal trash dumping to poaching deer. Did this woman happen to notice the make or model of vehicle?" Lacy asked. "Did she think they were dumping trash or hunting?"

"No. Only that it was a red car. I remember it was a car rather than a truck because I thought the same thing. Sometimes people *do* dump illegally or poach way out here, but those people usually drive pickup trucks. But what did you mean about the arms?" Beth asked.

"Nothing you need to be concerned about. What you said makes sense," Lacy said.

"The only other thing Mary Pearl mentioned was that Edward Lee, Pete, and Roy came running from the same direction shortly afterward."

"Hey, isn't that the Phillipses' kid? Oh, and the other kid from the peach farm?" Lacy asked.

"Yeah. Edward Lee works for Cooper," Megan said. "We can check it out tomorrow."

"But tomorrow's Easter. You have to be here," Beth said with a sulk.

"Don't worry, Beth, we'll both be here on time," Megan said. She knew the idea of working on a Sunday, let alone Easter Sunday, upset her sister. The problem was, that was the nature of her job. She had to act on evidence while it was fresh. It was up to her and Lacy to keep the community safe. If that meant working holidays, then so be it. She was willing to sacrifice her personal life for the safety of the rest of her community.

14

The blood coursed through his head with each pulse as he lay there staring into the darkness, unable to sleep. The air hung dense and heavy with humidity while the cicadas and tree frogs announced the coming rain with a deafening serenade. Even without nature, he could smell the storm was close. He breathed in the scent, savoring it. Rain was good for him. It would wash away his problems. The dust would disappear, and the air would be fresh and clean. It would help to erase the evidence of the body on his farm. He wished he could wash it from his mind as easily.

He rolled over onto his side and absently stared out the window. It was pitch-dark from the looming clouds that totally obscured the moon. He kept his gaze steady yet saw nothing. The weather paralleled his internal turmoil. His mind focused on Edward Lee and why the boy had run to the police instead of coming to him. He didn't know what to think.

Then last night, the boy showed up at his doorstep, obviously shaken. He could feel the tension radiate off the kid. Edward Lee was scared and unsure whom to trust. It'd taken a good hour before Cooper managed get him to open up and confide in him. Once he did, the whole story spilled out. Now, that conversation played over and over again in his mind.

By the end of the recount, the two sat on the top step of the porch, drinking a Coke next to Nelly. Edward Lee looked for some much-anticipated advice. Unfortunately, Cooper was at a loss. The more he thought about it, the more he realized how serious and complicated the situation actually was. It was difficult to discern how much the three boys had actually seen. They were scared, and fear tended to cause people to forget details. Yet once given a chance to calm down, these additional pieces of information often came out. But Cooper was thankful he'd regained Edward Lee's trust and intended to work hard to keep it. He wanted to keep an eye on him.

"So all you saw was a car?" Cooper had asked.

Edward Lee nodded solemnly. "Not even the whole thing. We don't know who the guy was, so it don't seem safe to tell the police anything. Heck, we could end up talking to the killer."

"Maybe the red car had nothing to do with the killer," Cooper pointed out.

"Then why was he back there with a shovel and a big black bag?"

"Maybe it was money from a robbery," Cooper suggested.

Edward Lee seemed to mull that possibility over in his mind. "I haven't heard of any robberies lately, but there have been two dead people found. If that guy is rotten enough to kill two people, I don't think whacking a few kids would bother him."

"You said Roy was with you?"

"Yes, sir, and Pete. But you can't tell no one. You have to promise. Our fort's a secret. We took a blood oath." Edward Lee showed him the scar on his hand.

Cooper remembered how important things like that were at that age. Now it was dawn as he looked over at the clock on his nightstand and groaned. He wished he could forget about the boys and the bodies and go to sleep, but his mind wouldn't let the conversation go.

"So none of you saw the man's face or license plate?" Cooper asked.

"No. We tried, but the leaves were in the way."

"What about the body found at Roy's place, you knew about that?"

"Yes, sir, I do now, but not when I was here yesterday. I met up with Roy afterward. That's when he told me all about how he and Rosie found the big bone. We ain't supposed to know they found the rest of the body in the woods."

Cooper nodded. From what he could tell, Edward Lee was being totally honest.

The boy looked over at Cooper with pleading eyes. "What am I gonna do? I'm all my mom has left with Dad gone. If that guy kills me, she'll be all alone. Who will take care of her?"

Cooper saw the redness in the rims of Edward Lee's eyes and heard the fear in his voice. The boy's lower lip quivered faintly, but he fought valiantly not to cry. For the first time, he seemed very small and vulnerable. Cooper vaguely remembered the boy's father, who had died of viral meningitis when Edward Lee was only four. Since then, the boy had had to grow up fast. He'd become quite aware that life didn't always have a happy ending. He saw how his mother struggled daily.

"I honestly don't know what to tell you, Edward Lee. You'll need to give me a minute on this one. I mean you still don't know that the man you saw was the killer."

"Not just a killer. You know he's a serial killer, don't you?" Edward Lee said emphatically.

Cooper sat upright, taken a bit off guard and shocked that Edward Lee was so knowledgeable of such issues. But then again, he was the one to find the body at the peach farm, with another one discovered at his best friend's house the next day. For the three boys to witness the mysterious man in the woods near their fort, it didn't take but a fraction of their imaginations to connect the dots. And those were only the bodies they knew about. They had no idea if there were others. Odds would have it, there were.

The child was terrified that the killer was already after him. Now he was here, asking for help. The only thing he cared about other than staying alive for his mother was the protection of the fort's location. He wished he could make it all go away and tell him that nothing bad would ever happen in this small quiet town. But it had happened, and Edward Lee knew it. They both knew it.

He remembered his attempt to reassure the boy. "It's possible the guy killed those people over some business deal. They might not have been random at all."

"I don't know, Coop. We only saw a part of his car and his legs," Edward Lee said. "But that man don't know that. What if he thinks we saw his face or the license plate? That's why we can't go to the cops. We don't know who he is. If we talk to the police, he might think we're telling them a lot more than we can, then come after us. Heck, I'm afraid to talk to anybody. I can't trust anybody but you. Despite what some folks may think, I know you're not the killer."

Cooper got a little choked up at the faith this boy had placed in him. He hated to admit how much it meant to him. So to lighten the moment, he said, "Why? Because you know I don't drive my daddy's old red car?" Then he ruffed up Edward Lee's hair.

"Hey, quit it," the boy said and smiled. He scooted over a little closer to Cooper.

Cooper reached out and wrapped his arm around the boy's shoulder. He felt the child's warm body touching his. He didn't know what he would do next, but he was glad the kid trusted him.

"Let's think about this calmly. I understand you're upset. You have reason to be. But that man couldn't have seen you. The three of you stayed hidden in the fort, right?"

"Yes, sir, that's true." Edward Lee didn't mention that he'd stuck his head out of the side of the fort to throw up. He figured the man couldn't have seen that. Besides, it was plain embarrassing. Not something to freely admit to.

Cooper noted that Edward Lee seemed to relax a little, so he kept going.

"So he doesn't know who you are. He can't kill you if he doesn't know who you are."

"Hey, that's right," the boy said, notably brightened by the thought.

Cooper leaned back and used Nelly as a backrest. The pig snorted once in acknowledgment, then nodded off again.

"All three of you promised not to tell anyone, right? If no one speaks about what you saw, then there is no way for that man to find you. Heck, he doesn't know anyone saw him. He might have thought the sound came from an animal in the woods. You'll be safe as long as y'all stay quiet."

"Well yeah, but I told you, didn't I?"

"That's different. You can trust me to keep it a secret."

Edward Lee looked up at Cooper, glad he had him to talk to. Roy was right; he was kind of like a big brother or maybe even like a dad. He wasn't so scared anymore. Now he had a grown-up on his side. Someone he could count on to keep him and his mom safe.

Despite how vague the information was, Cooper realized it was more than the cops currently had. "I know you're afraid, but you shouldn't say a word to anyone else, and I won't either."

That's when Edward Lee really landed the bomb.

"We're gonna try to find the guy ourselves," Edward Lee declared.

Cooper sat up straight again. "What?"

"Even though we're kids, we still know that what this creep is doing is totally wrong, and he needs to be stopped."

"So y'all plan to hunt him down?" Cooper shook his head. "I don't like it. It's too dangerous."

"We got a good look at the car, and we know what shade of red it is. It's like the same color as your dad's car. Besides, that's not something you can really explain to the cops."

Cooper nodded his head in understanding. He had to admire the kid's bravery although it was misguided. The boys were determined to catch the killer and save their community and each other from danger. Being best friends at that age really meant something.

"Besides, Pete said the guy more than likely lives close because who wants to drive around with a dead person very long?"

Cooper nodded again. "That makes sense. It sounds like y'all have thought about this a lot."

"I haven't been able to think of nothing else since it happened. We figured with the three of us, we can search the entire area. We'll find him."

"I still don't like the idea. I think you should let me handle it. You trust me, don't you?" Cooper asked and gave him a hug. "Promise me you won't do anything until I see you again. I want to do some investigation work myself, and I promise I'll keep an eye on you and your mother."

Edward Lee gave his word, and now it was early morning, and Cooper couldn't get his own promise out of his head. He had felt Edward Lee's fear. It was so real, he could almost taste it. Cooper rolled over onto his back and let out a sigh. What really concerned him was the other two boys. He hadn't spoken with them, and there was no telling who they'd talk to. When he'd talked with Megan earlier, she was certain the killer lived close to where the bodies were found. She considered him to be a neighbor, just as the boys had. Someone they'd known their whole lives.

Giving up on sleep, Cooper rolled out of bed and tromped to the kitchen in need of his morning coffee. To make use of the early hour, he decided to scout out the location Edward Lee described to see if there was any evidence left from what the boys witnessed. That was if the weather would allow. As he looked out the window in the predawn, he could see lightning in the far distance. The storm was headed this way fast. The rain would surely erase the evidence.

The coffeepot beeped, which took Cooper out of his thoughts and back to the present. He poured a large cup and got dressed for his trek through the woods. When he passed Nelly on the way to the jeep, she barely moved. She was tucked in the porch farther than usual. It would have been the perfect morning to sleep in, if only he could have.

15

Megan decided to skip her morning run due to the impending rain. Instead, she left her apartment before dawn to check out the story Mary Pearl had told Beth. It was early enough. She'd be able to be done in plenty of time to make the Easter festivities. With it being so early, the traffic was light, and it didn't take long the get to the location. She pulled off the main highway, onto the unpaved road, and noted the first large drops of rain. It was going to throw a crimp in many people's holiday plans. Within moments, it came down in a steady sheet, obstructing her view. The humidity caused the windshield to fog, which further hindered her sight. She looked around for something to wipe it away and came up with an old rag that made the situation worse.

Soon, milky puddles began to form in the rutted-out limestone. The lack of road maintenance reinforced how isolated this area really was. Not only was it an excellent choice for a secret fort but a plausible location in which to dump a body.

She came to a clump of palm trees and pulled off near a set of tracks previously left by another vehicle. As she did, she held her coffee out to the side in an attempt to keep it from sloshing out of the mug. Once she passed the drainage ditch, she threw the truck in park and hopped out.

The weeds in this field were tall, interspersed with young saplings. Another sign of disuse and abandonment. The woods had begun the slow reclamation of the land through succession. She took a sip of coffee, then set the mug in the truck to take a look around. A bald eagle soared above in a graceful low glide. It hovered below the fog, which had set in. For the moment, the rain began to ease up. She glanced up and down the deserted road, then focused on the area a few yards ahead. It held her interest because the beaten-down grass still showed evidence of a vehicle that appeared to have been driven at a good clip. In its wake was a spray of gravel and loose sod. The exit path swerved through the pasture, continued onto the limestone, and toward the main paved road.

She walked over for a closer inspection and squatted down at the edge of the tire marks. They looked fresh and by someone with his foot heavy on the accelerator. It didn't appear to be from a teenager fooling around either. There were no donuts or other marks. Only a single straight trail. It was her guess the tire marks were from the person Mary Pearl had spoken about. The red car.

Megan was unsure of what to do. It wasn't quite dawn on a gloomy Easter Sunday. It hadn't rained in weeks, and now the first tenuous piece of evidence was being washed away. If she called Lacy, the tracks would more than likely be gone or, at best, useless by the time she got here.

She stood up and felt a chill. She was the only soul out here, yet she sensed that she was being watched. The eagle let out a screech that made her jump. She looked all around but saw nothing out of the ordinary to give any credence to her unease. Only the low-lying fog, which lent an eeriness to the atmosphere. The eagle swooped overhead as Megan visually noted the trail through the tall grass and weeds into the woods and decided to follow it to completion.

Once she stepped through the thick underbrush that separated the field from the woods, it was like a different world. The rain was muffled and soft as it hit the canopy of leaves above. The walking was easier, but for a few yards she lost the tire tracks. Then twenty feet ahead, she noticed a patch of brimmed-up dirt and debris. She also noted one of the adjacent trees bore a recent scar with a streak of red paint. Not exactly proof of a crime, but it was enough to place a red car here, which in turn backed up Mary Pearl's story. Unsure what that meant, Megan turned to leave, not sure what else she could do or why she'd even come. As she did, another curious upheaval of fresh dirt caught her eye. She walked closer to investigate. It became clear this wasn't the result of any vehicle. Instead, it appeared to be a shallow grave that lay empty, waiting for the next victim. She stepped back and grabbed her cell phone. Luckily for her shaking hand, she had Lacy's number on speed dial.

"Hello. I don't know who the hell this is, but it better be good," Lacy grumbled.

"Lacy, it's Megan. I need you to see something right away."

Lacy glared at her bedside clock. It read 6:20 a.m. She was not happy. "You do know what time it is, don't you? That it's raining out? It's freakin' Easter Sunday? You realize all this, right?"

"Umm, yes, and I'm sorry, but you really need to get out here as soon as possible. The rain has made it urgent. This is about the serial killer and the evidence is being erased as we speak."

That got Lacy's attention. "Evidence? As in real homicide evidence?"

"I think so," Megan said and gave her directions. When she hung up, Megan smiled. Lacy had referred to it as homicide evidence. This was her first homicide case. She began to sketch and measure what she could before the rain destroyed it all.

* * *

Lacy rounded the last bend before she was to turn off the highway onto the limestone road. She looked down again to check her map when another vehicle pulled out and sped away in the opposite direction. It struck her as odd because she couldn't fathom any good reason not to be in bed right now. What was also weird was even with poor visibility, Lacy swore it looked like the same jeep she'd seen at Cooper's house the other day. Although it was splattered with mud, she recognized what appeared to be a Peach Farm logo painted on the side. It raised several new questions in her mind, and she hated unanswered questions or where these thoughts led her.

16

Lacy leaned over with her hands braced on her knees while she gasped for breath. Sweat poured from her body and left tiny craters in the sand all around her.

"I am so out of shape," she panted as she fought to gulp in enough oxygen.

Megan circled back around to stand next to her partner. "It's the humidity," she said. "It will take you awhile to get used to it. We can take it slower if that will help."

"How 'bout we walk. That would be a good pace for me," Lacy said.

"Oh, come on now, don't be like that. You agreed to go on a run with me."

"You know the only reason I'm doing this is to burn off a few of the zillion calories I ate at your sister's house today."

"So let's go then," Megan said and began to run at a slower pace so Lacy could keep up.

"I shouldn't have eaten those last peeps," Lacy admitted. "That was a mistake."

"I've never actually met anyone older than six who eats those things. I've always considered them something you put in the basket for decoration. Then you throw them away when they get hard as a rock."

"Right now, I would consider that sound advice, but I was nervous. I eat when I get nervous. With Beth so ticked off at us for showing up late, it got to me. So I couldn't help it. I overate."

"I guess that explains all the deviled eggs too."

"No, no. That's entirely different. That's because I love them and don't get to eat them that often," Lacy said. "But seriously, do you think Beth will be OK? She seemed pretty upset."

"She'll get over it. It's not like we could help it. I even hated to have to call you, but it was possible evidence," Megan said. "The rain was erasing everything as I watched."

"As much as I resented it, you were right to call. It's our job. This is one of the biggest cases we'll ever face. And I know it wasn't like we blew Beth off. Still I feel bad for all the hard work she went through and being late to help with the egg hunt. Not to mention it rained on her."

"Again, not our fault," Megan said. "It rained on everybody, not just Beth."

"Yeah," Lacy said. She ran a little farther and studied Megan. "Doesn't it bother you that Beth was so upset with you?"

"Sure, but unfortunately, I'm kind of used to it. It bothers me more that she's managed to drag you into her drama," Megan said. She ran with her eyes straight ahead.

"What do you mean?" Lacy asked, not sure if she should be offended.

"Beth has stressed you out over helping with an Easter egg hunt. You're the lead detective in the midst of a serial-killer case. As you already pointed out, this is probably the biggest case of our careers. You were dragged out of bed at dawn, in the rain. Beth should be the one worried about you. The kids didn't care what time you came, but the serial killer's next victim will."

"Wow," Lacy said. "Now you're starting to stress me out. What if I'm not there for his next victim?"

"That's what I'm worried about, not Beth," Megan said. "Beth hates anything that takes the focus off her. Or anything that has to do with me being a cop. It competes with her being the center of the universe. The ultimate mother, wife, and saint. The center-stage spotlight."

"Jeeze, that's a bit harsh," Lacy said. "I think candy makes you grumpy. You can't mean all that. She tries so hard to be the perfect hostess, wife, and mom. I think she really cares."

Megan glanced over at Lacy. "OK, I guess it was a little harsh. I think mainly Beth acts that way because she *does* care. She loves me and feels protective. I know she was upset about us being late, and the rain messed up her plans, but what came out as anger was actually concern over our safety. Especially after the two bodies were found so close by, people are scared."

"I can understand that. This case is more than a simple police investigation. It's about a serial killer who could live near her family. Worst of all, her baby sister is the one assigned to the case. It has to be nerve-racking for her. If you were my little sister, I would be scared to death for you."

"Really? Thanks. But you're right. The killer might be one of our own. That's enough to freak anyone out. And Beth is a good mother. She just forgets she's not *my* mother."

"I think once those maternal genes kick in, they don't distinguish who their target is. Anyone who stands in the path gets mothered and fretted over," Lacy said. "You should feel loved."

"That's Beth for you. And a part of me is flattered that she cares so much, but I also resent her hovering. It feels insulting that she can't respect my position as detective."

"I think I understand. That's family for you. Friends are different. They respect privacy boundaries. They're there for you when you need them and want to share. Families, on the other hand, don't seem to recognize those boundaries.

They give advice and criticize whenever. They insult and demean you without pause," Lacy said. "Trust me, I've been there. I think everyone has."

Megan thought Lacy hit her problem with Beth dead on, and it felt good to have someone she could talk to like this. When she looked over, it was Lacy who stared straight ahead this time. She felt Lacy was speaking from her own heart and not of her and Beth's situation.

"When Beth sits back and thinks about today, she'll realize there were a lot of people there that had a great time. All her hard work didn't get wasted. The place looked great, and I have to say the food was wonderful as usual," Megan said. "Don't worry about her. She always manages."

"You don't have to tell me about the food. I think I ate the equivalent of my body weight. Which again, is the only reason why I'm out here with you right now. I hate exercise."

They ran silently for a few minutes. The sound of crunching gravel and rhythmic breathing was hypnotic to Megan, but she was concerned about Cooper. "Did you notice that Cooper seemed kind of uptight today? He acted kind of weird," Megan said, almost to herself.

"That's something I wanted to talk to you about."

"Really? How so?"

Lacy told Megan about the jeep she'd seen near the site that morning. "I would have mentioned it earlier, but we got involved with the site workup, then had to rush off to Beth's house."

Megan stopped short. "You think Cooper was at the site this morning? But why would he be out there?" She left out the part that she'd felt watched as she looked around, all alone.

"So he wasn't with you? I thought you'd called him or something."

"No. My god, it was 6:05 a.m. when I got there. What in the world—wait a minute. Are you wondering if I spent the night with Cooper?" Megan asked and tried not to laugh.

"It would fit," Lacy said. "It was a rainy Sunday morning. Most folks would be in bed. The two of you were in a secluded area. I know your reason but not his."

Megan had to laugh. "Well, we weren't together. You do have an active imagination. Cooper and I are purely friends. You like him, don't you? Maybe that's why he acted weird all day today."

"That or he has something big to hide," Lacy said, ignoring the connotations of Megan's comment.

"Well, I'm not into Coop. I couldn't sleep last night, so I gave up. I figured I'd use the time to check out Mary Pearl's story. I didn't want to be late getting to Beth's house. That's the only reason why I was out there so early. When I found the red paint and the shallow grave, I called you. Why Cooper was out there, I have no idea. I never saw him." Megan again recalled the feeling of being watched but kept it to herself. She wondered why Coop didn't speak to her and hated the concern it brought about.

"So he never spoke to you? That's weird because I saw your truck right off, as Cooper would have. I think we need to talk to him. I would have at the party, but I wanted to talk to you first."

The two women were far from town, on the same abandoned road Megan had run on the previous day. Lacy had no idea where they were. What she did know was that she was hot, tired, and full of candy peeps that didn't sit well. That's when she came to an abrupt halt and regained her previous bent-over stance. The sweat dripped off her chin. "I've got to turn back. As bad as I want to pry into your life and get the inside scoop on Cooper, I've got to quit. I can't breathe. I'm too old for this."

"What are you talking about? You're only two years older than me. Thirty's not too old for anything. You're letting the peeps talk. You need to win them over. You're young inside."

"Bite me. I need a couch, bag of chips, and an ice-cold beer. Maybe a fan too."

Megan rolled her eyes at the dramatic remark but felt bad that Lacy looked so exhausted.

"How far have we gone anyway?" Lacy wheezed.

Megan looked around and really felt bad. They'd gone farther than she'd intended. "I'd have to say about four miles."

"What? You take me out four miles, knowing I have to run back four miles? Do you realize that means I have to go eight miles altogether? Eight miles! Are you crazy? This is attempted murder. I could press criminal charges against you for this. You got me up at dawn. This is abuse."

"Calm down. I'm really sorry," Megan said. "I got distracted with our conversation."

"That's because you're some kind of freak. I'm a normal person," Lacy said. "Besides, aren't you supposed to drink when you run in heat like this? I'm dying of thirst. Hell, I'm just dying."

"You're not dying. You're not acclimated. It's really not that hot."

"So why am I sweating so much? I need to drink something. I need ice. I need a medic."

"Sorry, here's the key to my apartment. You go back, I want to run a few more miles before I turn back. I've got some things I need to sort out in my mind. I'll see you back at the apartment."

"The rumors are right. You really are a freak," Lacy said. "I work my problems out on the sofa with a bag of potato chips and ice cream like normal people. That's how you handle stress. That's how you do it."

Megan suppressed a grin and took off in the opposite direction. She was used to people who gave her a hard time about running. Most people just didn't get it. Then she recalled Lacy's comment about Cooper. She noticed the way Lacy had stuck near him all afternoon. She had thought it was Lacy trying to gather information. Now she believed otherwise. Unfortunately she had no explanation for Cooper's actions. He had no reason to be at the remote site this morning.

She got to where the power lines crossed the road. There was a high-priced new development up ahead which consisted of ten-acre miniranches. They were actually more like estates or castles than farms. Everyone who lived there had a least one horse, housed in an opulent barn. The homes were huge and extravagant. Two SUVs, at minimum, were parked in each drive. It was beautiful in an uncontrolled-suburban-growth sort of way, but she never failed to be chased by a tiny yappy dog. Even though she loved animals, it was something she didn't care to deal with today. She was too edgy, with so many questions over Cooper in her head, so she turned back.

There was a slight breeze, which felt cool against her sweaty skin. The run had begun to relieve the tension in her shoulders. It felt good to be outside someplace other than at a murder site. The air smelled of wildflowers and vegetation. The birds chirped freely. She rounded the curve and was startled by Buddy Howard. He stood there, hands in his pockets, as if he'd been waiting.

Megan pulled up quickly in front of him. "Buddy, what are you doing way out here?"

She'd just passed this stretch of road going the other way, only moments earlier, so the only place he could have come from was the woods. But why? She knew he lived down the road from Mary Pearl's and Beth's farm, not in town.

"Out for a walk and a little peace and quiet," he replied. "Had to go over Sissy's parents' new house for Easter." He motioned with his head over his shoulder toward the new development, hands shoved deep in his pockets. "My wife's entire family's over there. Must be twenty damn kids running around, all screaming. I couldn't take it anymore."

Megan remembered that Beth mentioned Sissy's folks moved to one of the new ten-acre ranches. It wasn't very far to walk, but Buddy wasn't usually the nature type. And he looked miserable. Twenty hyper kids all hopped up on sugar and excitement could do that to anyone.

"Same for me," she said. "I just came from Beth's. She had a houseful too. I wanted to go for a run to clear my head."

"Too hot to run, don't you think?" Buddy said with a thin smile.

She noted how pleasant he was to talk to. He seemed timid and extremely attractive—nice body. She had to remind herself that he was married. God, her sister and Lacy were right. She needed a man in her life. "I'm used to it," she said.

They were in the middle of nowhere. There were no voters to impress out here. This had to be the real Buddy. She couldn't help but feel for him.

"Yeah, that's what I heard. You like to run."

That remark threw Megan. She realized people talked while other's had their back turned, but she wasn't aware Buddy Howard was one to make any note of her. Especially not to talk about an after-hours hobby. It didn't seem like a topic of riveting gossip. She tried not to be flattered.

Buddy shrugged as if this were common knowledge. "Everyone knows you like to run a lot. Marathons and stuff. People notice you."

As much as she tried, Megan couldn't help but be sucked in by his flattery. It caught her off guard. "Thanks," she said. Then was unsure. He said people noticed her. He didn't say if it was positive or not. She might have just made an ass out of herself. "Well, I'll let you get back to your peace and quiet," she said, then waved and headed back to her apartment.

She could feel his eyes on her as she retreated and noticed her pace was much quicker than it'd been before the encounter. She wished she hadn't been so sweaty and her hair looked better when she'd run into him. God, she hoped he didn't think she looked too gross.

Two miles from her apartment, Megan came up on Lacy, who limped down the road. The sight made Megan forget about Buddy altogether. Instead she felt a rush of guilt. She slowed down and took up pace alongside her partner.

"You come up with any life-affirming revelations?" Lacy asked.

"Not really. How about you?"

"Hell yeah. I've realized it's not worth running out in this heat so I can eat what I want without having to buy a new wardrobe. Hell, I like shopping. New clothes are good. Shopping's fun."

That got a laugh out of Megan. She often told people she ran so she could eat dessert, which was partly true. Also, she truly hated to shop for clothes, so running worked out well. Still, she mainly ran because she enjoyed it. It allowed her to think clearly, removed from all the daily stresses and obligations. To breathe fresh air and be a part of nature. It was an integral part of who she was. It let her witness nature in all different weather and seasons.

"Well, if you change your mind and want to go out again with me, just let me know."

"I wouldn't hold your breath," Lacy said.

They walked in silence for a few minutes before Lacy spoke again. "You know, I was thinking and wanted to ask you something."

"You see there, a run really does clear your head. I've solved many cases while I ran."

"That's really nice, but this doesn't have anything to do with work or running," Lacy said.

"Oh?" Megan asked. "This sounds kind of serious."

"Not really, and I know it's none of my business; but you've told me about your mother, yet you've never mentioned your father. Does he live around here?"

Megan looked over at Lacy, then straight ahead. "No, he died a few years back."

"Oops, I'm sorry to hear that."

Megan looked over at her. "Go ahead. I know you're about to die to ask what happened."

"OK, but if you're sure you don't mind," Lacy said.

"It's OK. There's not much to tell really. He loved my mother deeply and turned to the bottle to deal with the loss. He was struck by a car and killed on his way home from the bar, drunk as usual."

Lacy nodded. The catch in Megan's voice told her there was more, but it was obvious how raw the wound remained. She guessed Megan considered whoever killed her mother to also be responsible for her father's death. She'd find out the whole story from other sources sooner or later.

17

Nate sat at T. J.'s bar and nursed an ice-cold beer while NASCAR highlights were played across an overhead flat-screen TV. It was 6:00 p.m., Easter Sunday. Normally Sunday nights were slow, but tonight business was brisk. Holidays often had that effect on people. Expectations were held artificially high while nostalgia ran thick. Throw in a divorce or family member who doesn't enjoy the company of his fellow gene pool, and you end up with a recipe for disaster. From the conversation he'd overheard, such was the case this evening. Fellow patrons had a slice more of family life than they could digest for one day. This bar was a great place to escape, have a beer, and catch the latest sports news.

He glanced at his watch and gave a sigh. He was due back at the church in an hour for his nephew's play. Although he felt an obligation to attend, he was far too content to leave. T. J.'s had the coldest, cheapest beer in town. But more importantly, none of his family was here—namely, his two sisters. He enjoyed the days off for the school break. Anything that got him away from work was good. It did, however, give him an overdose of family time. Not that he didn't love them all—he did. It was a dosage issue. He had struggled with mental-health issues since the loss of his parents, and his current therapist had warned him about situations like today. The stress level had left his nerves frayed. If he didn't go to church, he'd pay for it later from both his wife and sisters. Then again, every choice in life had consequences. Take those women who were found dead, for example. At some point, they'd each made a poor choice and trusted the wrong person. They ended up paying the ultimate price—death, just like his parents.

Now the town was turned upside down. Everyone was suspect. No one knew who the killer was, only that he could be any one of them. Everyone had their own theory of who the culprit was. People had begun to see each other through distrustful eyes; and it was his little sister, Megan, who had stirred up the hornet's nest. He finished off his beer and signaled for another.

"Hey, Nate," Cooper said and slapped his friend on the back. He slipped into the stool beside Nate. "I figured you'd be here."

"What the hell's that supposed to mean?"

Cooper ordered a longneck, which the bartender promptly placed in front of him. He took a sip before he glanced over at his friend. "Just knew you'd be here is all. What's your problem?"

"Women."

Cooper chuckled. "Women? But you're married. I thought those days were over for you."

"Not until the day I die," Nate said and took another big swallow.

"Want to talk about it?" Cooper asked, looking up at the TV screen instead of at his friend.

"Not really. No point."

Cooper gave a shrug in reply. Content to sit in silence.

"I will say that you're lucky you don't have two sisters," Nate said abruptly.

Cooper nodded. He totally understood. He'd been witness to the whole drama. No one could have missed the tension between Beth and Megan. It'd made Lacy and him so uncomfortable, they ended up together, isolated from the main crowd. Exactly the opposite of his original plan, which was to avoid the detective altogether. But nothing had gone as planned for him lately. It made him feel out of control of his life. What was worse was he turned out to enjoy her company. He'd just come out of a bad relationship, his father's death, and with current tax problems, he didn't need a romance. He had to focus on keeping his property.

"I know what you mean," Cooper said with a shake of his head.

"Why does family have to be so complicated? I love both my sisters. Why can't they just accept that and leave me the hell alone? And don't even get me started on my wife."

"They do it because they're women. Women complicate everything," Cooper said. "They have this way of insinuating themselves into your life before you're aware it's happened, then *bam*! You're toast. They're picking out colors for the kitchen along with your clothes. Tossing out your favorite jeans and T-shirts."

Nate sat up a little straighter and turned to appraise his friend. "Is this still about me or you?"

Cooper gave a cursory look at Nate. "Your sisters, a wife, women in general, doesn't matter. They all complicate things." He waved his hand in the air as he said it. "They're all bad news."

Nate grinned. "I know that look. This isn't about me. There's a woman bothering you."

"Who doesn't," Cooper said. "They're everywhere. You can't escape their web."

The sharpness of the comment set Nate back. It occurred to him that Cooper had made reference to his ex-fiancée, who'd recently taken off when his father took ill. Here he'd gone on about how much trouble family was, but at least he had family close by who cared about him.

"I'm surprised you're not with the rest of the clan at the church play," Cooper said. "I was under the impression that everyone including Megan and Lacy were going to be there."

Nate started to respond, then sat back. Cooper mentioned Lacy. To bring up Megan was one thing. She was Cooper's friend and his sister. Lacy, on the other hand, was different. "It's Lacy," Nate said and slammed his fist on the bar in a declarative statement. "I saw you two together."

"I thought she was just hiding from Beth. You think she could be interested in me?"

"Hell yeah, man. And to think, all this time Beth has hounded me to get you to date Megan."

"Megan and I are friends," Cooper said. "She's like a little sister to me. I couldn't date her." He gave an involuntary shiver. He considered Megan untouchable territory, close to incest.

They sat side by side silently and sipped their beers. Each deep in their private thoughts. Nate was happy that even though he was miserable, Cooper had moved on with his life.

"What about being the serial killer? Does that mean she trusts you, or do you figure she was working you for information?" Nate asked.

"Damn, Nate. I don't know," Cooper said. He motioned for the bartender to get him another beer, finished off the one in front of him, and pushed the empty away. "We talked about it. She asked me several questions, but I never felt like she was fishing for information. But I've never really understood women. She seemed to be more interested in me personally, but I don't know."

"That's positive. Like something that should cheer you up. Why don't you seem happy?" Nate asked and looked over at his friend. There was an emotion deep in Cooper's eyes that told him his friend's worries went deeper than any doubt over Lacy.

"What is it, man?" Nate asked. He was concerned about his friend. "Maybe I can help."

Cooper shrugged his shoulders, unsure where to begin. "This whole situation stinks, man."

"What do you mean? You and Lacy? Sure she's a Yankee, but she's hot, and she likes you."

Cooper looked around to make sure no one was listening. "No. This is about the serial killer."

Nate leaned forward, ordered another beer, and asked, "Did Lacy tell you something?"

"I think the killer lives here in this county," Cooper said.

"Everyone thinks that. Even tight-lipped Megan told me that," Nate said and took another swig.

"Does she have any proof? Any leads?"

"Damn, Coop, now you sound like you're fishing. Does Lacy have you working for her?" Nate asked.

"Don't be ridiculous."

"OK, sorry. But seriously it's so obvious," Nate said. "Two bodies found within a mile of each other. Megan figures, who the hell would drive around with a dead girl in their car for very long? It increases the chance of getting caught, and it's basically creepy. Along that line, she assumes they have to be local. But they'll never find out who it is," Nate said and took a pull off his beer.

"Wow, you sound pretty certain," Cooper said. He wondered if his friend knew something that he hadn't shared, either because he suspected him to be the killer or something more insidious.

"Beth wants to believe it was one of those vagrants that ride the rails. The tracks run pretty close to your place and the Phillipses' farm," Nate continued.

Cooper nodded. "That's true. But it sounds like you know otherwise."

"I don't know. That rail track's pretty busy, it's possible." Nate watched the overhead TV for a minute then asked, "Hey, where were you early this morning? I called but didn't get an answer."

The abrupt turn in conversation caught Cooper off guard. This morning was a subject he didn't want to discuss. It was bad enough to have almost stumbled into Megan.

"My phone got knocked out by lightning. I haven't gotten a new one yet or an answering machine. Why? You need something?"

"No. Just wondered. I went to the Handy Way to get some coffee, and no one had seen you."

Cooper shook his head. "Rain made me lazy." It was his usual routine to stop off at the convenience store for coffee and a paper every morning. After he'd gone to the abandoned field and seen Megan's truck parked there, he'd hightailed it back to his place, not sure what to do.

"You need to get a new phone," Nate said. "You live too far out not to have one."

Cooper sat there nervously and sipped his beer. A few more patrons came. By now the place was almost full. Billy Ray was in the middle of a heated discussion with Buddy Howard over bass fishing at the far end of the bar. Gabe took a seat at the opposite end of the counter and nodded in acknowledgment to Coop and Nate.

The bartender took new orders as he worked his way down the bar. He stopped at the end to chat with Billy Ray and Buddy for a moment.

Nate turned his attention back to Cooper. "Megan went to some abandoned old field to check out a lead. That's why Lacy and she were late to Beth's house. Did Lacy mention anything to you about what they'd found or what kept them so long?" Nate asked.

Cooper froze for a beat. "No, she never brought up work. I didn't see her out there."

"See her out there? What are you taking about? Of course you didn't see her. Good God, who the hell would go out there unless they had to? I meant, did she tell you about it at the party?"

"I didn't know either of them were there. I figured they were at the station or something," Cooper said. "I don't know Lacy that well, so I didn't ask why she was late."

Nate nodded and took another sip of beer.

"I take it you aren't going to your nephew's play?" Cooper asked.

"I don't want to talk about that," Nate replied. "But back to Megan. She said they found some evidence they were excited about. Does that mean the police have a suspect?"

"Again, you got me. Lacy's tight-lipped about an ongoing investigation."

"Should I be worried about my sister?"

"Hell yes. I've been worried about her for years. The girl's not right," Cooper said and laughed. People glanced at them momentarily before they turned back to their own conversations.

"Seriously. I know she's a detective, and this is her job, but she's after a serious killer. She needs to back off, or she could get hurt," Nate said.

"Damn, Nate, that sounds like a threat against your own sister. Besides, what am I supposed to do? I can't stop Megan or Lacy from doing their job," Copper said.

Nate was already aware of his sister's stubborn streak. He also knew these crimes had changed the feel of the community. People had families to protect. They'd begun to lock their doors and windows each night before they went to bed. That had never been the case before.

He watched as the bartender spoke to a few guys at the end of the bar. Buddy looked up at him and smiled, raised his glass in the air, as if in a toast. *Always the politician*, Nate thought and saluted back to be civil.

"So do you think the killer lives close by?" Cooper asked.

"Hell, I don't know," Nate said distracted. "Megan said they found some red paint, but that don't mean much. There's a lot of red cars out there. That's the color of your dad's car, isn't it?"

"Yes. Pretty much the same as the Barracuda you fixed up. You got that running yet?"

Nate nodded. "The engine runs, but I'm doing some bodywork on it now. It has a few dents I want to get rid of. I figured it'd be cheaper to do myself."

"Makes sense. Easy enough to do at home," Cooper said and looked at the TV.

"You know the killer could just as easily live in Tampa or Orlando. He could dump the bodies here to distance himself from the crime. Both I-75 and Highway 441 run through here," Nate said.

"But who would want to ride around with a dead body for that long? It would be more logical to dump the thing close. Somewhere deserted, where it would go unnoticed," Cooper said then leaned back. "Hell, Nate, I don't know. That kind of question is best left for Megan. Maybe they drove from out of town and killed the women here. Because seriously, there are several areas of undeveloped land between Ocala and both cities, despite the growth. They could have left the bodies in some construction site and buried the bones with a backhoe in a place due to be paved. I don't know. There are no secondary roads that lead from either city to Ocala. You have I-75 and Highway 441. Both are very visible and busy. Ocala is an oasis between metropolitan areas. Gainesville would be the closest place to come from. But then again, there's a huge prairie in between it and Ocala."

"I see your point," Nate said then caught the attention of the bartender and ordered them another round. His last. He didn't want to be drunk when he got home. His wife was sure to get after him for not showing up at the church. He need not give her any more ammunition.

He contemplated what Coop said. It made a lot of sense. Then as he sipped his beer, his thoughts returned to Megan and what he should do about her. In his mind, she would always be his baby sister, but in truth, she was all grown up and had chosen a dangerous job. Perhaps this time it was she who had chosen poorly. He wanted to be supportive, but more than anything, he wanted her out of this mess. He wished Beth would win. Megan would find someone, settle down, get married, and leave the force. If not, and she pushed too far, she might face deadly consequences.

"Nate, all I can say is your sister has her work cut out for her. The guy's a serial killer. Murder is his thing. He kills then dumps the body as quickly as possible. If she gets in his way, she could be next. It's the talk around town," Cooper said.

Nate had been so deep in his thoughts he hadn't heard a word Cooper said. He sipped his beer quietly and nodded absently. Cooper looked at him expectantly, so Nate asked, "I heard something about Mary Pearl and Farley. What was that about?"

"This is exactly what I'm talking about," Cooper said. "That happened no more than a day ago, and here you already know about it. I'm sure you didn't hear it from Megan."

"No, Megan wouldn't tell me anything about her work. She knows I worry too much. I heard it from the crippled cowboy at the Handy Way. But I'm surprised they would use Farley as a source. You know—considering his current mental state and all. That was some sad business. Tragic."

"The crippled cowboy?"

"Yes, and before you say anything, I'm not being insensitive or politically incorrect. That's what he goes by. It's printed real big across the top of his business cards. I'm not making it up."

"What happened to him—a rodeo accident or stampede?"

"Naw, he got in a bad car wreck on Highway 441. Broke both his legs. Then last year he had a heart attack, so he's really not supposed to work. He collects disability, but he does work on the side by rounding up livestock to supplement his income."

"What? Wrangling cattle? Isn't that strenuous?"

"I guess, but I'm not his doctor. The point is, every now and then, he gets Farley to help him round up cattle to take to market. Farley told the cowboy what he saw while he was working in Mary Pearl's yard. I happened to hear him tell the story when I got my coffee this morning."

"You actually went to the Handy Way on Easter Sunday? I thought you were kidding earlier."

"What can I say, I'm a creature of habit. Besides, I needed the coffee to help me stay awake for the sunrise services," Nate said.

This new revelation worried Cooper. Not that Nate had an attention problem in church. He could understand that, but it reinforced his concerns for Edward Lee. If that boy told anyone else what they saw, the story would spread like water on plastic wrap.

"Hey, Coop," Buddy said from behind him. "I hear you had yourself a dead body out at your place. Do they know who it was yet? Come to think of it, I haven't seen that fiancée of yours in a while." He gave a wide grin and tilted his head back in a laugh.

Buddy's close presence had startled him, but his words cut like a knife. It made him question if there was anyone in the county who wasn't talking about him or the investigation. He felt the eyes of the other patrons on him and could feel the sweat bead up on his forehead.

"I wouldn't know. They don't keep me informed," Cooper said.

"That's not what I heard. The word around town is that you're pretty tight with Nate here's baby sister. You could do worse, that's for sure. She keeps herself up real nice. Has a nice body, and that new partner of hers is a real looker too. Maybe the two of them would spend a little time with me. We could discuss the case over dinner."

Nate tensed up at the remark about his little sister, along with the insinuation behind it. Cooper whispered under his breath, "Let it go. He's not worth the sore knuckles."

"Maybe, but it would sure feel good," Nate whispered back.

Nate tried not to let the commissioner goad him into an argument. He didn't like Buddy and never had. He preferred to tell himself it was all because Buddy had life handed to him on a silver platter. Whereas Nate had to work hard for everything. But in all fairness, Buddy's father was known to be a ruthless son of a bitch. It couldn't have been that easy to grow up under his shadow as his only child. Through it all, Buddy retained a certain charisma that his father lacked. He also had a talent for baseball and was the gem of their high school team. His father couldn't do that for him. Maybe he had to face the fact he was jealous, plain and simple, and didn't want to admit it. Even to himself.

"It so happens I saw your sister not too long ago. She was out on a run behind my in-law's place. She does look damn good in shorts. Nice legs," Buddy said. "I think she likes me."

"I don't think Sissy would appreciate that kind of comment about other women," Cooper said. He wanted to intervene before Nate jumped up and began to pummel Buddy's face.

"Aw, I didn't realize you were the sensitive type. But you don't have to worry about Sissy. That woman can bitch about anything. Why do you think I'm here? I had to get out of the house with all her relatives. Same reason I bumped into Megan. Had to get some fresh air."

"Hey, Buddy, I thought I'd find you here," a man said, walking up behind him. He gave him a slap on the shoulder. "We still on for fishing tomorrow?"

"Hell yeah," Buddy replied and walked away with him.

Nate watched the two men settled in at the other end of the bar. Buddy's attention was quickly diverted by the new conversation—fishing in the gulf.

"God, that man grates on my nerves," Nate said. He ran his hand through his hair and came up with several stray strands. "Jeez. This shit is making me lose my hair. Maybe it's from having two sisters, but the way he acts toward women gives all men a bad name."

Cooper glanced back over at Buddy, who was now engrossed in a lively commentary about the most recent grouper he'd caught, which could entertain him more than goading the two of them.

Nate looked down at his watch and jumped up. "I better get home before I get myself into more trouble than I'm already in. You take care, man," he said. He gave Cooper a quick pat on the back and tossed a twenty on the bar.

A few other customers noted Nate's departure and offered up their good-byes as he walked out. Cooper opted to stay and think. He signaled the bartender for another beer.

Buddy left moments later and made a slight detour past Cooper on his way to the exit. He stopped short behind Cooper before he spoke.

"You best stay clear of detective work and stick to peach farming."

"What's it to you what I do?" Cooper asked and turned.

"Votes. I don't want you to get in the way," Buddy said. "Of me, or my father."

His words were slurred, and his gait was unsteady as he made his way to the door.

Cooper didn't know what to make of Buddy's comment. He was obviously drunk, but not enough to discredit the remark, and that concerned him. By now the rain would have erased all evidence from the area near the boys' fort. The only thing the police had was two samples of red paint from two locations. That wasn't much to go on. He wondered if it was enough.

18

He drove the short distance home without the radio, needing the solitude to think. The rain had stopped, but the clouds persisted and blocked any moonlight from breaking through. He thought about his mother, and tears welled up in his eyes. Unsure if they sprouted from anger over being abandoned or love because he missed her, he tried to push the emotions away. Occasional flashes of heat lightning and a far-off rumble carried through the thick night air, a dark reflection of his unsettled mood. A heavy fog began to settle in, and he was glad to get home before it got too thick. He pulled around to the side of the house and noted the lights on in the bedroom and gave a quiet curse. His wife would be in wait, ready to bitch him out for not staying with the family. She would know that he'd hidden out at T. J.'s bar instead.

He drove another few yards to park next to the garage. There he sat in his vehicle and ruminated on what their relationship had become. It made him feel somewhat morose but more resentful than anything else. They'd met in college, both young and full of shared dreams for a bright future. She'd actually looked up to him back then. He was, after all, an athlete, and she was a cheerleader. They made the perfect couple and married at the end of his senior year.

However, once the reality and pressures of everyday life took hold, things rapidly went downhill. He was no longer a star ballplayer, with all the attention and glory to feed his ego. Their daily lives became a grind. Now his wife made a sport out of belittling him every chance she got. Nothing was ever good enough. Sometimes he would daydream about putting a pillow over her face until all the breath was extinguished from her body. It was the only way he could think to shut her up. But he also knew her friends and family would never allow him to get away with it. They were everywhere. The woman knew everyone in town. Yet those precious fantasies were what made it possible for him to get through the day; that, and his hobby.

Before he ventured into the house, he headed out to the shed. This was his private sanctuary. A wry smile crossed his lips as he pulled out the keys to unlock both of the padlocks on the door. It took him a minute as he fumbled in the dark, slapping at mosquitoes as he worked. Once inside, he felt around in the dark until he found the single string that dangled from the lone lightbulb that hung from the ceiling. The only two windows in the place had been sealed over, so there was no need for concern from his wife's curiosity. As added insurance, he'd convinced her this shed was infested with snakes, of which she held a deathly fear. Since he allowed the weeds in the area around the building to grow waist high, the story was probably more true than he cared to believe.

Whatever the risk, it was essential to keep this place all to himself. His wife or anyone else could never come near. The people in his life had caused him enough pain. Out here, on nights like this, he could enjoy the peace and solitude that helped ease his daily anxiety. He'd often sit and wait until his wife gave up and went to sleep. It was a small victory in their tumultuous marriage, but he relished it nonetheless. He swatted at another mosquito and made a mental note to buy more bug spray. His wife had already questioned the numerous bites and scratches on his arms. To hide the truth, he made up a lame story of helping a friend put up a fence. It was out of character for him to partake in manual labor, but skeptically, she let it go. The swamp was still his secret.

He pulled over a stool, grabbed a cold beer from the minirefrigerator, and sat down heavily. He was mindful of his feet, not wanting to knock over any of his treasures. He adjusted his seat back a few inches to get a better view of the collection. Before him, buried half-in and half-out of the ground, were all the souvenirs from each murder. Well, almost each. The first had been an accident. He'd panicked and been in shock. It hadn't occurred to him until later to take away a token. Now, in total, there were five sets of arms. But he yearned for more. It would have been a ghoulish sight to anyone else, but to his eyes, they represented justice. They lent him a sense of inner peace. Each amputated limb represented retribution for all the wrongs committed against him as a man. All the times women tried to invalidate and slap him down. It was evidence of his power and control. In the end, he'd dominated each of them. It made him feel omnipotent.

He distinctly remembered each woman, even the early ones. They'd acted all friendly, enjoying the drinks and the stories he told of his athletic prowess. But at some point, each and every one had rebuked his advances. As if they were too good to sleep with him. A slap across the face was what triggered his rage. It was their hands he hated most, with their long polished nails, ready to dig into his flesh to fend him off. But in the end, he'd showed them who had the power. He did what he wanted to them, then cut their arms off while they were still alive and aware of his actions. The memory of the horror on each one of their faces made him smile. It made him feel victorious. He finished his beer and crushed the can in his hand, frustrated.

Now new trouble lay on the horizon. Certain people had stuck their noses where they didn't belong. Their questions could destroy him. He had to do something about it before the situation got totally out of control. It was bad enough to have a wife always on his back, nagging him to take his medication.

He knew the pills were to control his mind, and he wasn't about to let them get away with that. The doctors at college tried to diagnose him as a sociopath. What the hell did they know? His mother left him. Something that haunted him every day. Then there was his father. No, he wasn't mentally ill. He reacted to his past, that's all. Now his present was no better.

With the ever-increasing pressures and responsibilities, he felt he could never live up to the standards and expectations others set for him. He cherished the release these women offered. The last thing he needed was some know-it-all detective from New York and Megan to ruin his fun. Recently they'd acted as bad as all the other women. The ones he'd been forced to murder. He didn't want to have to kill them. They were cops. To kill a cop was serious. Besides, Megan was special to him. He really didn't want to have to hurt her, but he would if she forced him to.

He had to be smarter to beat them. Throw them off his trail. Hell, he walked away with the other women's arms. He held all the power and ultimately controlled the lives of both detectives—or anyone else who messed with him, for that matter. He was better than all of them, invincible. It didn't matter that Lacy came to town, asked all kinds of questions, and acted as if she owned the place. He could bring a tear to her big brown eyes quick enough. Her arms would be a grand prize for his collection. Plus, it would be enough to scare Megan into leaving the force.

The trick, however, would be to kill Lacy without a trace of evidence left behind. After today, he knew exactly how to accomplish that. He would become the talk of the town. To have the lead investigator vanish and not know where her body was or if she was yet another victim of the serial killer. It would put everyone on edge. He grinned wickedly. The predator kills the hunter.

Then there was that damn bossy old woman down the road. He'd hated her since he was a kid. As long as he could remember, she'd been old and stuck her nose into everyone else's business. As a child, she'd yell at him for the least provocation, ensconcing herself as one of his root problems with women. A bossy old bitch who would shake a knobby finger of hers in the air. Yes, her time had come. He wasn't a child any longer, and it was time that she learned her lesson. With the entire town on alert, he'd have to be careful. But he was confident that with thought and effort, he would win over her once and for all. *The wicked witch would die.*

The best part of the whole situation was that no one suspected him. He lived and worked alongside the same people who were terrified of the elusive serial killer. His family wanted him around for protection. He loved it. They had no idea he was the object of their fear. Nor would they ever. He was smarter than all of them, cops included, and he'd prove it once again. He would rid the community of that pesky old bitch. Hell, that wasn't evil. It was a public service.

He ran his hand through his hair and noticed a few stands fall to the floor. He hated the thought of losing his hair. It wasn't fair. He wasn't old enough for that. He remembered back in high school how thick and wavy his hair was. It represented his virility. Something his wife constantly challenged. The girls loved to touch it and touch him. They could use their hands for pleasure or for pain. And he could take those arms away as he pleased.

He looked back over his collection that stuck up out of the ground. It brought about a gnawing urge to add another trophy, to right the wrongs that women had done to him. But first, he'd take care of the old woman.

19

Megan woke with a start to the sound of her alarm, which she'd set at full volume, just in case. Turned out it was a good thing. She hadn't slept well the night before, something that had now became more of the norm than an exception. Worries over the serial killer played through her head. She wondered if the killer really was someone from their very own community, or had he years ago deliberately chosen their quiet town to use as his garbage dump. She got out of bed with dry, gritty eyes and stumbled into her bathroom to splash cold water on her face. It didn't help. What she needed was a hot shower and caffeine. Lots of caffeine. The more the better.

She turned the shower to Hot and went to get a towel. Today she and Lacy planned to question people who lived in the areas where both bodies were found. Surely someone would have seen or heard something. She wanted so badly to be able to go to her boss with some positive information. Rationally she understood it took time, but she was disappointed with the progress thus far.

By the time she got the coffee started, grabbed a fresh towel, and made it back to the bathroom, it was like a sauna. She peeled off her pajamas and climbed in. The water felt good as it flowed over her body but did little to ease the tension in her shoulders. Thoughts of Beth swam through her head. How she'd gotten all in a twist over her and Lacy being late. It wasn't that Megan needed the complete adoration of her family, but a tad of respect and acknowledgment for her attempt to catch a serial killer would have been nice. And it wasn't her fault it rained, yet Beth acted as if she'd ordered it personally out of spite. But regardless of how righteous Megan felt, her role as youngest sibling forced her to succumb to guilt. And boy, could Beth heap it on. She'd even managed to make Lacy feel bad, which really irritated Megan.

Puffy eyed and grumbling, she toweled off and padded back to the kitchen. The more she thought about yesterday, the more indignant she became. She poured herself a cup of coffee in her favorite mug and slid two Pop-Tarts into the toaster. Basically the extent of her culinary skills. At least Tim from the crime scene unit could make spaghetti. He wasn't bad looking either, she remembered. Then she thought about Buddy. He was married and a player, but Megan could understand why women fell for him. Something about his self-confidence made him sexy.

The Pop-Tarts clicked, and she plopped them on a paper towel and sat happily at her counter. She savored the hot coffee. With her notepad and pen handy, she jotted down a few items of what she hoped to accomplish for the day. For one thing, she'd call Beth to get that out of the way. Family stress was a distraction she couldn't afford. She needed to stay focused.

Then there was Jerry. He might have information on a number of outstanding issues. She knew he was usually good to call right away. But it never hurt to follow up. Patience wasn't her biggest virtue, and she felt useless waiting. She jotted down Lacy's name when her doorbell rang.

"Gee whiz, it's freakin' six thirty in the morning," she mumbled as she went to answer the door. She looked through the peephole before she released the deadbolt. There stood Lacy, with a big bag from the local bakery. Megan threw open the door so fast, she stubbed her toe.

"Ouch, dang it," she said, hopping around on one foot. "Lacy, come on in."
"You OK?"
"I will be in a second," she said when she realized Lacy held a bag of goodies.
"I hope you don't mind me here so early. But I did bring breakfast and hot coffee," Lacy said.
"I see. I feel better already. It smells wonderful."

Megan noticed a stiffness in her partner's gait as Lacy walked through the room to set her bag of goodies on the counter. "What's the deal with you? Why are you walking like an old lady?"

Lacy whipped her head around, placed her hands on her hips, and said, "Trust me, girlfriend, you don't want to go there, Ms. Running Queen. This however," she said and sniffed the hot pastries, "is my form of compensation for the pain and suffering you inflicted on me yesterday with that insane eight-mile run. I mean, what were you thinking? You're lucky I'm a forgiving person."

"Ohmygod, this smells so good. I love you for this," Megan said, drawn to the aroma.

"Good. I was afraid you'd want to sleep in or something since it's kind of a holiday. I mean most places are closed on Easter Monday. I don't want to be one of those bosses," Lacy said.

"Yeah, like we have that option with a serial killer on the loose. The chief expects answers, along with every other elected official and voter," Megan said.

"You can't blame them for that. The community that elected them wants answers. Hell, I want answers, and I've only lived here a month. This situation ain't right."

Megan broke off a piece of cinnamon roll and popped it into her mouth. She let it melt away as it left a tantalizing flavor of orange, yeast, cinnamon spice, and sweet. "Oh god, this is so good."

"Tell me about it. Why did you let me rent an apartment less than a mile away from that place? It is a disaster waiting to happen to my waistline and thighs."

Megan peeled the lid off one of the coffees and breathed in deeply. She savored the aroma before she took a sip. "Ooh, this is so much better than my own. I almost feel human again."

"Not to interrupt a private moment here, but where do we stand on this case?" Lacy asked.

Megan looked up with a frown. "Do we have to go there just yet? I was having fun."

"I noticed, and it was getting a little too personal if you ask me. Besides that, we've got a monkey on our back, whether you want to acknowledge it or not. I say we hit this investigation head-on. We got some good stuff yesterday. I know it wasn't enough to break the case wide open, but we can't let this psycho win. You've worked up a profile. We have a history that he's a repeat offender. It's my opinion that, given enough time, he'll commit another act of flagrant turpitude."

"We're gonna be the ones to stop him," Lacy said, waving her finger in the air dramatically.

Megan stood there blinking. The intensity with which Lacy spoke denied the early-morning hour.

"This isn't your first cup of joe, is it?"

"Hell no. I'm on my third, but I couldn't sleep last night. I was worried about what Mary Pearl said. Not about the red car but the little boys coming from the same area afterward. What if the person in the car was the killer? And what if he saw those children? He might be afraid they could identify him. He could hurt three little kids. That's not right. We've got to stop him."

Megan became serious. Besides her own trepidations over the investigation, she was deeply concerned for Edward Lee and his friends. She shared Lacy's concerns.

"You're right," Megan said. "Let's get to work. The only way to keep those kids and everyone else in this town safe is to catch this lunatic."

Megan took out a couple of notepads and pens. She tossed one to Lacy and kept the other for herself. "I've already spoken to Jerry about the evaluation of the two older cases. He'll do it as soon as possible. Heck, he might have already figured it out by now. That will confirm or deny if it's the same perp or someone new."

Lacy looked up from her pad. "This must be hard for you. I mean, if this killer is the same as the one eight years ago, that means he's either a long-term resident or someone who has used your town to discard his refuse for years. It very well might be someone you've known your entire life. It could be Cooper for that matter, and that little boy who works for him really trusts him."

Megan shook her head defiantly. "It's not Cooper. He would never harm Edward Lee. The creep we're after may live near my family or think our community is his dump, but it's not Coop. Both Nate and Beth live within a couple of miles of where all the bodies were found. It keeps me up at night, going over and over it in my mind. I can't think of who it could possibly be."

"But you admit you can't fathom who it is. That makes Cooper a suspect to me," Lacy said.

"That's ridiculous. By that reasoning, Nate and Mather would be suspects as well."

For a moment, Lacy said nothing. Then she looked Megan in the eye and said, "Sorry. It's my nature to question." At this moment, she felt like an outsider, the only one who could be objective.

"I understand. I would have done the same thing in your situation. I should have done the same thing. It's just that Nate is my brother, and Mather . . . Hell, you spent the day with him. He may be physically capable of that sort of violence, but he's gentle as a kitten with a kind heart."

"I'm sure that's true of both Nate and Cooper too. I overstepped. Let's move on. We also need to follow up on the presence of adipocere in the dirt from the first body," Lacy said.

"Oh yeah, the grave-wax stuff," Megan said, glad for the new direction.

"I also want a rush put on the paint chip and hair analysis in both cases," Lacy said.

Megan looked up over her pad. "You better be careful, or you'll get a reputation like mine."

"I should be so lucky," Lacy joked.

"So he did find hair in the remains from the Phillipses' place?" Megan asked

"Only two strands. I'll call Jerry on all of that. I can also have him run the Coke can again for prints since he'll be dealing with old evidence already," Lacy offered.

Megan suddenly looked up. "Maybe we should wait until this whole mess is over with before we pursue that."

"If the chief questions it, I'll tell him I want to look into all the unsolved older murders to see if they could be connected to this guy. If the old remains come back positive for chain saw marks, which I believe they will, the Coke can will be the least of his worries," Lacy said.

Megan began to protest. Her mother's case was technically not a murder. It'd remained a missing-person case. However Lacy was right: to run the prints wouldn't take any of their time. And who knew, they might come up with a match this time.

"Great, you take care of that, and I'll talk to Mary Pearl and her yardman, Farley."

"Perfect. Since you know the woman, she's much more apt to share information with you than she would me. Where do you want to meet after we get this stuff done?" Lacy asked.

Megan thought about her sister's house but wasn't so sure that was a good idea. "How about I swing by the station, and we can interview the others together?"

"That sounds good to me," Lacy said. "I've got your cell number, and you've got mine. Call me when you finish up."

*　　*　　*

Things did not work out the way Megan planned. First off, the gas gauge in her truck read empty. Something she'd neglected the previous day. Then she got stuck behind a school bus that seemed to stop every twelve feet, and she couldn't pass. By the time she made it to Mary Pearl's, she was certain her blood pressure was in the danger zone, and she was ready to stoke out from a stress induced blood clot.

She paused outside the house to regain her composure before going around back. She started up the porch steps when she noticed the door was ajar. She looked around but saw no evidence that the elderly woman had been outside recently. With senses on alert, Megan crept toward the opened door. She hesitated, heard no sound, so she peered through the slight opening. This gave a glimpse of a soiled dish towel on the floor. For Mary Pearl, a clean fanatic, this was equivalent to total disarray. She pulled back and drew her Walther PPK from her waistband. The way things were progressing, she didn't know what to expect, but her years on the force overrode her unease.

With a slight nudge of her foot, Megan coaxed the door open the rest of the way. She held her gun tightly as she entered. Seconds later, she spotted Mary Pearl, facedown on the kitchen floor. Megan noted traces of dried blood matted in her friend's hair and reached down to feel for a pulse. As suspected, there wasn't one. The elderly woman was cold and definitely dead. The emotional impact was strong, but Megan couldn't allow it to get to her now. There would be time for that later. Her first thought was the possibility that the killer might still be in the house. With a tight grip on her pistol, she proceeded to check out each room. She came up with nothing. The killer was gone, and strangely, there was no sign of forced entry. Did that mean Mary Pearl knew her killer? Or was there even a killer? Mary Pearl had to be at least eighty. It was possible she'd slipped in her own kitchen, hit her head, and died; but Megan's gut told her otherwise. This was too coincidental. One day the woman voiced information about suspicious activity; the next, she's dead. Mary Pearl had more spirit and gumption than most people half her age. Something wasn't right. What had happened to their quiet little town? She took her cell out and called it in, then called Lacy.

Once off the phone, she began the usual crime-scene workup while she waited for the others. She measured various distances of Mary Pearl's body from the door, the window, and the counters. She noted the inside and outside temperatures and jotted down whatever she thought might prove to be pertinent. All the while she worked, she couldn't shake the gnawing feeling that Mary Pearl had been murdered to silence her. The woman did speak her mind, even when it wasn't exactly appropriate. Who was this person? He killed young and now old, but why?

She walked out to the porch to get some fresh air and wait. The smell of fresh-cut grass hung in the air, a sure sign of spring. A season Mary Pearl would never again be able to enjoy.

*   *   *

The ME and crime scene unit came, did their thing, and left. With everything so straightforward, it didn't take long to work up the site. With everyone but Lacy gone, Megan slumped against a nearby kitchen cabinet and placed her head in her hands. She felt much older than her twenty-eight years.

"Something tells me you don't agree with the ME, that she had a heart attack," Lacy said.

"With no sign of forced entry or struggle, I understand. But you're right, I disagree."

At this point, Megan was so tired she actually wasn't sure herself why she questioned the ME. Maybe she was paranoid. But whatever the reason, her instincts screamed otherwise. "The last thing this community needs is another unsolved murder, and this one would have to be considered a random and violent home invasion," Megan said. "That's the worst it gets, big-city crime."

"I know the stats for home invasions are greatly elevated in the other cities in Florida, but so far, you guys have been fortunate here. So why do I sense a 'but' in your comments?" Lacy asked.

Megan looked up. Her face splotchy from where she'd rubbed it with her hands. "I feel it. I could feel his presence when I walked in. He did this to shut her up."

Lacy went to the sink and wet a paper towel and came back to her partner. "Here, clean your face up. You look like hell. As far as Mary Pearl goes, we'll know more after the autopsy. Who knows, she was old. Maybe she got confused with her medications and killed herself by accident."

Megan wiped her face with the cool, wet towel. "Thanks," she said. "Your right about the autopsy but not the medications. Mary Pearl didn't believe in taking any medication, prescribed or over-the-counter.

"How do you know?" Lacy challenged. "She was eighty—she had to be on something."

"Not last I knew," Megan said.

"I wasn't aware the two of you were that tight. Maybe she didn't share everything with you."

Megan realized Lacy was right and slumped back against the cabinet in defeat.

Lacy leaned back next to her and took a deep breath. Then she sat bolt upright. "I know one way to find out before autopsy," Lacy said. "We can do a bit of snooping. You check her medicine cabinet. I'll cover the kitchen cabinets and frig."

Megan looked up, surprised. "You believe me? You don't think I'm crazy?"

"I never said that. I believe Mary Pearl took medication, and I hate to be wrong," Lacy said.

Megan smiled at the challenge. They each headed off in different directions and both came back empty-handed. Megan had a huge grin plastered on her face, and Lacy was confused.

"I don't understand. Was she a Scientologist like Tom Cruise or something?"

"No, she was healthy and stubborn, but I think you mean Christian Scientist. They don't use modern medicine. The killer got to her before we could ask any questions," Megan said.

"Hey, maybe it wasn't him. It could have been the farmer she turned in over the sewage use."

"No, that was almost fifteen years ago. If he'd planned to kill her, he'd have done it back then."

"They say revenge is a dish best served cold," Lacy said.

Megan shook her head. "No. The timing is too perfect. This was the work of our serial killer."

"I hate to even bring it up, but you seem so insistent. If it was the serial killer, why did Mary Pearl get carted out of here with both arms intact?"

"He's cunning. She wasn't his quarry, only someone that needed to be silenced. He did that."

"What about the yardman? Do you think Farley had anything to do with this?"

"Farley? No, he's very gentle. I can't imagine him involved. He wouldn't hurt anyone."

Lacy hesitated, "What about Cooper? As I arrived, I saw him drive away from the site yesterday. He knows Nate, Matt, and Beth. He could have heard about Mary Pearl's story."

Megan looked up, not sure what to say. Lacy was right. "I don't have all the answers, but my gut tells me this was a murder. Since Farley saw exactly what Mary Pearl did, his life's in danger too. Same as those three children."

* * *

Ten minutes later, Megan and Lacy pulled up to the local Handy Way.

"Why are we stopping here?" Lacy asked.

"To find Farley."

"He works here?"

"No, but Edwin does. He pretty much knows the scoop on what's going on around here, like the local squire. People stop in for their morning coffee, exchange anecdotes, and get the latest news. Edwin hears it all. If Farley's around, he'd know where."

"I'm gonna grab a Coke while you talk to him. I'm really thirsty," Lacy said and disappeared down one of the cramped aisles.

"Edwin," Megan called out.

A head popped up from behind the counter. Edwin was in the midst of stocking a shelf. "Megan. I haven't seen you in here for a while, not since you moved into town. What's up?"

"I moved to be near the station. I stay busy, mostly work. How 'bout you?"

"I can't complain. But it's a shame about Mary Pearl."

Megan was taken aback by the remark. How could Edwin already know about Mary Pearl? Her body had been removed less than an hour ago. But then again, the parade of CSU, ME, and ambulance would have gone right past this store. A few probably stopped in for coffee.

"It truly is a shame. I had no idea the woman had heart problems," Megan said. She was fishing and wanted to hear Edwin's take on the situation.

"Heart problems? Is that what they said? Shoot, that woman didn't have any heart problems. She was as strong as a mule and just as stubborn at times. Could be a pain in the neck."

Megan was reassured that someone else shared her belief over Mary Pearl's health status. However, documentation from a physician would carry a lot more weight than Edwin's opinion. She hoped the autopsy would warrant such weight in favor of her suspicions.

"Maybe you could help me. I'm looking for Farley. Do you know where he's at today?"

"Sure, he's out at your sister's place, picking peanuts. Mather stopped in the first thing this morning to put the word out he needed pickers. Farley was here when he came, so they rode together. You know he's not allowed to drive anymore. I wouldn't let him on my tractor."

Megan nodded. "I know. It's sad. Thanks for the info," Megan said and walked out to the truck where Lacy waited.

When Megan climbed in the cab, she looked over at Lacy. "Damn, girl, did you need a cart for all that?"

"Don't even start with me," Lacy snapped. "I'm stressed out, and they had a sale."

"Sales are good," Megan agreed.

20

"I can't believe you're actually going to eat that junk," Megan said. "And I thought my standards were low."

"They *are* low. I've seen your pantry. This stuff isn't any worse," Lacy stated in defense.

"At least Pop-Tarts are fortified, and I always have peanut butter on hand. That's a good source of protein."

"Yeah, well, last I heard, that stuff's full of those trans-fatty things that kill you."

"Maybe the Pop-Tarts but not peanut butter. That's heart-healthy," Megan said. "So is my butter spread."

"Just the same, sometimes a person needs a snack as a pick-me-up. You know, to help make it through a stressful period. I happen to favor Ring Dings and Coke. They go good together. Besides, I had no idea we were going straight to your sister's when I bought them. I thought our plan was to talk to Farley. You should have told me. This is all your fault."

"You going to blame me for your eating indiscretions?" Megan asked incredulously.

"Sure, why not?" Lacy asked.

"Because that's not fair. I was busy with Edwin when you bought all that garbage. I had no idea Farley was with Matt, and you said you were gonna get a Coke. I don't see how any of that makes this my fault."

"OK, whatever, but the thing is, now I'm in a bad situation. I have too much stuff to eat before we get to your sister's house," Lacy said, taking the treats out of the bag.

"Why two packs of Ring Dings anyway? What happened?" Megan asked.

"They were on sale, buy one get one free. What was I supposed to do? It only makes sense to get two. It would be stupid to pay for one and refuse the free one."

Megan had to concede that point. After all, it was value shopping. "That's true. If it costs the same to get two packs as it does one, it would be foolish not to get both."

"Now I feel obligated to eat them before we get to Beth's house. If I leave them in the truck, the heat will make the chocolate outer coating stick to the cellophane wrapper. I hate when that happens. It messes up the chocolate, cake, and filling ratio. I'm sure a lot of research went into that, and if you ask me, they got it just right. It's not the same when you have to scrap the chocolate coating off with your bottom teeth. Not to mention it's messy."

Megan again had to give her that. "It would be a shame to let them go to waste. Since you blame me for this, how about this—I eat one pack, and you eat the other?"

"That sounds like a good solution to me," Lacy said and handed Megan one. "But don't expect me to run it off later with you. No more running for me."

"Fine," Megan said and took a big bite. She hadn't eaten one in years, and it tasted wonderful.

The two ate in blissful silence for a few moments. Then Lacy said, "You know, if you're right about Mary Pearl, and we talk to Farley, he might end up dead next."

"Believe me, I've thought about that," Megan said. "Along with the three children."

"Oh, and what about Beth? She's the one who told us about Mary Pearl and Farley to start with. Maybe I should have the chief put a uniform on her," Lacy said.

"I'm scared for them all. But what's he supposed to do? My theory about Mary Pearl's death has nothing to back it up yet. Everyone's scared, and we can't put protection on them all. The entire community's in danger. The chief already knows there's a serial killer loose out there."

"And if you put someone on your family, it will look like favoritism?" Lacy asked.

"And it would be, don't you think?" Megan asked.

"No. Not if what you say is true. Beth put herself directly in the path of the killer without realizing it. Then there's Edward Lee and the other boys. They very well may be in grave danger."

"Remember that's only our theory, until we can prove Mary Pearl died of something other than natural causes. For now, we've got squat, and the chief won't want to hear it."

"OK, so what do you think we should do?" Lacy asked.

Megan froze and wondered why Lacy, the lead investigator, asked her opinion? Was this a test?

"We're dealing with three little boys. You know kids love to talk about adventure," Lacy said.

"Yeah?" Megan agreed, not sure where Lacy was headed.

"How long do you think it will take for one of them to leak the story? It's a pretty big secret for a ten-year-old to keep inside for very long," Lacy said.

"That only makes our job more urgent."

"Oh, I almost forgot. When you were checking for the meds at Mary Pearl's, I found a clump of hair on the kitchen floor. I bagged it for evidence," Lacy said.

Megan brightened. "Why didn't you mention it? It may match the other samples. Maybe our guy's getting careless," Megan said with a wry smile.

"Careless and hairless," Lacy said with a chuckle. She took a sip of her Coke before she continued. "I was primarily in search for medications when it caught my eye. It looked as if Mary Pearl grabbed a fist full of hair and pulled it out by the roots. Maybe during a struggle."

"That sounds like Mary Pearl. She was a fighter. I think we should request a full autopsy on her, not just a medical run-through to determine if there was presence of pathology or not."

"A medical-legal autopsy? That would have to be ordered by the medical examiner. Then again, I don't see him having a problem with it. Her death was unexpected, sudden, and she was alone. With no history of medical problems, that raises a red flag for me. Sooner or later, this creep is gonna mess up, and we'll be there to catch him," Lacy said.

"I think he already has with Mary Pearl. I'm certain something of interest will be revealed on autopsy. I only hope the lab won't take too long with the results."

"Ah, speaking of lab results, I spoke to Jerry earlier. He wanted me to tell you he had dinner with his mother last night. Afterward, he went home, took two Advils, and had to lie down. You want to tell me what that's all about?"

"Nothing really," Megan said but had to suppress a grin. "What did he have on our case?"

Lacy gave an audible sigh. She knew that was all she'd get on that subject. With a flick of her wrist, she flipped opened her notepad. "OK, let's see here. The first ground sample came back negative for adipocere. The second was positive but minimal. That means the first body was dumped clean. The one at the Phillipses' place had at least some flesh still on the bones when it was partially buried. Both indicate the killer did not murder the women on site. Then there's the formation of the remains—they were basically in a pile."

"Interesting. So that means he committed the murders elsewhere, but where?"

"Good question. But what I also find of interest was that he dumped clean skeletons. What happened to the flesh and cartilage? Were they allowed to decompose elsewhere?" Lacy asked.

"I wondered the same thing. It's possible he did something to speed up the decomposition."

"To throw off the time of death? Like pour acid or bleach over them?"

"That or even to minimize the stench of death. A rotting carcass does tend to draw attention. Even something as small as a dead dog or opossum can really stink," Megan said.

"Oh, that's so gross. Can we refer to them as remains? I just ate. I don't feel so good."

"It's the Coke. I told you soft drinks were bad for you."

"No way. Coke's supposed to soothe your stomach."

"That's a myth created by the syrup manufactures," Megan said.

"Are you always this cynical?"

"Pretty much. Anyway, I agree with you. I think this joker selects his victims, kills them someplace secluded, then does something to their bodies to end up with pristine bones. Maybe Jerry could determine what. It has to be something he pours over the cadaver to dissolve the soft tissue. What we've found is the end result," Megan said. "But I still think the murders occurred close to here. Even if you're crazy, you still wouldn't drive far with a body in your car. It's too risky, and something tells me that although this guy is insane, he's not stupid."

"OK, I see your point, but it isn't uncommon for criminals to use remote, distant locations to rid themselves of evidence. He might live in a nearby city," Lacy said. "Big-time criminals do it all the time."

"Humm," Megan said and mulled this over. "My gut tells me if he knew of the abandoned limestone road, he was local. It's too far off the interstate or main thoroughfare to be a random dump site for a criminal from another county," Megan said.

"You do have a good point," Lacy said and smiled. "You're thinking like a detective now."

"Thanks. So what's next on your list? What about the paint samples?"

"Tallahassee told Jerry they ran both samples through scanning electron microscopy and the FBI's National Automated Paint File and got a match. Both are standard issue from Ford. Unfortunately, the company doesn't distinguish the make, model, or year. And it's been used since the sixties. Without a suspect vehicle, they can't make a positive ID. However, they did state that the height for both samples was consistent with the prominent contours of the car models and not their trucks or SUVs."

"That corroborates Farley's, Mary Pearl's, and Edward Lee's stories," Megan said. "I like when things fit."

Lacy could appreciate that. She hated discrepancies.

"It would be nice to have a make or model, even a year, but I guess you can't have everything."

"Well, at least we have a match," Megan said as she pulled up to her sister's house. "Let's stop by to say hi to Beth. She'll know where they're picking today. Two hundred acres is too big to look around until we find Farley. Beth can save us a lot of time."

"I hope she's over yesterday, because if she's not, I'm serious about not going on another run with you to blow off steam. I'm still sore. Ring Dings and maybe potato chips are my favored treatment modalities. I like the ridged ones. They have a better crunch. That kind of chewing helps reduce pent-up stress and anxiety. Too bad they weren't on sale."

Megan rolled her eyes and got out of the truck.

* * *

As usual, Megan knocked first, then continued into the house without a response. Lacy followed, with Cleo close at her heels, amazed that no one around here seemed to lock their doors. Quickly her thoughts shifted when she breathed in deeply. "Oh, I smell something yummy."

"Hello," Megan called out then turned to Lacy, "I can't believe your appetite."

"In the kitchen," Beth called out.

"At least she doesn't sound mad," Lacy whispered, not sure if you could tell such a thing from three inane words.

When they walked in, Beth was bent over the oven, pulling out a pound cake. She placed it on the counter next to two others.

"Girl, I'm telling you, with the way you bake, you should start up a bakery or some kind of catering service. You could make a fortune from home," Lacy said. She walked over to the counter and took in a deep breath of the rich aroma. She waved her hand over them, so the smell would waft up to her nose. It was intoxicating.

"Lacy, you flatter me, but I don't think I could run a business from home with two small boys running around underfoot."

"Sure you could. Women like you do it all the time. The key is to work on your own terms. If you get too busy, then turn people away. Before you know it, it will be a kind of a status symbol to be lucky enough to have you cater a party. I saw a whole segment about it on *60 Minutes*."

Beth looked at her. "You really think so?"

"Positive. Besides, the other day you told us you felt like you need something else in your life."

"It seems like a great idea. You should seriously consider it. I know Mather would be all for it. You definitely have the talent. It would be a shame to let it go to waste," Megan added.

"Really? But to run an actual business? That seems hard, and I'm already so busy with the boys," Beth said.

"What do you mean? You run this household like a business. You're the one who makes sure everyone has clean clothes, healthy food, homework done, and gets to school on time. You name it, the list goes on. You are the CEO of this household. You have upper management skills. You even do the bookkeeping for the farm and the house and pay all the bills," Megan stated.

"I guess I do, don't I?" Beth said. She turned back around to free the cake from the pan, then went over to the sink to wash it. "It wouldn't hurt to look into it."

"Why so many cakes? You hungry or something?" Lacy asked.

Megan walked over to the refrigerator and took out the iced tea and poured out three glasses.

Beth wiped her hands on the dish towel that hung on the handle of the oven door and took a seat at the table. "Oh, it feels so good to sit down. But to answer your question, the cakes aren't for me. The Humane Society needed them for a bake sale."

"Do they pay you for them?" Lacy asked.

Beth laughed. "Of course not. It's for charity. Sissy Howard called last night and asked me if I would bake them. She's their chairperson this year. They want to build an expansion. Then she had to tell me all about this new horse of hers. She said it had already won several awards. I'm sure he cost a fortune."

"I didn't realize she was involved with the Humane Society," Megan said.

"You two are missing my point," Lacy interrupted. "People come to you to bake for them. You need to charge for your services."

Her enthusiasm was infectious. Beth thought over what Lacy had said about the cookies, along with doing so much for others at the expense of her own family. It was all true. So, with a glint of mischievousness in her eye, she surprised herself. "Only two are for the charity. One is for us. I say we have a slice right now."

"Oh, that wasn't why I brought it up. We just stopped in to look for Farley," Lacy said.

"Farley?"

"Yes," Megan said. "Edwin said he went off with Mather this morning. I thought you might have an idea where they were going to work today."

"They planned to start picking on the back forty and work their way up from there."

"Thanks," Lacy said. "As much as it pains me, we'll have to take a rain check on that cake."

Beth got up, went to the cabinet, and took down a prescription bottle. She popped two tablets in her mouth and swallowed them dry. "I've had such a headache lately," she said and leaned against the counter. Megan thought she looked very tired and thin.

"Maybe it's too much caffeine," Lacy suggested.

Beth nodded. "Maybe." She turned and busied herself at the counter.

"Just out of curiosity, what kind of addition is the Humane Society building?" Megan asked

"It's a facility to be able to take in more horses. I guess they get a fair number of large animals from people that buy thoroughbreds in the hopes of raising a winner. They don't anticipate the full cost of upkeep or the room they require.

I'm sure you've seen it off 441," Beth said and added, "please take these to go." She handed them each a warm slice of pound cake on a napkin.

"Oh, thanks," Lacy said.

"That makes sense. I know Sissy's really into horses," Megan said. She took a bite of the warm cake and moaned. "Lacy is right, Beth. You have to sell this. I don't know how you do it. Mine always come out like crud."

"Thank you, but it's all in the addition of the flour and eggs. You have to add them slowly. You blend each one in really well before you add the next."

"You tell me this like I would understand what you're talking about," Megan said.

"Well, you should learn to cook if you ever hope to get married and have a family," Beth said.

"Especially with those clothes," Beth continued. "There's absolutely nothing feminine about them, or the shoes. You know a skirt every now and then wouldn't hurt, or a little makeup."

Megan tried to shrug it off. "OK, Beth. Thanks for the cake and the info. We have to get back to work now." She almost left it at that; but when she got to the door, she turned and said, "You know, Beth, this isn't the fifties. A lot of women live happy lives married or not. Some may not even know how to cook. That's why Lacy's idea to start a catering business is so great. That way, women such as myself could call you up and order the things we want to eat but can't, or don't have time to make for ourselves."

She loved her sister, but at times, Beth was exasperating. One moment she nurtured and fussed over her; then next, she was irritable. She'd also noted her taking a lot of prescription medication lately. With her complaints of frequent headaches, Megan was concerned that the everyday responsibilities of the house and children, combined with the threat of a killer on the loose, were already more than enough. Maybe a business would put Beth over the edge. Or it was possible it might be just the thing she needed to refuel—give her life new meaning, direction, and purpose.

Megan and Lacy walked to the door with Beth close behind.

"Thanks for the cake. You really should think about a start-up business," Lacy said. "It can be small-scale at first, then you could expand as needed."

"And please take care of yourself, Beth," Megan said. "A lot of people depend on you."

Beth looked at her sister and nodded absently. She noticed her hands were shaking. She looked out the window and watched Megan and Lacy disappear into the rows of peanuts. She couldn't remember a time when she felt more vulnerable and alone. Why did her sister choose a job that put her life on the line for others? Didn't she realize she was needed too? She needed her, more than ever.

21

That afternoon, Megan and Lacy found themselves in the small reception area outside the chief of police's office. It wasn't by their request, and neither one was real keen on the idea. They both had an inkling it wouldn't be a happy meeting for any of them.

"What did he say again?" Megan asked.

Lacy shrugged. "He wants answers, and I'm sure he wants a complete update."

"That doesn't sound real encouraging. The majority of lab work won't be in for days. With Mary Pearl's death thrown in, I have no idea what to tell him."

"So I'm supposed to do all the talking?" Lacy asked.

Megan gave her a wry smile. "You *are* my superior, big-city cop, and all that. It's your show."

"Well it might not be either of ours if he decides to pull us off the case."

"Why would he do that?" Megan asked.

"For one thing, this mess started out as unidentified skeletal remains. It was unknown if it was even human. It could have been a deer or a hundred-year-old anthropological find. Since then we've presumed there to be one more recent victim and two past. So now the man has a serial-killer case on his hands. This is your first homicide, and I'm new to the area. He might want to rethink his personnel assignments," Lacy explained.

"I never looked at it that way."

"What I hate the most is how he ordered us here right away, then makes us wait. I don't have time for these kinds of power games. We could be chasing down leads."

"What leads?" Megan asked. "We don't have any real leads."

"He doesn't know that yet. I think I'm getting an ulcer," Lacy said and rubbed her stomach.

"It's more likely from the Ring Dings, cake, and soda," Megan said.

"There you go again with the soda thing. I think you have unresolved issues."

Megan noticed how the secretary, who was trying hard to look as if she were actually busy instead of eavesdropping, had to stifle a giggle. Megan suspected the woman enjoyed someone else being the target of her boss's scrutiny. But before she could say anything, the intercom buzzed. Their presence was needed in the inner sanctum. The two reluctantly did as instructed.

When they entered, Megan was shocked to see Jerry already seated at a small conference table. The chief towered over him, eyes intent on the papers spread across the table. She wondered why they hadn't been included in this private assembly. She feared Lacy was right in her assumption that they might be taken off the case, and she walked past in a daze.

Jerry looked up with an unusual expression on his face. Megan realized it was the lack of confidence he normally held when he was at work in the lab.

"Take a seat," the chief barked and gestured to the table.

Lacy swiftly claimed the seat the farthest away from her boss. Which only left two others. One had a suit jacket draped over the back. Megan assumed it belonged to her boss and dared not disturb it. The other touched it, but since it was the only available choice, Megan grudgingly pulled it out and sat. She managed to gain a few feet of space in the act, a tiny bit of solace. She glared over at Lacy and slunk deeply into the seat.

"Tell me what you have so far." the chief asked. He glowered at the two newcomers.

Megan looked up quickly, taken off guard by the abruptness of the question. For some reason, she expected some type of preamble, like, "Hello," or, "How ya doing?" before broaching the main issue. This guy wasn't giving her a chance to gain her bearings. She felt his eyes bore a hole right through her. Already emotionally drained from the death of Mary Pearl, worry over her sister, and her family's safety, her defenses were down. She opened her mouth to speak, then hesitated.

"Well?"

"Not much, sir," was all Megan could say, and that came out more as a squeak than words.

"Not much? We've got a serial killer out there in our community, and you've had the case five days. Is that all you can say for yourself?"

"It's actually been four, sir," Lacy spoke up. "And one was a holiday, Easter Sunday. Which we worked through, I might add. We worked our asses off over this. As a matter of fact, you would have no idea we were dealing with a serial killer if it wasn't for Megan's off-duty research."

The chief stood up straight to his full height of six feet, two inches, all 230 pounds of him, and stared directly into Lacy's eyes.

Lacy met his gaze without hesitation or fear. She might be new on this force, but she wasn't in the mood to let this guy mow over her or Megan. There had been no point in belittling Megan in front of coworkers. That was intolerable. If he chose to take them off the case to put some team with more experience in, fine. What she wouldn't accept was for him to say they hadn't tried. She stood, hands on the table in a stare down. "You have something to say, I think now would be a good time."

Megan couldn't believe Lacy would talk back to the boss. It was as if she was watching a train wreck. Horrified yet fascinated at the same time. The chief moved closer to Lacy, leaned in on the table with one arm so he was eye to eye. "It sounds like you're the one with something to say."

Megan sat straighter as she watched Lacy hold her ground. "First of all, we thought we were dealing with unidentified remains. They weren't even known to be human. They could have been a vagrant or missing person who died of exposure. Not a lot to go on, sir. No more than a pile of bones, and the second one wasn't in much better condition. As far as we know, Mary Pearl's situation is up in the air."

"Oh, well then, I'll just call a press conference and tell the community we're working real hard, but this case is just too tough for our detectives to solve without a body in better shape. Maybe the killer will hear our plea and accommodate us."

Lacy slammed her fist down on the table. "Damn it! That's not what I said, and you know it. A case of remains in poor condition always relies heavily on lab results. They haven't come in yet, which I'm also sure you're already aware of after your private conference with Jerry. You can call a press conference and tell the community we're working around the clock to keep them safe. But I can assure you that you already have the best on this case."

Megan watched the chief turn and pace for a moment, afraid to move. She knew he hated excuses, but what Lacy offered was different. It was a valid reason.

Although agitated by the way the chief addressed them, Lacy understood his position. He had a county full of upset constituents with no answers. She felt a degree of sympathy for him being in the spotlight. This was a tough investigation for everyone. Forensics and extensive lab work all took time, more than five days. The outcome of the case would be based on that information. Despite all that, he still tried to place the blame on her. It was hard not to take it personally, and she wasn't going to stand for it. They needed to work together, not against each other.

"So you say Detective Callingham noted the connection with the older cases?" the chief asked.

"That's correct. I noted the marks on the remains found at the peach farm. Megan put the rest together," Jerry said.

"Tell me about this, Callingham," the chief said and turned abruptly to look at her.

Megan didn't exactly enjoy being in the hot seat, but it did give her the opportunity to convey the work their team had put in so far. "I reviewed all of the unsolved older cases in my free time. I went back twenty years. As I did, two cases stood out. They occurred around the same time, both eight years ago. They were both intact skeletons except for the arms. After the recent cases, I began a criminal profile. Jerry's determined that our second victim might have been strangled, as well had her arms removed."

This information seemed to capture the chief's attention. He actually appeared to listen, instead of wait for a chance to criticize.

"I really think there's a strong chance the perp may be a longtime resident," Megan said.

"How so? Who's to say he isn't from a nearby big city?" the chief challenged.

That's when Megan realized she should have stopped when she was ahead. Apparently, while the chief would listen to evidence, he was not interested in Megan's musings. "These types of murderers often change their MOs, but they keep their signature the same."

"And you're telling me his signature is to cut off both arms, and he lives here?"

This time the chief posed the question as a sincere inquiry and not a veiled accusation.

"Yes, sir."

"Why both arms?"

"That I cannot answer. And it's true he could use our community as his trash dump, but I think he lives here. The locations the bodies were found at were remote, even for locals in town. They are miles from any major road, with areas that appear desolate in between. It wouldn't make sense to risk travel with human remains for any longer than necessary."

"Well, I can appreciate the fact you've thought long and hard over this," he said and went over to look out the window.

"Yes, sir. We would like to reevaluate the remains from the two past cases as well. That would determine if my theory's right or not about the killer being the same. I would like to be certain."

"But wouldn't the lab people have picked up on something like that back then? I mean it seems like a pretty damn obvious thing to me," the chief said.

He was getting agitated again. He talked over his shoulder but never moved from the window. It looked out over the town square on a beautiful sunny day. The grass was green and neatly trimmed. The walkways were free of debris. Interspersed between the paths were gardens that overflowed with blooms in various vibrant colors. A mother pushed a stroller, stopped briefly to readjust her infant and his teddy bear, then continued on. Not the place you would expect to find such egregious crimes. That was a bloody image and reputation he didn't want for this town.

Jerry broke the tension-filled silence. "I wasn't around back then, but it would be my guess that due to the state of the remains and the fact they were obviously out in the field so long prior to discovery, the absent limbs were attributed to intervention of the local wildlife. They didn't see any reason to suspect such a disturbing violent crime."

The chief nodded. "How long will it take to make the determination?"

"Once I get them in my lab, one hour," Jerry said.

"Then do it. I want to know the answer by the end of the day," the chief said, then turned back to Lacy. "So what else can you tell me besides we have a serial killer running around our community that hideously mutilates his victims. That's not something I want made public before we have a name. It would be widespread hysteria. People would end up hurting themselves or each other. I need someone we can make an example of to make the voters feel safe again."

"Give us forty-eight hours," Lacy said. "We've managed to get a good estimate of the time of death in the first victim. The one found at the peach farm. We ran it against the missing persons and came up with four possible matches. We haven't had a chance to question the families yet. That's what we were doing when you called us here."

The chief walked back to the table to face all three of them. "Fair enough. Forty-eight hours it is, and we all meet back here for a full report. If I'm not satisfied, I'll put you on watermelon crime."

Megan felt better about the situation now. At least the chief had to know they were trying.

He leaned in close, almost nose to nose to Lacy, and said, "I expect a name. A face to plaster on the front page. Longtime Killer Captured," he said as if he viewed the headline. "I want the community to see us out there. They must feel our presence and feel safe."

"Yes, sir," Lacy said. "Then with all due respect, we need to get the hell out of here and do some police work."

He stood, towering over them. Then an unexpected grin crept across his face. "Please do."

The three of them wasted no time in their departure. Jerry uncharacteristically scooped up an armload of papers, with no regard to their order. That was something he'd straighten out later. Someplace safely out of the chief's view.

Once outside and out of earshot of the nosey secretary, Jerry said, "Man, Lacy. You kicked ass in there. You are the bomb." He gave her a high five, as did Megan.

"Thanks. We didn't deserve his shit. What the heck does he think? He knows darn well it takes time to solve a case like this. He was asking for is a miracle."

"Then a miracle we shall provide," Jerry said. They all gave another high five, and he turned to leave when Megan stopped him.

"Oh," Megan said, "I want you to rush through the lab results on Mary Pearl's autopsy when they come in."

Jerry folded his hands across his chest and leaned on one hip. "Why? The forty-eight hours isn't tight enough for you? You want to up the ante? She was old and died of a heart attack is what I heard."

"I know she had no heart problems. I believe she was murdered," Megan said.

"People don't publicize their health problems, Megan. Besides, it's not unheard-of for someone to show no symptoms, then die suddenly of a massive coronary at that age. Heck, she could have thrown a clot," Jerry whispered. He looked around to make sure no one was close enough to hear.

"Then what about this clump of hair Lacy found at the scene? It looked as if it were ripped out of the assailant's head," Megan said and held up the bag.

"What? Are you crazy? Why wasn't this with all the other CSU evidence?"

"They missed it," Lacy said. "But I bagged it in the presence of another officer. It's usable."

Jerry looked from one to the other. "Fine. It's evidence. I'll do the best I can."

"It might be a sample of the killer's hair, his DNA. A clue to his identity," Lacy said.

"What? Now you think the serial killer killed an elderly woman?"

They both nodded.

"Fine. I'll do a quick look-see under the scope before I send it off. I can tell color and race."

"Thanks, Jerry, I knew we could count on you."

"Yes, it's so convenient that I don't have a personal life," he grumbled as he walked away.

"I kind of get the feeling he's not too happy with us, or this situation right now," Megan said.

"Sometimes life's tough. You have to learn to deal with it. For us, forty-eight hours will come soon enough. I say we get to work."

22

Megan and Lacy walked to her truck. "What did the chief mean about watermelon crime?"

"Oh, that happens every year around this time. Unfortunately it's started early this year."

"What the heck do the criminals do? I mean, so they steal watermelons and spit seeds at people? That seems more like a kid's prank."

"It's actually big money. Last year the growers claimed over three million in theft."

They were almost to her truck when the exit door to the station slammed open, and a uniformed cop raced toward them. He called out to them.

Automatically, Megan stopped and pivoted around.

"We almost made it," Lacy mumbled.

"The chief told me to give you these," he said and handed Lacy a new set of car keys.

They both looked at them, confused. "There must be some kind of mistake. He never mentioned anything about a new vehicle."

The fellow officer nervously put his hands in his pockets and avoided eye contact with both Megan and Lacy. "There's no mix-up. He said specifically for me to give those to you. He wants you to drive one of the new prototype cars. It'll let the community know our presence."

"But—"

"The number's on the tag, and it's parked in the side lot," he added, then turned and walked away at a brisk pace.

"I don't understand. Why didn't the chief tell us about this when we were in his office?"

"He did say he wanted the police presence to be visible," Megan said.

"Man, it's hot out here. Maybe a new car will come in handy. It will have air conditioning, unlike your truck," Lacy said. "Maybe even a better radio."

"Hey, don't start with my truck. I like it, and I've had it for years," Megan said.

"It looks like it too. Besides, I'm just trying to be positive."

The two women walked up to the vehicle with the matching number and stared in disbelief.

"I think you got the wrong number. Let me take a look at those keys," Lacy said. She took the set back from Megan and read the tag again. Then turned the tag upside down, which didn't help.

"This has to be some sort of joke," Lacy said. "It's smaller than a Mini Cooper."

"I'm afraid it's for real," Megan said.

"Well shit. I can't ride in that. How are we supposed to come across as tough in something the size of a golf cart?" She walked around it and balked.

"It's one of those new environment-friendly prototype vehicles," Megan explained. "I heard our station had been chosen to test one out. They're electric and supposed to save the taxpayers thousands of dollars in fuel cost, plus be environmental friendly. I think for the next forty-eight hours, we have no choice. Besides, like the chief said, it has an emblem on the side. People will notice us," Megan said, trying to follow Lacy's positive lead.

"Hell yeah, they'll notice us all right. Everyone that sees us is going to laugh their ass off. People will snap pictures of us on their camera phones so that even their friends in other states will be able to laugh at us," Lacy complained.

"You're small and still manage to be tough. It's all in the attitude. Maybe this car has attitude," Megan said and climbed in. It was a tight fit for her long legs, but she managed. They pulled out of the side lot with the window down in anticipation of a breeze, but the tiny vehicle couldn't seem to get up enough speed to create much of one.

"I feel ridiculous," Lacy said.

"That's probably because we look ridiculous."

"Why don't you roll up your window so we can use the air conditioning? It's the only amenity this little thing has to offer."

"If I roll up the window, I won't have any place to put my left arm. Besides, I'm afraid it would suck too much power. We're already going slow enough as it is."

"Trust me, I noticed. If we get passed by a moped, I'm getting out. I have my limits on how much humiliation I can handle."

The two sat silently at a stoplight and tried not to notice the unwanted attention they drew.

"I hate being stared at," Lacy said, breaking the silence. She looked straight ahead, willing the light to change.

"Just because they're curious doesn't mean they think the idea of an electric police car is bad. This is something new. It's bound to spark interest," Megan said.

"Well, it makes me feel more like a meter maid than a detective."

"Like it or not, we're stuck with it for now. We might as well make the best of it."

"Yeah, yeah, I know. Does this thing have a radio? Maybe we could listen to some music. Good music always cheers me up," Lacy said. She fiddled with the various knobs on the dash until she got a light-rock station that came in clearly.

"I wish Farley had more to say," Megan said.

"What did he tell you? You never got to finish telling me because of the chief."

"Unfortunately, Farley's mind doesn't belong to this world anymore. He's happy enough, but he didn't remember even being at Mary Pearl's—much less a red car. If he *did* see anything, it's floating around somewhere in the great abyss of his mind."

"Well, that might save his life. If it was the killer that got to Mary Pearl to silence her, Farley won't be any threat to him."

"I hope you're right, but that would suggest he knew Mary Pearl's predilection for gossip. He'd have to be a local to know how Mary Pearl spoke her mind, regardless of what others thought."

"Like me?" Lacy asked. "You think I use my mouth too much. I can tell."

Megan chuckled at that. "At times. But my point is, you suggested he killed to silence Mary Pearl. That meant he had to know her—which, in turn, meant he had to live or work in this area."

Lacy mulled that over. She liked solid evidence rather than to rely on a hunch, but what Megan said made sense. "Maybe we should run down all her acquaintances, friends, and family."

"That might be difficult. Mary Pearl was invested in everyone around her and in the community as a whole. She was always willing to get involved. She didn't have money, so instead, she gave of herself. She was involved in the church, library, community events, political issues, and various societies. The only aspect we can eliminate is family. On that front, she was alone. Her husband died in the war, and she had no children or other relatives that I know of."

"That's kind of sad," Lacy said. "So if the killer thought she might be able to recognized him—"

"It wouldn't mean anything," Megan finished. "She knew everyone in town. We can't gain a lead based on who she knew. We have to think of another angle."

"You mentioned societies. Would the Humane Society be one of them?"

"Ohh yes. I should stop by and give Sissy my condolences," Megan said.

"That's not a bad idea. You could ask Sissy if Mary Pearl told her anything. One thing I do know for sure is the homicide of a prominent citizen is a PR nightmare."

"It still hasn't been relegated as a murder," Megan pointed out. "We'll know more after the autopsy, which I plan to sit in on, if that's OK with you. I know we're pressed for time."

"It's OK. The autopsy should tell us if it was homicide or not. If so, and she was so involved with social work, and the Humane Society is having a big drive, there's a chance Sissy was one of the last people to speak to Mary Pearl alive," Lacy said. "I'd like to question her."

"Good idea, but let's cover our list of the possible matches to our peach-farm remains first. We can swing by and talk to Sissy last. She lives near Beth. It'll take awhile to get there in this thing."

Lacy scanned the sheets of information from the folder on her lap. In it were all the lab results and site drawings of the case. "The first potential match is Kelly Warren." She read off an address.

"I sure hope at least one of these four leads pans out," Megan said.

"You and me both. It won't ID the killer, but to know the victim would be a step in the right direction." Lacy said, scanning the info. "She was reported missing the day after Christmas."

"Let's cross our fingers," Megan said.

Lacy and Megan drove down the old road located in the center of the historic district. Both sides of the street were lined with huge oak trees that created a canopy of shade. The homes were all restored, well maintained, with manicured lawns and flower gardens in full bloom.

"Wow, this area is beautiful. It's so peaceful and quaint," Lacy said.

"I know. As a kid I used to love to drive down this street during Christmastime. All the houses were decorated so beautifully. It seemed like a fairy-tale land. Oh, here we are," Megan announced.

They pulled into the driveway. Megan had to pry her long legs out of the vehicle. She felt stiff but tried to ignore it. They had an interview to focus on, a killer to catch.

"I feel like I'm getting a cramp," Lacy said as they walked up the drive. "You know they warn people about that. You can end up with some sort of deep-vein thrombosis and die if you sit too long without being able to move around."

"We were in the vehicle for twenty minutes, tops. It's not that bad," Megan said and continued on to the front door. She noted an angel birdbath with a bluebird that took flight as she passed.

She knocked and tried to compose herself. This would be an interview of a family with a loved one missing. A subject she was all too familiar with. If Kelly Warren was not their girl, she would still be at large, and Megan would feel responsible for reopening a raw wound for naught. If it was their daughter, then she was the bearer of terrible news. The girl had died a hideous death at the hands of an assailant they had yet to capture. She didn't care to deliver either message. It was in moments such as this that she seriously questioned her career choice.

The door slowly opened and brought Megan back to the present. The woman in front of her had a sallow, grayish-green complexion, sunken eyes and guant frame. "May I help you?" she asked in a feeble voice.

Megan was taken aback by the woman's appearance. She realized that was exactly what she'd looked like all those years ago to the officers who came to her home. A haunted, empty shell.

Lacy stepped up at Megan's hesitance. "Sorry to bother you, ma' am. I'm Detective Andina, and this is my partner, Detective Callingham. We're trying to find your daughter."

"Please, come in then. Can I get you something? Anything to drink?"

"No, thank you, but I would like to ask you a few questions. It won't take long," Lacy began. "An unidentified woman's body who fits the general description of Kelley has been located."

The woman went ashen and sunk into the closest chair. Her worst fears had come true.

"Do you happen to have a photograph of Kelley?" Megan asked. "It might not be her."

The woman nodded and picked up a frame from the end table next to her. She glanced at it, touching it briefly before she handed it over to Megan. When she did, their fingers brushed, and Megan was shocked by how cold they were for such a warm, sunny day.

Megan pulled her eyes away from the mother and focused on the photograph. The girl was laughing, but that wasn't what drew her in. It was the girl's eyes that tugged at her heartstrings. They reached out to her. She was so alive and vibrant, but now she was gone. "Who's the child?"

"Kelley's boy. He's all we have left of her now. He'll be two this summer."

Megan and Lacy shared a knowing look.

"So your daughter had a son? He's not adopted or anything?" Lacy asked.

The woman looked up confused. "Why, no. She was eighteen when she had him and single. Why would she adopt a child? I don't understand. She was still in school. It was a struggle."

"It's just that the woman we found was believed to never have had a child," Lacy said.

The woman brought her hand to her mouth and gasped. "So she's not my baby girl. She may still come back to me."

"We will keep looking for her," Lacy said.

Megan turned back to the mother as they made there way to the car. The woman's eyes were pleading, and Megan felt her pain. She wanted to tell her it would be all right, but she was on the job in an official capacity. Such promises couldn't be made. She had to stick to facts.

Back in the vehicle, Megan said, "One down, three to go. Let me look at the list to see if any are close by. With our forty-eight-hour time limit, we need to be as efficient as possible."

"I'm all for that. The less time in this egg, the better."

Megan had calculated the shortest route to their next interview when her cell phone rang.

"Callingham," she said in a clipped voice. She hadn't meant to be so short, but that last interview had dredged up old feelings that were best left buried. Being empathetic was good to a point; after that, concern become crippling. It could drain the life out of you.

"Now, Megan, why do you always sound so defensive when you answer the phone? You need to work on that," Jerry said. "Presentation is everything, dear."

Just the sound of his voice brought a smile to her face. "Sorry, not the best day so far."

"Well, I've got good news."

"You do sound cheery. What do you have for me?"

"I think you're gonna like this. But remember, it's not official."

"OK, I'll try not to get too excited."

"I looked at the hair sample Lacy gave me from Mary Pearl's place under my microscope before I sent it off to Tallahassee for analysis."

This immediately changed Megan's mood. She sat up straighter and bumped her knee in the process. She managed to stifle a curse as she got out her pen and pad.

"I'm 99 percent certain it's a match to the other hairs found at both crime sites, and it's brown. I saved a tiny piece of all three so you can see for yourself, but if you want my opinion, they're from the same person. The final say, however, will depend on the DNA results, and they take at least two weeks. Of which I knew you couldn't wait with the forty-eight hours over your head."

"So that means it has to be the killer's because the victims would all have different hair."

"You got it, babe."

"Thanks so much, Jerry. I love you for this."

When she flipped her phone shut, she looked over at Lacy, who waited in anticipation.

"So?" Lacy said.

"That was Jerry. He thinks the hair sample you appropriated from Mary Pearl's belonged to the killer. It's brown—not much help, but all three samples matched and were sent off for testing."

"So that pretty much proves you're theory that Mary Pearl was murdered, or the serial killer was there."

Megan looked at Lacy. "You're right. It could have been someone involved closely with the police or rescue teams. A lot of people were involved. That hair could have been from anyone."

"True. But if it was, it was a plant because it was a clump, a fistful, not a stray strand of someone passing through. If it was an arbitrary stand, that would be different. It had to be the serial killer's. It matches the other two skeletal remains," Lacy said.

"That makes sense, but I'm not so sure it's a good thing."

"I know. Too bad the killer wasn't a redhead. You don't see as many of them. If you combined that with someone driving a scratched red car, we might have something. Speaking of which, I wonder if our search on that has come up with anything," Lacy pondered.

"Maybe you should call and ask. They might have something significant and not even realize it," Megan said.

"We'll see. I had them put a call into every auto-body repair and paint shop in town to see if anyone has recently brought in a red Ford car for repairs."

"Of course you realize there are a large number of citizens around here that are capable of doing their own home repairs."

"Really? Paint too?" Lacy asked. "That's the kind of man I need. Someone handy with his hands. Good with plumbing too."

"Well, both Nate and Cooper worked at Parker's garage part-time in high school."

"Really?" Lacy said again. She wanted to ask why Megan's truck looked so bad but thought better of it. "Thing is, if the perp's not from here, we're out of luck too. Tampa, Orlando, and Jacksonville have too many auto-body shops to canvass."

"But he had to know Mary Pearl personally, and she has no family from out of town."

"You said she was involved with numerous charities. If someone from a nearby city, such as Tampa or Orlando, came for a mutual cause, he could know what she's like," Lacy said.

"True, but most people pick charity work close to home. Let's finish up with these interviews," Megan said and pulled into an apartment complex. It was the parent of their next possible match.

"What's her name again?" Megan asked.

"Tina Simpson," Lacy said. Then she looked at her partner with her head cocked. "You OK? I know this has got to be hard on you."

"Yes," Megan said. "I'm fine. It's part of the job. Let's figure out who this woman is."

23

Lacy and Megan sat in a dingy living room while their host excused himself for a moment. In the back, they heard a toilet flush. Shortly afterward, their host reappeared. They all shook hands before sitting down. Megan hoped the dampness of the offered hand was from a fresh washing.

"So what can I do for you, Detectives?" he asked with bushy eyebrows floating about.

"We're here about your daughter," Lacy stated.

Immediately the man's demeanor changed. It wasn't exactly hostile, but it was certainly guarded. "What about Tina?"

"We think we may have found her," Lacy said.

Before Lacy could finish, he interrupted, "Is this some kind of joke? I know damn well where my child is and how it happened. You don't think that's painful enough you feel the need to taunt me?" The old man stood up and teetered before he spoke again. "Get out! Get out of my house!"

Megan stood as well, stunned. She had no idea what had caused this turn of events. "Please, we didn't mean to upset you. We only want to find your daughter."

Seeing the sincerity in Megan's eyes and the way it came through in her voice, the man was somewhat placated. "So why are you here then? They told me yesterday my daughter was found, dead at the bottom of a lake in Gainesville."

Megan glanced at Lacy, then back at the man. "I'm so sorry we had no idea. We're from Marion County. They haven't updated the missing-person file yet. We had hoped we found your daughter. Please excuse us," Megan said.

He sat back down heavily, as if defeated. "It's not your fault. It was a fisherman who found her. He hooked his line on her wheelchair."

"Wheelchair?" Megan asked, transfixed as she sat back down as well.

"Yes. Her pelvic bone was fractured in an automobile accident in November of last year. It caused her to miss a great deal of school, so she stayed on campus after the usual break to make up her missed work and take finals. She was very independent and didn't want anyone to feel sorry for her. She was a varsity volleyball player," the man said with pride. "Here's her picture."

Megan held the frame in her hand. Staring back at her was a confident, energetic young woman.

"She went to a New Year's party. She drank too much, they said, which I find hard to believe. She didn't like to drink and was on medication for her fracture. They told me she lost control of her wheelchair and ended up in the lake. From there the gators took over."

"What?" Lacy asked. "I thought gators didn't usually bite people."

"They don't," the man said. "They told me she was dead already when they began to eat her."

"Ohmygod," Megan gasped. "I'm so sorry." Even after she said it, she knew it was inadequate, but words escaped her. There seemed to be nothing that could console that sort of loss.

*   *   *

They left the man to mourn in private and climbed back into what they now fondly referred to as the miniegg. Lacy situated herself the best she could and tried not to complain. A serious challenge, since it was totally against her nature. "That was creepy."

"For sure. His daughter's been missing for over three months, then yesterday he was informed she was dead. It's a very hard thing to deal with. The rest of the world goes on as normal while yours has come to a screeching halt. He knows to the police it's officially a closed case. To him it will remain a festering wound. I only wish the other department had been quicker with the communication. We could have spared him this extra pain. What a horrible way to go."

Lacy nodded. She presumed her partner spoke from personal experience. "You know, sometimes it's best to let the past go, especially if it adversely effects the present," Lacy said.

Megan looked at her and said, "You're right. We have forty-eight hours and two possible matches to go. I need to forget my connection to these people. I can do this. I can catch this son of a bitch."

"It's OK. I thought this was the girl too. Disappointment and frustration are normal for cases like this. But I have to say, this one threw me for a loop," Lacy said.

"I know, she physically fit the profile so closely. Then to find out her pelvic bone was broken in a car accident this past November. If we'd known that, we wouldn't have had to bother."

"And that girl had it all together. She was an athlete, good-looking, and smart," Lacy said. "I'm surprised she drank that night."

"I think that was part of the problem. She wasn't used to it. Along with her medication, she might have lost perspective," Megan said. "It was New Year's Eve. Everyone was drinking. She might have had very little, but it was enough to throw off her reflexes."

"Champagne can go straight to your head. I wish someone had walked her home."

"I imagine that's one of the many 'what ifs' that runs through her friends' minds constantly."

"Too bad she hit her head on that rock. She might have survived otherwise. That wheelchair must have weighed her down. But what about the gators? I thought you said they don't bite."

"They don't usually. But that lake is infested. They're big and not afraid of humans."

"I have to tell you, it freaks me out. I never heard of anyone being eaten by gators."

"As he said, she was probably already dead before they began to feed on her. That lake has a lot of benches around where people eat lunch. They get used to equating humans with food."

Lacy gave an involuntary shiver, shook her head, and said, "Alright, Melissa Stanley is next."

Megan read the address then consulted a map. "Her family lives across town."

"I say we eat first. I'm starving. Not to mention disappointed. That always makes me want to eat. I need food. Besides, it's half past twelve."

"OK, OK. We can stop up here and grab a sub," Megan said.

"That sounds good, and ice cream too. There's nothing better than ice cream to drown out your sorrows and console yourself."

Megan rolled her eyes and pulled in the parking lot of the sub shop when Lacy's cell rang. Reluctantly she answered, only because it was the chief.

"Andina."

"What is this I hear about some hair sample?"

"Oh shit."

"What? What did you say?"

"Nothing, sir."

Megan didn't have to wait for her partner to tell her who it was or what he wanted. The man yelled so loudly, she could hear him clearly from where she sat.

"That old woman wasn't connected to these murders."

"Yes, sir. We're working on it now, but it seems as if she might actually be connected."

"Well, for god's sake, come up with some damn proof. I've got the mayor and Justice Howard breathing down my neck. I don't want the fear of home invasions or vigilante action. I understand people want action. The courts take time and are backed up, then there's plea bargains. I need you to find this killer."

"Yes, sir," Lacy said.

"Do something, and do it fast."

187

Lacy heard a click. She pushed End on her cell, then looked over at Megan.

"I heard," Megan said before Lacy could speak.

"I think that man needs some ice cream real bad. He seriously needs to chill out."

"He's in a tight situation. He's being pressured," Megan said. "Everyone wants answers."

Megan could feel her eye begin to twitch again. Why was it always her left eye?

"He has to understand we're doing all we can," Lacy said.

"He's anxious. He has a lot on his plate."

"Your eye's twitching again," Lacy said. "That's not good. You realize high blood pressure can kill you. Have you had your pressure taken lately?"

"I've been kind of busy. Besides, I'm more worried about a stroke than a heart attack."

"We can stop in one of those drugstores and take it after lunch," Lacy said.

Megan sat there for a moment, blankly staring at the brick pattern of the building in front of her. It gave no answers to her life's questions. Then an answer arose to one of her problems. "Oh, an outside outlet!" Megan said, brightening. "You think they'd mind if we plug the car in while we eat? I think the battery's low."

"I don't see a problem with it. It can't use much power."

Megan hopped out, unwound the cord, and plugged the car in. Then they walked into the small sub shop and took a booth in the back where there was less traffic, and they could talk freely.

"I plan to sit in on Mary Pearl's autopsy," Megan said. "The cause of death may be cardiac arrest, but the manner of death lies up in the air. My bet is homicide."

Lacy was about to say something when the waitress came. They gave their order and waited for the woman to leave before they continued.

"All the power to you. We need to ID the killer soon," Lacy said.

"I worry about Beth. She and my nephews live in the middle of all this, and right now Mather is busy picking peanuts. He's hardly ever at home."

"Well, hopefully one of these last two missing persons will be a match. Once we get a name, we can work on who saw her last. You know, the usual friends-and-family interview stuff."

The waitress brought their food, and Lacy wasted no time digging in. Megan watched in amazement. "How do you eat like that and stay so tiny?"

"What are you talking about? You're the same size as I am," Lacy said. She wiped at a big glob of mayonnaise with her napkin and set back to work on her sub.

"I have to watch what I eat. *Plus* I run every day, and my life sucks from constant stress."

"I read if you exercise too much, you actually increase your risk of getting cancer."

"What? That's not true. People who don't exercise made that up," Megan said.

"No, really, I'm serious. It's supposed to affect your immune system. In this instance, more is not better. The research states mild to moderate exercise stimulates your immune system, but excess exertion suppresses it. It leaves you more susceptible to things like colds and even cancer."

"Well, that still doesn't explain why you can eat so much and not have to buy new clothes."

"Good genes. I have a naturally high metabolism. I plan to enjoy it while it lasts," Lacy said. Then took another bite of her sub.

24

The dried palm fronds rustled in the breeze, creating an eerie sound. Night was falling fast, and the shadows grew deeper by the second. He crept through the dense undergrowth, crossed the dark tannic waters of a small creek, then headed toward the house. It was the dry season, so the movement of the water was lazy. An almost imperceptible pace. The banks were dense with rotting vegetation, weeds, and hyacinths. He tried not to make any noise as he cut through the thick muck, but it was so viscous it threatened to suck his shoes off with each step. He realized he'd have to find another way out if a quick escape route was necessary.

He was close enough to smell supper cooking. His nerves were on edge, and he noticed a slight tremble in his hand. The faint sound of muted voices and country music floated from the home. This was not how it was supposed to be. His intentions were to come here when no one was home. It seemed simple enough earlier that afternoon. But now, actually being here, it became apparent he hadn't thought things out so well.

It all started when he'd spotted the car at Parker's garage. The place was on his path home from school. They had a drink machine that was not only the coldest in town, it was still only twenty-five cents, which fit his budget. He bought his usual, then sat on a pile of tires to drink it. Parker's daughter, Katie Elizabeth, would often come by, which was an added bonus. She had the bluest eyes he'd ever seen.

While he looked around, trying to act real hard like he didn't care if he saw the little girl or not, he spotted the car. Not just any red car, but *the* red car. The same one he and his friends had seen while they'd been hidden in the fort. He was almost sure of it.

It was up on one of the lifts, and Gabe, the head mechanic, was pounding out a dent in the rear quarter panel. Edward Lee's heart froze for a moment, and he almost choked on his drink. He wasn't sure what to do, only that he had to do something.

He willed himself to calm down. There was no use to panic. He could be wrong. Odds had it, the car probably belonged to someone other than the killer. After all, red was a popular color for a vehicle. He'd given it considerable thought and planned to get a red sports car when he was old enough, and he certainly was no killer. He'd almost talked himself into letting it go. But the thing was, the timing was too perfect. This was the first business day after the Easter holiday.

He knew about the red car scraping a tree because Coop had gone out there Easter Sunday to look for evidence to back up his story and found it. His friend reassured him that he'd told no one about what happened in the tree fort, but that the killer would still be caught. Although Edward Lee appreciated Cooper's loyalty and not betraying his confidence, he wasn't sure how he could be so sure the killer would be caught without telling the cops what he knew. If this car did belong to the killer, evidence was being erased as he watched, and he was the only one that understood the significance. He couldn't stand by and do nothing, so he sauntered over to Gabe.

"Hey, you. You're not supposed to be back here in the work area," Gabe scolded as soon as he noticed the boy from the corner of his eye. "You better git before we both get in trouble."

"I know, but I wanna watch. I'll be careful and stay out of your way, promise."

Edward Lee's voice cracked from nerves, but Gabe didn't seem to pay any attention. Perhaps he attributed it to his age, or it was also possible he plain didn't care.

"So whatcha doing?"

This time Gabe stopped and looked over at Edward Lee with a frown on his face. "What's it look like, boy? I'm working, trying to fix a dent."

Edward Lee didn't want to push his luck. Gabe had a reputation of not getting on with kids all that well since he had none of his own. He seemed especially grumpy today. He also didn't want to be obvious. That might lead to unwanted attention and questions. All he needed to know was who owned the car, and that would be on some sort of paperwork.

"Sorry, didn't mean to sound stupid. I was thinking about being a mechanic when I grow up. I think it seems like a real cool job. I like cars, especially fast ones."

Gabe glared over at Edward Lee, shook his head, then turned back to his work. "It's all right I guess. It pays the bills, and you could do worse. If you getcha a good fan, the heat's not so bad in the summer. Nice to have a radio too."

Gabe ducked underneath the vehicle to work from the inside, so Edward Lee took advantage of the opportunity and looked over the papers on the side bench. He couldn't see a name, but there was an address. It was close to his house, on the same road.

That's when he made the decision to come here. He wanted to figure out if this was where the killer lived. If it was, he could tell Cooper about it. He would end up a local hero. Katie Elizabeth would have to notice him then.

But as he hid in the deepening dusk, it didn't seem like such a smart idea. At least not to come alone. He should have asked Roy or Pete to come along for backup, but he'd been in a hurry. He felt his jeans for the cell phone his mother gave him. It wasn't there. He must have left it in his school pants when he ran home to change. He could kick himself for his stupidity now. This was too dangerous. He was in way over his head. He didn't even know if they had a dog. The one thing he did believe was, if this was the killer's house and he got caught, the man would kill him, just as he had murdered the others. No one would ever know because he hadn't told a soul where he was going.

He started to back away. Slowly at first, then as the distance increased, so did the speed of his departure. He crossed through a patch of light that cascaded down from a window. His pulse was rapid and his breath shallow. He feared that if he breathed too deeply, they would hear him. Within seconds, he was back in the shadows against a shed. It smelled terrible. He figured they must dump their trash or something out here.

He could see a figure move about through what he believed to be the kitchen window. He assumed it was the guy's wife. She must not have noticed him, or she would have hollered. This made him feel better, and he took a deep breath in relief before he turned to go.

It was in that instant he felt a large hand cover his mouth. He couldn't see his assailant, but in his gut he knew exactly who it was and that no one would ever hear from him again. He struggled with all his might, but he was no match for his captor. He was being dragged around the corner into the dark shadows. With a wet rag placed over his nose and mouth, there was no way he could cry out for help or even breathe. No matter how hard he fought, he couldn't manage to get free. His mind became foggy, and his limbs became weak. Then his world went dark, and he thought and felt nothing.

25

Cooper walked outside into the breaking dawn. The air smelled clean from the recent rain, and the grass was a lush, vibrant green. Nelly looked up and snorted, then put her snout in the air to sniff for food possibilities. Coop sat down on the top step next to her and scratched her head. It was hard to explain to people why he had a pig for a pet, but darned if he didn't love her, along with all her peculiar ways and eccentric personality. The animal made little grunting noises of appreciation as he rubbed her, content to let it go on for as long as her master had time.

He stood to begin the day's work when Megan drove up in her old truck. He watched curiously as she parked and strode over. Nelly rocked herself back and forth in an effort to stand. The animal recognized the sound of the truck and instantly correlated it with a tasty treat.

"What brings you out here this early?" He glanced at his watch. "It's not quite 7:00 a.m."

"I came out to check on you and make sure everything was all right."

Nelly ambled over to Megan, snorting, and rooted in her pocket for the treasure she was certain would be there. Megan, being one to never let anyone down, even a pig, came through and retrieved the sought-after treat. "Here you go, girl," she said, then walked up to Cooper.

"I'm fine, but you look like you lost your best friend," Cooper said. "And where's your boss?"

"She's home. I plan to swing by to pick her up after I leave here."

Megan looked over at him curiously. If she didn't have such a pressing concern, she might have pursued his interest in Lacy. Unfortunately, what brought her out here was far more serious.

"I'm out here on official business."

"Oh? That doesn't sound good. Especially considering the hour. This isn't about zoning, is it?"

"What? No. I tried calling but didn't get an answer or the machine. What's up with that?"

"House got hit by lightning in the storm Sunday. I haven't had a chance to replace them yet. What's so important? You seem pretty damn anxious. Are you here to arrest me over the bones?"

"No. It's Edward Lee. His mother called the station late last night to report him missing."

Cooper stared at her in disbelief. His worst fears were being played out, and he couldn't stop it from happening. "Are you sure?" he asked and sat down heavily on the steps.

"Yes, but I had held out hope he was with you or that you might have some idea where he was. That was until I saw the look on your face just now," Megan said and walked over and sat next to him. "I swear, Coop, I know you didn't have anything to do with this."

"What? Is that what people think still? That I'm the killer? That I would hurt a child?"

"OK, here's the thing. We know a killer is using this area as his dump site. There is reason to believe he might live in this area as well. I know it can't be you. You love Edward Lee like a son."

"Why do I sense a 'but'?"

"Because Lacy saw you Easter Sunday leaving the area we had a lead on."

"The abandoned peanut field," Cooper stated deadpan. How could he explain that?

"So you admit you were out there? But why?"

"Edward Lee told me this crazy story. I needed to check it out."

"Why didn't you say anything to Lacy or me?"

Cooper ran his hands through his hair. "I don't know. Stupid I guess. I didn't want the boys caught up in this. I figured if I went out there I could find something to go to the police with, and they would be removed from it. I saw the red paint and tire tracks, and after the party, I was gonna tell you about it, but I got distracted by all the commotion. It wasn't much, and it could have been there for years for all I knew. Well, not the tracks. But a lot of tractors are red, and it used to be a farm. I figured the tracts were from a poacher more than likely."

"Well, I know your tractor's not red."

"But my father's car is. It's out in the shed, if you want to take a look at it."

"I don't have to. I believe you. Besides, a lot of people have red cars. Even Nate," Megan said. "Tell me more. What happened? What was the crazy story Edward Lee told you?"

Cooper went on to explain the entire story. Then how he went to verify or deny the children's accusations. And how they planned to capture the killer on their own. "So now it's your turn."

"I wish I had answers. That's what I've been trying to figure out all night. He was at school yesterday, and one of the teachers saw him head off in the usual direction. His mother worked a double shift at Angel's diner and didn't get home until past ten last night. At first she thought he was in bed asleep, since he'd apparently never made his bed that morning, it was lumpy. She didn't turn on the light when she checked on him, afraid it would wake him," Megan said.

"Then about two o'clock last night, she got up to get a drink of juice. When she opened the refrigerator, his supper was still there, untouched. That's when she realized something was terribly wrong. She said that boy never misses a meal. Even if he ate over Roy's house, he would have still eaten the meal she'd left for him. She said she could barely afford to keep enough food in the house. She ran to his room, flicked on the lights, only to reveal a messed-up, empty bed."

"Oh, shit," Cooper said and ran his hand through his hair again.

Megan noted his reaction and continued, "The sheets were cold. She'd hoped he'd recently gotten up to meet his friends or something. Anyway, she was out of her mind with worry by the time she called the station. They, in turn, called me since they figured I know both her and you."

"Me? Because they think I took him?"

"Some do. His mother doesn't. Others know he works for you, so if he ran away, he might have come here. But I think the general consensus is he ran away on some adventure. His mother is on a major guilt trip for having to work all the time, and he's kind of a latchkey kid. There's even a question pending about lack of adult supervision of a minor."

"You mean she may be in trouble? But it's not her fault. She's a widow. She loves that boy."

"I know, and so do you," Megan said.

"What do we do now? We know what the boys saw. Are the other boys in danger too?"

"I'll give their folks a call, make sure they're safe, and advise them to stay near their parents."

"The bastard got him," Cooper said.

It was the same thing Megan felt deep in her heart, but she couldn't accept it, not yet anyway.

"You don't know that."

"Edward Lee doesn't take off by himself in the middle of the night. If he was on an adventure, he would have left a note, or Roy or Pete would be with him. He wouldn't worry his mom like that. He loves her too much. He's all alone out there somewhere," Cooper said. "Something bad happened."

"We'll find him. And Edward Lee has you to count on too. If the killer took the boy, he must live close by. If he has him, he's within a few miles of this house. We'll find him."

"This is all my fault. He trusted me, and I let him down. I should have shown you the paint."

"Stop it. Lacy and I found the paint on our own. Edward Lee came to you for help, and you did that. The only doubt we had was why you were out there so early on a Sunday morning, and you answered that. So the only way you could have let him down was to be the killer. This has nothing to do with you," Megan said. "You're not thinking clearly. This is no time for guilt trips: focus!"

Cooper sat up straight, then turned to Megan and said, "You're right. We need to find him. Send out a search party or something."

"First, let's think this through. He was at school and left in the usual direction. He must have seen something on his way home."

"Heck, he might have tried to call me, but like I said, my phone was out," Cooper said.

Megan sat there, thinking. A child was lost, possibly abducted by a serial killer. She had to take her own advice and focus, remain unemotional. This wasn't about her, it was about Edward Lee.

"It has to be something to do with the car," Megan stated. "That's all they saw right?"

"Maybe he saw it at school and recognized whose it was. Maybe it was a teacher's. You said it might be someone who lives close to us. Edward Lee knows everyone who lives around here. He might have even felt safe enough to talk to the creep or followed him into his home," Cooper suggested.

"It could have been in the school parking lot, the pickup line, or it might have drove past him on his way home. He had to be on foot. What's his usual route home from school?" Megan asked.

"I'm not real sure. We need to talk to Pete. They go to the same school, and they live close by. He might know the way Edward Lee walks home. If we retrace his steps, we just might see the same thing he did," Cooper said.

However, the fear lingered in both their hearts that even if they did find the child, it would be too late.

26

Megan paused outside the two large metal doors. This was where she had to make a decision. Her responsibility was to find a serial killer, and she had less than forty-eight hours to do it. To further complicate matters, a little boy's fate lay in the balance. By her sitting in on an autopsy of what seemed to be an unrelated case, it might appear to others as a waste of time, but her gut told her that both Mary Pearl's death and Edward Lee's disappearance were connected to the killer.

But as Lacy had pointed out, she needed proof. It was her bet the autopsy would reveal such. She took a deep breath and forged on through the double doors to enter the morgue. As she did, one of the assistants looked up. At first, Megan didn't recognize her friend through all the required protective gear of surgical gown, gloves, mask, and hairnet. The huge body on the gurney in front of her didn't help either as it created an obstructive mound.

"Hey, Megan," a petite woman said from behind the covered corpse.

Immediately Megan recognized the voice. "Hey, Beverly. I haven't seen you in a long time. How's motherhood?"

"Great. What's not so wonderful is coming back to this place on a few hours of sleep a night."

"It does look as if you've got your hands full."

"Yeah, I just weighed this guy. Do you believe he came in at three twenty? I had to make sure I wasn't standing on the scale pad with him. So what brings you here anyway?"

"A case I'm working on." It was a bit of a stretch, but Megan didn't see the point in explaining the nuances of her minor deception. "I wanted to sit in on the Mary Pearl Harkin autopsy."

Beverly cocked her small head to the side. Megan wasn't sure if it was in confusion. As a general rule, if a person dies while alone, such as Mary Pearl had, an autopsy would be performed to determine the cause of death. If foul play is suspected, then a more complete form of autopsy would be carried out, which would involve further toxicology tests. If the manner of death is determined to be homicide, then a detective is assigned to the case. Megan had not been assigned to Mary Pearl's case, so technically, there was no reason for her to be here.

"Let me think—that's right. She's set up ready to go in suite B. Rodney's the assistant for Doc Evans today."

Megan headed off in that direction, relieved by her friend's lack of interest. Evidently, she had more important things on her mind.

"Oh, Megan, wait," Beverly called out.

Megan stopped dead in her tracks, then turned slowly around to find Beverly staring at her, hands on her hips. *Great,* Megan thought, *she realized I have no business with Mary Pearl's autopsy.* Megan was about to say something in defense when Beverly beat her to it.

"Evans won't be in suite B yet. He's with Rodney in D. They're finishing up on a little boy," she said.

"A boy?" Megan asked. It came out more like a croak. Her stomach knotted, and her breath was jagged.

Beverly noted Megan's distress. "Yeah, it's tragic when we get them so young."

With that, her friend turned and gave a strained effort to wheel her oversized load around the corner. Megan momentarily stood frozen, unable to move. She had come to view Mary Pearl's autopsy, not Edward Lee's. Her knees felt weak, and her stomach lurched.

She had an urge to turn and bolt. Take herself back into the sunshine and fresh air. To leave the cold ugliness of this place far behind. But that wasn't possible. She had an obligation to those women who died. The victims all had loved ones whose lives were forever changed by their death. It was up to her to assuage their doubts and find the answers to their unresolved questions. The only way for her to deal with this was to face it head-on. If it turned out to be Edward Lee in there, people had to be notified. Answers had to be found. With renewed determination, she spun around on her heel and took off in the direction of suite D.

When she got to the door, she peered in the small square window before she entered. From that vantage point, she viewed Rodney arranging samples on the side counter, labeling them with fastidious care. She assumed they were to be sent off to histology, pathology, toxicology, or some other laboratory for evaluation. She saw Dr. Evans's wide back. He was hunched over a small body. It was evident from the mass of blood and body parts lying on the table that he'd been at it awhile. It made the corpse impossible to identify. Megan knocked softly and walked in.

Rodney nodded in acknowledgment. The doctor looked over his shoulder at the sound of the door. "Ah, an audience," he said in a pleasant voice, which was his usual temperament.

It fascinated Megan how the man could remain so easygoing and cheerful under these conditions. "I hope I'm not bothering you," Megan said.

The doctor had classical music playing softly, but the harsh lighting along with all the stainless steel and odorous chemicals took away any soothing effect.

Intermittently, the drain which sucked away the body fluids from the trough at the foot of the autopsy table gurgled. She found it unnerving. In contrast, Evans seemed quite relaxed and content as he continued to work, elbow deep in the child's intestines. He was in his element and well suited to his profession.

"What can I do for you, Detective?" He didn't bother to look up as he spoke, which was also his custom. Megan had sat in on several of his autopsies in the hopes of one day making detective. He worked in a similar manner to Jerry. He liked to narrate as he went about his duties. Megan found this not only informative, but it helped to detract from the macabre reality.

"I had a missing boy come across my desk as a case last night. I wanted to verify if this was him or not," Megan said.

"Pull up a stool and take a load off. I'll tell you what I know so far."

Megan did as instructed but cringed when the stool made a hideous squeak as it scraped across the tile. The sound ricocheted off the stainless steel counters like a bullet. Rodney shot her an annoyed look, then went back to his labeling. He'd yet to speak.

Evans continued without pause. "I don't have a name. You know how it is with kids—don't carry wallets, let their parents pay for everything. Got to love them."

Again, it was a good-natured comment, meant in mirth. It reminded Megan that the doctor had two daughters in college. "How are your girls anyway?"

"Good, good. They work hard at school, make good grades. I can't complain. I know other parents who have kids on drugs, getting into trouble, having babies when they hit puberty. No, I can't complain. I've got two great girls. They make me proud."

As Megan listened to him, she felt envious of his daughters. To be loved like that was something she would never know again. With both parents dead, that part of her life had ended. She shook off her personal melancholy and focused back on work. It was always safer ground and what she felt more comfortable with.

"So what do you have?"

"I plan to find another piece of that information out right now."

The doctor pulled out his Stryker saw, and Rodney plugged it in. He proceeded to cut through a piece of bone, which left a cloud of nasty dense funk in the air. Megan watched as it moved across the room toward her. She didn't want to act like a wimp, but the last time a cloud of bone dust hit her, it took two days to wash the hideous smell off. Todd, her ex-boyfriend, wouldn't have anything to do with her. Definitely a situation she wished to avoid if at all possible. She leaned as far forward as she could while the vile cloud floated past.

"I set the PMI at twelve hours when they found him," the doctor said.

"Him?" She had held out some hope it was a girl. That way it couldn't be Edward Lee, clear and simple. Unfortunately, the postmortem interval, a term used to indicate how long a person has been deceased, fit into the time of disappearance for Edward Lee.

"Yes. Unlike with adult assault cases, where the majority of victims are female, this is a young male."

Megan felt her throat tighten.

Evans, unaware of Megan's distress, continued with his monologue, "Yes, his body temp was 80.6 when they found him, so with the ambient temp, I place him at twelve hours. In children under thirteen, which is my guess for this lad, the most reliable age indicator is the degree of wrist development. I had Rodney snap a few radiographs for me. This would be a good time to take a look-see. I could also show you the initial preop snapshots. You might be able to determine from those if this is your boy or not if you have a visual for comparison."

Megan was only able to nod as she watched the doctor walk over to the sink and wash up. He cleaned off in a methodical fashion, as with everything else he did, while he continued to speak.

"Rodney should have those films for us shortly. In the meantime, I noted the stage of tooth development in this case. He was beginning to get his first premolars but not his canines. That would make him around ten. However, I am seeing an acceleration of development in some ethnic populations."

"Did Rodney take any dental radiographs?" Megan asked.

"Yes, yes, of course. I run a tight ship here. I run poor Rodney ragged."

"Oh, I didn't mean to imply," Megan stammered.

Doctor Evans held up a cleanly scrubbed hand. "No need to explain, dear. I understand. I must say though, this child was from a low socioeconomic group."

"What makes you say that?"

"His dental condition. He had poor oral hygiene. Sad, really. It's so easy and inexpensive to brush one's teeth on a daily basis. A child just has to be taught, that's all, very simple."

"Maybe it's a family thing. He might have been going through a rebellious phase," Megan said.

"It's more than that. He had stainless steel crowns on permanent teeth. That's just not done anymore unless a child is on public assistance."

"You mean Medicaid?"

"Exactly. No fee-for-service doctor would ever place a stainless steel crown anymore. They have been replaced by more modern and aesthetic resin or porcelain crowns. Of course they cost more, so the government adheres to the archaic, cheaper version. This poor child had several. That means for one, his home care was poor; and secondly, his dental care was government based."

Megan's stomach did a flip. Edward Lee and his mother were struggling financially. She was forced to work long hours. Did that mean there was no one there to make sure he brushed every morning or at night before bed? Had he had dental problems? She didn't know. For some reason, it caused a stab of guilt. She lived in a community she wanted to think of as tight-knit, but in reality, she didn't really know her neighbors or their private struggles.

"Was this child a minority?" Megan said.

"No, Caucasian," Evans said. Then he turned and picked up a stack of photos from the counter. "This is what he looked like."

Megan was afraid to look, but before she could turn away, the doctor had the photos in front of her. The little boy had reddish hair and hazel eyes. Megan breathed out a sigh of relief. Edward Lee had dark brown hair and eyes. This child couldn't be him. It still didn't answer the question of where Edward Lee was or who the child on the slab was. Yet to find out it wasn't Edward Lee gave her a slight bit of consolation.

Dr. Evans looked at Megan and leaned against the counter with his arms folded across his chest. He had noted her behavior. "Now, are you going to tell me what this is really all about?"

Megan should have expected this. Evans was sharp and missed nothing. That's what made him so good at his job. He was also a fair man, who tried to remain nonpolitical in his work. She had no reason to be less than forthright; she could trust him.

"I was actually here to sit in on the Harkin autopsy when Beverly told me you were in here working up a child case. A little boy I know showed up missing last night. He was last seen leaving the school grounds yesterday. I believe his disappearance and the Harkin case are connected."

Evans shot one bushy eyebrow up in question. In the past, he'd equated Megan with good, sound judgment. This, however, seemed a stretch. "Really. I haven't started the Harkin case yet, but the prelim notes given to me indicate the woman more than likely died of a heart attack. Surely you don't think the child had anything to do with it."

Megan's eyes widened for a moment. "No, no, that's not what I meant."

"Perhaps you should explain while we wait for Rodney to return with the radiographic data," Dr. Evans said while gesturing to a stool as he took an adjacent one.

Megan perched on the offered seat. "Of course. You see, I don't believe Mary Pearl's death was purely natural." Megan paused to watch what effect these words had on the doctor. He seemed to listen and remained unfazed by her suggestion. She ventured a guess that at this point in his career, he'd seen it all. Every possible act of depravity and violence one human could inflict on another. She explained about Mary Pearl's story of the red car and the evidence Lacy and she had found to verify it. "It's information that might ultimately lead to the killer's capture."

"And the boy? How does he fit into all this?" the doctor asked.

Megan hesitated for a moment. "I'll give you the abridged version."

Evans nodded, not moving from his listening stance.

"The boy saw the same red car. His story backs up, or I should say, backed up Mary Pearl's."

"The same information that you think got the Harkin woman killed."

"Yes," Megan said.

"I'm almost through here. You're welcome to sit in on the next case, but I must warn you, don't push me. I find what's in front of me, not what you, as the detective, want to hear."

"Yes, sir, I understand."

Evans wasn't sure that he agreed with the connections Megan had made or the fact that Mary Pearl died from anything other than natural causes. That would be determined soon enough. "I know how you get when you get your teeth into a case such as this one, Megan. I feel it necessary to reiterate my warning and add that anything I say in there is off the record, unless specified."

Megan nodded and knew enough to keep her mouth shut. She would accept whatever Evans determined. He was thorough, unbiased, and wanted the same end result as Megan. That was for Ocala to once again be safe and free from the evil that currently stalked their community.

"As you know, Detective, it would not be appropriate to speculate on the manner of death prior to performing a complete autopsy and evaluation of all the lab results. It's the combination of the details of both the clinical and diagnostic findings that I use to ascertain the true cause and time of death. I don't want you to jump to conclusions and going off half-cocked, leaving me to explain your actions."

"I promise not to push. I'm sorry if I came across that way. It's just that this is not only a serial killer we're dealing with. He's a monster. He tortures, possibly rapes, then dismembers his victims while they are still alive so they can suffer and witness their own death."

The doctor nodded his head. "Yes, I consulted with Jerry about both sets of skeletal remains. I appreciate and understand your desire to catch this person as soon as possible. And, of course, I'll do whatever I can. I have a family and live in the same community as you. I have the same fears and concerns. Give me a few minutes to tie up a few loose ends here and let Rodney ready suite B."

"Thank you," Megan said and left Rodney and the doctor to finish up with the child. At least now she knew the boy wasn't Edward Lee.

27

While Megan stayed at the morgue to wait, she called Lacy. They'd decided the best use of their time was to split up. Megan was to sit in on the autopsy, and Lacy planned to interview the last possible missing-person case. Megan paced as she waited for her partner to pick up.

"Lacy," a cheery voice answered.

"Wow, you sound like you're in a good mood," Megan said, still pacing.

"I am. I'm with Jerry at the lab. I think we might have our first real break," Lacy said.

"Please tell me. I could use some good news for a change."

"That's what you get for hanging around the morgue."

"Very funny."

"The last girl on our list could be a match to the remains found at Cooper's peach farm."

"You're kidding. What's her name?"

"Heather Daily, and so far she's a perfect fit. The height was right on, the time of disappearance is off, but then again our guy might be messing with that. Anyway, no births or notable history of trauma, and you'll like this the best." Lacy paused for effect.

"What? Do you expect a drumroll?"

"God. Sometimes you're just no fun," Lacy said. "Anyway, I got a hair sample from the girl's brush. Jerry's doing a preliminary evaluation to see if it matches the hair found at the site."

"I thought Jerry said that was the killer's."

"That was there too, but remember the CSU found a few other strands. One was in the Wal-Mart bag, and the other was in the muck at the Phillipses' place. So far, Jerry thinks the peach-farm one could be a match. He's going to send them off for DNA comparison."

"Wow, that *is* encouraging but not exactly within our forty-eight-hour time frame. Those test results will take weeks."

"True, but I'm on my way to the girl's dentist with the postmortem radiographs. We should know within the hour if we've identified our first victim or not. How's that for speed?"

Megan spotted Dr. Evans down the hall. He gave her a come-along gesture with a beefy arm before he disappeared into suite B. "That's great, but I've got to go," Megan said and snapped her cell phone closed, turned off her ringer, then scurried off after Dr. Evans.

She practically entered the room on his heels, spotted a stool close to the examination area, and claimed it in the hopes it would be out of their way. Evans had already begun to assess the body on the table. Rodney had previously taken the obligatory photographs. A set with the victim, as delivered, and one naked. Mary Pearl lay prone on the cold stainless-steel table in preparation for her autopsy. They went through a few minutes of run-of-the-mill dictation. The older woman's height, weight, age, and general overall impressions were given by the doctor.

Megan's breath caught in her throat with her own impressions as Mary Pearl lay lifeless and cold on the autopsy table, under harsh fluorescent lighting. The woman, who was once so dynamic and vibrant, looked small and frail. A mere fraction of what she'd been in life. The powerful personality she displayed as recently as yesterday was drained from her body, just as her life had been. Now a faded memory.

With the aid of Rodney, Evans arranged the body on its side to evaluate the back. "You can see there are no signs of trauma here," he said, more or less to himself and the tape recorder which he used to reference and make notations. "The purple discoloration is due to livor mortis. This pooling of the blood demonstrates that she was on her back at the time of death. Which, as the report indicates, was how she was found."

Since Megan was the one to discover her body, she already knew this but restrained from remark. Dr. Evans was methodical and thorough. He liked to proceed in a certain order, and she didn't want to disrupt his thought process or irritate the man.

The two returned the body to its original position. Megan was again struck by how tiny the woman seemed in the doctor's gloved hands. Nonetheless, her back made a slapping sound as it met with the flat metal table.

Next Evans went to the head. Megan's eyes were fixated on the doctor's movements, searching for the proof she knew had to be there. Hoping for something to back up her theory.

"The scalp appears to be within normal limits," he said as he gently moved the hair around to better view the skin beneath. Then he paused. "Humm, this is a bit odd."

"What? What do you see?" Megan asked. She leaned in as close as she dared.

"Looks to be a small patch of petechiae here on the temporal aspect of her scalp."

"What does that mean?" Megan asked, confused. "Did that mean Mary Pearl had dandruff, or was it something more relevant?"

Dr. Evans flipped down a pair of loupes he wore strapped around his forehead. The small but powerful magnifying eyepieces allowed him a closer view of the area in question.

"No, this looks more hemorrhagic with slight crusting. Rodney, we need to get a few photos of the area."

"So she has a scab on her head? Could it be from a fall?"

"You mean like she collapsed and hit her head when she had the heart attack?"

"Something like that, or maybe she was pushed," Megan dared to suggest.

"No, that would leave an entirely different kind of mark. This was caused from a patch of her hair being pulled out. It happened while she was still alive. Thus, the slight scab."

"Could it indicate a struggle?"

Evans surprised Megan with a slight chuckle. "Yes, more than likely. You hear of people pulling their hair out, but from my experience, it doesn't usually happen. However, Detective, don't jump to any conclusions. It's my understanding that her home was broken into, and she had a heart attack as a result. A struggle would fit in with that scenario," the doctor stated.

They both watched while Rodney did his thing with the camera before Dr. Evans resumed his efforts.

"There was no remarkable amount of blood at the scene," Megan said.

"We're talking about a fistful of hair. That doesn't cause an overt hemorrhage. We have mild irritation and a minor scab in the involved area. It may not amount to anything," Dr. Evans said.

Megan sat there and couldn't help but notice that Mary Pearl's eyes were sunken in, the expression on her face frozen in terror. Was it because the criminal startled her? Had she recognized the intruder and feared him? Megan thought not. The older woman feared no one. Perhaps she did have a heart attack and realized it was fatal. Would she be afraid to die? Again, Megan thought not. Mary Pearl was a devout Christian. Although she might not want to die, death was something that would be accepted and welcome if her Lord chose to call her home.

"Ah, this may be something," Evans said. It shook Megan out of her thoughts.

Megan leaned in closer to see what the doctor was talking about and whispered, "What?"

"A broken nail. Recent I would say. All the others are trimmed and polished smooth. This one has jagged edges."

"As if it were broken in a struggle?"

Evans shot her a warning look.

"Sorry."

"It's possible," the doctor conceded. "I should have noted it on general impressions. It slipped past me. Anyway, it could have been broken in any number of ways. The woman lived in the country and was very active. She liked to garden. Grew the finest tomatoes I've ever eaten."

This was the first remark that revealed Dr. Evans knew Mary Pearl personally. It was more than just the Harkin case to him as well. He knew she enjoyed work in the garden. He had eaten the result of her efforts. If that was true, he would also realize if the woman's nail had been broken off in the yard earlier that day, she would have smoothed it off. She was a neat freak.

It seemed the doctor already had similar thoughts because he began to take samples from underneath her nails. That indicated he gave some credence to foul play and sought true answers.

The external exam went on as such for the next thirty-five minutes without event. Then Dr. Evans flipped his loupes down once more. Megan leaned forward to see what was going on.

"Rodney, the camera," Evans barked.

Megan leaned even farther, so far she slipped off the stool but managed to catch herself before she fell to the floor. She wanted to ask what he was talking about but feared being exiled.

"What do you want me to photograph?" Rodney asked.

Bless you, Megan thought.

"This," Evans said, pointing. "It's a recent injection site. On the back of the upper arm."

"That's hardly an area Mary Pearl could access herself," Megan said. She regretted the words as soon as they were out of her mouth. She'd thought out loud.

"True, Detective, but more important is the fact that this individual did not have a history of diabetes or any other condition that would require injection-type medication. She also displays no other needle marks other than fairly old ones in the medial aspect of her arm. That's the normal site of routine blood retrieval for medical testing."

Megan let out a deep breath in a sigh of relief. It seemed as if she and Dr. Evans were now on the same page. "Are you going to do a toxicology screen on her?"

"Circumstances dictate it now. This is no longer a simple cardiac arrest. This needle mark could indicate foul play. We may be dealing with a homicide here. That requires a complete toxicology workup. I don't like the look of this."

Megan didn't know whether to be relieved, thrilled, or scared to death for her family. If Mary Pearl was murdered by the serial killer, no one in their community was safe, especially Beth.

"Rodney, take a quick sample for me. I want to run a test for cocaine."

"You can't believe Mary Pearl took drugs," Megan said, aghast.

"No, of course not. However, it would be a quick way to kill an old woman. You see, cocaine is a potent vasoconstrictor. It reacts with the heart muscle by stimulation of catecholamines."

"In English please, Doctor."

"Cocaine can easily cause a myocardial infarction due to arterial spasm. I suspect it's what caused Ms. Harkin to have a heart attack."

Megan watched intently as the doctor fiddled with a small vial of blood. When he was done with the testing, Evans held it up and announced, "It's positive."

Oh my god, I was right, Megan thought. Evans went on with his dialogue.

"Cocaine is continuously metabolized to benzoylecgonine, along with other compounds. The concern is, this breakdown occurs not only in the body but even after death in the test tube. Therefore, we've got to rush these samples through. Time is of the essence. The other stipulation with this type of toxicology samples is I can't take them from the chest cavity."

"Why not? It seems just a good a place as any. Maybe even better because it caused her heart to fail," Megan said.

"It's because, in the chest cavity, it may be mixed with pleural effusion fluid or even gastric contents, depending on the cause of death. These can produce erroneous or misleading results."

"I can't believe Mary Pearl could have cocaine in her system. It seems so surreal."

"That's probably something the killer counted on and hoped we wouldn't think to check an elderly woman for. But, as I already stated, these samples taken now, at autopsy, will be changed by the time they are analyzed," Evans said. "They were much higher when she was found."

Megan nodded in confusion, dazed, as she watched Rodney rush around to fill various tubes with body fluids, then rush off to the gas lab.

"But I thought samples taken postmortem were stable," Megan said.

"Some substances are quite stable, such as alcohol. It mainly only continues to be metabolized while the subject is alive. Once the blood sample is taken or the person dies, metabolism all but ceases. Therefore, it's a good indicator of the premortem levels—that is, until decomposition sets in. Once that occurs, all bets are off."

"Do you think you will be able to determine if the level in her bloodstream at the time of death was enough to kill her?" Megan said.

"Probably not definitively. However, I will have a sample of her hair sent to toxicology to be analyzed. That should show no history of narcotic use. If you add that with no past needle use and a fresh injection site, I think we have something substantial."

The remainder of the autopsy went past in a blur, with Megan's mind reeling. It had been Dr. Evans's determination that Mary Pearl had been dead roughly twelve hours when she found her on the kitchen floor. That would make the time of death approximately 8:00 p.m. the night before.

Evans felt reasonably confident in this determination. For one, her body was completely stiff from rigor mortis, and her abdomen had a slight green discoloration from the action of bacteria in her intestines. But she hadn't begun to swell yet. Then Evans had explained something about a rise in the level of potassium in the vitreous fluid. The doctor told her that this begins soon after death and proceeds in a predictable fashion.

The clincher was the degree of digestion of her stomach contents. This was something Megan had provided some information on. She happen to know that Mary Pearl ate dinner at 6:00 p.m. every evening while she watched the nightly news. She also knew that she ate slowly and took her time. When Dr. Evans opened up her stomach, the presence of a fair amount of undigested food indicated that she had died within one to two hours of her last meal.

Again it angered Megan that something so egregious could occur in their quiet community. The hours between 6:00 p.m. and 8:00 p.m. should be a safe time to relax at home. *Heck, home itself should be safe,* she thought. Yet it hadn't been for Mary Pearl. The woman was murdered in her own kitchen, probably cleaning up from dinner. There were no dirty plates in the sink, so her meal hadn't been interrupted. Had the killer watched her from the window and waited?

Megan sat on the stool, contemplating the events, when Evans motioned her over to the side counter where the victim's effects were stacked. Mary Pearl had been wearing a pink nightie, which Rodney had photographed and folded neatly. *No stress there,* Megan thought. She'd been set for an evening in, all comfy in her favorite jammies. Then something caught Megan's eye.

"What's this here?" she asked and pointed to a mark on the front of the gown.

Evans chuckled. "Well, it's not blood, if that's what you figured. The best I could tell was it's hot chocolate. CSU said there was a mug of it next to her recliner."

"But that's not like Mary Pearl to wear anything with a stain on it," Megan said. "May I?"

Evans did a shoulder shrug and watched as Megan donned a pair of latex gloves and investigated the garment more closely.

"Everyone spills a drink from time to time," the doctor said. "It may not have anything to do with the crime."

"But you knew Mary Pearl and how fastidious she was. You know she would have changed."

Evans chuckled. "Why do I feel like you have me on the stand, Detective?"

"Sorry, didn't mean to be pushy," Megan said.

The doctor dismissed her apology. "That's OK, no offense taken. I understand this case means a lot to you." He leaned back against the counter and folded his hands across his ample stomach. "There's a possible version that Mary Pearl surprised someone in a break-in attempt. The scare caused her to have a heart attack. They could have struggled before he fled."

"I didn't buy that the first time I heard it. After her autopsy, I'm sure it's a bunch of garbage," Megan said.

The doctor nodded but said nothing.

"This means something," Megan said in reference to the stain on the garment. "Mary Pearl was neat as a pin. She would have changed her nightgown if it had a stain half this size. Just as she would have immediately smoothed off a broken nail."

"But she was home alone. It's possible, since no one was around to see, she let it go. Or maybe she went to the kitchen to clean up, and that's when she spooked the burglar."

Megan nodded. What he said made sense, so why didn't she believe either scenario?

"We'll know more with the lab results," Evans said. "Between the hair, blood, and bile, we'll get evidence of cocaine. That will speak for her. This woman never used drugs that were not prescribed to her, certainly not cocaine. That was injected into her system against her will."

"True, and I appreciate your allowing me to sit in on this one."

"It's personal with you, isn't it?"

"I'm afraid they're all going to be personal with me, Doc, but this one especially so. I've got to catch this guy. The community of Ocala deserves to feel safe again. We all need to feel free to get back to our daily routines. Mary Pearl's death remains an admonition of how easily it could have been anyone of us. We're all vulnerable, and she didn't deserve what she got."

"But, Detective, you forget that only you and I are cognizant of that. The public believes she died of a heart attack. Which was indeed the cause of death. Be careful what you say."

Megan nodded and watched Dr. Evans go with Rodney to finish up. She saw Rodney replace Mary Pearl's organs and the doctor suture up the intestinal cavity. On the surface, it was all protocol. Megan had experienced the other side of the situation. Mary Pearl may have very well died of a heart attack, but that wasn't the end of the story. The mechanism of death was lethal injection, and the manner of death was homicide.

She was sworn to serve and protect this community that was now hobbled by fear. They deserved the truth to be able to protect themselves. But she wasn't the one to make that call. That was up to the chief, and he had his own worries and concerns—confirmed proof and vigilantes ranking high on his list.

28

Megan pulled up outside a formidable two-story Victorian-style home at the same time as Lacy. She'd called her partner as soon as she was finished with Dr. Evans, and they decided to met here, which was their next interview. Megan got out of her old truck and walked over to meet Lacy.

"Nice place. Hard to believe someone who lived here could be murdered so violently."

"I know. But unlike the last two interviews, I already know it's her. I just finished speaking with her family dentist, who confirmed it. I'll tell you the details at lunch when we finish here."

"Any word on Edward Lee?" Megan asked as they stood by their vehicles.

"None. I've tried calling Cooper several times but no answer and no machine. I don't like the coincidence of him being unavailable at the same time the boy turns up missing," Lacy said.

"Not to worry. His phone got knocked out by lightning, same with his answering machine. He refuses to carry a cell. I'm not sure what that's all about, but he went off retracing Edward Lee's trail from school on foot. We can talk about that over lunch too. So what's the scoop here?"

"Name's Heather Daily, nineteen-year-old college student and volunteer. A political science major," Lacy said, reading off her notes. "The whole thing's a damn shame. She had her whole life in front of her."

The two detectives walked up the meticulously landscaped brick path to the front door. Lacy was the one to ring the bell, which actually turned out to be a chime.

"That's pretty," Megan said in appreciation, looking around.

Lacy looked over at her, but before she could respond, a butler answered the door.

"May I help you?"

"Yes," Lacy stammered. She'd never actually spoken to a butler before face-to-face. "I'm Detective Andina. This is my partner Detective Callingham. We're here to speak to Mrs. Daily."

"Yes, madames, please come in. She's expecting you along with Ms. Tina.

"Ms. Tina?" Megan whispered to Lacy as they followed the butler.

"I think she was Heather's best friend."

The butler ushered them through a huge library-type room, past a set of large Corinthian pillars, and on to a poolside room. In a chair off to the side sat a slender elderly woman. She was well dressed and poised in a wingback chair. She didn't rise when they entered but gave a polite nod. She picked up a tiny porcelain cup and took a sip before she spoke. "Welcome, Detectives. I hear you have news of my daughter's death."

The statement threw Lacy off. She wasn't aware the woman already knew they'd identified her daughter's remains for certain. It had only been an hour ago. Then again, she'd spoken to their family dentist. It was possible that Dr. Klein called ahead out of consideration.

"Sorry to intrude on your time of mourning, but we do want to find the individual responsible for your daughter's death," Lacy said.

The woman's rouged lip quivered slightly at the remark. "As do I."

There was an awkward moment in which neither Lacy or Megan knew what to do. The butler reappeared with a young woman. "Ms. Tina," he announced.

The girl went over to the older woman and whispered something. They gave air kisses, and the girl sat down. "Please, sit, y'all. Would you care for any tea?"

"No, thank you," Lacy said. "We won't keep you long. I had a few questions about Heather."

At the mention of her best friend's name, Tina brought her hand to her lips. "Sorry, I'm still emotional over her loss," she said, waving her other hand in front of her in a flutter.

No doubt, Lacy thought, *since an hour ago she was missing, not dead.* "Can you tell me about Heather's interests, how she spent her free time?"

This time it was the mother who spoke. "Heather was a volunteer for several local politicians."

"Anyone we might know?" Lacy asked.

The mother snickered. "I would hope so. Senator Shaw for one. Another, more recent, was for Justice Angus Howard. I'm certain you know of him."

"I do. In what capacity did she help the judge?"

"She planned out his entire campaign strategy," the mother said. "It didn't get into full swing until this week, but my daughter was the brains behind it all."

"Heather was real personable. Everyone just loved her," Tina added.

"When was the last time you saw your daughter?" Lacy asked the mother.

"That would be two days before she disappeared. She was an adult. She led her own life. We weren't what you'd call close. But I loved her just the same. She was an only child."

"Can you tell me anything else?"

"I hardly think so. Like I said, we weren't close."

Lacy nodded and flipped her pad closed. "Thank you for your time."

"I'll show you out," Tina offered and popped out of her seat.

The two detectives followed the girl to the door. When they got there, Megan stopped and asked, "Was Heather dating anyone at the time she disappeared?"

Tina looked around to make sure the butler wasn't near before she answered. "Yes, but I don't know his name. All I know is she met him at one of her campaign jobs or the school. She wouldn't tell me who he was or which campaign. I think she wanted to keep it a secret because he was married."

"Thanks so much for all your help," Lacy said. She gave Tina a card. "If you think of anything else, give me a call."

Tina looked at the small paper square reverently. "Sure thing," she said. Her sorrow gone from her face. It was aglow from being the brief focus of attention and a source of sought-after information.

Megan and Lacy walked back to their respective vehicles. Neither was the egg.

"I thought you took the prototype car?" Megan questioned.

"I did for a while, but it got too slow. I plugged it in behind the station. The plug near the side door. They will think one of us is in the office," Lacy said.

Megan nodded with a smile. "Smart thinking. Let's go to Hogan's subs and compare notes."

"Sounds good," Lacy said. "I've got a lot to go over with you, along with a few questions."

*　　*　　*

They both ordered large glasses of iced tea to go with their sandwiches. Megan sipped on hers while she watched Lacy organize notes of the meeting with the missing girl's dentist.

"As you're aware, the remains found at the peach farm belong to Heather Daily," Lacy declared. "There was no doubt in Dr. Klein's mind. He told me in cases such as Heather's, where total decomposition of soft tissue has occurred, the teeth and jaws may be the only effective means of identification. But it surprised me that her mother seemed to already know."

"Dr. Klein might have felt obligated to call the family after speaking with you," Megan said.

The waitress came with their subs, and Megan picked out her pickle and crunched on it while she listened to Lacy.

"True, but at least he's absolutely sure. Dr. Klein told me that a person's dental condition is like a fingerprint. Each person has a unique and individual presentation."

"How so? We all have thirty-two teeth. They're all in our mouth. What's the big deal?"

"Not that simple," Lacy said. She paused in her explanation to take a bite out of her sandwich, then wiped her fingers on a paper napkin before she took a glance at her notes and proceeded.

"Humans are supposed to have thirty-two teeth, but there are those of us who are born with some missing or even a couple extra. Then, each tooth can vary in size, shape, and orientation in the mouth from person to person."

"What do you mean by orientation?"

"You know, how some people have a crooked tooth or a space between their two front teeth?"

Megan nodded yes because her mouth was full.

Lacy looked at her notes again. "Dr. Klein called it a diastema. The point is, each tooth has the propensity to be tilted, twisted, or misaligned in some unique fashion."

"I guess that's why braces are the big thing," Megan said. "So what's your point?"

"My point is, there can be a lot of potential variation with thirty-two teeth. Each one has five surfaces that can have either a filling, a cavity, or a marking of some sort. Then you have the alignment of these teeth together as a whole in the mouth. Even without the dental radiographs, you end up with an infinite combination of possibilities. Each one is particular to that individual, thus, the fingerprint analogy. Only difference is, it can document changes throughout life."

"Wow, I never thought about teeth as being so individualized."

"Me neither, but Dr. Klein set me straight. He also added that there are some people with chipped or missing teeth who never get them fixed. The affected tooth becomes part of that person's personality, their look. Kind of like a trademark."

"Yeah, I knew a guy in school who chipped a front tooth. I think he would have looked weird to me if I saw him with it fixed," Megan said. "It was from a bike accident."

"The thing is, I had the dental radiographs from the peach-farm remains. Dr. Klein pointed out information on them that could only be specific to Heather. No doubt."

"Like what? An x-ray is an x-ray."

Again Lacy referred to her notes. "Not really. There is something called a sinus print that is different with each person."

"How do you determine that? Everyone has sinuses, and I didn't think they had anything to do with your teeth."

"They don't exactly, and I can't tell you that I totally followed everything Dr. Klein told me, but it goes something like this. The maxillary sinus is in close proximity to the top teeth. The lower border of this sinus is scalloped. This scalloping is quite individual. If you superimpose one panorex radiograph over another, you can determine whether they are the same individual or not."

"Really? That's pretty cool. Did he do that?"

"Yes, as a matter of fact he did, and it was cool."

"Do all dentists know how to do that?" Megan asked.

"Not really. Dr. Klein took a few forensic classes in school. He also compared the pulp chambers of her molars and premolars. They can vary greatly from one individual to the next. Heather happened to have a few distinguishing characteristics."

"Such as?" Megan said while munching a chip.

Lacy read through her notes with her finger, then stopped when she got to the place she wanted. "Let's see. There was a small cyst near the apex of her number 22 that Dr. Klein has been watching and a dilacerated root on her second premolar."

"What's a dilacr . . . what?"

Lacy looked back down at her notes again. "A dilacerated root is when the tooth gets bumped or injured when the root is forming. The result is a curvature at the end. It's a very personalized distinction."

Megan looked over at Lacy with her eyebrows raised. "Wow. You like this guy or what?"

"He's married. But Dr. Klein said it really is all very distinctive. There's no doubt that Heather is our peach-farm remains, and that I liked." Lacy beamed at her across the Formica table. "It's our first positive ID."

Megan was pleased by Lacy's accomplishments. But it also saddened her that although they could identify the victim, they were still no closer to the killer. A little boy had disappeared, and an elderly neighbor woman was killed by lethal injection. Now she feared Coop was missing.

"I want to notify the campaigns Heather worked on, ask questions of everyone involved. Primarily about when she was last seen, with whom, and who she hung out with."

"That sounds good," Megan said. "What about the schools?"

"That was too vague. All I could do was call the National Crime Information Center and tell them we found Heather, since she was listed on the NCIC missing-persons list."

Megan nodded, took one last bite of her sandwich, and pushed it aside.

Lacy cocked her head to the side and evaluated her partner. "So, droopy face, what's the deal? I think we've done pretty good today."

"You did great. It's this situation. I feel like we're getting closer to this pervert but still can't nail him. Like he's watching and laughing at us, and our forty-eight hours is running out," Megan replied.

"Look, I realize this is happening in your hometown, but now it's my home too. You're full of advice about sucking it up and gutting it out in a marathon, but when it comes to the real world and your own life, you're a shrinking violet. Get a grip. Put some of that 'face adversity' shit into practice. You give the rest of us women a bad name. We're not all a bunch of wimps, you know." Lacy threw back the rest of her tea and added, "You worked hard to be a detective. Act like it."

Megan stared at her, blinking. "You're right. Absolutely. We still have the rest of the day and tomorrow to prove ourselves."

"Great. So tell me what the forensic pathologist said."

"Dr. Evans isn't a forensic pathologist. Actually, he's not even a pathologist. He's a retired physician, but he is good at what he does. At least he's not a coroner. When we were under that system, the man in charge was a funeral director. That's when the other two cases occurred."

"No wonder," Lacy said. "What's a funeral director going to do with a pile of unidentified bones? There's no one to bill for the services. I imagine that was the end of his interest." Lacy looked at her empty glass, then around the room. "I need more tea."

Megan cast a wary look while Lacy flagged a waitress down. She came with a refill.

"You know, you might want to go easy on that stuff. They make their tea strong here. You'll be wired all night."

"I'm good," Lacy said. "I can handle it. We're on a tight timeline. I need the energy."

Megan thought that was probably what most addicts said but let it drop. "Anyway, I think Dr. Evans was less than enthusiastic on my thoughts at the beginning, but he agreed to allow me to be present. He's actually a very nice guy. I've worked with him before."

"Did he find anything supportive of your theory?"

"Yes, as a matter of fact a few things. First of all, he discovered a patch on Mary Pearl's scalp that had a small scab. It appeared to have a clump of hair pulled out."

"Did you tell him about the hair under the table we retrieved? I'm certain it wasn't hers," Lacy said, "so she must have matched his efforts."

"No, not at that time. I was more interested in what he said. I told him that Mary Pearl didn't have any blood on or near her head that I remember when I found her. But he said it occurred before she died, and the involved area didn't bleed much. At that point in the autopsy, I think he was still stuck on the idea she died of a heart attack but was less sure than when he began."

"What do you mean 'at that point'? Did he change his mind?"

"Yes, but although Dr. Evans is good at what he does, he's not trained in forensics. There are very few of them in our state. Evans was a physician. He knows how to diagnose cancer, heart disease, high blood pressure, ulcers, that sort of thing. He's not geared to homicide."

"Ah, I understand the problem. New York City has a team of forensic pathologists, but the outlying areas are lucky to have someone like Evans. At times, I've had cases that overlapped. But considering that pathology is a medical specialty, doctors are trained in evaluating cells under a microscope to determine if there are any deviations from normal, such as cancer. Whatever the diagnosis ends up to be, the causes are all natural. With them, homicide cases get the same treatment. On the other hand, forensic pathologists are specialized. When you get into foul-play territory, it's a different beast altogether. They work alongside with us as detectives to get a prosecution. They have education above and beyond the basic pathologist and physician."

"Exactly," Megan said. "They must be a dedicated group. How many years of college does it take? I mean a physician is at least eight-plus years."

"Not sure," Lacy said. "But they add a lot in investigation of unnatural deaths, homicides, suicides, and accidents. They have legal, criminal, as well as medical concerns on their minds when they perform an autopsy. They know they will be asked to testify in a court of law in front of a jury. They understand the need to be able to back up their findings under cross-examination."

"So if someone, such as Dr. Evans, who is not familiar with the criminal element, performed the autopsy, they might miss something important?" Megan asked.

"It's possible. The damning evidence may be something subtle that a physician would overlook, yet the same thing would be obvious to a forensic pathologist. Sometimes these missed clues are an integral cog in the prosecution's case. The one tiny piece of information that puts the criminal away for life or allows him to go free. But from what you tell me, I think Evans was on his game. It sounds as if he was looking for evidence of foul play. So what did he find?"

"A recent injection site on the back of Mary Pearl's arm. Her blood came up positive for cocaine, so he ordered a complete toxicology screen for her blood, hair, and bile."

"Wow," Lacy said and sat up straight. "He doesn't suspect she was a user, does he?"

"No, of course not."

"So he *is* on the ball. To find evidence of cocaine in her blood, something's going on."

"He attributes her heart attack to the drug, not natural causes." Megan said.

"To inject someone with cocaine?" Lacy said and slumped back in her seat. "That had to be premeditated. People don't walk around with a loaded syringe full of a lethal dose of drug. He purposely went after her. He wanted to shut her up."

"Afraid so. That means she had to be someone he knew or someone close to us," Megan said.

"Maybe not us. Beth was the one who relayed the story. It's possible the killer got a good look at Mary Pearl and knew she'd talk. You said she's lived there a long time. If he got a glimpse of her in the yard, he could have also easily found out who she was without knowing her well."

"True, but I think he was very familiar with the community and its residents."

"You're probably right. At first I considered the killer used this county as an isolated dump. A location separate from his residence to distance himself from the crimes. Now, I'm starting to agree with you," Lacy said. "He very well may be a longtime member of this community."

"Did you ever mention the clump of hair?"

"Yes. After Evans was done with the examination, I brought it up. He'd already planned to send a sample of Mary Pearl's hair off to verify that she'd never used narcotics. He said Jerry should send the other evidence for DNA testing."

"Did he find anything else?"

"Minor defense wounds that indicate a struggle. But then again, as he pointed out, that could be explained in any number of ways."

"I think our Dr. Evans has had forensic training. He seems on the ball in anticipating answers to possible court questions. You know the chief isn't going to be pleased with another death that could be attributed to the serial killer, but he has to be satisfied with the forensics and lab analysis we've all done," Lacy said. "We're making the best of our forty-eight hours."

"He can't argue that the injection site on the back of Mary Pearl's arm isn't a damning piece of evidence. Most B and Es occur from people who try to get money for personal drug use, not to inject their victims with a lethal dose," Megan stated.

"What are you going to do about Beth? What if it was she who informed the killer?"

Megan locked eyes with Lacy. "We need to protect her without her freaking out. If this man is that familiar with the local residents, he knows she's a gossip. He knows where she lives and that she has two small children. Possibly even where Campbell goes to school."

"So you feel pretty sure he's the one who nabbed Edward Lee?"

"Yes, I do. So does Coop. The timing is too coincidental for us to think otherwise."

"I have to tell you I find it worrisome that Coop's disappeared right after the boy and is not around for questioning. All I'm saying is that it raises questions," Lacy stated.

"The only reason why Coop took off is to find Edward Lee. He loves that boy like his own."

"OK, so you're the local. What do you suggest we do?" Lacy asked. "I acquiesce to your knowledge and trust your judgment."

29

Lacy sat next to Jerry in the lab. She'd stopped by after a brief meeting with the chief to tell him about Heather and return the radiographs he'd lent her for her meeting with the dentist.

"Are you sure the means of obtaining this hair sample was copacetic?" Jerry asked.

Lacy shot him a mischievous look. "Yes. The CSU missed it in all the commotion, but I followed procedure in retrieval, bagging, and labeling. Megan was there when I did it."

Jerry had plans to compare it against the sample of Mary Pearl's hair Dr. Evans had given him. She watched eagerly, awaiting his decision. He seemed to take his time with it under the scope.

"So?" Lacy asked impatiently, unable to keep quiet any longer.

Without looking up, he said, "You know, you and Megan are cut from the same bolt of cloth."

Lacy smiled. Perhaps she did have more in common with her partner than she'd first believed. "Is that so bad?"

This time he sat up and turned toward her with a grin. "No, but you keep the pressure turned on high. But to answer your question, it's not Mary Pearl's hair."

"I knew it, I just knew it," Lacy said and did a little end-zone dance.

"I'm going to request a toxicology screen on it along with a DNA profile. Hair can hold the history of a person's drug or medication use. It's what I like to call invisible clues."

Lacy had discussed this over lunch with Megan. Dr. Evans planned a similar mode of action with a sample of Mary Pearl's hair. It made sense to do one on the suspect's hair as well.

"How does a DNA test work anyway? I mean, doesn't it take like two weeks?"

"Yes, it takes time and is costly, but this case warrants its use. DNA, or deoxyribonucleic acid, is a double-helix stand that contains the entire genetic instructions of who we are."

"You mean whether we become a serial killer or not?"

Jerry chuckled. "No. That would be more of a nature-versus-nurture issue. I'm talking more along the lines of hair and eye color. Some people want to use it for medical information. For example, to find out if a woman carries a gene for breast cancer. It could influence the choice of treatment. Or pretreatment, for that matter. On the other hand, it could destroy lives."

"But we already know this joker has brown hair. What are you looking for?"

"We can get a lot of information out of this sample. One would be his drug use, but that doesn't involve the DNA."

"How do you actually get the DNA out of the hair anyway? I mean, hair is like a thin stand."

"True, and you extract it out of a cell, but at a follicle, not the colored part. It can be done with a hair follicle, blood, bone, or even saliva. DNA typing is a conclusive piece of evidence. People are convicted or exonerated on the results. That's why I asked about how you obtained this sample. If the defense thought it was improperly collected—"

"I'm aware of the protocol. The CSU team only missed it because they were told she was an elderly woman who died at home, alone. No foul play was suspected. They did a quick sweep and packed up. I happen to spot it when Megan and I took another look around."

"So what's your take on what happened?" Jerry asked.

"From learning that Doc Evans found an area on Mary Pearl's head, I believe the killer got in a scuffle with her. She fought back, and they both got a fistful of hair before he injected her with a fatal dose of cocaine. But for sure, that old woman went down with a fight."

"That sounds like Mary Pearl," Jerry said with a chuckle.

Lacy sat back looking at him, stunned. "I didn't realize you knew her personally. I'm so sorry."

He shrugged his shoulders.

"Does everyone in this town know each other?"

"Not like it used to be. The town's growing by leaps and bounds. Still, if you don't know someone, then one of your friends or family usually does. It just so happens Mary Pearl and I went to the same church. We sang in the choir together."

"Seriously? I never would have pegged you for a choirboy. I guess it's your devilish grin."

"Every Tuesday-night practice. It's really a lot of fun as long as they don't try and make me sing a solo. I hate that, but I really like the holiday presentations we put on. They make the different seasons more fun. But don't let that fool you. I still have a little bit of wild side in me."

Lacy could definitely understand Megan's attraction. "Well, I *am* sorry—about Mary Pearl, that is, not you being in the choir. I think that's cool to have interests outside work."

"Thanks. Actually, Megan and I grew up together too. Along with Beth and Nate of course. I'm a couple years older, but we went to the same schools. She was a cute kid."

"Cooper too?"

"Not so cute. We were on the same baseball team. Nate, Cooper, and Buddy Howard, the county commissioner, who turned out to be the most talented and famous player on our team. Of which my mother often reminds me."

"You keep in touch with any of them?" Lacy asked.

"Not really. I see Megan at work and the others around town. I enjoy my work, this case in particular. I have a stake in this community. I want to see justice done."

"With everyone so close, you must have a deep sense of belonging here," Lacy said. "I envy that."

Jerry finished off the paperwork for the tests and set the package down. "You sound like family and community are important to you too."

Lacy nodded. "They are."

"So why the big move to Ocala?" Jerry asked and raised one of his bushy eyebrows as he did.

"Long story," Lacy said. "But I sympathize with the sense of violation these crimes must cause, since they occurred in your own town."

The quick change of conversation away from her personal life, back to him, didn't go unnoticed. He was about to ask another question when a chirp of Lacy's cell phone interrupted.

"Oh, I've got to take this. I'll see you later," Lacy said, hopped off the stool, then was out the door before he could respond.

He stood there, somewhat thrown. The next chance, he was going to bring the subject of her move back up. He liked Lacy as a friend, and any unanswered question drove him crazy. There was a reason she uprooted herself from New York and set up home here. He intended to find out what it was.

30

Lacy pulled up to Beth's house just as the two little boys tore around the corner. The front yard looked as if a toy store had recently exploded. The children appeared to be playing cowboys and Indians, but it was hard to tell, since they were out of sight before she could even say hello. She got out of her vehicle and was in the process of scaling the porch steps when they came screaming past again. This time, they headed in the opposite direction. In an instant they were gone.

"Don't run with sticks in your hands," Beth hollered after their wake. She was at the front door, with a large box in her arms. She acted as if she'd been expecting Lacy.

"Can I help you with something?" Lacy asked, unsure if she'd missed something.

"If you could get the door for me, that would be nice." Beth walked on past to Lacy's car.

Lacy did as asked and ran to catch up. "What's going on?"

"I want to put this box in your trunk. Then I really need a ride to Sissy's if you could."

Lacy hesitated briefly, then said, "OK." She opened the hatchback for Beth to stow the box.

"Thanks, I appreciate this so much. I tried to get in touch with Megan, but she hasn't answered her phone. Neither has Cooper. And Matt's in the middle of a peanut field somewhere as usual," Beth said and walked around to the passenger side and got in.

Lacy wasn't exactly sure what was going on, but apparently, Beth did. She was going to meet Megan here, but apparently her partner got sidetracked, so she figured she might as well go with the flow. "Are the boys going to be all right?" Lacy queried as they ran screaming past yet again.

"Sure. They're just hyped up on Ovaltine," Beth said with a wave of her hand as if it were a daily occurrence. "Arlene's inside. She'll probably let them run themselves out shortly."

When Lacy got in the car, the aroma of pound cake filled the air. She was a competent woman but had a weakness for riding with food. "So what's the emergency?"

"It's not an emergency exactly, but remember I promised Sissy I would make these cakes for the Humane Society fund-raiser? She was going to pick them up this morning but never came. It's really hard for me to get away with the children, so I called her. No one answered at her place the first two times, so I thought maybe she was still on her way. Probably got delayed."

Lacy pulled out of the driveway and headed down the road, confident Beth would direct her where to turn. She seemed to like to give directions.

"Do you think I'm wrong? I mean, don't you think it was enough I baked her three pound cakes from scratch? Well, two, since we ate one. Still, I don't think I should be the one to have to run them over there, do you? If they don't get to the bake sale soon, it will be all over with, and I would have wasted my time and effort. And I have to tell you, the ingredients aren't cheap."

Lacy looked over at Beth, who seemed strung as tight as a bowstring. It was possible she'd helped herself to some Ovaltine as well. Lacy decided to look into the stuff for herself once she got home. It appeared to work better than iced tea or crack.

"I don't think you should have to drop them off yourself after all that hard work you went through. Maybe you should keep 'em, and we can eat them. It would teach her a lesson."

Beth looked over, wide-eyed, aghast at Lacy. Then a smile crept over her face that spread to her eyes. "You are bad girl, but I like the way you think. The thing is, I finally got in touch with Buddy right after I called you. He said Sissy got hurt. So I can't actually be mad at her. I feel bad that I got upset to begin with, instead of being worried about her. I shouldn't have assumed she neglected me. Instead, I should have worried about her. That maybe she was in an accident."

"That's natural. It doesn't make you a bad person. So what happened? She get in a wreck?"

"No. Some sort of barn accident. I don't know. Buddy didn't say, but he sounded really weird. I really do feel bad that I thought she blew me off when she was actually hurt. But I don't want the cakes to go to waste. I figured I'd go over there myself, but my car's in the garage."

"Hey, I don't mind at all," Lacy said. "I like riding with food. It's one of my favorite things."

"This is it. Turn here and follow the left fork in the road," Beth said. "It's over this hill."

"I thought Florida was supposed to be all flat and sandy, with bugs the size of Rhode Island."

"I guess some of Florida is that way, but Ocala is hilly. Maybe not California hills, but they're hills nonetheless. Now the bug thing is true. Especially the palmetto bugs. They look like roaches, but they can fly. Luckily they're usually content to stay outside in the palm trees."

Lacy squirmed at the image as she pulled onto an oak-lined drive. Paddock fences lined both sides of the winding lane. "I guess being county commissioner pays well."

"Selling mobile homes does. That's where the money came from—Sissy's family. She married Buddy for respectability. Her family got the money from their mobile-home dealership in town."

"Really? That's interesting."

Lacy's curiosity ignited Beth's gossip fuse. "Oh yes, her family owns Uncle Ray's Mobile Homes. They make a killing from trailer sales. In fact, their family lived in one until recently."

"You mean before they moved into that fancy neighborhood with ten—and twenty-acre ranches? The one with really nice houses and everybody owns at least one horse and two SUVs?"

Beth looked at her with her head cocked to the side. "Yes, how did you know about it?"

"I went running with Megan near there. She said she ran into Buddy, who'd been visiting his in-laws. He'd snuck out to take a walk, get some peace and quiet."

"Well, that doesn't surprise me. The two families don't get along at all. Sissy's dad thinks 'Sweet Home Alabama' is the national anthem, and her mother washes her turnip greens on the rinse cycle of her washing machine. Buddy, on the other hand, comes from old money. Everyone in his family is well educated and let's just say more sophisticated than Sissy's relatives."

"So she met Buddy and latched on?"

"Basically, yes. Sissy wanted more out of life. She's a social climber. Buddy could offer her that—you know, become a prominent member of society. His daddy's a judge and has connections and respectability. They knew the right people. She would be invited to all the right social galas."

Lacy wasn't sure she totally understood since she was raised in a lower-income blue-collar family herself but nodded in agreement. It seemed to make total sense to Beth, if not her.

"Sissy wanted to advance in society, and she did the day she married Buddy. The fact that he also had a little money too didn't hurt," Beth said and laughed. But her laugh was extinguished when they rounded the bend to the house.

Before them was an EMS vehicle, lights flashing, siren off. Next to it was Megan's old truck. She'd obviously chosen to ignore orders again and not drive their assigned prototype facade of a vehicle. *This must be serious,* Lacy thought. This was why Megan called and said she'd be late.

"Oh no, Sissy must be really hurt," Beth said, knuckles clenched to her mouth.

Lacy didn't want to point out the fact that the EMS wasn't in motion. That meant that, more than likely, poor Sissy had already bit the big one. "It had to be one hell of a horse accident."

"I don't understand," Beth said. "Sissy's an expert rider. She's won all kind of awards."

"Take Christopher Reeves. He was Superman, knew all about horses. Look what happened."

Right after Lacy said it, she did a mental head slap. The look on Beth's face was horrified, then it turned into an effusion of tears.

"Wait, Beth, we don't know what happened here. You wait with the cakes. I'll go check it out."

Beth nodded and reached into her purse to retrieve a handful of tissues.

Lacy got out of the car and again told Beth to stay put. The first person she spoke to was one of the EMS drivers, who confirmed that Sissy was now one of the newly departed. Next to him stood Buddy. She could appreciate his appeal with the public. He was tall and handsome. He had an ease about him and radiated a charm even when he was bereaved. Yet he didn't exactly seemed to be all that bereaved. Not like a man whose wife had died tragically moments earlier, which Buddy confirmed in a brief conversation with Lacy.

From where she stood, Lacy scanned the scene in search of Megan. Off in the far distance, away from the ambulance and the commotion, she spotted her partner entering a long horse barn. Lacy looked back over her shoulder at Beth, who seemed busy with her tissues, so she followed after Megan.

Moments later, Lacy called out, "Hey there," before she stepped into the dark barn. It took her a few seconds for her eyes to adjust to the darkness.

"Lacy, what are you doing here?"

"I came with your sister to deliver the cakes for the fund-raiser. She wrangled me for a ride. I figured, I was close enough, and you were still busy."

"Ohmygod, Beth is here?"

"Don't worry, she's in my car with the cakes. She's fine. Did you get in touch with Cooper?"

"No, and I'm starting to get concerned. Was there any word at the station about Edward Lee?"

"No, sorry. What's the deal here? What happened to Sissy?"

"I don't know for sure, but I don't like the look of this," Megan said and gestured to the stall where the accident was to have occurred.

"I know. It's always sad when someone so young dies tragically."

"This wasn't an accident," Megan stated. She stood there with her hands on her hips.

Lacy looked around. She saw horses in stalls, horse poop outside of the stalls, then neat little swept poop piles. On the wall were numerous horse-type thingies hung neatly on hooks, all undisturbed. Nothing looked out of place, mysterious, or deadly, just very smelly and horsey. Just as one would expect in a barn.

"Not seeing the problem," Lacy said.

"I saw evidence of blunt-force trauma on Sissy's skull."

Lacy had already spoken with Buddy when she arrived, and he'd told her what happened. The newest horse his wife acquired was feisty, and Sissy thought it was what would make him a champion. Buddy worried the animal was too dangerous and told his wife as much, but she assured him she could handle the creature. Now it appeared Sissy was wrong. The stallion had caused her demise.

"A kick to the head from a horse is blunt-force trauma," Lacy said, still not seeing a problem.

Megan stood there and shook her head. "I know his story, but it doesn't ring true. She didn't die from a horse accident."

Lacy looked around the barn to make sure no one else was in earshot. "This is crazy, Megan. You may have been correct in your hunch about Mary Pearl, but you can't mess with this one. Buddy's a county commissioner, and his dad's a freakin' judge, for god's sake. We're already walking a tightrope as it is. What are you trying to do, get us fired? I didn't move here for that."

"No, but I *am* a detective. The statistics are against this one, Lacy. Very few people die from a horse kick. Even in the head. Even here in Ocala, the horse capital of the world."

"But it does happen, right?"

"Yeah, but it didn't here. Not this time"

"What makes you so damn certain? Who reported the death?" Lacy asked.

"Buddy. But again, something's not right. I think he called it in hours after it occurred."

"Maybe because that's when he found her. Did he ever state he was here when it happened? What makes you so sure he's lying? Because I'm telling you, Megan, that's a serious accusation. You better have more than your gut to back it up." Lacy stood with her arms folded, impatient.

"First of all, Sissy was an expert rider. She knew horses. She knew what she was doing."

Lacy opened her mouth to interject when Megan held up a hand to stop her.

"This is the spot where Buddy claims to have found his wife," Megan said. She pointed to the wall of the nearest stall and walked in.

Lacy looked around, a bit anxious for the animal that had recently perpetrated the crime in question. She enjoyed all the animal shows but really didn't relish any real-life interaction with a creature that could kick her butt or cause her tragic death.

Megan picked up on Lacy's apprehension. "Don't worry, the animal's out to pasture."

"Out to pasture? They put it to sleep already? Ohmygod, that's terrible."

"No, of course not. The horse is really out there in the pasture," Megan said and pointed out the window at a beautiful black stallion.

Its mane blew in the wind as it made its way along, grazing on the lush green grass. It didn't seem possible that something so majestic could kill so easily. Even though Lacy didn't feel comfortable getting close to the animal, she was relieved it hadn't been destroyed.

"Look, this is what I'm talking about," Megan said and stepped to the far side of the stall. She took a pen from her pocket and used it as a pointer while she spoke. "This blood here on the wall doesn't match Buddy's story."

"What exactly is his story?" Lacy asked.

"He said he found Sissy up here with the horse going wild in the same stall. He said he wasn't sure how long she was injured before he got there."

"Injured? Does that mean he states Sissy was alive when he found her?" Lacy asked.

"No. I asked him the same thing. He said he was upset and didn't realize she was dead when he saw her. It took a few minutes to get the horse out before he could get to her and feel for vitals."

"That makes sense. I sure as hell wouldn't have entered the stall with something that big going crazy. So when was the last time he saw her before that?"

"That morning, at breakfast. He came home at lunch and went looking for her when she wasn't in the house."

"So far it all sounds reasonable. He never claimed to be here when it happened."

"True, but that would place the postmortem interval at no more than four hours."

Lacy nodded. "And?" She knew Megan was going somewhere with this, but she didn't think she was going to like the final destination.

"Buddy rarely came home for lunch. Even if he had today, Sissy was busy with the fund-raiser for the Humane Society. She more than likely wouldn't have been home anyway. No reason to get concerned that she wasn't in the house. Sissy was a busy woman. If she wasn't out and about, I'm sure she was often at the barn caring for her animals. She was not a couch potato."

"He could have forgotten about her plans for the fund-raiser. Husbands do that sort of thing. Or maybe he'd called her and said he was coming home, and the two of them were going to have a little joy in the afternoon. I don't see anything sinister here, Megan."

"Then take a look at this." Megan pointed to the blood pattern on the wall.

Lacy studied the marks. "It looks like a little bit of blood from her hair smudged on the stall as she fell," Lacy said.

"Or as she was placed here," Megan suggested. "For a kick violent enough to cause Sissy's death, I would expect more of a splatter of blood droplets up here," Megan said and outlined an area in the air with her pen. It was much larger and higher than the blood that existed on the wall.

"Humm. As much as I hate to encourage you, I think you're right. How tall was Sissy?"

"I think around five feet four inches. But I'll need to check into that to make sure. Still, the blood splatter from a skull injury would be much higher up. There is no splatter here, only a smudge."

"What if she fell, then received the blow."

"I guess that's possible. The angle of the indentation in her skull compared to the position of her body should reveal more of what happened at the autopsy," Megan said. "It's not just my gut this time. When I got here, rigor was already setting in."

"But that still fits Buddy's story. Rigor mortis begins within two hours of death."

"Exactly. It would have begun no later than 10:00 a.m. Rigor progresses in a head-to-toe direction."

"Yeah. It's first demonstrated in the small muscles of the face, such as the masseter. The mandible becomes stiff, and the victim's jaw will not open. Dr. Klein told me that," Lacy said.

"Well, I bent down to touch Sissy, and her elbows were inflexible. Her knees were also beginning to stiffen. If you figure that the entire body will demonstrate rigor at eight hours, it doesn't fit. Sissy was past the four-hour mark. It doesn't coincide with Buddy's story. I would place her at a postmortem interval of at least six hours or more."

"It's not that large a difference. It's more like you're splitting hairs. Postmortem changes can be modified by environmental conditions and body habitus," Lacy said. "She could have been hot and sweaty from working with the animal. This is something better left for Dr. Evans."

"I know, but I was practically here when the call came in. I felt compelled to investigate."

"What was the body temp when the EMS got here?" Lacy asked.

"Eighty-eight point six Fahrenheit. That puts her death at six hours or more, not less than four. Same as all the other stats."

"God, Megan, I don't like this. Can't we just stick to our serial-killer investigation?"

"Yes, I know, but I got the weirdest feeling when I showed up here. I couldn't put my finger on it, but something was off. I don't know what part if any Buddy has to play in this, but I suspect there's foul play involved in Sissy's death."

"Oh god, here we go again with your gut. Are you saying Buddy killed his wife?"

"Not exactly, but I believe someone did, and he's lying. He certainly doesn't act bereaved."

Although Lacy had to agree that Buddy didn't exactly seem torn apart when she and Beth arrived, she couldn't equate that with guilt of foul play. "That's a serious accusation," Lacy said.

"I know, but when I got here, livor had begun as well," Megan said. "You know—the settling of red blood cells. That takes eight hours to be fixed."

"Again, something best left to Dr. Evans," Lacy stated.

"OK. I'm just telling you my impressions. I didn't do anything to interfere with the autopsy. Although I did request the EMS guy take a sample of the vitreous fluid for a potassium analysis."

"Ohmygod, Megan. Why? You're setting yourself—no, us—up for the firing range."

"You know why. The level of potassium in the vitreous humor can be used as an indicator for the time of death. Something that will be key in this case."

"This case? Megan, that's pretty much an out-and-out accusation of murder of his wife. Besides the potassium rise postmortem can be inaccurate. This is a nightmare. Didn't you tell me the chief and Angus Howard were buddies? And how do you plan to link Buddy to the crime scene? He lives here. He can refute everything. Oh, this whole situation reeks of disaster. I feel sick."

"Don't worry. Neither the chief or Angus know about it yet. That won't come out until autopsy. And it's my guess, by then, the shit will hit the fan anyway. Besides, if his wife was murdered and Buddy's innocent, he should want to find out what happened. He should be happy we're on top of things."

"The shit will hit the fan, all right, and guess who will have the crap all over her face," Lacy said.

"Wait," Megan said and grabbed her by the elbow. "I know we already have our hands full, but we can't look the other way on this one. We owe Sissy that much."

"Fine. The chief can handle it. If he feels there was a homicide, he will assign it to someone."

"We *are* that someone."

"OK fine, this is a pissant force. We have a serial killer to catch. If Buddy killed his wife, well, that's definitely wrong. But he's not a danger to the community in general. We know where we can pick him up once all the lab work comes in," Lacy said. "But I can't deal with it now."

"It will be OK. You'll see," Megan said.

"You're insane. You *do* realize that, don't you?" Lacy said.

"So I've been told. But still, I believe we can look into Sissy's death along with investigating the serial-killer case. Who knows, Buddy may be innocent, and we'll be heroes."

"I hope you're right. But I better go check on Beth. The cakes she baked are sitting in my car, calling my name. That's the way I deal with stress."

"Ohmygod, I forgot about Beth. She shouldn't be alone."

The next thing Lacy knew, Megan took off at a run toward the house from the barn. Since she knew snakes fancied barns, she took off after her, not wanting to be the only one left behind.

They ran toward the main house where they found Beth in the middle of a group of men. Most were lingering cops and EMS workers, but with his height, they saw Buddy next to Beth.

"Ohmygod, what in the world is she up to now?" Megan asked.

"Megan, Lacy," Beth called out. "I was just talking to Buddy here. I gave him one of my cards and left a pound cake for him. He said he's going to hire me to cater Sissy's funeral and service."

"You have cards?" Megan asked.

"Yes, I had them printed up the other day after our conversation." Beth waved one in the air.

"Hey, can I have one of those?" Lacy asked.

Megan shot her partner a look, then grabbed Beth by the arm and pulled her over to the side. The men all went back to their discussion and ignored them. "What do you think you're doing?"

"I decided to take advantage of an opportunity, just like you told me. Remember you said not to be afraid to branch out and try new things? I decided to try a shot at being a caterer."

Lacy stifled a giggle. She figured Megan's encouragement lectures would land her in trouble sooner or later.

Beth only gave her a cursory glance. "I decided you and Lacy were right. I want more out of my life than being a mother and wife—not that I don't love it. I just want a part of my life to be more about me. To improve myself and grow as a person. You understand, don't you?"

Megan nodded. She wanted to be supportive but really didn't have time for this right now. "Yes, I understand all that. But what I meant was, why did you come here? To Buddy's farm?"

"I already told Lacy, I had cakes to deliver. Buddy told me Sissy was hurt," Beth explained.

"Buddy called you?"

"No, silly, I called because Sissy was supposed to pick up the cakes this morning, and she never did. I was wondering what was going on. I called, and I'm glad I did."

"What time was that?"

"Let me think. I called earlier in the morning, but there was no answer. Then about two hours ago, I got through and spoke to Buddy. It took awhile to get a ride. My car's in the shop, you know."

"OK, here's the deal," Lacy said. "Beth, I'll take you home so you can get started on your first catering job. Megan, you swing by and see if you can find Coop. I have a few errands to do. Then, Megan, you meet me at the station."

The three women nodded, and Beth watched Megan get into her truck. "Hey, I thought y'all were supposed to be in some new type of electric police car?"

"We're not talking about that," Lacy said, not breaking stride.

Beth shrugged and followed her ride. Evidently the stress was getting to both of them. *That's why they're so touchy*, she thought. *If only they would find jobs more suited for women.*

31

Megan sat on what had become her usual observation perch, close to Dr. Evans. She didn't particularly have a good reason for being at Sissy Howard's autopsy, but the doctor didn't seem to question her presence. The man enjoyed talking while he worked, and Rodney seldom spoke, so an interested audience was always welcome.

"You see, the muscles stiffen as urea, carbon dioxide, and other cellular by-products of metabolism accumulate because they are no longer removed via the circulating blood," Evans explained.

"So that begins at the time of death?"

"Precisely, after the last heartbeat. This is why rigor develops more rapidly if the deceased was involved in any vigorous activity prior to their demise. It throws off the time of death a bit."

"That's what Buddy suggested. That Sissy had been working the horse."

The doctor looked up from his work for a moment and made eye contact with Megan from underneath bushy gray brows. "I take it you question the statement, along with her death?"

Megan shifted uncomfortably, concerned she was developing a bad reputation with the doctor.

"Well yes, in part. At least Buddy's story of the last time he saw his wife alive."

"I assume you realize you're getting into sticky territory with such talk."

"I know. He's a community leader and public figure with a powerful father. It could cause a lot of backlash, so I hope all this is off the record."

"You're safe to speak freely with me," Evans said. "Actually, I have a few questions myself."

"Really?" Megan scooted her stool closer. This time she made sure it was done quietly.

Rodney looked over at her, annoyed by her dramatics. Evidently, he wasn't a people person. At least not with the living.

Evans, totally oblivious to anything other than the task before him, continued. "It's really more of a subtlety than anything else, but in death, the muscles first relax. They succumb to gravity. In other words, they assume a gravitational dependent position almost immediately. However, if a body is moved after rigor sets in, then the new position does not completely correlate. No matter how careful the criminal is. It's obvious here, there are slight discrepancies that are inconsistent with gravity and the description of how the body was found."

"Could you show me?"

"Certainly. Now you have to understand this is closely based on the livor changes. They occur as the red blood cells settle in the small vessels according to gravity, just as the muscles do."

"You mean the pooling of the blood?"

"Yes, many people refer to it as that. The science of it is after the heart stops pumping, the blood begins to settle from gravity. You can ascertain what position a person was in after death. It is my estimate that this woman was moved between thirty minutes and an hour after her death."

"I knew it," Megan said and slapped her hand on her knee, then remembered where she was. "Sorry," she said, "I get excited when things work out and make sense."

Rodney rolled his eyes to convey his annoyance before he turned his back on her.

Megan ignored him and said, "I'd figured Sissy died more like 6:00 a.m. I don't know what the circumstances were, but I got the feeling Buddy has something to hide."

"Well, you're the detective. It's not my position to solve crimes, if indeed this actually is one. I'm here to determine time and cause of death. The manner, if not natural, is really on your side."

"I understand, Doctor."

"However, I live in this community too and want to see justice done as much as anyone. But there is something I have to ask you. Did you by any chance touch her body in any way? The reason I ask is, within the first couple of hours after death, finger pressure on the lividity produces blanching. Then, as I already stated, if you move the body, the blood will shift, but not to totally correct for a change in posture. Since I see evidence of that, I wondered about the finger pressure."

"I did test for rigor when I got there. Her elbows were fixed, and I got her knee to bend slightly, but at no time did I reposition her. The EMS was already there, and everyone considered it an accident scene and treated it accordingly, not as a homicide."

"Everyone but you?"

"Yes, afraid so. I can't help it. Being a detective isn't something you can turn off."

"I'm pleased to know you understand rigor can't be determined by the feel of the skin or muscle tissue. I can't tell you how many police officers I have to explain that to."

Megan nodded, trying not to look too pleased with herself.

"From what I can detect from the degree of rigor, livor, and the body temp, this woman *did* perish at approximately 6:00 a.m. Now I understand the legal contingents will pose the exercise component. Yet I see no evidence that this woman was involved in vigorous-enough movement to throw off her PMI. I've evaluated her cutaneous glands, and they show no evidence of such activity. The lab will tell more on that. But the real clincher is her fist."

"Her fist?" Megan asked, curious. She was ready to hear some intriguing explanation of the unknown secrets the fist could hold in death.

"Yes, she was found holding a wire brush. I presume it's the type to groom a horse. The funny thing with rigor, though, is that you can have instantaneous rigor demonstrated in a hand if it was in use during a violent death. It's referred to as cadaveric spasm. The way I heard it, this woman was grooming her horse when he acted up and accidentally kicked her, causing her death."

Megan nodded. "That's the same story I was told as well."

"Something's not right here. If she was vigorously brushing her horse, she would have been grasping this brush. Instead, it appears to have been placed in her already rigor hand and the fingers pressed into place. She didn't die with it in her hand. It was placed there, postmortem."

"So she was murdered?" Megan asked.

"I wouldn't go that far. All I'm saying is, there does seem to be something going on here. I suggest we have a closer look at her skull. It should give us a great deal more information."

The doctor brushed the victim's hair out of the way to better view the area of trauma. Unlike Mary Pearl's situation, Sissy's hair was caked with dried blood. "As a general rule, you will find that injuries to the scalp in blunt-force-trauma cases bleed heavily," Evans explained.

He moved aside to allow Rodney to snap a few shots of the area before he proceeded. Megan was impressed by how smoothly the two worked in unison with so little conversation.

"These areas can include abrasions, contusions, or lacerations. I wouldn't actually expect to find an abrasion in this situation though. That's actually where the top, superficial layers are scraped or rubbed off of the epidermis. You see that more in car-accident fatalities."

Megan watched closely, hoping the doctor would discover evidence that would answer some of the questions she held regarding Sissy's death.

"However, what I would expect to find, and I don't see here, is a hoofprint," Evans continued.

"Would that really show up through all the hair?" Megan asked. Sissy was one of those woman blessed with an profusion of beautiful thick, lustrous hair, and every strand knew its place.

"Most certainly. A contusion or ecchymosis which results from an injury that causes hemorrhage beneath intact skin usually reflects the specific imprint of the inflicting object. In this case, according to Buddy, that would be a horse's hoof. One that packed enough force to kill her. To make the situation even more certain, Buddy has identified the actual horse in question."

"Therefore, if an impression was taken of that horse's hoofprint, it would theoretically match the contusion on Sissy's head?" Megan asked. "In a similar manner to bite marks?"

"Precisely, my dear, in size and shape. Something you might also find of interest is that the contusion pattern produced by something, say, like a pipe or baseball bat, is very different. It usually consists of parallel lines separated by a central area of pallor."

Evans stepped back to allow Megan a better view of what had aroused his curiosity. He hoped it would enhance her knowledge and experience base. Unlike Megan, he hadn't walked into this autopsy with any preconceived ideas. But it appeared the two would leave with shared concerns.

"Ohmygod," Megan gasped. Her eyes shot up to meet the doctor's. "It was a pipe, not a hoof."

"It could have been any number of objects found around a barn. But I agree it wasn't a horse hoof. If you look closely at the very tip of the injured area, you can see a slight laceration."

Megan looked but wasn't quite sure she saw what the doctor did. His eyes were trained to see things she had no knowledge of. Lacy was right when she said the time of death was best determined by this man. She'd taken a few courses whereas he'd had years of firsthand experience.

Evans flipped his loupes down and bent over the area. "Yes, that's what I thought," he said.

Megan's anxiety increased tenfold. She wanted to jump up and ask, "What? What did you see?"

That's when the doctor stood back up and pivoted toward her. "As I previously stated, blunt force trauma can produce tiny tears in the tissue or, as we call them, lacerations. The force of the object actually rips the skin apart. What's helpful about that is, at the edge of the laceration, the tissue is undermined. Which in turn reveals the direction of the blow."

"So what does Sissy's injury indicate?" Megan managed to ask, almost in a whisper.

"That the force came from a cranial angle. That means, the blow initiated from above her head. If a horse was to kick her, as stated, the blow would come from a lower angle."

Megan nodded. "So it looks more like someone taller hit her on the head with a blunt object?"

Evans gave a chuckle. "Now, now, Megan. You're not going to get me to say that. Such issues are left up to the court to decide. I will say, however, that even if she fell prior to the kick, the lacerations would not be from above. In that case, I would expect the impact to be more medial or lateral. In other words, from the side. And of course the injury wasn't from a horse."

"I need to send someone out there to look for the murder weapon," Megan stated.

"Let's look at the skull first. Not only does blunt-force trauma leave its mark on the epidermis, it does so on the underlying skeletal aspects as well."

Evans used a scalpel to incise through the skin of Sissy's head. Then he reflected the tissue from the bone as if he were peeling off a mask. The sound it made was sickening, but Megan dared not move for fear she'd miss something. The one thing that could bring down Sissy's killer.

Once Evan finished, the skull was visible under the bright light. "Hoof imprints have a characteristic shape, just as a hammer does. When you examine the bone, it becomes apparent what sort of object was the cause. It also should directly coincide with the soft-tissue injury."

This all made sense to Megan, but she wanted to fast-forward Evans to get to the punch line. But she knew enough not to interrupt and break the physician's train of thought. Which happened to be heading directly where she wanted to go. Only not as quickly as she would have liked.

"These skeletal injuries also reveal the direction of force, and once again, I must say it had to have come from above. You might want to snap a few photos of the blood pattern and measure the height of her head in the stall. I'll have Rodney measure the injury from her heels."

Megan took this as Evans's subtle way to state they now dealt with a homicide.

"I see an almost-circular fracture, but not as much as you would with a hoof or a hammer. If I were to guess, and this is off record, I would go with a pipe or tire iron. If you find the assaulting device, I can easily compare it to what I see here, which is most definitely not a hoofprint."

From that point on, Evans did a routine autopsy exam. He determined the contents of Sissy's stomach, which revealed no food at all. The doctor explained that the digestion and movement of food from the stomach through the intestines proceeded at a relatively predictable rate, the stomach emptying in two to three hours. Since hers was empty, she hadn't eaten breakfast.

Buddy stated he saw his wife at breakfast, around 8:00 a.m. It couldn't be possible for Sissy to have been present—she'd already been dead for two hours. The defense might try to state that Buddy was confused due to the emotional impact of hearing of his wife's sudden death. A reasonable argument for lunch, perhaps, but as far as Megan was concerned, a person couldn't confuse 6:00 a.m.

with 8:00 a.m. At this time of year, 6:00 a.m. was pitch-dark while 8:00 a.m. was bright and sunny. Still, if Sissy was at breakfast, she hadn't eaten. Not all that unusual for someone in Sissy's situation. Upward moving, social conscious, she might have wanted to lose a pound or two to fit into a dress for some event. She couldn't nail him with that, but it was one more discrepancy.

"OK," Evans said, breaking Megan out of her thoughts. "This is what I think."

He walked over and sat down next to her. His fingers were tip to tip, and he lightly bounced them off each other.

"Blunt-force trauma to the head as severe as this woman experienced results in several types of injuries. First, there are characteristic skeletal injuries. Their pattern can aid in the identification or rule out the causative agent. In this case, you can rule out a horse's hoof. The fracture is more typical of what you would find from a pipe, tire iron, or possibly some sort of farrier instrument. The type used to remove the shoes of a horse. I understand this often isn't obvious at the scene, but here, in the progress of this autopsy, it has become very clear."

"I'll go back and look. No one did today. Like I said, they believed it to be an accident."

Evens nodded, then continued. "Also, this victim exhibited cerebral contusions that lie directly beneath the area of impact. You may see areas in the brain directly opposite the impact region as well. They're commonly referred to as contrecoup contusions. This occurs when the victim is forcibly hit, then falls back from the impact displacing the brain to the opposite side of the skull."

"Such as a horse kick to the side of the head. That makes sense. That would cause enough force to propel a person backward with momentum," Megan said.

"Correct. However, I did not find any evidence of this."

The wheels in Megan's head turned as she made a few mental notes.

"What I *did* find was a subcutaneous, subarachnoid hemorrhage, accompanied by cerebral contusions and a laceration that I'd pointed out to you. She had an epidural hematoma outside the tough dural membrane of the brain as a result of a blow to the side of the head. It fractured the squamous portion of the temporal bone, which lacerated the middle meningeal artery."

"Wow, so the blow to the head knocked her out and caused her to bleed to death in the brain?"

"Basically, yes. These injuries caused swelling of the brain as well and a predictable chain of events. First, it resulted in an initial focal increase in intravascular cerebral blood volume. That, in turn, led to herniation and compression of the brain stem. Which then leads to a compromise of respiratory centers and finally death. So even though the initial event was a blow to the head, first her brain bled, swelled, then after a few minutes, she lost the ability to breathe. Whichever way you look at it, there was no evidence of a horse being involved at all," Evans said.

"I appreciate your honesty, Doctor."

"What makes it worse," the doctor added, almost to himself, "was she didn't die immediately. She could have been saved after the initial blow if she'd been taken to a hospital instead of hidden away in a barn. It's truly a shame. She was a sweet girl. She had her whole life ahead of her."

Immediately it came back to Megan that Buddy stated Sissy was hurt when he found her, not dead. *That's not a common mistake. He knew she was alive.* It caused an involuntary shiver to run down her spine. Marital problems or not, to be witness to someone's death without offering help was beyond heartless and cruel. If Buddy had acted on impulse and caused the injury, he could have righted the situation by seeing that his wife received help in a timely manner. Instead, he chose to hide his malfeasance. It changed the way she thought about him considerably.

32

Lacy sat at T. J.'s bar and nursed a beer while she waited for Megan. The day had been a bust. It started out good by getting an ID on the peach-farm victim but went downhill from there. Their forty-eight hours were dwindling, basically halved, and now a boy was missing; and a prominent citizen had died, possibly murdered. It was all very counterproductive. She'd met up with Megan at the station, who insisted she stay in town to sit in on Sissy's autopsy. Lacy had a few more leads to run down; since it wasn't a two-person job, she agreed. She could understand Megan's drive to make a name for herself as a detective. She wanted the same. Problem was, fate was not cooperating. It was barely dusk, and she was worn-out.

She absently watched the 5:00 p.m. news on the plasma TV above the bar when a story caught her attention. As best she could tell, the piece dealt with some local produce company.

"Could you turn that up, please," she asked the bartender, curious from the chief's comment this morning.

"Sure," he said and reached up to adjust the set. He leaned against the counter and watched along with her.

"Hey, that's Walter's Produce, just down the road," he said. "They must have got hit again."

"It was a daring heist," the anchorwoman said. "Over three million dollars worth of melons were stolen. The speed and efficiency with which the criminals made off with so many melons suggests it was well orchestrated by professional thieves."

They showed a uniformed cop taking notes as he spoke to an older man. Lacy presumed he was either the owner or the manager. Neither one looked all too happy.

"The police are baffled by the absence of any clues or major leads. Initial forensics test found no fingerprints on any of the few remaining melons," the woman stated.

Then the picture scanned the empty docks. Lacy was impressed by how large the facility was. She had no idea produce could involve such big money. She worried if this case didn't pan out soon, homicide might be her past, and what she watched was her impending future. Not that that sort of crime wasn't serious, it's just not what she envisioned for herself.

The story changed to the upcoming local elections, and the bartender turned back to his work. "The same thing happens almost every year," he quipped. "All they need to do is look for the trucks loaded down with the melons. They'd be headed north. Seems like they'd be easy enough to spot. It's not like you can hide them in a closet. Plus, they have those agricultural checkpoints."

Lacy merely nodded. She was fairly certain it wasn't that simple, but that usually didn't stop people from their opinions. Before the guy could say anything further, Megan walked in and plopped down next to her. She ordered a beer and proceeded to fill her partner in on Sissy's autopsy. It didn't take long to get the gist across. The woman had been murdered.

"So who do you think did it?" Lacy asked and took another sip of her beer.

"I don't know. Buddy said a few things that didn't add up, but I don't see why he'd kill her."

"Did you drive the egg here?"

"No. It's getting dark and it might rain. I was afraid to drive with the lights on, let alone the wipers. It goes slow enough as it is."

Lacy felt as the superior, it was her responsibility to carry out the chief's commands. Thing was, she didn't like the car and didn't care all that much at the moment. She was more intent on solving the increasing number of murders they had. The test car could wait. "Where is it?"

"I plugged it into an outside receptacle at my apartment building. It's around back, so no one will see it. The super said it was all right. I guess he figured it was so small, it couldn't suck much electricity. I'll tell the chief it ran out of power if he asks."

"Maybe we should move over to a booth. It'd be more private to discuss our notes. Besides, I wouldn't mind something to eat. What's good here?"

There was only one booth open due to the hour. Most of the locals were getting off work. A few chose to eat. The rest mulled around the bar and poolroom, which was standing room only.

"Just about everything. I think I'm going to get a chili dog and cheese fries," Megan said.

Lacy looked at her sharply. "You can never again get on my case about what I eat."

"I know, but I'm stressed out, two autopsies back-to-back. Besides you eat like a horse."

"I'm not a white girl like you. So unlike you, I'm not afraid of having curves and looking like a woman, which is why your selection surprises me."

"Well, for now I need comfort food. We have a serial killer out there who murders women for fun and evidently old ladies and possibly children who get in his way. Plus another killer who got Sissy. When this is all over, I'll go back to my health-conscious diet and run regularly."

Lacy rolled her eyes at Megan; then they both ordered their food, and Lacy got another beer.

"So you don't think the husband did it?" Lacy asked. "They usually do."

Megan bit her lower lip in thought. "I don't know. Buddy has everything going for him—intelligence, money, power, social position. Sissy was beautiful. I don't see the motive there."

"What about money? If he wanted a divorce, would that be an issue?" Lacy asked.

Megan sipped her beer and thought. "I don't really see it. His family's loaded."

"That's my point. If he got divorced, he'd have to share the wealth. Is this about you not wanting to acuse Buddy because of what your father went through in your mother's disappearance?"

"No. But that's what was really weird. Buddy didn't appear to be in grief."

"Maybe they got in a heated argument that got out of hand. He might have killed her by accident," Lacy suggested.

Megan mulled that over. She'd considered the same thing. "For all the things Buddy is, an animal lover isn't one of them. I don't see him up at the barn for any reason," Megan said.

Their food came, and Megan squirted a planet-sized glob of ketchup in her basket. She looked up to see a quizzical Lacy. "What? Ketchup contains high levels of lycopene, along with other antioxidants."

"So now you're worried about your prostate?"

"Very funny," Megan said.

After a few minutes, Lacy asked, "You get in touch with Cooper yet?"

"No, but I taped a message on his door to call or meet us here. If he gets it, he'll show up."

"What about Edward Lee? There's been no word at the station. It's like the kid vanished."

"Sorry, but I've been shut up in the morgue. No one knows anything there about the living."

Lacy nodded. "Yeah, I didn't want to say anything, but you kinda smell like the morgue."

On instinct, Megan smelled her sleeve and shrugged. "At least Sissy wasn't a floater."

They ate for a while before Megan looked back up at her partner, thinking.

"What?" Lacy asked. "Do I have ketchup on my face?"

"No, just thinking. Like what it would be like if you got together with Cooper."

Lacy sat up straight and took a swig of beer before she answered. "That's kind of out of the blue but, yeah. I am a little attracted to him I guess. But I doubt it could develop into anything."

"Why's that?"

"We're too different. Different backgrounds, jobs. And he's so, I don't know, country."

Megan laughed. "There's a lot more to Coop than you know. For starters, he teaches at the University of Florida in Gainesville. Not full-time, but he's considered an expert in horticulture, primarily peaches and blueberries. People from all over the world seek him out for advice."

"Wow, I'm not sure what to say. Did he graduate from there?"

"Yes, but he lived here the entire time he went. He had to help out on the farm. The majority of his knowledge and wisdom is empirical. He loves to read and is self-taught on many aspects of farming and history. He loves history and watching PBS."

"Wow, for some reason, I wouldn't have thought that," Lacy said.

"It seems like there's always more to people than what lies on the surface," Megan replied.

"As I am really beginning to understand from this small town. When I got here, I thought I had everyone pegged, but I was wrong. It's made me ask if Sissy was another victim of our killer?"

Megan almost choked, totally caught off guard by the remark. She looked around to make sure no one was listening. "Are you crazy? You think the serial killer took Sissy out and not Buddy? Why?"

"Why not? Sissy was one of the ladies of the community," Lacy made quotation marks in the air with her fingers as she said it. "She lived in the same area as the others. She was involved in charity events. She might have seen something that would compromise the killer. If he was aware of that, what would keep him from killing her as well? She might be collateral damage."

"Like Mary Pearl? The location and time may be right. But Sissy was a social climber, not a gossip. She spent all her time on their farm. If she saw something, she wouldn't be aware of it."

"The killer might not realize that."

"So you're suggesting that Buddy's innocent?" Megan asked.

"Not exactly. It could have been him or the serial killer. You can't negate either one."

Megan shrugged her shoulders. "Everyone knew Sissy and Buddy had marital problems. The victim is almost always acquainted with their killer in some manner. They often have close family ties. Then you have to consider she wasn't merely murdered but killed, then her body moved to make her death look like an accident," Megan said. "That doesn't sound like the serial killer."

"Really? It sounds a lot like Mary Pearl's death to me. He tried to cover his tracks there too. Maybe we should question Beth. She was one of the last people to talk with Sissy. If we ask her a few questions, it may spur a memory. I happen to know she's home. I dropped her off there to work on her catering job, remember?" Lacy asked.

"Beth's always home. That's what makes her so dissatisfied with her life."

"Oh, don't start that again. Beth was really upset about Sissy. But I should add that Buddy didn't appear all that torn up over his loss," Lacy stated. "Then again, we all grieve individually."

Megan knew too much about grief. The kind that may get better with time but never actually leaves you in peace. She looked down at her cheese fries and half-eaten chili dog. They were also the result of grief. It was a subconscious act to defy death. She couldn't stop thinking about Mary Pearl lying on that cold stainless steel slab. Or Sissy with her perfectly groomed face that was peeled back to reveal the cause of her violent death. Did either woman know their fate?

"Megan? You all right?" Lacy asked.

Megan shook off her thoughts, embarrassed. "I'm sorry, I drifted off for a moment there. Lost in space," Megan said, trying to make a joke of it. "Hey, weren't you going to talk to Jerry?"

Lacy was concerned for her partner. Dealing with death on a daily basis could take its toll. They'd had classes about it at the academy, but she let this event slide for now. You can't help someone who doesn't want it or realize they even need it yet.

"Yes, let me see here." She took out her notepad, flipped it open, and scanned the entries.

"OK, for lab results, we have quite a few. Jerry put a rush on everything, and someone in Tallahassee owed him big-time. First of all, they confirmed there was no adipocere at the first remains site at Cooper's and only a slight amount at the second one near Phillipses' house."

Megan listened intently. "OK, go on."

"Jerry seems to think that although this is within reason for the time frame it takes soft tissue to decay, he said the bones didn't look right. Something about staining or lack thereof. He said they appeared too pristine. His gut says the killer did something to speed the decomposition process."

Megan looked up at Lacy. "Ohmygod. That's exactly what we both thought."

"I know. When he told me, I was excited. Then I began to consider what it actually meant."

"What did he say? Does he have any theories?"

"Yes, but it's really creepy."

"Everything about this case is creepy."

"OK. As we know, in hot, humid weather, bugs along with animal and bacterial activity can skeletonize a body within days. Being somewhat below ground diminishes that rate. However, these bones were completely free of any tissue matter. Completely for the first, almost complete for the Phillips place."

"Especially the ones found at Cooper's," Megan said. "They looked as clean as the teaching specimen."

"Exactly! It sparked Jerry's memory. He told me about these companies that utilized bug pits he saw when he lived in North Carolina. They were huge commercial specimen producers that sold to schools and universities for science classes. What they did was place dead animals in pits filled with flesh-eating bugs. Within twenty-four hours, the skeletal remains are pristine and ready for shipment. There are no stains, as is the case in normal decomposition. He wants to pursue that," Lacy said.

"Oh, how gross." All of a sudden, the heavy chili dog and cheese fries didn't sit so well.

"The killer wants to make sure we don't have any evidence or clues," Lacy continued.

Megan remembered something. "He won't get away with it. Dr. Evans told me there are over two hundred bones in the human body. Each bone can hold a clue. Together, they will tell the story. The story of a person's life. Things such as the foods we've eaten, broken bones, past diseases. All are spelled out in the matrix of our bones. He won't get away with it," Megan repeated.

"I hope you're right, but at the moment we haven't any idea who this creep is. There are no entomology, microbial, or chemical clues we can trace due to this enhanced decomposition. With nothing other than clean bones, the postmortem interval or PMI is hard to pin down."

Megan was about to speak when her cell phone rang. She didn't recognize the number but answered anyway. As a detective, she never knew who the call was from, but anyone could bring forth valuable evidence. "Callingham."

On the other end, all she heard was breathing. Annoyed, she hit End, then tucked her phone back away.

"What, wrong number?"

"No, it's some moron that keeps calling me and breathing."

"How long has this been going on?"

"Since yesterday. I had the guys at the station put a trace on it, but he calls from a different pay phone each time. I have no idea who it is. I give my number out to anyone who might call back with information on a case."

"I don't like this, Megan. You should have mentioned it."

"I kinda thought you had your hands full. Besides, I can handle it. So we were talking about?"

"Right, the bugs. I think he's doing it to erase any evidence," Lacy said.

"He also might do it to rid the body of flesh so no one smells the corpses. Who knows, someone this insane may enjoy watching the beetles devour his victims."

Lacy shivered at the thought and finished off her beer.

"Where does a person purchase flesh-eating beetles anyway?" Megan asked.

"Jerry said that companies who supply research specimens sell them. You could also raise your own easy enough in a warm, humid environment such as Ocala. Oh, and while I was at the lab, Jerry told me some lab results came in from the hair we found in Mary Pearl's kitchen. It revealed the person took medication. Let me see," Lacy said and referenced her notepad. "Some type of cholesterol-lowering drug. They also had a history of cocaine use for months."

"The cholesterol drug doesn't rule out much of the population, but it would indicate we're more than likely dealing with an adult, not some teenager," Megan said.

"Yeah, but a lot of teens have high cholesterol and use street drugs."

"True, but if it were a random B and E, they would keep the cocaine for themselves, not inject their stash into an old woman. I think this was very personal."

"Makes sense. The perp shows a history of cocaine use. He has access to the stuff. Jerry also ran a sample of Mary Pearl's hair that came up negative for both the cholesterol medication and cocaine. No surprise there. She doesn't exactly fit the profile of a user. Not to mention someone her age wouldn't be limber enough to be able to shoot up on the back of her upper arm."

"Heck, I don't think I could give myself an injection on the back of my arm," Megan said.

"I don't like to think about my upper arms while I eat," Lacy remarked. "The other day when I brushed my hair, they did this kind of old-lady-wiggle thing. It kinda freaked me out."

"You should exercise more," Megan said. "Work out your triceps. Upper-arm extensions will do the trick."

"I don't think so. It sounds painful, and I don't like pain. Long sleeves is an easier way out. But back to Mary Pearl's hair. Jerry informed me that hair grows at a rate of one centimeter per month. He had them do a segmental toxicology analysis on both samples. Mary Pearl's came up clean all the way, not just recently."

"I don't think Mary Pearl has ever been on any medication. She said it was against God's will."

"Was she a Christian Scientist?"

"Heavens, no. A Southern Baptist. But she thought if you took anything stronger than an aspirin, you would end up a heroin addict."

"My Grandma Rose was like that. We had to fight with her to get her to take her heart medication," Lacy said. "Anyway, there was one really offbeat thing Jerry brought up. He said he found what seemed to be a cinnamon Tic Tac in the bottom of the Wal-Mart bag. Remember, the one found at the remains at the peach farm?"

Megan nodded. "He mentioned that to me, but I don't know how it factors into our investigation."

The waitress came and renewed their drinks and cleared their plates out of the way, then left quickly to tend to the growing crowd in the poolroom.

"I didn't either until he told me he went to Mary Pearl's."

"Get out! Jerry left the lab? I thought he had a room in the back and secretly lived there."

"That's funny. He said the same thing about you," Lacy said and laughed. She came close to spitting beer out of her mouth. "Sorry. But seriously, I think that after he evaluated the samples, he had a hunch foul play was involved and that perhaps the CSU had missed a small shred of evidence. He actually knew the woman, you know. They sang together in the choir."

"Jerry sings in a choir? No way!" Megan said, obviously shocked.

"That's what he told me. Said he loved it. Anyway, he checked her house out himself. He thought about calling you since you're the detective, but he didn't want to get you in trouble."

Megan was touched that Jerry cared enough to want to protect her and help solve his friend's death. He really was a sweet guy. But here he had this whole other side to him that she didn't know about. She had no idea he held an interest in singing. "He'd never mentioned choir to me."

"He probably wouldn't have mentioned it to me if it weren't for Mary Pearl's death. Anyway, he went to her house to look around. And in the kitchen, under the counter, he found a cinnamon Tic Tac. That's how he figured out for sure what the melted thing in the Wal-Mart bag was. He recognized the smell."

Megan leaned back in the booth, struck by how this substantiated what she'd suspected. The serial killer was the one who killed Mary Pearl. It wasn't just the hair, or that breath mints were all that uncommon, but to find one in both locations was something that couldn't be overlooked.

"So it was personal. The serial killer murdered her," Megan said.

"OK, so now that you know all that, do you see why I suspect that Sissy might be another victim?"

Megan nodded. "It does seem as if our man has two sets of victims and MOs. One quarry for pleasure, where he removes the arms before he kills his prey. The other set is to keep his dirty little secret. This just keeps getting worse. But what did Sissy know?"

"Oh, you're gonna love this then," Lacy said and sat back with her arms folded across her chest. "Remember when the chief said he wanted Jerry to look at the two older cases ASAP?"

"Yes, at the meeting. Right before he gave us the egg to drive."

"Guess what? Jerry did a quick eval of the remains, and they came up the same. They were missing both arms, with similar marks on the adjacent bones that would indicate they'd been removed by a chain saw. The chief already knows, and he's not happy. It confirms that we now officially have four bodies to contribute to the serial killer, and if you count Mary Pearl, five. Sissy's death is still up in the air as a homicide but not necessarily a casualty of our serial killer."

"Oh man, I feel sorry for the chief. What's he going to do when the press gets ahold of this?"

"I think he's planning a speech for a press conference. He wants to avoid a widespread panic. Jerry, on the other hand, plans to send the old remains off to the University of Florida in Gainesville for further evaluation."

"Oh, the C. A. Pound lab. It's the premier forensic anthropology lab in the country. They work closely with law enforcement departments all over the nation. They've done numerous high-profile cases. So what else do you have in that little pad of yours?"

"OK, let's see," Lacy said finding her place again. "He also ran a luminol test on the old Wal-Mart bag with the melted Tic Tac in the bottom."

"I wasn't sure you could do that with something that was weathered," Megan said.

"I know, I wondered about that too, but Jerry informed me that it's only the luminol mix that must be fresh. The blood is actually better old. Plus, it doesn't contaminate blood typing, which he also did. The blood on the bag was Heather's, so that really wraps that up."

"So as of this moment, we know the killer had brown hair, does cocaine, drives a red car, and favors cinnamon Tic Tacs. Oh, and how could I forget, he cuts women's arms off with a chain saw for fun and possibly lives near my friends and family," Megan said.

"Don't forget the possibility of the large flesh-eating bug pit, waiting to be fed."

"I knew it would come in handy to have a partner," Megan said. "But do not fear, I have a plan."

The sparkle in her eyes as she spoke gave Lacy hope. "Please enlighten me. I could use a good plan right about now."

33

Lacy and Megan showed up on Beth's doorstep less than a half hour later. Megan gave a knock and a holler, then went on in the wide-open door. The place smelled of furniture polish and floor cleaner. The kind her mother had always used. She breathed the fragrance in deeply and smiled. The scent made the house feel like a home. It also meant Beth had gone on a cleaning binge.

"This place is immaculate," Lacy said. "Look, you can see where the carpet in the living room has been vacuumed, so there aren't any footprints. That's serious housecleaning there. She had to back out of the room to do that. Definitely premeditated."

Megan nodded and looked around. It was true. The hallway floor shone to a high gloss, and there wasn't a bit of dust anywhere.

"This is weird," Lacy said. "I don't smell any food. She was supposed to start on her first catering job."

"When Beth goes on a cleaning spree, it means one of two things. One, she's either anxious about something, or two, she's ticked off beyond belief. This doesn't look good. She even got out the buffer. I mean, just look at the shine on this wood floor," Megan said.

"You're not kidding. I'd hate for her to ever see what my apartment usually looks like. Maybe Sissy's death finally hit her. Maybe we should leave. It's not like she's going to get in our way if she's here cleaning toilets."

"No, I need to find out what's going on. This has to be more than Sissy's death."

Megan called out to her sister again.

This time Beth answered, "Back here, in the pantry."

"Maybe she's getting organized first," Lacy said. "You know, making sure she has all the ingredients before she begins. It's good business sense."

The two walked back to the kitchen. Lacy sat down at the table while Megan peeked into the pantry. There she found Beth, on hands and knees, scrubbing the floor with a toothbrush.

"I know I'm not the best housekeeper, but what in the world are you doing? I've heard of people who brush their pet's teeth but not the floor," Megan said, confused.

"I'm scrubbing the grout," Beth snapped. "It's not that uncommon."

"And may I ask why you're doing that instead of cooking for Sissy's funeral service?"

"Because I got fired, that's why. I will be stuck as a prisoner in this house forever. My one chance to get out and prove myself, and I blow it. *That* will teach me to dream."

Megan went over and helped Beth up, then gave her a hug. They had their differences, but she did love her sister fiercely. She hated to see her this unhappy.

After a moment, Beth backed away and said, "Thanks. I could use a drink." She stripped off her plastic gloves and went into the kitchen. When she spotted Lacy, she instinctively brought her hands up to her hair. "Oh my, I'm so sorry. I look a mess."

"You look fine," Lacy said, then realized that wasn't exactly true. "OK, we're friends now so maybe you do look a little rough, but you've got good reason. You just had your dream crushed."

This brought a smile to Beth's face.

"I'll get the tea while you tell us what happened," Megan said.

"It's pretty simple, actually. Buddy hired me on the spot to do the food for Sissy's memorial service, but when her family found out about it, they were outraged," Beth explained as she leaned against the counter.

"Why? Do they have a problem with you?" Lacy asked. "It can't be your food."

"Not me personally, but they hate Buddy."

"Then I don't think you can count that. They're doing it against Buddy, not you," Megan said.

"Megan's right. Besides, you can't give up your dream because of one setback."

"Do you really think so?" Beth asked, looking at Lacy.

"Most definitely," Lacy said. "You have a talent that shouldn't go to waste."

Beth took the tea from Megan and downed two pills before she joined Lacy at the table.

"Anyway, since you're not busy, we have a few questions for you. You were one of the last people who talked to Sissy. Did she say anything that stands out in your mind?" Lacy asked.

"No. All we talked about were the cakes for the fund-raiser and how nice the new facility would be. She was excited about the expansion to accommodate more large animals. She really loved animals," Beth said. Her eyes began to get glossy as she fought back the tears. "She had names for all her animals. Who will take care of them now? And what about Willy?"

Megan and Lacy exchanged a wary look. "Who's Willy?" Megan dared to ask.

"He's a baby goat Sissy found abandoned and homeless. She hand-fed him from a bottle every so many hours. She said he's growing like a weed."

Megan knew her own living arrangements disallowed animals of any kind. They would certainly frown on Willy as a tenant. "What about Buddy? He could take care of all her animals, including Willy. They live there already. He could feed them."

Beth shook her head adamantly. "He hates animals. It's something Sissy and he fought about often. He says he's allergic, and that's why his hair's falling out. Willy might starve to death."

"Take it easy, Beth. It will be OK. We can go get Willy right now if you want," Megan offered.

"Really? You would do that for me?"

"Sure. We can either bring him back here or keep him at Cooper's. If Sissy's family wants him, they can come get him anytime."

"Sissy's family will take her horses, but their subdivision is kinda upscale and doesn't allow goats, chickens, or pigs. It's some kind of deed-restrictive covenant."

"What about the kids?" Megan asked. It was almost eight, and she hadn't heard them since she'd got there.

"Don't be silly. They allow children to live there," Beth said, exasperated.

"No, Beth, your kids. What about them? We can't leave them alone," Megan said.

"Ah, don't worry. They're over at Arlene's. They'll be excited to come home to a new pet."

The three walked toward the door when Lacy pulled up short. "Wait. Beth's car's in the shop, and we left your truck at T. J.'s bar. How are we going to get Willy here?"

"He's just a baby goat. I'll hold him on my lap," Beth offered. "It'll be OK."

*　　*　　*

They got to the Howard's farm within minutes. The place looked dark. They could see no lights on in the house. Lacy parked her car under a large oak, and the three women got out.

"Are you certain about this, Beth? I sure as hell don't want to be accused of stealing Buddy's goat. Maybe we should come back tomorrow," Megan said.

"No. Willy could be dead by then. I think baby goats have to eat every few hours," Beth insisted. "Besides, Buddy just lost his wife. He won't be thinking of a baby goat."

"I don't remember a goat at the barn today. But then again, we weren't looking for one," Lacy said. "It might have been sleeping. Babies do sleep a lot. I say we head there first. No need to bother Buddy."

They walked through the darkness toward the main barn. "This is kind of creepy," Beth whispered. "It's so dark out here, and it smells really bad."

Lacy hadn't noticed it earlier that day, but she agreed with Beth. But in Lacy's case, there was little doubt what the stench came from. It could only be rotting flesh. But that piece of information she chose not to share with a civilian. For all she knew, it could be a dead deer at the edge of the woods. The wind shifted, and the odor was gone. But her trepidation lingered. She needed to get Beth out of there and fast. She glanced over at Megan and nodded. It seemed she, too, had recognized the smell of death.

*　　*　　*

Lacy, Megan, and Beth were crammed into the front seat of the hatchback, while Willy took up the entire backseat and munched happily on a flake of hay.

"I thought you said he was a baby," Lacy snapped. "Babies are tiny. He's not tiny."

"That's the way Sissy made it out. He could be a baby. I don't know that much about goats," Beth said. The truth was, he weighed at lest eighty pounds and had a mind of his own and pooped freely.

"Well, he looks full grown to me," Megan said. "And he certainly doesn't need a bottle."

"What do you think his sharp little goat hooves will do to my upholstery?" Lacy asked.

"Humm," Megan said. "It's not that far of a drive, and he is kind of little."

Lacy shot a dagger look at her partner. Beth, being stuck in the middle, both physically and figuratively, felt the uncomfortable tension, not to mention where the gearshift was with respect to her hindquarters. "That place stunk," Beth said, wanting to change the subject.

"It was a barn, and now one of its main inhabitants is stinking up my backseat," Lacy said.

"Let's drop Willy off at Cooper's. It's the closest," Megan said.

That seemed reasonable to Lacy, who had planned to use her car for a trade-in as soon as she could afford it. She didn't know if it was calculated in the blue book value or not, but she had to assume goat doody didn't add to a vehicle's worth, no matter what the mileage.

"No, really, it wasn't a barn smell. It was more of a cloying, sickening odor," Beth said.

"It's not for you to worry about, Beth," Lacy snapped again. "You probably breathed in too many chemicals earlier. Willy's your problem." Lacy didn't want a civilian getting involved with what she suspected might be going on at the Howard's farm.

Beth nodded. She did have a tendency to mix whatever was handy when she cleaned all upset.

"You're probably right. I did feel a little woozy earlier. That's why I propped the doors open."

"So what will Coop think about his new pet?" Lacy asked, having never given away a goat.

"I'm not real sure about that," Megan said. "I never thought that far ahead."

"I'd gladly take him, but with his horns and all, I was afraid for the children," Beth said.

"Ohmygod, the horns," Lacy gasped.

Just as she said it, all three women heard a loud rip.

"Oh, that can't be good," Beth said and twisted around.

Willy looked at her. He had a mouthful of hay, and the cloth liner of the car roof hung from one of his horns.

"It's OK, dear, just keep driving and don't look back," Beth said and patted Lacy on the knee. "We can fix this. I have a glue gun at home."

34

He sat in his shed quietly. Alone, except for the collection of human arms and the memories of the women they'd belonged to. Now they were his. The small lump in the sack remained still. He didn't know if the boy had died yet. The truth was, he really didn't care. He wasn't any fun, not like the women had been. They were each a thrill in their own separate ways. The chase, the seduction, then the dominance. All had wanted him. His money, power, and influence. Then he controlled them. The boy, on the other hand, was merely an annoyance. Someone who needed to be taken care of.

He popped a cinnamon Tic Tac in his mouth and tried to relax, but for some reason, tonight he couldn't. He couldn't shake this sense of foreboding. It was getting warmer every day. The summer heat would be here soon. Too soon. With the high heat and humidity, any woman he killed would be completely decomposed within days. There would be no use for the bug pit, and that was something he enjoyed so much. The occasional chicken or scraps he got from the local butcher and threw in there to keep the little beauties happy between corpses wasn't the same. Sure they were still fun to watch, but with the women, it was different. That was special.

He got a shiver when he thought about the last woman he had thrown in there. Within seconds, the flesh-eating scavengers covered her body. He could hear them eat away at her carcass as she held onto life. What once had been a pretty face had turned into a skull right before his eyes. The scene excited him, as did the memory. Each time, it'd been hard for him to pull away from the activity and close the lid on the intense excitement of the tiny carnivores. It was the beauty in nature's way. When they were finished, there would be no odorous, rotten flesh. Only clean, easy-to-dispose-of bones. Virtually nontraceable evidence, and the length of time the woman were dead was totally obfuscated by the insects. It was only his treasures that could cause him trouble, but he couldn't part with his collection. They gave too much enjoyment, with each set of arms in a different stage of decomposition. Otherwise, they were all perfect murders. So much so, he'd been able to repeat it several times in the same community for years, without an eyebrow raised toward him.

That's actually what made his secret hobby that much sweeter. No one suspected him. He drank coffee with them in the morning and had beers with the guys after work, but still, they harbored no idea. The cops scrambled around, chasing their tails. He was one of the good guys. Part of the system. He was untouchable. A hometown boy.

Then the lump in the corner moved. He cursed and went over and kicked it. A tiny moan emerged from the sack. The boy would be dead soon enough. Maybe the heat would be good for something. However, it was making his arm collection rank. He didn't mind it so much himself since he enjoyed the smell. However, he did notice others had sensed it while they were at his house earlier. Perhaps he could put out mothballs. They were overbearing and smelled enough to cover up the putrefied rotting flesh. Since the little white balls were known to dissuade snakes, no one would question their use. Snakes were a known nuisance in the area; everyone knew that. Between the moccasins, rattlers, and copperheads, they were everywhere.

The wind gusted outside, and a branch rubbed against the metal shed with a screeching sound. He hated the wind. It was the second time that night it sounded like someone was close by. Someone could sneak up on you when it was this windy out. The hair on the back of his neck stood up. After catching the boy in his yard, he'd begun to get a bad feeling about things, and it caused him to feel claustrophobic. He got up and began to pace like a caged animal. He could not get caught. For the first time, his shed felt too small and closed in.

He feared his fate was more precarious than he had originally thought. That he might not be invisible anymore, and it was all his wife's fault. He'd seen Megan and that new detective at T. J.'s. The thought of kidnapping Megan and telling her about his first murder made him laugh. Oh, that was a glorious day, so long ago, but still vivid in his mind. They say you never forget your first time, and it was certainly true for him. Of course with her, it hadn't been planned. Thus, there was no anticipation, but that didn't detract from his pleasure.

However, with Lacy, that could be a different story. To add her arms to the collection would be a joy beyond any he had known as of yet. But it would also be risky. He couldn't hurt Megan in the process. At least, not yet. Megan was special.

35

After the two detectives dropped Beth off at her house with Willy, they swung by to pick up Megan's truck. With Beth out of the way, Lacy was free to talk.

"That smelled like rotting flesh back there," Lacy said.

"I noticed that too but didn't want to say anything in front of Beth. It wasn't as bad as a decomposing human, but it definitely smelled like something rotten. We should check it out."

"After Sissy's autopsy, we might be able to get a search warrant. Even though that stench wouldn't have anything to do with her death, it would let us look around. I'll talk to the chief about it. Right now, I'm due to meet with the lead investigator in one of the old cases at the station. You want to come along?"

"No, I need to go for a run and clear my head," Megan said. "In the meantime, I plan to try and get in touch with Coop. Then I'll check in with the station about Edward Lee. I can meet you there. Call me when you finish. It's 6:30 pm. Now. I can be there by 7:30."

"Sounds good." Before Lacy drove off, she asked, "You said Angus Howard and the chief are hunting buddies, didn't you?"

"Megan briefly glanced around and stepped closer to Lacy's car. "Yeah. They're pretty tight."

"Do you think the chief would give Buddy special consideration because of that?"

"Whether he does or not, we have no evidence against Buddy, only speculation that Sissy was murdered. Her death poses several questions we have no answers to. If anything, Buddy will push to find those answers and prosecute someone for her death."

"You have a point. The crime scene wasn't exactly secured. Anyone could have walked through there. A good lawyer could put a twist on any evidence found now," Lacy said.

"Whoever the killer was, he'll more than likely walk on this one," Megan said.

"God, I hate shit like that."

It was the first time Megan had heard contempt in her partner's voice. She wondered if it was specifically directed at this particular case or more of a summation of all the unsolved cases she'd worked throughout her career. She knew that kind of frustration. For her, the anger began when no one ever paid for the loss of her mother. It became a driving force in her life.

"Buddy's smart, intelligent, and knows how to lay on the charm. His family's reputation can't be challenged. I can't see him crumbling on the witness stand. Or for that matter losing it enough to kill Sissy. His style's to blow off steam, to go out drinking with the guys, maybe hook up with a young girl. He may be a charmer, but I can't picture him as a killer," Megan said.

Lacy thought about that. She didn't know Buddy as well as her partner, but what she'd seen of the man, so far, matched what was said. "I see what you're saying. With all that behind him, he would have no motive to kill his wife. Maybe she was involved with another man?"

"Could be," Megan said and backed away from Lacy's hatchback and waved. "See ya in an hour."

36

Cooper followed Edward Lee's usual path home twice over and had come up with nothing. Not even a trace of the boy. No one could remember exactly when they saw him last. The holiday had thrown everyone off. He was about to give up when he stopped off at Parker's garage to grab a cold soft drink. It was past closing time, and Gabe was finishing a job when he looked up.

"Hey, Cooper, haven't seen you in a while. You need a new tire for that old tractor of yours?"

"No, just a cold drink," he said. "Looks like a bad flat you're working on."

"Yeah, got flat from a critter bone," Gabe said.

"What's that again?"

"People drove over some kind of roadkill. Got a critter bone stuck in the tread. It's fixable though. Happens more than you'd think."

Cooper plunked his quarter into the machine, made a selection. A second later, an ice-cold drink tumbled out into his hand. He pulled the tab back and drank half of it down in a single swallow. "Man, that tastes good. I was darn right parched."

"Yeah, you can feel the summer heat coming. I think it got up to eighty-six degrees today, and the humidity's creeping up with it. I'm gonna have to get out the big fan soon 'nough."

Cooper wiped his forehead with the back of his hand and sat silently for a moment.

"So how's the peach crop coming along this year?" Gabe asked while he packed up his tools.

"Good. Real good. That rain the other day helped a lot, but my watermelons are a loss."

"You hear about the big robbery over at Walter's produce?"

"Yeah, stuff like that really ticks me off. You work your butt off all season, and some jerk comes along and steals everything. It ain't right."

"Well, they'll more than likely catch 'em bragging at T. J.'s after a few too many."

Cooper nodded, finished his soda, and tossed the can in the recycle trash. He turned to leave when a thought struck him. "Hey, Gabe, have you repaired any red cars in here lately?"

Gabe considered it an odd question, coming from a peach farmer, so he wiped his hands off and walked over to Cooper, thinking as he did.

"Actually, yeah, yesterday. Had one of those big Ford Thunderbird's in here. It had a dent on the back right panel. Owner said he was goofing around after he went to T. J.'s place and got a little out of hand. Kind of wanted to keep it hush-hush."

"Anyone I would know?"

Gabe laughed. "Considering you know most of the folks that live out here, I would have to say yes. But in this case, most everyone knows him. It was Buddy Howard. You know how he likes to drink. He thinks no one else notices and that those damn cinnamon mints hide the smell of the alcohol on his breath."

Cooper nodded as his stomach did a flip. Buddy lived near him, Edward Lee, and the Phillipses' place. But Buddy couldn't be the killer. He was a county commissioner, and his dad was a judge. He shook his head, then realized Gabe was staring at him expectantly.

"You OK?" Gabe asked.

"Yeah, just thinking." Cooper was about to leave when he added, "By the way, have you seen Edward Lee lately?"

"Yeah, now that you mention it, he stopped off here yesterday to get a drink after school. Why? He not show up for work or something?"

"I think he might be in trouble."

"How so? He stops in here a lot after school. No big deal. I think he has a crush on little Katie. Can't say I blame him. She's a cute kid. I feel sorry for Parker when she turns sixteen. That man's gonna have his hands full."

"By any chance, did Edward Lee see that Thunderbird?"

Gabe rubbed the stubble on his chin with his hand. "Well yes, now that you mention it, I was fixing it at the same time he stopped in. He acted all interested. Told me he might want to be a mechanic when he grows up."

"Did he know who the car belonged to?"

"I don't know. I sure as hell didn't tell him, but a lot of people see Buddy driving that car around. He lives out by y'all. Who knows, he might have seen the work order. Heck, I don't know. I wasn't babysitting the kid, I was working."

"I understand. Thanks," Cooper said. When he turned to leave, he got his answer. There on Gabe's tool bench was the work order for the tire he'd been fixing. It was in plain sight for all to read, as would the work order for Buddy's Thunderbird have been. Just as clear, in easy-to-read print, was the name, address, and phone number of the vehicle's owner.

That had to be what happened. Edward Lee stopped in here after school to get a drink, saw the car, along with the work order. The crazy kid saw the work order and thought it was the killer's car, so he went after the killer himself. But still, Cooper couldn't make himself believe it could be Buddy Howard, of all people. He'd never liked the man, but he also never felt him to be that emotionally unstable. Surely he wouldn't hurt a child.

Hopeful to now have a lead on finding the boy, he also feared for Edward Lee's safety. He took off to his truck at a fast pace with a feeling of dread heavy in the pit of his stomach.

"Coop, you all right?" Gabe called after him.

"It's not me you need to worry about," he said over his shoulder and kept going.

37

Megan actually hadn't intended to go for a run, but she knew if she said that, Lacy would let it drop like a stale biscuit after a picnic. She had meant what she said about Buddy, but she'd recognized that smell, the same as Lacy. It wasn't merely rotten meat. It smelled of death. Human death. There was something not right at the Howard farm. She sensed it earlier when she was at the accident scene, then again when they went to rescue Willy. Beth noticed it too. Perhaps not articulated in cop words, but she was a keen observer. She was a mother with skills. She noticed everything that went on around her. Nothing got past her eagle eye. Lacy had tried to write it off as a chicken carcass or two, but Megan knew better. She could smell a lie almost as well as Beth.

Now the main objective was not to get caught snooping. Her presence on Buddy's farm would be hard to explain and much easier accomplished alone. After her encounter with Dr. Evans, she'd planned to go there to photograph the blood pattern on the stall. A picture of the scene would be needed to back up his findings. Even though Lacy told her to wait, she felt compelled to go now. Her concern was that it would be erased before dawn.

She parked her truck down the road, in the woods, and cut through at a diagonal. She tried to be quiet, but except for the rain on Easter, it had been dry. On every step, leaves crunched and twigs snapped. The wind rustled the leaves above. It was a clear night, and the moon shone brightly against her shirt. It helped light her way but also made her feel exposed. She wished she'd chosen darker-colored clothes. Then again, this excursion hadn't been planned.

She heard a distinct noise directly behind her and froze. It came from the bushes. Close by was another loud rustle. Then a twig snapped, but not from her feet. Her heart pounded. She came close to giving a yelp of fear and silently chastised herself. She was a detective. This was her job. Still she couldn't ignore the deep feeling inside that warned she was in mortal danger.

Before she could react, a family of opossums emerged from the underbrush. A mother with her three babies in tow. They paid her no heed as they passed. Megan sucked in a deep breath, then let it out slowly in relief, but the sense of impending danger persisted.

She looked around, took another deep breath, trying to calm her jagged nerves and think of the positive outcome. Yet all her mind conjured up was that someone was hunting her. Perhaps it was all the talk earlier of the serial killer, flesh-eating bugs, and arms that had been sawed off. It had given her the heebie-jeebies. So why, she asked herself, was she in the deep woods, in the dark, alone? But she knew if she waited for Lacy to ask the chief then clear it with Buddy, the stall would be scrubbed clean. Perhaps to cover up evidence or just to cover up a painful memory. Just as the evidence they'd had on the serial killer was washed away by the rain. She wasn't about to let another opportunity slip through her fingers. Even if it was a little creepy.

She took in a deep breath to gain her composure. When she looked up, she noticed a curious glimmer of light through the trees. It wasn't far, so she decided to check it out. The breeze blew toward her, and it carried an unpleasant stench. Beth was right. It was a cloying odor, and it wasn't from the barn. Instead it seemed to emanate from the area around the shed. It smelled of decaying human flesh. A scent that once experienced, a person never forgets. That's why Lacy had picked up on it so fast.

Obliged to continue, she crept forward. This was no longer about photos of blood patterns or Sissy's death. It was the nagging feeling that had haunted her all day. It was the dead calling out to her. There was something evil on this farm, and Buddy Howard had something to do with it. It went against what she'd previously thought of the man, but the sense she got now was too strong to ignore, especially after Sissy's autopsy. Megan intended to find out exactly what part he played in his wife's death, if in fact there were some connection. It might be as innocuous as someone else killed Sissy, and wanted to cover it up. He stumbled upon her body and reported it as stated, with no foul play on his part. Buddy could be totally innocent.

As she stepped out of the woods into the yard, the security lights from the house cut on. Megan had been so engaged with her thoughts, she didn't realize how close to the home she'd gotten. Frozen and exposed, she blinked as the bright lights shone in her eyes. She prayed they would shut off, and no one would notice. However, that hope was soon extinguished when she heard a voice holler from the back steps.

"Who's there?"

"Oh crap," Megan murmured.

The screen door opened with an audible creak. There on the back stoop stood the silhouette of Buddy, shotgun in hand. She had no doubt it would be loaded, as he also appeared to be. She saw him put his hand up to shield his eyes from the spotlight. He seemed to look straight at her.

"I know you're out there, whoever you are. Might as well come out."

His words were slurred. The way Megan figured it, she had two options. One was to run like hell through the woods and hope to God Buddy didn't shoot her, or that she didn't run headfirst into a tree. The other was to speak up. Problem was, she had no plausible excuse for being there. She had no warrant. Without a clue as to what she was going to say, she stepped forward.

"Hey there, Buddy, it's Megan," she said and stepped further into the circle of light.

He dropped his gun to his side and smiled. "Megan. How nice to see you."

She walked another step closer and stopped. The air was heavy with evening dew, and it held the unmistakable scent of rotting flesh. She pretended not to notice. She watched as Buddy came staggering down the steps, obviously drunk. Some might say that was understandable, considering his wife had died tragically only hours ago. Whatever his reason, it made her anxious. She felt around for her cell phone and silently cursed when she realized she'd left it in the truck.

Buddy's gun rested against his side as he glared down at her. "I should use a mint to hide the smell of alcohol on my breath. Oops, I wasn't supposed to tell you that. You're a cop."

"It's OK, you're not in a vehicle," Megan said, taking a tiny step backward.

Buddy stepped closer. He reeked of overpowering aftershave, which made her nauseous. Especially mixed with the stench of the decayed flesh and alcohol breath. He leaned heavily against the muzzle of the teetering gun. Megan wished he'd fall over and pass out.

"I can't have my constituents know I drink," Buddy said.

"I won't tell anyone," Megan said as she inched back toward the woods.

"Baby, I know you won't say a thing to anyone."

Megan gave an involuntary shiver. When she'd spoken to Buddy in the past, he'd made her feel special, like one of the pretty girls. This time, she felt dirty. He was so sure of himself and acted as if he were some kind of celebrity. They were totally alone, and he acted much different than he did the last time they met. She also noted his formidable size. Again, she mentally kicked herself for being stuck out here without her phone, no backup, and no one knowing where she was. Not very well thought out. At least Lacy expected her back at the station by 7:30 p.m.

"I'm sorry about Sissy. It's a shame her own horse killed her."

"Flash. That's his nickname. Noble Warrior was too long. He was a handful, that's for sure."

"I would think an experienced rider such as your wife could handle an animal like that."

"What do you mean by that, Detective? You want to insinuate something?"

"No, it's just that Sissy was an expert rider. She knew horses, and it's hard to believe she was killed by one of her own. Seems she would know not to get in the stall with an agitated animal."

"I don't like your tone, woman. You better be careful what you say."

At this point, Megan knew she was on thin ice, but her view of Buddy had changed. He was not the charismatic charmer he appeared to be in public. Evidently, a private audience received different treatment. Perhaps that's what happened to Sissy.

"What are you doing here anyway?" Buddy asked.

Megan wondered when he'd get around to that. "I came to look for Willy's hairbrush. We forgot it when we were here earlier, and he really needs it. His fur has hay all stuck in it. But I didn't want to intrude on your grief, so I came around back so I wouldn't disturb you." The story was full of holes, but it was the only thing Megan could come up with. She was surprised she could speak at all.

Buddy didn't question that the barn was fifty yards in the other direction. Nor that Willy had seemed to have never seen a hairbrush. He was a goat. He lived his life in a barn. Who the hell cared what he looked like. Then again, Buddy was shit-faced drunk, so none of this occurred to him. A fact that Megan wanted to take advantage of.

"Well, I hope you're doing all right. I'll leave you alone now. I've got to get going," Megan said and backed away. "I'm supposed to meet my partner at the station."

"Sorry about your sister."

Megan's heart lurched to her throat. What about her sister? She was fine an hour ago. "Beth?"

"Yeah, the catering thing. I didn't mean to get her hopes up and then have Sissy's family crush them. They don't like me, but they shouldn't take it out on her. I told them that, but her parents wouldn't listen."

"That's very kind of you. I'll tell her that," Megan said. She was actually relieved to think he cared about her sister that much. She breathed in again. She had no reason to be scared. Of course he wondered who set the security lights off in his yard. Sure he'd been drinking, but his wife died that morning. She felt empathy toward him. He seemed sincere. She was free to leave.

It was as if Buddy read her thoughts. "Not so fast there, cupcake," he said, reaching out to her. He took her arm firmly in his hand. He was a large man, not exactly in great shape, but still much more powerful than Megan.

"What are you doing? Let go of me." She wished she had her nightstick or pistol.

"Relax, sweetness. I'll walk you over to the shed. That's where Willy's brush is. No need to get upset."

Holy crap, Megan thought. *The stupid goat does have a brush. You certainly wouldn't have known it by the look of him.* Now she wasn't sure what to do. Buddy wanted to be helpful. But as soon as she got that stupid brush, she was out of there.

"You look tired," Buddy remarked.

"I've been busy lately."

She didn't want to tell him she went to bed exhausted, only to lie there wide awake until dawn. She'd become afraid of sleep for fear of what her dreams would hold or what the next day would bring. She couldn't shake the feeling that someone she knew was the killer. A neighbor.

Buddy walked slowly as he held onto Megan's arm firmly with one hand, the shotgun tight in the other. She assumed his grip was due to the amount of alcohol in his system and needed something to stabilize himself. *Get the brush and leave,* she told herself. *The brush, then leave.*

God, this place stinks, she thought. "You kill a bunch of chickens lately?" Megan asked. She knew they had chickens, and it was necessary every now and then to cull out the ones that no longer laid eggs. Most folks she knew let the older hens go free range as a reward for the years of fresh eggs. After what Beth had told her, she wondered if it was possible that Buddy snapped their necks and left them rot. It would be a perfect way to upset Sissy. It's possible that's what started their last fight.

Buddy stopped abruptly and spun Megan around to face him. "Why would you ask that?"

Megan tried to keep her composure despite the growing sense of dread in her gut. It seemed as if Buddy had another side to him that she'd never known. Perhaps Nate and Cooper's dislike of the man lay deeper than jealousy. Maybe they'd seen this side of him on the baseball team. Perhaps it was displayed in the locker room.

"Sorry, I didn't mean to upset you. I just thought I smelt a bad odor. It was probably the trash. I'm sure with all that went on today, you had other things on your mind."

Buddy stood there and glared at Megan for a few beats before he nodded and said, "Let's get you that damn brush."

When they approached the door to the shed, Buddy turned again and offered her a wry grin. Something about it made her skin crawl. Only days earlier, she'd found him somewhat alluring. She noted the smell here was worse, but it didn't seem to offend her host. Then again, he was inebriated.

She stood there as he fiddled with the two locks and wondered why a shed like this would have such high security. From her experience, a stolen goat brush didn't bring much of a price on the black market. But perhaps expensive horse tack did.

"What's with the locks?" she had to ask.

Buddy looked over at her with a smirk and said, "You'll see, darlin', you'll see."

"You need to cut the grass around this place, or it'll end up infested with snakes."

This made Buddy howl with laughter. The reaction surprised Megan. It wasn't what she'd expected, and her nerves were on edge. She began to think that Buddy might not only be drunk but insane as well.

"I don't understand what's so funny."

"You—showing up here tonight for one thing."

He fished around in his pocket and pulled out a small container. It made a familiar sound as he shook it over his hand. He tossed back whatever it was in his mouth. "Want a Tic Tac?" he asked and held them out.

Megan felt her lower lip quiver and fought to remain calm. "What kind?"

"Cinnamon."

Her legs grew weak, and she stumbled slightly before she righted herself again. "No, thank you," she managed to say. For a moment, she was so overwhelmed with fear, she couldn't hear. The realization that she was alone with the serial killer hit her. She noticed Buddy glare at her. She couldn't afford to lose it now. Her life depended on it. She had no backup.

"Something wrong, sweetness?" he asked.

"No. It's just that I don't like cinnamon candy."

"That's too bad. I've gotten fond of them. Carry them everywhere I go."

Megan recalled him popping something in his mouth the day she ran into him near his in-laws' house. But hindsight was no help now.

"I was going to go after your partner first, but this works out just as well. You will solve all my problems, and I get to have a little fun in the process," Buddy said.

Megan turned to bolt away.

Buddy reached over, grabbed her by the hair, and pulled her face close to his. At first, she thought he intended to kiss her. Then he opened up the door to the shed and shoved her in with so much force she stumbled and fell to the ground on her hands and knees.

The door slammed closed behind her, and she was left in total darkness. She could hear Buddy laugh as he locked the door behind her.

"I'll be back soon, sweetheart. We have unfinished business. Try not to miss me too much while I'm gone."

Then silence, and dread took over.

38

It was pitch-dark, and the stench of decayed human flesh assaulted Megan. She didn't need light to realize there was a dead body in the same room where she was held captive. Cautiously, she felt around, almost afraid of what she would touch. The floor was dirt; that much was readily apparent. She continued, trying to gain her bearings. Yet one thing was very clear. She'd totally misjudged Buddy. Now she was in serious trouble. At least he hadn't bothered to tie her up.

If being locked in the same space as a decaying body in the pitch-dark wasn't creepy enough, she knew that if she didn't find a way to escape soon, she would be right alongside the rotting corpse. She could kick herself for being so stupid. She had no cell phone or revolver. Both were safely tucked under the seat of her truck, not more than a quarter mile away. A rookie mistake. To make matters worse, Buddy hadn't bothered to check for either. If she wasn't a total idiot, she could have called for help by now. How could she have let a complete drunk outsmart her? She hated when she made dumb mistakes, and this one very well might cost her life. Silently, a tear ran down her face.

She couldn't afford to feel sorry for herself or panic. But the only person who expected her was Lacy. As easygoing as Lacy was, she'd accept Megan being late or not showing up at all. She didn't know Megan well enough to realize how out of character her being late the other day was. Cooper might call, but since they hadn't spoken recently, he wouldn't think much of her not answering. He'd figure she was busy. She did another mental head slap. This wasn't getting her anywhere. She had to focus. This was a life-or-death situation, and she was prolife on this issue.

Then she thought of Beth. It would be her sister who'd freak out when she didn't hear from her. As much as her sister's constant interference in her life bugged Megan, she now became her best chance at a rescue. Still, Beth would have no idea where to look for her. It was possible by the time anyone came, it would be too late. Buddy was sure to return soon. "Oh shit," Megan said.

A branch hit the side of the shed and scraped along the metal. Megan froze, petrified.

"My god, you are so stupid," she said out loud and actually hit herself on the forehead. "Stupid, stupid, stupid." She so wanted to be a tough-ass detective, but here she was, a wimp. The fact was, she was scared to death.

Then a little mew from the far corner caught her attention. "Hello?" she called out.

That wasn't the wind, she thought and listened intently. The blackness heightened her other senses, including fear. It could have been a large rat, and she hated rats.

A slight rustle of cloth, then the same noise again.

Was it possible another woman was being held captive as well? Another victim?

That's when reality totally sunk in. Buddy's remark about his intention to get Lacy first. She now knew Buddy was the serial killer and must have realized they were close. Lacy was to be his next victim.

Events started to fall into place. Jerry commented that Buddy had been at the lab, asking about the evidence. It wasn't because of his father's political campaign. It was to know what the police knew. It fit the profile perfectly. Buddy enjoyed being close to the chase. Watching the police scurry around after him. That was until Lacy and she started to get too close. Now the detectives became his prey.

It also explained how he met Heather. She worked on his father's campaign. She was in the wrong place at the wrong time. An innocent victim. She could understand how Heather fell for his deception. A charismatic well-dressed man who acted interested. He had social power and status. It had worked on Sissy, a beautiful woman in her own right. Megan, as well, had almost fallen for it. Buddy used his charm and status to pick up impressionable young college girls. No one suspected him. Either then, or now. She had to escape to warn everyone and stop him.

While he appeared concerned about his community, he ate away at its belly. He played varsity baseball with Nate and Cooper. Then he went off to college and on to serve in the military. He came back eight years later, a decorated soldier. It all made sense and appeared so upright. But his absence explained the serial killer's eight-year hiatus. He'd been able to keep his sick life a secret, separate from his public persona. *That was until now. I have to stop this monster,* Megan thought.

The tiny sound, once again, came from the corner, snapping Megan out of her reflections. A part of her hoped it was another woman and not rodents. She didn't want to be alone in this utter darkness. Not in her last hours of life. Detective or not, she was human and scared to the bone.

"Hello?" she said, barely a whisper. She began to crawl through the blackness toward the sound. She inched her way across the floor, gaining a newfound respect for the blind. The complete absence of light scared her to the core, but she continued to scoot over the dirt. She hit something that stuck up out of the ground. Unsure of what it was, she felt it with her hand. It was wet and gooey. She put her hand to her face to smell, then retched severely. She had just touched the source of the rotting flesh. She had pieces of dead human stuck in between every finger.

"Ohmygod, ohmygod," she chanted and frantically wiped her hand in the dirt to get the rotten flesh off. But it was all over her and had dripped onto her wrist. "Oh my god," she said again. She'd never been so repulsed. Where was Beth now with those damn alcohol wipes? She heaved a few more times before she heard the tiny voice once more. That was what she had to do, focus on that noise. She was a detective, not a victim. Even if it was a kitten, she intended to save it.

Megan resumed her slow crawl through the dark. Every few feet she would hit something that stuck up out of the dirt. She immediately recognized the stench, having already learned that revolting lesson the hard way. She wondered how many women had Buddy killed. And was one still alive?

"I'm on my way to help you," Megan called out to the darkness.

Another squeak came from the corner. Megan scooted faster, now with a more defined purpose. It did not sound like a rat or kitten but a human.

"Hold on, I'm coming to save you."

OK, she thought, *that might be a bit grandiose since I'm stuck in here too, but a prisoner needs hope.* She'd learned that in her police training. It certainly wouldn't help anyone to admit that they both might soon die a hideous, painful death at the hands of a maniac with a chain saw.

"Help," a weak voice eked out.

"I'm on my way," Megan answered. She could now tell it was a voice not an animal. Not only was it human but of a child. Within moments, she reached the small bundle. Blindly she felt her way to untie the ropes and released the contents. A small hand reached out and grasped her fingers. She reciprocated the touch with a vengeance. It gave Megan hope to learn she wasn't too late. There was not only life but a great deal of spirit left to save. She now had two lives to live for.

Spindly little arms wrapped around her, and a small face buried itself in the crook of her neck. Quiet whimpers escaped the diminutive figure, and Megan tried to console the child with a rocking motion. Until that moment, she hadn't realized she actually had any maternal instincts. But they were there, and they were fierce.

"He's a bad man," the child sobbed.

"Yes, honey, I know," Megan said and stroked the child's head. "I won't let him hurt you anymore. I came here to save you."

She actually had no way to keep that promise, but she meant it deep in her heart when she spoke it. Buddy would have to kill her first before any more harm came to this little person. A newfound resolve and determination to protect and preserve life surged through her.

"We have to do something quick because that mean man will come back. We have to work together," Megan said.

"He has dead people's arms in here, and they stink real bad," the child said.

"I know, baby. We need to get out of here. Do you know a way out?

Megan didn't need light to know the child's answer. His body language told her everything as he melted in defeat at the question.

"Not to worry, we'll make our own way out," Megan said. "We can do it together."

"My name is Edward Lee," the child said.

That set Megan back on her butt, shocked. She hadn't expected to find him a hostage here. Then again, she hadn't expected a lot of things that had happened so far that evening.

"I'm Megan," she said. "We'll get out of this. Coop and your mom have been looking for you."

"Really?" the boy said. "They have?"

"You bet, and we can't make them wait any longer. This is what we're going to do." She remembered Jerry told her that the humerus was the longest bone in the arm, which was what Buddy collected. She decided to use the resources on hand to dig their way out. She hoped that one day she'd be able to look back on this experience an learn from it.

The two went to work, feverishly digging next to the wall of the shed. Megan assumed since it was a basic dirt floor, the building would have no footing. If they dug deep enough, they could create a space large enough to crawl out to freedom. She once owned a dog that was an expert at it. From there, her truck was close enough to run to.

The problem was, it wasn't as easy as she'd hoped. Edward Lee was weak, and a bone was nowhere near as effective a digging implement as a shovel. It was more like scratching at the dirt. With Buddy's imminent return hanging over their heads, she had to think of another way.

Then a ray of hope popped into her mind. They were in a shed. People kept shovels and other tools in sheds. "Edward Lee, is there a light switch in here?"

"I think so, but I don't know where. He kept me in that sack the whole time."

"No matter. You keep digging. I'm going to search for a shovel and possibly a light."

As Megan crawled off, another thought crossed her mind. What she'd told the boy earlier wasn't a total fib. Cooper was actually searching for him. It was entirely possible that he'd find them. But it had to be soon. The boy was dehydrated and obviously weak. If Buddy didn't kill him, the conditions under which he'd been held captive would. She felt like Dorothy in the *Wizard of Oz*, watching the hourglass in fear of the witch. Then the locks on the shed door rattled.

"Hurry," Megan said. "You get back under the tarp and don't say a word. Pretend you're dead, no matter what. Promise."

"OK, I promise, Ms. Megan."

"I'll sit over here. We don't want him to know what we've been up to."

"OK," the boy said.

They each took their assumed places. Megan thought of trying to overpower Buddy but knew the chances of success were slim. She had the boy to think about. Therefore, when Buddy strode in with a Budweiser in his hand, Megan sat on the ground and glared up at him. She seethed with rage. He flicked on the overhead lightbulb and sat down on his stool. Luckily the dim wattage didn't extend to the area where they'd dug or to the disturbed arms. Their efforts went unnoticed.

"Party time!" he said.

Megan took advantage of the light to search the room for a shovel or any possible weapon but tried not to make it obvious and draw suspicion from Buddy. Although he was drunk, she'd already underestimated him once. She sat close to his stool to keep his attention. It was the best way to protect the child. However, with the small enclosure illuminated, it was impossible not to notice the rows of human arms in various stages of decomposition. It was the stench they'd picked up on earlier. It also explained why it was less than a whole human body. She shivered in disgust.

"Hey there, darling, ready to have some fun?"

She maintained eye contact in a battle of wills. No matter what, she wouldn't let him break her.

"What's the problem, princess? You don't look so happy," Buddy said. He leaned over and cupped her chin in his hand. "I have so much to tell you. So much to share."

Megan's first instinct was to spit in his face, but she reined in her emotions. It was imperative that for once, she kept them in check. If she indulged him and let him talk, it would retain his attention and keep it away from Edward Lee. In doing so, it would buy as much precious time as possible. As an added bonus, she might gain information to use against him once they were free. That was what she remained focused on. Freedom.

"I have so much to tell you," he said then took a swig of beer. "You see, I know you've been all over town trying to catch me."

"I had no idea you were the killer until tonight," Megan said.

"Yes, darling, it was me all along. And you know what I loved best?"

Megan considered it a rhetorical question and made no effort to interrupt. He seemed to be in his own world of reminiscing. Then she noticed the pistol shoved into the waistband of his jeans, along with the shotgun that conspicuously leaned against him. She wondered what her odds were if she lunged for either. One well-placed shot was all that was needed.

Then Buddy looked directly at her, and she lost her nerve. She sat in the dirt, hugging her knees tightly against her body. She was scared, but mostly she wanted her one move to count. A hesitation would cost both her and Edward Lee's life.

He finished off his beer, crunched the can, and threw it at Edward Lee. It bounced off the blanket and landed in the freshly overturned dirt. The child made no sound, and Buddy didn't notice the dirt. He was busy enjoying himself.

"Good, the little shit's finally dead."

He reached to grab another beer from the refrigerator. "I have many stories to tell you."

"You're disgusting," she said then stopped short. She was giving him exactly what he wanted. She was a professional detective with a will to survive. If Edward Lee, a small child, was strong enough to rein in his emotions and play dead, she could do the same. Not only to survive, but prevail and bring this murderer to justice.

"Did you kill Sissy?" Megan asked to divert the subject off her lack of self-control.

"Hell yes. I had to," Buddy said. He sat down heavily on the stool, beer in hand. It was hard to tell if it was the result of so much alcohol or the weariness of so many deaths on his shoulders.

"What happened?" Megan prompted. She was surprised how gentle her voice came out despite her rage. She cared about Sissy and truly wanted to know her story.

He looked up. "I never meant to kill her. We loved each other once. I still love her actually. We were happy when we first married."

Buddy looked straight into Megan's eyes. She saw genuine sadness there. "What happened?"

"She never forgave me for not being able to father a child. We got tested. That's when we found out it was all my fault. I let her down in the worst possible way. She loved children."

This was a piece of information Megan didn't need to know, but Buddy's defenses were down.

"You could have adopted or turned to a specialist."

"Yeah, yeah, we did all that except for the adoption shit. The whole drawn-out process killed our closeness. They gave her hormones and a schedule. She'd call me up when her temperature was right. We'd go at it, but nothing happened. Every month I had to face her relentless tears and disappointment. We became two people who lived in the same house but didn't know each other. She turned to her horses while I had politics. It worked. We went our separate ways."

"So why kill her then? Was it your indecorous behavior with other women?"

Buddy took another swig of beer. "Hell no. As long as I didn't bother her, she didn't care whom I slept with. It was this damn shed. She had to go snooping around."

"I don't understand," Megan said, encouraged by his heavy drinking. It evened the field.

"Sissy had no idea of my hobby," he continued and waved his arm in the direction of the severed limbs, sticking out of the dirt. "I kept her away from the shed by letting the grass grow long. I told her there were snakes out here. She was terrified of snakes. Did you know that?"

"No, I actually didn't know Sissy very well." Now it made sense to Megan why he'd laughed so hard when she told him he should cut the grass.

"It was all my fault. I borrowed a damn tool from her and left it in here. She needed it for one of her horses, so she came to look for it."

"And she found more than she bargained for," Megan stated in understanding.

He nodded with his head held low. "Yes. I was on my way out of the house when I spotted her screaming as she ran. If I thought she was disappointed the day the doctor told her I couldn't father a child, this was worse. When I caught up with her, the look on her face was of stunned disappointed and repulsion. I knew I had to kill her even though I loved her. I still do."

Despite her hatred of the man, a part of Megan felt sorry for him. He was hurting and seriously messed up. Yet that didn't negate the fact that he'd killed several woman, one being his wife.

"Did you kill Mary Pearl too?"

He looked directly at Megan when he answered. "Yes. Yes, I did. I hated that bitch."

So much for any warm, fuzzy feelings of compassion, Megan thought.

"They know she was murdered," Megan said with a bit of satisfaction.

"What are you talking about? The cops already determined it was a natural death."

"The cops at the scene, perhaps. Their opinion doesn't count. The autopsy does."

"Autopsy?"

This was something Megan could enjoy.

"Yes, autopsy. It's required by law when anyone dies not under the care of a physician. Or if there are suspicious circumstances." She purposely didn't distinguish which imposed the autopsy. Let him have his own doubts. Anything to throw off his game.

"She died of a heart attack. They had to discover that on autopsy," Buddy said.

He was becoming agitated, so Megan backed off. "They did. She died of a heart attack," Megan said in an attempt to calm him down. "But you already admitted you killed her."

"All you need to know is, she was a problem with a big mouth who needed to go away."

"So what about Sissy? Did you think she had a big mouth too?"

"Yes. She would have told her family. They hate me because I can't give them grandchildren."

271

"Maybe they hate you for other reasons," Megan said with a raised eyebrow.

"What? You mean because I run around? I have needs. I like young girls. They like me. It wasn't behind Sissy's back. She refused to sleep with me. I never made an oath to be celibate."

Buddy finished off his beer and reached for another. Megan watched, encouraged.

"I figured since this was the horse capital of the world, a horse accident wouldn't look suspicious. Everyone knew she worked with the damn things every day. It was her life."

"I understand your reasoning, but the thing is, death by a horse kick is really rare. Even here."

Buddy sat up straight for a moment. "Well damn, I didn't know that. Seriously?"

"Seriously," Megan said.

"Well shit. It seemed like the thing to do at the time," Buddy said. "Hell, I panicked. Then you came into the picture yet again. You're like a dog with a bone. I knew I had to stop you, but I wasn't sure how to go about it. You being a cop and all, I had to be careful. That's why I decided to go after Lacy first. You've got family all over the damn place. She's new to town. I hoped it would scare you off, but then you so kindly showed up on my doorstep."

"Were you the one who kept calling me on my cell?"

Buddy raised his beer in the air as if in a toast. "That would be me, darlin'. You enjoy it?"

"Yeah, breathing is real stimulating conversation," Megan said.

"Oh, baby, don't be like that."

"You had to know people would question Sissy's death. She has trained and owned horses all her live. She was an expert rider."

"Then you have Christopher Reeves, look how bad he got hurt," Buddy said. "Then he died."

Megan rolled her eyes. "Yes, he's the poster child for horse accidents."

"Look, I had no choice. She was all freaked out. I had to shut her up."

Megan so badly wanted to interject a comment or two but felt that at this point, sarcasm would only be counterproductive. Her goal was life.

"I don't know what happened. I guess I panicked. Before I knew what happened, I hit her on the head with a crowbar. I didn't mean to kill her. It was an accident. Just like your mother."

"My mother? What do you know about her?"

Buddy looked into Megan's eyes and continued. "They were both accidents. When I realized she was hurt so badly, I didn't know what to do. I couldn't take her to the hospital. If she regained consciousness, she would tell the doctors everything. She had to die. I saw no other way."

Megan wasn't sure who he was talking about but went with Sissy. It was safer ground for her. "So you left her there while she was still alive? She was still breathing, gasping for breath."

"Stop. Yes. I didn't know what else to do. When she finally died, I figured I could make it look like an accident. It seemed like the best way to go. So I carried her body to the barn and put her in the same stall as the stallion. Then I called 911 to report it. It worked too, until you came along."

"They can tell it wasn't a horse that caused her death from the autopsy, you know. That and her body was moved after her death," Megan said. She wanted to squelch his self-confident image of being invincible. To be the one who planted a seed of doubt in his overconfident ego.

"Doesn't make any difference now. Sissy's body will be cremated in the morning. Whatever the autopsy claims, can't be disputed. But I doubt it will ever come to that. Even if they say the horse didn't kill her, they can't pin it on me. My dad will be on my side. Besides, you know the deal. Neither Mary Pearl or Sissy's deaths were considered homicide. The crime scenes were never taped off. Nothing gained from there would be admissible in court, so there's no evidence."

God, Megan hated him. He was so smug and cocky and totally right. He would get away with both murders, and no one else knew he was the serial killer but her. Soon she'd be dead. His secret kept safe.

"So how many people will you kill to hide your sick hobby?" Megan asked.

"As many as it takes."

He got up and retrieved another beer from the small refrigerator, which made Megan happy. The more he drank, the easier it would be to either overpower or outsmart him. Then there was the option of basically waiting him out. Eventually he'd pass out, unconscious.

He sat back down, popped the tab on his beer, and guzzled half the can in one swallow. She gained hope for the last option. No matter how much a person was used to drinking, sooner or later they had a physiological limit. Buddy had to be close to his. It seemed that as many people as he'd killed in the past, Sissy's murder was the one that had finally gotten to him.

"I gotta go take a whiz," he said. He wavered as he made his way to the door but was still of mind enough to douse the light. "Be back soon, darlin'." Then he locked her back up.

Megan breathed a sigh of relief for the reprieve. Buddy was not only getting more inebriated by the moment, he showed a hint of a conscience, albeit buried deep inside. She had to find a way to access it and use it to her advantage. With any luck, it might offer an opportunity for her and Edward Lee to escape. She extinguished her own fears and planned to use every second Buddy gave them. She leapt up and accessed the same bulb he'd diminished.

39

Lacy finished up the interview with the retired detective in time to meet Megan as agreed. But for the second time, her partner never showed. Lacy held her cell phone, ready to call when it rang. The caller ID revealed it was Cooper. Unsure if this was about Willy, she answered.

"Hello, Coop?"

"Lacy, I need you to meet me at Parker's garage. I have a lead on Edward Lee."

Cooper gave Lacy directions, and she covered the distance in less than ten minutes. Once there, Cooper filled her in on everything he'd learned from Gabe, including the distinct possibility that Buddy Howard, the respected county commissioner, was the local serial killer. A multifaceted individual of the worst kind. It also concerned her that he hadn't heard from Megan either.

"We can leave the vehicles here and follow the same path the boy took through the woods."

Lacy grabbed Coop by the arm, not sure she'd heard correctly. "Wait up a second, cowboy. Why trudge through the swampy woods in the dark if we already know he's at Buddy's?"

He looked down at her as if she were a total dimwit. "Because I can't be sure he made it there. I can only assume he was headed that way on foot from here. I need to make sure he didn't get hurt along the way. And we can't waste any more time. Every minute could be his last."

He took off at a brisk pace. Lacy followed as best as she could, but with her short legs, it was a challenge. She could understand Cooper's concern. If the kid had gone after the killer on his own, through this hazardous swamp, any number of things could have happened. If Buddy didn't get hold of him, a poisonous snake or gator very well might have. The upside was, she figured if Cooper spooked a snake, or any other creepy crawly, she'd have enough warning to run the other way. Her eyes were focused on the ground as Coop stepped past a thicket. As he did, a branch swung back and snapped her on the forehead. It struck with enough force to cause her to yelp.

"Jeez," she said and brought her hand to the area. She noted there was blood.

Cooper turned to see what was wrong and realized what had happened. Quickly he took out a handkerchief and dabbed at the wound. "Oh god, I'm so sorry," he said. "I'm so damned worried about Edward Lee, I wasn't paying attention to what I was doing."

"That's the kind of thing that can get you killed," Lacy said. It was something drilled into their head during police training. Loss of focus could cost your life, but in this case, she'd been just as guilty. She'd watched the ground at the expense of all else. They both needed to be more cautious.

"You're right. Buddy's dangerous, especially if he knows we're onto him. We've got to be careful."

"Will the blood attract gators?" Lacy asked. She looked at the slightly soiled piece of cloth.

"No. That would be sharks," Cooper replied.

"You do realize it's dark, don't you?" Lacy said, leaning on one hip, gesturing with her arm.

"Yes, that's one reason why I'm so concerned. I want to find the boy before another night passes. His mother's worried sick. Anything could have happened to him out here. If he's out here hurt, I have to find him. Driving to Buddy's won't do us any good."

As much as Lacy hated to admit it, Cooper was right. And she could tell the boy's mother wasn't the only one worried sick. Cooper was beside himself. Just the same, a trudge through the Florida wild in the pitch-dark did not appeal to her. Beyond her fear of all things slimy, Jerry had recently shared new information with her that made the situation worse. It was entirely possible they were already too late to save the child, and now her partner was missing.

"The bleeding stopped," Cooper said. "No need to worry about sharks. We need to get going."

Lacy grabbed his wrist. "Wait."

Cooper, unsure how to read the gesture, looked down at her. Their eyes locked momentarily, and the concern in her gaze was readily apparent. "What? What haven't you told me?"

"Jerry called me right after I hung up with you. He wanted to give me the results of a lab test we ran. It turned out to be rather disturbing."

"And?"

"It doesn't bode well for Edward Lee if he went after Buddy Howard by himself. Your hunch about Buddy being the killer has more merit than just a dented red car. There were two older cases similar to the one at your farm and the Phillips place."

"I don't understand what that has to do with Buddy," Cooper said.

"The old cases were down in the basement. Megan's mother's case was there as well. Out of curiosity, I looked through it," Lacy said.

Cooper was becoming impatient. "What does that have to do with Edward Lee? Megan's mother has been gone for over . . . what? Eight years? Ten? I'm not saying it doesn't matter, but right now, we need to find Edward Lee. I can help you with that latter."

Lacy continued despite Coop's protest. "There was a Coke can on the porch of the house the mother was painting. It was considered the last place Helen was seen. The drink was half full."

"That doesn't make any sense. Megan's mother didn't drink soda or allow any of the kids to drink soft drinks. Nate used to complain about it, said it made him feel like a freak."

"Exactly. They ran the prints on the can back then. They came up with nothing. They were not the mother's or in the data bank at the time. But like you just said, that was over eight years ago."

"OK, so how does this tie in with Edward Lee? We're running out of time, and in case you haven't noticed, this isn't the best place to stand around and talk."

"I had Jerry run them through the NCIC system again. It has greatly improved over the last eight years. Now anyone in any type of public service is required to be printed and entered into the National Crime Information Center. It is a computerized compilation of not only criminals but service personnel, public service individuals, even volunteers."

"So?" Cooper said, impatiently pointing to his watch.

"OK, let's walk while I explain," Lacy said and gestured Cooper to lead the way.

She spoke as she made her way through the thick vegetation. "Jerry had the prints on the Coke can run through the system again. Buddy Howard came up as a match."

Cooper stopped dead in his tracts and pivoted around to face Lacy. "Why the hell didn't you say this earlier? You said Jerry just called you? When? You should have told me this."

"Calm down. Jerry called right before I pulled up to meet you. I told him to notify the chief. Other than that, no one else knows. I wasn't sure what it meant besides he was on the porch that day when Megan's mother disappeared. But when you told me about the car, I got a bad feeling. I think that not only is Buddy the serial killer, I think he killed Megan's mother too."

"And now he's got Edward Lee? But we went to school together. He was seventeen back then."

"I know. He's been at this for years. Back then, his age protected him, and he had no prints on record. Since then, he's served in the military and public office. Now his prints are on file."

"This is crazy. Just because his fingerprints showed up doesn't mean anything, does it? After all, he was on the same baseball team as Nate and I. Maybe he stopped by for a reason."

"It's possible. I don't know for sure. Like I said, until you brought up the car, I wasn't sure what to think. Now I think it's enough to question him. Besides, there's more."

"Go on, you definitely have my attention."

"Buddy got in trouble for voyeurism when he was in high school," Lacy said.

"What's that?"

"It's more commonly known as being a Peeping Tom."

"I never heard about it in school," Cooper said.

"That's because his daddy made it go away. They said he wanted to surprise his girlfriend with a birthday serenade. The thing was, it wasn't her birthday. And the girl didn't have any idea who Buddy was. She lived in Gainesville. But, since he was a juvenile, the records were sealed."

"Teenage boys do a lot of things to get a look at girls," Cooper said.

"True, but that kind of behavior crosses the line. It's often a foreshadowing of more aggressive actions that often lead to violence. I think Buddy killed Megan's mother. Now from what you tell me, it's possible he's the serial killer. If Edward Lee went after him alone, he's in serious danger."

"Holy crap. I didn't want to believe it could be true. I wanted to see the car for myself. We need to go find him now. I won't rest until he's safe in my arms," Cooper said.

"I understand your reaction, but we have to keep our heads straight. I think we need backup. This guy is a serial killer. We can't run up to him and demand he give us the kid. Someone will get hurt. Besides, we don't even know for sure he has Edward Lee."

"You're right. Maybe we should split up. I can go on foot through the swamp to make sure he didn't get hurt on his way, and you could go back to your car. We're not that far in the woods. Do you think you can find your way back to Parker's? And we can try Megan again to meet us there as backup."

"That's another problem. I've tried Megan several times. She's not answering," Lacy said.

Cooper ran his hand through his hair and paced in a small area. The swamp muck swished with each step. "That's not like her. I don't like this at all. Maybe she's at Beth's house."

"Maybe. But we were supposed to meet at the station, and she never showed," Lacy said, her concern mounting as she watched Cooper's reaction.

"She could have turned off her cell for some reason, and she'll call soon. In the meantime, I'll continue on foot. You head back to your car. I think you should call Beth," Cooper suggested.

"Great idea. I'm close enough to swing by there. She'll more than likely knows where Megan is. I'll meet you, with backup, at Buddy's." Lacy held out hope that both Beth and Megan were busy fussing over Willy.

Cooper nodded and headed off. It didn't take long for him to disappear into the darkness of the thick vegetation. She watched him vanish into the black abyss. That's when she realized where she stood. She was all alone in the swamp. She took off at a brisk pace back to her car. She was afraid of the creatures that lurked in darkness of the wild. But an even deeper-seated fear of the animal they sought sat in the pit of her stomach. Buddy faced the threat of serious prison time. People cornered in a situation like that often reacted in drastic ways. With his substantially violent past, it wouldn't surprise her if he tried to take someone down with him, and Megan was missing.

40

Megan heard the rattle of locks on the shed door and cursed Buddy's return. She told Edward Lee to stay quiet no matter what. She reached up and turned off the light, then scooted back to her original position. They were close to freedom. She figured another fifteen minutes and the space would be large enough for the boy to escape and get help. Then, with the objects in the shed, Megan planned to create an illusion of Edward Lee under the tarp. Since Buddy thought the child was dead, lack of movement from his corner wouldn't arouse any curiosity.

Buddy walked in, reached up to pull the string that turned on the single light. He didn't seem to notice it was already in motion prior to his touch. It swung back and forth and cast an intermittent light from one side of the shed to the other that risked exposure of all their hard work. He looked around, appraising the surroundings. As he did, Megan held her breath. They'd created a formidable mound of dirt next to their hole. Evidently, the alcohol was their ally. The arms were in place, so Buddy remained unaware. He took a swig of beer and sat down heavily on the stool.

"Miss me, darlin'?"

"I managed," Megan said curtly. She couldn't hide the contempt in her eyes.

Buddy was unfazed by her hostility. He seemed to exist in his own world.

"I never actually set out to kill anyone," he began.

To Megan, the comment came out of the blue. Evidently, the ghosts of all the dead had begun to haunt her captor. That knowledge made her feel better, yet it did little to abate her loathing of him.

"It didn't stop you from killing over and over again. Why didn't you stop? Get some help?"

"It's not like that. I couldn't stop. It was the only time I felt in control. But I have to tell you, the first one is always the best. I'll never forget Helen, your mom," Buddy said in a wistful voice.

Megan's head jerked up at the mention of her mother's name. "What are you talking about? How dare you speak my mother's name." She sensed it wasn't a taunt. With her own death looming so close at hand, she wanted to know the truth. The mystery had haunted her entire adult life. If Buddy knew something, she needed to hear it before she died.

Buddy spoke into the air in a trancelike state. It was as if he were making a final proclamation. Megan might have contemplated making a move on his gun but was completely drawn into the story. For years, the questions surrounding her mother's disappearance plagued her. Now Buddy was ready to reveal the answers. She couldn't help but listen.

"It was a beautiful summer day," he began. "My dad had been on my ass all week and sent me on one of his errands. I went out to y' all's farm to sabotage your dad's tractor. I don't know exactly why, but that's what my father ordered."

"But my dad was a plumber and part-time farmer," Megan said, more confused than ever.

"Ah, but your father found out a nasty little secret about Angus. I learned that after the fact. The Honorable Justice Howard had a staunch reputation to uphold in the community. He resorted to whatever means necessary, even terrorism. He controlled and intimidated everyone under his reign, either through verbal threats or evil deeds. Since I was in high school, he used me for much of his dirty work. He figured he could keep his hands clean. If I got caught, he could attribute it to an adolescent prank. The worst-case scenario was my record would be closed because I was a juvenile. It was all kept in the family. That's where he held the greatest ability to control. And believe me, he exercised it."

Buddy finished the beer and chucked the can at Edward Lee. Again, no sound came from the boy. Megan hoped he had heard all of this, so he could later corroborate the confession.

"What in the world did my dad find out? I don't even see how their paths ever crossed."

"Ah, my father was not only a judge but a land developer. He bought large tracts of land cheaply from area orange farmers who were about to go under and lose everything. He used privileged information as a judge. 'Prey on the weak' was his motto. As a lawyer, he understood how to work the system. He turned around and plotted the large tracts into much smaller lots for his housing communities. It was something the average landowner wouldn't be allowed to get away with, but my father was in tight with the zoning board. Money and favors exchanged hands—all under the table of course—and presto, it was recorded without question. But that wasn't enough for Angus. He wanted more. That's where your father came into the picture. He had the unfortunate character flaw of being honest, along with having a backbone."

"I still don't understand." Megan said.

Buddy chuckled and said, "Neither did your father. You're a lot like him." He looked at her for the first time without animosity. "Honest and loved by your family, same temper."

"How is that bad?"

"My father had a plan, and your dad wouldn't go along with it and accept the bribes. Your father was a hard worker. Unfortunately, in the middle of one of my father's many housing developments, he was told to install the required household plumbing. After inspection, he was to pull out all the expensive copper pipes and replace them with inferior, substandard lead-based ones. A definite code violation. My father did it with electrical wire, hurricane tie-downs, you name it. Anything to make more money."

"That's horrible."

"That's exactly what your father thought. He was intelligent enough to realize my father's greed would endanger the health and lives of those families who unknowingly bought the new homes. But the main mistake your father made was to go up against Angus."

"So your father sent you out to sabotage the tractor?"

"It was meant as a message. If that didn't work, the threats would escalate."

"But why kill my mother?"

This time Buddy didn't gloat as he spoke. "That really was an accident."

"An accident? How do you accidentally kill someone?" Megan noted he didn't say he was sorry.

"We had a baseball game that day. Your mom was always at the games for Nate. I remember she would bring us fresh-baked cookies and cold water, no Kool Aid or soda. I skipped out of my last class and went straight to your place. I didn't expect anyone to be home."

"She was painting the porch that day. She must have run late," Megan said.

"Yeah, she was painting it a pale yellow. She saw me walk past on the way to the barn and called out to me. She wanted to know what I was doing out of school. I told her I came by to borrow Nate's glove. Said he'd left it at home in the barn. The coach let me come get it because I had study hall, but Nate had a math test. She saw I had a Coke in my hand and proceeded to give me the usual lecture. You know, how it would rot my teeth and give me diabetes."

This brought a smile to Megan's face, despite her current situation. Buddy was describing her mother perfectly. For a moment, Helen felt so real; and Megan missed her so much, it hurt.

"I walked over and spoke to her before I said I had to go. After all, I had a job to do for my father. If I didn't accomplish it within the given amount of time, I'd pay. So I circled back around and ducked into the shed. She must have watched me out of the corner of her eye."

Megan nodded. That was so like her mother. The woman had three children. She wasn't easily fooled. In that respect, Beth was very similar. "My mother was an expert at figuring out the truth. She never would have bought such a lame story."

"Well, that's something I had no experience with. My stepmother ignored me while my father used me. Neither actually cared about me. I didn't expect a friend's mother to notice what I did."

Megan listened intently to Buddy's words and almost felt sorry for him. Almost.

"She actually followed me. I was in the process of tampering with the tractor when she walked up behind me. She scared the bejesus out of me. I had a wrench in my hand, and on instinct, I swung it. It hit her square on the temple. She fell back and hit her head against a cinder block. It killed her instantly. I freaked out; unsure what to do, so I ran to the house and called my father. For him, it was business as usual, and he took care of everything. I knew you and your sister would be home soon. I wiped my prints off everything I'd touched as instructed by Angus. Then I went to the game for an alibi."

"So the Coke can was yours."

Buddy nodded with his head held low. "Do you know how hard that was to sit next to your brother on the bench that day and look at him?"

Rage flooded Megan. "Do you know how hard it was to not have a mother? Or know what happened to her?"

Megan was a boiling pot of emotions. She was relieved to learn her mother hadn't run off and abandoned them as some believed. On the other hand, she'd found out Helen had been murdered, taken away from them, and the person responsible sat before her. For years she'd fantasized of what she would do or say if faced with such a scenario. Now that it was here, words escaped her.

"So now you know," Buddy said and crushed his beer can. He threw it at the mound in the corner. Again, no movement. This time Megan's concern grew. Perhaps Edward Lee wasn't acting or being as clever as she'd given him credit. It was possible he was actually dead from heat and dehydration.

"If my mother was an accident, why keep killing?" she asked. She wanted to buy more time, keep him talking.

"Because once I learned I could get away with it, I felt this overwhelming power. For the first time in my life, I felt important and in control. Until then I was impotent next to my father. My stepmother constantly slapped me in the face when I didn't do as she wanted. Or when she had a bad day, which became increasingly more frequent. She never wanted a child and made sure I knew it."

For a moment, Megan considered it to be a worse fate to actually have parents who didn't love you than to have them taken away. After all, how does a child explain or deal with that? It would make him feel as if they were unworthy instead of what it was—a character flaw of the parents. She wondered if Buddy would have turned out differently if he'd had other parents. He was obviously dysfunctional and in pain. She'd had the experience of being loved unconditionally, and that was something Buddy could never take away from her. Her parents would live on in her heart, and she would always know they loved her.

Although it was a relief to finally understand what had happened, she vowed to make Buddy pay. Not only for her own family's pain but for all the others he'd torn apart by his malevolent acts of violence. Tears stung her eyes over the emotions that surfaced from past memories. She would use that anger to fuel her conviction to escape.

"Why didn't my father tell everyone once my mother was gone? He had nothing to lose."

Buddy laughed, but it held no mirth. "He had his children to think of. You were loved by both your parents. Not just your mother."

Megan could feel the resentment pour off her capture as he spoke.

"I know my father loved me. What does that have to do with anything?"

"It had everything to do with it. You gotta understand the way Angus works, both then and now. Rule number one, threaten harm to those you love. You see, this works real well for him because no one can retaliate. He loves no one other than himself. Your father, on the other hand, loved his three children. He held onto y'all desperately after your mother's death."

"You mean Angus actually threatened to kill us?"

Buddy tapped his finger to the side of his nose to indicate Megan got it right.

"On top of that, he promised he would take your family's farm by eminent domain if a word of incrimination was ever voiced against him."

"I don't understand. What is that?"

"That, darling, is legalized, modern-day piracy. It's where the government states it has the right to seize private property for the good of the community as a whole. Believe me, it wasn't an idle threat either. As other local farmers sold out to the greedy developers, the county tax base increased. But so did its budget. My father was in a position, along with his zoning and county commissioner cronies, to take over your family farm. With it subdivided into single-family units, or even apartments, all nonagricultural exempt, the tax money would pour in. There were developers clamoring for land. Everyone wanted to get rich quick. As the population of the state soared, so did the need for available housing. The county needed the land and increased tax base. Your family held part of the solution. It was all very simple."

"And all very crooked."

"It all depends on the way you look at it."

"I see it as misuse of power and greed. Angus threatened my father, just like they're threatening to do to Coop now. He may lose his farm over politics and greed."

"Hell, yes. Greed runs through my father's veins like blood. But he and his friends did face a real problem. You see, the millage rate in this county is frozen, but each time a parcel of land changes hands, the appraisal value can increase drastically. It was all about money, then and now. Some things never change, and neither would your father. He wouldn't risk any harm to his children or their future. Your future."

"So he drank himself to death with the secret," Megan said.

"You would hope, but my daddy was good that way."

"What do you mean?" Megan asked. She wasn't sure she could handle any more information, but her curiosity got the best of her.

"He was indeed drunk that night. But being killed by a hit-and-run driver wasn't an accident. It was more like insurance to my father. I was away at college, but as I understood, your father was known to get boisterous when he drank. He was also predictable when he showed up at T. J.'s and when he headed home each night. At first, Angus figured his grumbling could be written off as a disgruntled blue-collar worker. But then your father became more vocal. Anyone who actually listened to him could have easily checked out the facts. That, to Angus, was intolerable. Your father needed to be removed. So he was, and his death wasn't even questioned."

Megan felt a surge of nausea roll across her, and her eyes welled up with tears. She'd always believed her father's death to be from his drinking. That he'd turned his back on his children and, in his weakness, had turned to the bottle. Now she knew otherwise. He died for them. She could taste the bile rise up in her mouth.

"Your father's a son of a bitch," Megan spat.

Buddy chuckled. "Now that's something we can both agree on."

"And to think our community regards the two of you as upstanding citizens."

With another chuckle, he said, "I've always found that humorous too. What can I say? We both have a talent for chicanery."

Megan balled up her fist, furious. It was all she could do to maintain her composure. She planned to live to see this man tried for his crimes. That would offer a much greater satisfaction.

"You're such a bastard. I know you plan to kill me."

Buddy threw his head back and howled. "Not only plan but relish the thought."

Megan noticed the bundle in the corner scrunch up at the loud noise. Edward Lee was still alive. There was still hope.

"Women are evil," Buddy spat back. "All of you bitches deserve to die a hideous death."

The rancor of his retort was unexpected. And it angered her further. Here, this completely nefarious individual who went around killing innocent women had the nerve to call all women evil. She had to remind herself to stay focused on the goal of getting out of there alive. This was no time to lose her temper. This sucker had to pay.

"Why cut off their arms?" she asked. As long as she kept him talking, she had a chance.

"I got sick of being bitch-slapped in the face as a kid. For years, my mother slapped me in the face for no reason. Next came my stepmother, then girlfriends. Damn, I got sick of women and their impossible, never-ending demands. They always expected me to be someone who I never claimed to be. That's why I cut their fucking arms off. I did it while they were still alive to feel the agony. I enjoyed watching them writhe in pain as they bled to death. It was the same pain they tried to hold me down with, but in the end, I won. I showed each and every one."

"What about the clothing? Did you remove it to destroy evidence, or was it merely a perversity?"

Buddy cocked his head to the side. "I hacked off their fucking arms, and you ask about their wardrobe? Who the hell cares? The clothes could have rotted by the time the remains were found," Buddy said. He took another gulp of beer. "You think you're so damn smart, you tell me, Detective. What happened to their clothes?"

"It wasn't from rot. There wasn't a zipper, snap, or bra hook anywhere. Cotton does decay fairly quickly, but metal doesn't. I say you stripped them."

"Yeah, and raped them. So why aren't you more concerned about the arms? That's a big deal."

"I am. I guess I just want to understand before I die."

Buddy shrugged his shoulders. "I don't know. I like a clean crime scene. The less evidence left behind, the more you cops have to scramble around chasing your tails. I enjoyed the show you put on. I burned all their clothes out behind the house in a can. Nice and neat."

Megan wasn't a fool. Buddy was freely giving her ammunition to send him to prison. Information that could easily be verified. But just as it had ended for her father, they both understood he had her death planned. If Buddy didn't pass out, or Cooper show up soon, both she and Edward Lee would be dead. Their clothes would end up in that same burn barrel, and Megan's arms would soon stick out of this very same dirt. No one would be the wiser because Buddy, along with his family name, was invincible.

But until that happened, Megan would hold out hope. "I know you said my mother was a mistake, and Mary Pearl had to be silenced, but what made you choose the other girls?"

"Convenience. The first two, eight years ago, were college freshmen. It was back in the eighties, and women were easy to pick up. With Heather, she worked for my father's campaign, then for another commissioner. I asked her to work on mine when the time came. We were alone together a lot. She was the one who first came onto me. Sissy wouldn't put out at home, so I wasn't about to turn her down. But when we were alone in my car, the bitch turned on me. She was a tease, slapped me in the face, and told me to stop when I touched her. I mean she's the one who initiated it," Buddy said. He was agitated again and threw his empty beer can against the wall with force. "Damn bitch." He got up to get another but came up empty-handed. "Shit."

Megan thought this was it. She was going to die. In an attempt to divert Buddy's attention, she asked, "Why were all the bones so clean? There was no rotten flesh."

"Now that's a better question than the one about the clothes. I'd like to hear your deductions." Buddy sat back down and folded his arms across his chest, ready to listen. He appeared amused.

Satisfied for the moment that her plan had worked, Megan continued.

"Jerry thinks you used flesh-eating bugs. With what you said earlier about a clean crime scene, it fits. The bugs not only got rid of the flesh but the smell and blood, leaving behind pristine bones. That's what caught Jerry's attention by the way. They were too clean. No stains whatsoever. It's something you might want to keep in mind for the future," Megan said. She hoped by the mention of Jerry and evidence back at the lab that Buddy would think twice about killing her. She wanted to plant the seed that she was not only a cop but that others were searching for the serial killer.

"Give Jerry a free beer, he's right. Too bad his intellect will cost him his life. I can't allow him to remain on these cases. You've confirmed he's gotten too close. He won't be a problem, but he'll have to wait until I'm through with you. I'll even show you my bug pit. I can throw the kid in as a demonstration. We can watch the beetles devour him. The sound of them crunching as they strip the carcass is amazing."

Megan tried hard to keep herself from a visible shudder in front of Buddy. It was bad enough to know that after watching the boy being decimated, she was next. But what was worse was to think she might be the cause of Jerry's death. Her lower lip quivered as she fervently fought back the tears.

"Well, angel, I have to take another whiz and get some more beer. Then our private party can get going in earnest."

He wobbled slightly as he reached up to turn off the overhead bulb. The room plunged into darkness. She heard the door lock from the outside before she dared to move. Then she launched into action. She'd memorized the room while Buddy spoke. First, she clicked on the light and ran to the fridge. The last time Buddy had opened it to get a beer, she'd noticed a bottled water. It was just the thing she needed for Edward Lee. The boy was close to death from dehydration. Next to the water was a candy bar. She grabbed both and made her way over to him. If they had to hide in the swamp for hours, he would need it for strength.

"Edward Lee, hurry and drink this," she said, shaking him.

It took a moment for the child to respond, but when he realized it was safe, he ate and drank ravenously.

"We have to get out of here. We've got to finish our tunnel."

The boy mumbled an agreement in between bites but kept eating. Megan dug furiously with a small trowel while she explained her plan of escape once they were free from the shed. She told the boy where the truck was and hoped he could get there quick enough. This was their last chance. Their lives hung in the balance.

41

It didn't take Lacy long to hightail it out of the swamp near Parker's garage to Beth's house. She hated to leave Cooper alone to trudge through the wilderness without a phone, but he insisted she keep hers in case Megan called. The way she figured, if anyone had to be alone in the swamp at night, it was best Cooper. He was used to it and seemed to know what he was doing. The creepy crawlies didn't even bother him.

When she pulled up to the farmhouse, she tried Megan one last time. Again, with no success. She tossed the phone in her purse and headed up to the house. Who knew, even though she didn't see Megan's truck, her partner might be busy with Willy out back or at Cooper's place.

Arlene answered the door on the second knock. The woman looked pretty young to be a grandmother twice over. Lacy thought she must use one of those expensive age-defying moisturizing creams. Without thought, she touched her own neck, worried the wrinkles had already begun. Tyler was in Arlene's arms. His hands were wrapped tight around his beloved blanket and bear. The child seemed almost asleep even though it was early.

"Sorry to bother you. Is Beth here?"

"Sure, she's in the kitchen. I need to get him upstairs for his bath before he falls asleep on me. Do you think you can find the way?"

"No problem."

The scene of domestic tranquility caused Lacy a pang of remorse. Her biological clock gave a kick to her side. She questioned the move to Ocala and leaving her life in New York behind. If she'd stayed, she'd be well on her way to having children. That's what everyone had expected. After all, Vinney and she were childhood sweethearts, destined for marriage and family. The problem was, she didn't love Vinney. Not after she'd learned he'd "loved" half the other women in town on a regular basis. Everyone else still thought he was wonderful, including her family, who acted as if her opinion didn't matter. She was certain she would have loved their children. But it wasn't the life she'd pictured for herself. It was easier to leave than deal with a husband who was constantly unfaithful. It was a humiliation she didn't care to endure. In fact, she found it such an embarrassment. She'd never even mentioned it to Megan.

Lacy took a deep breath to clear her mind and headed back to the kitchen. She still had plenty of time for kids. Then the aroma of food hit her. No one could argue that Beth could cook.

"Something smells heavenly," Lacy said.

"Oh, Lacy. It's lasagna you smell, along with fresh-baked bread for supper. Where's Megan?"

"Megan? I'd hoped she was with you. I haven't been able to get in touch with her since we dropped off Willy. She went for a run. I had an interview."

Beth stopped what she was doing and cocked her head to the side. "That's weird. Did you try Cooper? Maybe she's over there."

Lacy looked around to make sure there were no little ears nearby. "I just talked to Cooper. She's not with him. I just popped in here to check, but I need to go. I'll call you later."

Beth noted the seriousness in Lacy's manner. There was something big going down, and her little sister was smack dab in the middle of it. "Wait, have a seat. I'll get some tea," Beth said and motioned to the table.

Lacy shook her head. "I really can't. It's late. You have a family to feed."

"You're worried about Megan. I can hear it in your voice. What is it, Lacy? What's wrong?"

"Nothing, Beth. I don't know that anything's wrong. I was supposed to meet Megan at the station, and she didn't show. She could be doing anything," Lacy said. "But I do need to find her."

Beth nodded. "But she's not with Coop?" she asked and walked to the cabinet to get her medicine. She shook out a few pills and downed them with her tea.

"No. We've had a lot of interviews lately. She might have had to follow up on one. You have a nice evening," Lacy said and headed toward the door. To her surprise, Beth didn't protest.

"OK, have Megan call me."

Lacy left in her compact. She had no idea where Megan was. She called the station, but her partner wasn't there. She requested an officer check out her running trail. Then she headed to Buddy's farm to meet Cooper. Who knew, Megan might have gone there. They both recognized the scent of rotten human flesh when they were there to get Willy. Even though she'd specifically told Megan to wait for a search warrant, it would be just like her to go off to investigate alone. After what both Jerry and Cooper had told her, she didn't have a good feeling about it.

*   *   *

Lacy crept up the drive that led to Buddy's house with her lights off. She pulled to the side of the road and got out. She closed the door as quietly as possible. Once out, she checked to make sure she had a flashlight, gun, and then turned her cell phone to silent mode. She wasn't that familiar with Florida wildlife, but she wasn't about to allow her fear get in the way of her job. Especially since a young boy's life depended on it—and possibly her partner's too.

Silently, she sliced through the night. It was a slow closure of ground between her and the main house. Then there came a horrific noise. Lacy spun around to spot a huge tractor headed straight for her car. Seconds later it stopped, and Beth hopped off.

"What the hell?" Lacy asked.

"It's fast, isn't it," Beth said, walking up to Lacy. "I'd have followed you in my car, but it's in the shop, remember? I'm still not so good at shifting gears though. That's what made that noise. SORRY."

"Shush," Lacy said. "You need to take my car and go back home to your kids. You can't be here."

"Not to worry. Arlene's with them. I told her it was a girls' night out."

"What? No. You don't understand. This is serious, Beth. You need to go home."

"It's all right. I told Arlene dinner's in the oven, ready to eat whenever. We can rescue Megan."

"We? No. What are you talking about?"

"Damn straight, we," Beth said. "I figured it out. My little sister's missing, and you came straight here. I know it's police business, but I'm not leaving without Megan."

Lacy had never heard Beth cuss and was a bit stunned. "But this isn't about Megan. We're afraid Buddy has Edward Lee, not Megan. This is dangerous. You're not a cop so you need to go."

"What? Why would Buddy have Edward Lee? I know you're trying to trick me. I already told you I figured it out. I know he killed Sissy, and you're worried he has Megan too. That's why she hasn't answered any of her calls."

"I don't know why Megan hasn't answered her cell. All I know is that Buddy's dangerous, and you have a family to think about. You need to go home," Lacy said.

"My family is exactly who I *am* thinking about. I have two small innocent children, and I want them to live in a safe community, not one where the county commissioner can get away with the death of his wife. So what's the plan? You might as well tell me," Beth said. She looked Lacy straight in the eye, arms folded across her chest. "I'm not leaving!"

Lacy's eyes darted to the enormous tractor Beth rode in on, then back to her. She realized Beth wouldn't be cajoled into going home or waiting in her car. If she didn't allow Beth to tag along, Lacy was certain she'd probably end up getting them both killed. She didn't have time for this.

Lacy gave the sign of the cross before she began. "OK, OK. But you need to know a few things. I left Cooper a short while ago at Parker's garage. He thinks Buddy has Edward Lee."

Beth sighed. "That's just ridiculous. Buddy doesn't like kids." Then she stopped. "Seriously?"

Lacy brought her fingers to her lips. "Shush. Just listen. Cooper plans to make his way through the woods on foot. He wants to make sure Edward Lee didn't get hurt on the way here. I'm supposed to meet him here as backup. I only stopped by your place to see if you had heard from Megan. I have no idea where she is. We have so many pending leads, she could be running any one of them down. Right now, I'm here for Cooper and the boy."

"I say we get a move on," Beth said. "I've left several messages for Megan to call me, and she hasn't. That's not like her. What if she figured out the boy was here and went to check it out on her own?"

It was one of the fears Lacy held but would not share with Beth.

Beth started off at a good clip before Lacy caught up and grabbed her arm. "We may already be too late to save the boy. This could get ugly. I seriously advise you to turn around. You could help by getting backup."

Beth nodded. "That's sweet, but, honey, this is my sister. Could you turn your back if you were in my place? Walk away and hope for the best instead of trying to save your own sister? I think not."

Lacy dropped her arm. She had no ammunition against that argument.

"You know what really ticks me off," Beth continued, "I think I voted for the bastard last election."

Lacy could understand Beth's reaction. Her sister was missing, and a man they'd known their whole lives had possibly killed his wife and taken a child. She was upset, confused, and angry. Often, things were not what they seemed, and evil lurked everywhere, even small towns. Lacy didn't want to bring up the possibility that Buddy was the serial killer and also her mother's murderer as well.

"We need to be quiet. Remember, Cooper's out there somewhere, and I can only hope that Edward Lee is with him. It looks like Buddy's home because his car's in the garage. Don't underestimate how dangerous he can be. He faces serious prison time. People react irrationally under those circumstances. I don't want to spook him and have to rescue you along with the kid."

"Now what's that condescending remark supposed to mean? Really, you sound like Megan."

"Sorry, we're both cops. Goes with the territory to worry about a civilian's safety."

"Fine, but don't treat me as if I'm two. I can handle this bastard. I say we kick some ass."

Lacy stifled a smile. There was no doubt in her mind it was true. Heaven help Buddy if Beth got hold of his butt. She had a score to settle.

"Ohmygod. What is that terrible odor?" Beth said. She brought her hand to her nose.

Lacy smelled it too as soon as they'd stepped out of the woods. At first, it seemed to come from the horse barn, where Willy had been housed. However, she'd had an up-close-and-personal experience with Willy. Although she knew for a fact that the animal did stink, as did her car now, this was much worse. More pungent. This was no doubt human flesh in the process of decaying.

Lacy stood silent. Her senses heightened, alert for danger. The trees bent their limbs as they yielded to the force of the wind. Another storm was on the way. She felt the moisture in the air. On it rode the unmistakable odor of death, making her stomach lurch. With renewed fear for the boy and concern over her partner, she pivoted around to better discern the true direction of the offensive, putrid scent.

Beth watched her quizzically. "What is it?"

"The smell of rotting flesh."

"You mean like roadkill or a dead person?" Beth asked.

"I don't know yet," Lacy lied. She reached to feel for her Glock. It was safely tucked in her jeans.

"Beth, do you have a cell on you?"

"No, I left it at home. Is that going to be a problem?"

"No, just needed to make sure the ringer was off. We don't want to advertise our presence."

"We're good then," Beth said, giving two thumbs-up. "Remember, if an alligator takes after you, run in circles. They can't do that so good, and there's a lot of swamp around here, so there's a good chance one will be around this time of night."

"Where the hell did you learn that?"

"Oh gosh, I don't know. Kindergarten I guess. Everyone that lives here knows that," Beth said. "You really need to go by the library and get a book on Florida wildlife."

Lacy looked at her dumbfounded but managed to say, "Sure, next chance I get."

"Zigzags are good too," Beth added, trying to be helpful.

"Thanks, I'll keep that in mind."

Night was fully upon them. The moon created shadows from the big bald cypress trees, which were the dominant canopy species. The resurrection ferns were full from the recent rain. They lined the live oaks and added a thickness to their camouflage. The combination offered cover. Anything to lessen the chance of Buddy spotting their intrusion. The two women stood quietly, hidden in the dark of the breezy night.

"What do we do now?" Beth whispered.

"Shush," Lacy said and sniffed the air, this time only picking up the musty scent of earth and rotten vegetation. The wind had shifted. She worried it could give away their presence by carrying the scent of their perfume toward anyone who lurked outside. There was a tiny shallow stream that moved slowly in front of her. It occurred to her that everything in Florida was connected by water in some form or fashion. It seemed to be everywhere.

A slight rustle of branches close to her right shoulder startled her. She pivoted quickly and pulled her loaded Glock out in the ready position.

"Sorry," Beth said from behind a bush. "Don't shoot."

"What in the world are you doing?"

"I have to pee. Ever since I've had children, I have to pee when I get nervous. That or when I sneeze. Sometimes when I laugh real hard, which hasn't happened lately."

Lacy rolled her eyes, but it was wasted in the dark. "Well, hurry up, and try to be a little more quiet. I'm anxious to cuff this bastard. He deserves to rot in prison."

"Prison? Honey, we have Sparky. And I think he deserves to meet Sparky, up close and personal."

"Sparky? He's not another goat, is he?"

"Heaven, no. That's what we call our electric chair."

"What? Why?"

"Because one time when they used it, the person caught on fire. Well, really just his head. But it was one-and-a-half-foot flames and ever since, its been nicknamed Sparky."

"I forgot you guys have the death sentence."

"Dang straight we do, and we use it."

"OK, who am I out here with, Rambo or Beth the homemaker?"

"If my family's in danger and a little boy's life is at stake, you can consider me Rambo. I say let's kick some butt."

Beth smiled, pulled up and zipped her pants, and said, "Let's do it."

The wind direction switched again, back to the fetid redolence of decomposing human flesh.

"I say we head in this direction, but try to be quiet. We want the element of surprise to be on our side, not the other way around," Lacy said and headed toward the source of the stench.

The primordial surroundings of vegetation in various stages of decomposition couldn't compete with the putrid odor which prevailed. Through the shadows they crept. The scent of death grew stronger with each step. She had a better appreciation of why Cooper insisted on searching for the boy on foot. It would be easy to get lost or wounded in these mysterious surroundings. The trees above created shadows that reached down. A blanket on top of the already murky dark water.

The two women pressed onward through the darkness and across the tainted farm. They were beset by the macabre knowledge this place was marked by Sissy's murder. The absolute isolation allowed Lacy to understand how Buddy was able to accomplish such egregious acts. Deeds that, if performed anywhere else, would certainly draw attention. Like the roar of a chain saw. The screams that fell on the silent night.

The hairs on the back of her neck stood on end. The man they were after was truly insidious. She thought of Megan and the prank caller. Could that have been Buddy? She knew Megan was attracted to the man. Could he have lured her out here under false pretenses? She fought to put those thoughts out of her mind. She didn't need distraction. There was evil here; she could feel it. She had to focus on Cooper and the boy.

Beth walked silently behind Lacy, watching every shadow and movement. When she saw Lacy look back, Beth said, "You know the Lord won't let him get away with this."

Lacy didn't want to dispute Beth's beliefs. It obviously gave her the strength to overcome her fears. Yet on the other hand, she didn't want Beth to become overconfident. "Look, Beth, the prison system isn't overflowing with Mensa candidates, but Buddy's different. He's cunning. So much so, he's been able to evade prosecution for eight years. For all we know, he's stalking us at this very moment."

Beth grabbed her sleeve. "What do you mean eight years?" she whispered with her head cocked to the side. "I thought you said Buddy had Edward Lee?"

"I'll explain later. Where in the heck is Cooper?" Lacy asked. She walked with her hand poised over her weapon, nerves on overdrive.

"The stench is getting worse," Beth mumbled, covering her nose with the collar of her shirt.

They both knew they were getting close to the source. She could tell Beth was trying to be brave but also appeared on the verge of losing it.

"It's coming from this way," Lacy said. "The shed."

They walked a few more feet when they heard something. A faint noise. Lacy pulled Beth down behind a bush. They lay flat on the ground and listened.

"Stop breathing so loudly," Lacy snapped.

"I can't help it. I think I'm gonna cry," Beth whispered back.

"You make a sound, and we may both end up dead. Something I personally want to avoid, so pull yourself together. Think of your children. You're doing this to keep them safe. Stay focused and keep hold of yourself. Remember Edward Lee and Megan."

Beth nodded silently, but a single tear rolled down her cheek.

Lacy looked through the darkness in the direction of the sound. The shed door swung open, then Buddy staggered out. He was hard to make out in the darkness with only scant moonlight. At first the detective figured he was taking out the trash. But when he turned around and locked the shed behind him with double padlocks, she knew otherwise. No one locks up their garbage.

"See you soon, sweetheart. Then we'll have some real fun," Buddy called out and proceeded into the house.

"Who was he talking to?" Beth asked.

"I don't know. Be quiet."

"Maybe he's hallucinating since he killed Sissy. He certainly wouldn't talk to Edward Lee or Cooper that way. Buddy's a notorious ladies' man. He's not gay," Beth said.

"Well, I plan to go find out who's in there. You stay here as my backup. If anything happens, I need you to be able to go for help. This is serious, Beth."

"You mean stay here all by myself?"

"Yes, I'll be right back. Here are the keys to my car. Whatever you do, don't make a sound. Buddy can't know you're here no matter what. If he does, we're both liable to end up dead. I need you to be free to get back to my car and get help."

Beth watched in horror as her only form of protection made her way across the lawn to the small shed. She was concerned she was going to pee her pants out of fear. She wasn't especially fond of the dark or feeling particularly brave at the moment. It'd seemed like such a good idea when she started out, but with Lacy the detective and her fancy weapon gone, she was flat-out scared.

Suddenly a large rough hand clamped down over her mouth. Her eyes grew wide as she struggled to scream, but only a tiny whimper escaped the tight grasp.

"It's OK. It's just me," Cooper whispered in her ear.

"Cooper! Where have you been? We needed you. Now Lacy's off checking out the shed. We think someone's inside. Besides that, you just made me pee my pants. Now what am I supposed to do? I can't go fight crime with a wet spot on my pants," Beth said.

Cooper wasn't exactly certain what he'd expected, but being scolded wasn't one of them. Then again, this was Beth he was dealing with, and he hadn't expected her to be hidden in a bush.

"Sorry, but now it's my turn. What in the hell are you doing here?" he asked.

Beth filled Cooper in on everything and how they saw Buddy come out of the shed. "I'm sure he has someone in there. I bet it's his next victim. I'd help, but Lacy told me to wait here."

"That was an excellent idea," Cooper said with a glare. "I hope we're not too late."

"It would be my guess we're not. I don't think he would talk to a dead body," Beth said.

That made sense to Cooper. He crawled over so he could better watch what was going on. He could see Lacy circle the shed. Then she stopped short, bent down to the ground, and began digging frantically with her bare hands.

"What the hell?" Cooper asked.

Before Beth knew what was going on, Cooper was up and running. She wanted to go with him, afraid to be alone. Then she remembered her pants. What if the wet mark was big enough to see? It was a darn-right embarrassment. It was all Tyler's fault. That kid had such a big head. Motherhood certainly had its joys, but there was also a price to pay. So instead she watched.

Within seconds, Cooper joined Lacy with the digging. They'd obviously found something, but what? The next thing Beth knew, the screen door of the house swung open with an audible protest, and Buddy staggered out. He let the door slam shut behind him. It was something she'd always got onto the boys for. She followed his movement to the shed. He held a beer in one hand and a chain saw in the other. A shotgun was slung over his shoulder. To top it off, he was obviously drunk as a skunk.

"Oh, dear Jesus," Beth whispered. "This can't be good."

Her eyes remained focused on the scene that unfolded before her. Both Cooper and Lacy had been so intent on their task, neither had heard Buddy's approach. But luckily, since they were around the back of the shed, Buddy had no idea of their presence either. Beth hadn't a clue as to what to do. From her vantage point, she could see the whole thing clearly. It was like watching a train wreck with no way to stop the inevitable crash. For a moment, she considered a mad rush up to Buddy, screaming. That would give Lacy and Cooper some warning. But as heavily armed as Buddy was, it was possible that she'd only scare him, and they would all wind up shot. Besides, Lacy was very specific for her to stay put and remain absolutely quiet. It made sense. Lacy had detective training, and someone needed to get help if things went wrong. Beth wanted to be brave. That was definitely her intention on the way here, but actually being faced with such danger gave her a different perspective and a new respect for her sister's occupation and the danger Megan faced every day. She was scared of getting shot. It had to hurt and would leave a nasty scar. She hadn't realized how brave her little sister was until this moment. She wanted to tell her that, but she wasn't here.

"Here I come, baby," Buddy sang out.

Beth saw Cooper and Lacy freeze. *Good, they heard that,* she thought. At least now they know to stay hidden. She watched as Lacy dropped to the ground and Cooper tucked against the shed.

That's when Buddy spoke up. "My sweet little Megan, I've come to have some fun with you. I even brought some toys for our little party."

He was at the door now, fidgeting with the locks. It took a second for the words to register with Beth. The person Buddy held captive was her sister.

That's who Lacy and Cooper had been frantically trying to dig out while she idly watched. That's why Megan hadn't returned any of the last seventeen calls. Or any of Lacy's calls.

Sheer naked rage overtook Beth. Without thought, she jumped up and bounded toward Buddy at a wide-open run, linebacker style, straight toward her focus of hatred. Just before she reached him, she yelled out, "You son of a bitch, I'll kill you if you've laid a hand on my baby sister!"

Buddy, drunk as he was, still had reasonable reflexes. He pivoted around to see the mad woman charging aggressively. With an ingrained, practiced aim, he swung the shotgun around and fired. Beth dropped like a rock. Buddy had bagged her as easily as he would have a deer. She rolled over once and groaned. Then there was dead silence.

Seconds passed as they all looked on in horror. That was all except Buddy, who leaned back and let out a whoop of laughter. When he turned back around to face the shed, he said, "You're next, baby doll. You and your sister can both go into the bug pit together. Sisters to the end."

As the smoke and smell of gunfire wafted through the air. Lacy walked around the corner with her 9-mm Glock raised to Buddy's temple. "Not so fast, asshole. Drop your weapon and put your hands in the air."

Buddy knew it was over, but out of spite, he shot off a single round at Lacy's foot, hitting her little toe. It wasn't a mortal wound by any stretch of the imagination, but it was certainly painful, and that gave him some satisfaction. Which he made apparent in a wise-ass grin. "Sorry."

Lacy's anger overrode her pain. She never dropped her weapon or wavered from her target, despite her personal agony.

Her tenacity seemed to amuse Buddy. He allowed his shotgun to slide to the ground. With an air of arrogance, he held his hands up high. "Shoot me now, and it will go on your record as firing on an unarmed man who'd already surrendered. Besides, I'm grieving and not responsible for my actions. Besides, I think I may be drunk."

Lacy knew Buddy was insane. She couldn't let him goad her into making a mistake that might allow him to walk away from this. She willed herself to maintain focus. She had a partner and a little boy to rescue. The man before her was a sociopath who held no fear of killing a cop. But before Lacy could question Buddy, he passed out—totally inebriated.

Without a second wasted, she tossed her cell phone to Cooper and instructed him to call for an ambulance. Then she reached down and grabbed the keys to the shed from Buddy. "You check on Beth."

Cooper made the call, then rushed over to Beth, who lay dead still. Not being one to cope with blood—his or anyone else's, Cooper grew light-headed. He wanted to help but wasn't sure what to do. There was so much blood. Then all went black as he collapsed on the ground next to Beth.

When Lacy exited the shed with Edward Lee in her arms and Megan leaning against her, they saw three bodies on the ground. They all stepped over Buddy. Lacy had to let Edward Lee down as he scrambled to get to his beloved friend Cooper. In tears, Megan ran to her sister. Lacy knew that Buddy had passed out drunk, Cooper, she assumed, from the sight of blood, so she joined Megan at Beth's side.

Megan looked over at her pleadingly.

Lacy nodded. "Don't worry. She's our main priority. An ambulance is on the way. Her pulse is strong. She's gonna make it. Just think about the stories she'll have at the next PTA meeting."

Megan stifled a half cry, half laugh. "Thank you, Lacy. I owe you my life. I was so stupid."

The two hugged with ferocity. "Beth loves you, Megan. She risked her life for you without thought."

Megan pulled away and said, "I love her too. I know I complain about her all the time, but if the truth be known, I don't know what I would do without her. She's the one constant in my world. My rock. I need her so much."

Megan brought her fist to her mouth to help contain her emotions. This wasn't the time to let go. Ten minutes ago, she was assured of her and Edward Lee's death. All the secrets and confessions Buddy had spilled were sure to die with them. The next thing she knew, there were gunshots. She hoped it had been at Buddy. At no point had she ever consider her sister to be in danger. Yet on her first breath of fresh air, she saw her sister lying on the ground. It was all an emotional roller coaster. In the distance, she heard the sound of a siren. She grasped onto her sister's hand and whispered a chant into her ear, "It's all right now, Beth. You're gonna be OK. Just hold on."

Megan was stroking her sister's hair when she passed out on top of her.

Lacy ran to greet the driver.

"What the hell happened here. We've got . . . three down and one hovering. OK, four down. Call for backup," he yelled over his shoulder.

Lacy gave him the brief rundown of recent events. She led him over to Beth. "She's been shot. Her sister just passed out. I imagine from the emotional overload but needs to be checked out."

"Take this one out first," he called out. Then he turned to Cooper. "We got a vasovagal over here. Who's the little monkey on top of him?"

Lacy was anxious. "The little boy's name is Edward Lee. He was being held captive in that shed. He needs medical attention as well. What's that vasovagel thing? Is he going to be all right?"

"You need to get out of the way, Officer. We'll take it from here."

From there, Lacy was ushered away.

42

Megan slowly came to in unfamiliar surroundings. Her mind was fuzzy and confused. Everything was white. She struggled to make sense out of where she was. It couldn't be in the shed anymore—it was too bright. Maybe this had all been a terrible dream. Then she saw the IV in her arm. Her anxiety mounted, unsure what flowed directly into her veins. And who had hooked it up? She didn't agree to this. Did Buddy do it? God, she was thirsty. Her mouth felt like dirt.

She scanned the room for water. There was a pitcher on the side table, but her muscles were fatigued and weakened from all the digging. Her hands were bandaged.

Jerry, who had been asleep in a chair next to her, stirred from her movement. It took him a moment as well to gather his bearings.

"Let me get that for you," he offered, his voice husky from sleep yet soothing.

Megan turned to see him for the first time. His intense, deep-set eyes were focused on hers. She could tell he hadn't shaved recently. "Jerry? What are you doing here? And where are we anyway?"

"Munroe Regional Hospital. Here, sip this," he said and held the cup up for her. It had one of those bendy straws that she liked so much, which made it easier.

"How did I get here, and how did you know about it? Megan asked.

A smile crept across his face. It was one of relief and affection. "The same old Megan. One question after another. But to answer your question, Brian told me. He was the doctor on call when you and half of your family and friends came into the ER last night. He remembered that I'd wanted to speak to you, so he gave me a call. Hey, go easy on that. Don't drink too fast."

"Sorry, I'm just so thirsty." It took a moment for her to remember that Brian was Jerry's roommate, who happened to be an ER doctor.

She propped herself up to a sitting position, and her head began to clear. She reached up to feel her hair. As suspected, it was jutting out in every direction. "Oh, God, I have a serious case of bedhead. I must look horrible."

"At least you're among the living, with both arms," Jerry said.

"What happened? All I remember is going to Buddy's looking for clues about Sissy's death."

"Lacy's the one that should tell you. It's more her story, but since I know you won't rest until you know everything, I'll fill you in on what I do know. She can fill in the blanks later."

Megan smiled. It was weak, but it was a smile nonetheless.

"Buddy must have caught you snooping around because he had you captive in his shed. Turns out he's been a very busy man. He had his chain saw all ready to go when you were rescued."

"So it wasn't all a bad dream," Megan murmured. Her head was still foggy, but bits and pieces started to come back to her. "It all seems so muddy. I want to remember, but I can't."

"That's because of the medications."

Megan brought her hands up to her mouth and gasped. She recalled Buddy's confession of the murders. Then another flash. "Edward Lee," she shrieked. "Buddy had him in the shed too. He was waiting for him to die. I told him to hide in the corner under a tarp. Did they find him? I told him to hide no matter what. What if he's still there," Megan said trying to climb out of bed. "He may still be there hidden."

Jerry gently pushed her back down and tucked her in. "He's fine," Jerry said, taking her hand. "He's in pediatrics. Mainly dehydrated, same as you. Plus he had some internal bruising from where Buddy kicked him repeatedly in the side. Brian said you'll both be out of here today. They only kept you here last night for observation. He wanted you on an IV because you were suffering from dehydration as well as exhaustion. That's part of the reason you're so groggy and can't remember. They gave you something to help you rest. It'll wear off soon."

"Oh god, I feel like I screwed up so bad. Are you sure Edward Lee's gonna to be OK?"

"Good as new. Tough little kid and smart too. He may be sore for awhile, but he'll be OK. You helped to save him."

"What about Lacy and Cooper? I remember their voices. Oh no, then shots. Beth was lying on the ground, bloody. Ohmygod, this is terrible. Why in the hell was Beth there?"

"Take it easy. You need to calm down. Like I said, Lacy knows the whole story. But from what people have told me, Cooper went looking for Edward Lee. He figured out the boy spotted Buddy's red Thunderbird being repaired at Parker's garage. The crazy kid went after the guy himself. Cooper tried to call you, but since you were locked in Buddy's shed, no one could get in touch with you. So he called Lacy instead."

"It wasn't because I was in his shed. It was because I was so stupid, I left my cell in my truck along with my pistol. I don't know what I was thinking. I wanted to take a look around. Then I was going to meet Lacy at the station. I had no idea Buddy was the serial killer until it was too late. But how does Beth figure into this mess? She's a homemaker with children, not a cop. Is she gonna be all right? I can't believe I let my sister get hurt. She never approved of my job. She said it was too risky, and now, she ends up the one who gets hurt. God, I feel so guilty."

Jerry shifted uncomfortably in his chair. He really didn't want to be the one to tell Megan about her sister or that her partner had been wounded. Then there was the mess he'd wanted to talk to her to begin with, of Buddy's prints on the Coke can. He looked at her and said, "OK here's the deal, but don't kill the messenger. Lacy was shot in the foot. Cooper's with her now."

"That's terrible, but I don't remember any blood on her. I thought she helped me out of the shed. And what about Beth?"

"She was shot as well. They expect her to make a full recovery."

Megan felt light-headed and fell back against the pillows. "Oh, I feel sick. Are you sure Beth's all right?"

"Positive, Brian told me so himself. She bled a lot, but the bullet only grazed her shoulder."

"I'm such a bad partner. None of this would have happened if I'd listened to Lacy. She told me she planned to get a search warrant for Buddy's farm, but I wanted to make a name for myself."

"Well, Lacy will be fine. The bullet only winged her little toe. Buddy did it out of spite, and she's pretty ticked off about it. Cooper's with her. I'm sure they'll stop in for a visit before you leave."

"Ohmygod, Cooper. Is Cooper all right? He hates hospitals. I'm surprised he's here."

"It wasn't totally voluntary. Both you and Cooper pulled a vasovagal response, so you both had to be brought in by ambulance."

"What the heck does that mean?" Megan asked, sitting back up.

"You both passed out. Cooper, from the sight of blood. You, from the sight of your sister lying on the ground, shot. You see, emotional stress can cause cardiac vulnerability. The person appears cold, clammy, then goes unconscious from a hypotensive reaction due to fear or extreme emotion. Luckily, for the both of you, it was temporary. On occasion, it can lead to death."

"God, I feel like such a wimp. But Buddy told me everything. He's not only the serial killer but he killed Mary Pearl, Sissy, and my mother," Megan said.

Jerry took a deep breath. He was relieved Megan already knew about her mother. "I'm surprised he confessed to anything."

"I'm not. He didn't plan on my living to share the information. But I would have expected you to be a bit more surprised. I take it you figured it out already?"

Jerry nodded, "It was pure conjecture at first. Remember the Coke can?"

Megan nodded. She enjoyed hearing the way Jerry's mind worked.

"Well, the results of the prints came back positive for Buddy. After reading that report, I went to the break room to get a drink. There were two guys there from the sheriff's department talking about Heather Daily."

"She matched up with the remains we found at the peach farm," Megan added.

"Correct. They were talking about how smart she was and how much they missed her help on the current campaign. They assumed she'd left to concentrate on her studies and no longer had time to volunteer any longer. It got me thinking. I knew I'd missed something. It was like those women called out to me. Then an idea hit. I went back to reevaluate all the remains, especially the pelvic bones. On every one, there was no lens evident on the ischium portion," Jerry said. He leaned back and spread his hands out in a gesture as if the information was comparable to the Rosetta stone, unlocking the key to language.

Megan stared back, blinking. "Maybe it's the medicine, but I don't understand what that means."

"It means that all the victims were in a tight age range between postteens and early twenties."

"College age."

"Exactly, just as Heather had been, but I still didn't have all the answers. I was in the process of reviewing the hair-sample analysis when I got a visitor."

"The chief?"

"No, Buddy. He was fishing around for information about the Mary Pearl Harkin case. Since she died of a heart problem, on a whim, I inquired about Buddy's cholesterol levels. He looked at me as if I'd lost his mind. Then he shrugged his shoulders and told me it was fine ever since he started on this medication to control it. It was the same drug found in the hair samples."

"And that's when you figured it out?"

"Almost. Right before he left, he offered me a breath mint, a cinnamon Tic Tac. Then Doc Evans stopped by to ask me to run some quick tests on Sissy's tissue samples. We got to talking, and it came out he suspected the woman was murdered. From that, I extrapolated it was Buddy."

"Wow, you're amazing. And here I thought I was going to shock you with Buddy's confession. But now I need to break the news to Beth, including what happened to Mom."

Then Jerry grew serious again and wiggled in his seat.

"What? I don't like that look on your face," Megan said.

"It's your sister. She's OK from being shot, and they expect her to make a full recovery."

"Why do I sense a 'but'?"

Jerry placed a comforting hand over Megan's. "But she has a Ritalin-use problem."

"What?" Megan asked in disbelief. Yet she knew Jerry wouldn't lie to her or make it up.

"Yes, she told Brian she took it on the advice of some other soccer mom. At first, it was a way to have more energy to get everything done. Then she realized it helped her lose weight. Before she realized it, she was taking several a day. Unfortunately, Beth isn't an isolated case. Brian told me it's actually becoming an epidemic across America, even in small towns like Ocala."

"That must have been the prescription bottle I always saw her with. I'd assumed it was headache medicine. I feel so stupid that I didn't realize what was going on. I figured it was all the caffeine in the tea that made her so jittery. Is he really sure she'll be all right?"

"She's in good hands with Brian. He said it will take a few days to clear her system, and she needs plenty of rest, just as much as you do, I might add. You're supposed to be asleep now."

"But that still doesn't explain how she got shot. Was it some kind of drug deal to buy Ritalin from Buddy? Is that why was she there?"

"No, no. she was with Lacy. Lacy went to Beth's house in search of you. Evidently, Beth followed Lacy to Buddy's on a tractor. Lacy tried over and over again to get her to leave, but Beth loves you and wouldn't hear of it. She could sense Lacy was worried about you. She risked her life to rescue you." Jerry gave her hand a brotherly squeeze.

"I can't believe she risked her life for me."

"Without hesitation," Jerry said.

Megan was speechless. A lump formed in her throat, and she fought back the tears, knowing once they started, she would make a fool out of herself in front of Jerry. She regretted every ugly thing she'd ever said or thought about her sister and vowed to be more understanding and to help Beth more. She could take the boys on day trips more often to give her sister some personal time.

"I need to see her," Megan said.

"Sure, there will be time for that. She's resting now, which is what you should be doing. Remember, Brian said you were not only dehydrated but suffering from sleep deprivation."

"This case made it kind of hard to sleep," Megan admitted. She was embarrassed by how deeply it had invaded her personal life. A good cop was supposed to remain objective.

"What about Buddy? Did he get away?"

"No. He's in police custody. It's all over for him and the Honorable Angus Howard. Too many people know about their actions for a cover-up. Angus may not be culpable for the serial murders, but he has his own skeletons. Along with the county commissioner whom he was in collusion with. Buddy is telling all, not holding anything back. Evidently he has ongoing issues with his Daddy."

"Buddy told me Angus had my father killed. I hope he gives up enough information to put them both away forever. They deserved to be punished for what they did," Megan said.

This was the first Jerry heard of Megan's father. "I'm sorry for your family's loss, but I feel confident that there are enough people who are willing to confirm Buddy's allegation. He's told that Angus ordered the copper pipes to be removed, then replaced with cheaper, unsafe ABS, and even lead plumbing after the inspections," Jerry continued, unaware of Megan's inner turmoil. "Buddy is voicing all the family secrets as a deal to avoid the death sentence. Plus, we found the bug pit out back, along with the partially buried arms in the shed and the burn barrel. Brian called and postponed Sissy's cremation so further evaluation of her body can be preformed. They say that dead men tell no tales, but that's not actually true. Skeletal remains can speak volumes under the trained eyes of a forensic anthropologist."

"You don't do so bad yourself."

"What I do is more of a cursory once-over. Once the C. A. Pound Human Identification Laboratory in Gainesville gets a hold of the bones, there'll be few questions left unanswered," Jerry said. "Buddy will meet Old Sparky for sure."

"Will that lab be able to handle that many bodies all at once? We have like six in all."

"We found another. So it's actually seven."

"That must have been the one the boys saw him try to bury," Megan said.

"Seven cases is nothing for that lab. They're set up to cover all twenty-four medical examiner districts in the state as well as high-profile cases from around the world. It's the busiest forensic laboratory in the nation. They handle anywhere from 100 to 150 cases a year. They can handle plane crashes. I've already had all the remains transported there."

"Wow, it sounds like everyone else has been busy while I slept, including you and Brian."

"You and Lacy paved the way. Heck, even the chief's acting human again, thanks to your hard work. He wasn't even upset when he found the prototype car hidden behind your building."

"Oow, he wasn't supposed to know about that. But seriously, can I ask you something personal?"

"Sure, we're friends," Jerry said.

"Brian isn't merely your roommate, is he?"

Jerry chuckled, shaking his head no. "We're lovers. Have been for years. I thought you knew."

To Megan, viewing the situation in hindsight, it all fell into place. She felt kind of foolish to have a crush on a gay guy. How could she have not recognized the signs?

"I may not be in the closet, but Brian and I like to keep a low profile. Ocala's still a small town in many ways," Jerry said.

"I understand," Megan said. It was amazing how sometimes you think you truly know someone, but yet only see them from one perspective instead of the multidimensional individual they actually are. With Jerry and Beth, she had seen what she wanted. With the desire to be a good detective, it was a real eye-opener.

"One more thing."

Jerry rolled his eyes in exasperation. "You just aren't going to go to sleep until you have *all* the answers, are you? I can completely understand your state of utter exhaustion now."

"Sorry, I can't help it."

"I understand. I'm pretty much the same way when I run across something that doesn't fit, or I just can't figure out. The legal system hangs on our findings, and families insist on answers. That's a pretty heavy-duty responsibility."

Megan nodded, and a smile crept over her lips. "This is a less serious issue," she said. "What I was wondering was, what happened to Willy?"

"Ah, the now-infamous Willy. I saw what he did to Lacy's compact and the smell." He gave an involuntary shiver. "Some things never wash out, and I think goat stink is one of them. Lacy said Beth promised to fix it, but after this fiasco, I don't think Mather will let her hang around the two of you. He was pretty upset about his wife getting shot. I can't say I blame him. Cooper, on the other hand, was so relieved that Edward Lee was safe, he welcomed Willy with open arms. He told me that Nelly even seems to tolerate him. I guess because they don't like the same food."

"I think Lacy's good for him," Megan said.

"Oh, I almost forgot to tell you about that. Lacy bought Cooper a yellow Labrador puppy this morning. I think they're in love."

"Who? Cooper and the puppy, or him and Lacy?"

"Probably all three at this point."

"I'm glad. That means Lacy will stay," Megan said.

"She has to," Jerry said.

Megan raised an eyebrow in question. "And why is that?"

"Because like you, I don't like unanswered questions. Lacy has a history, some reason she picked up and moved here, and I don't think it was the weather. However, I'm certain that in time, I'll wheedle the whole story out of her."

Megan laughed and said, "If you don't, Beth and I will."

Then Jerry gave her a high five before he left her alone for some much-needed sleep.

THE END

Printed in the United States
122373LV00013B/106-111/A